Jackie **Ball** · Maddi **Gonzalez** · Mollie **Rose** · Nimali **Abeyratne**

Welcome to WANDERLAND

BOOM! BOX

Series Designer
Michelle Ankley

Associate Editor
Sophie Philips-Roberts

Collection Designer
Chelsea Roberts

Editor
Shannon Watters

BOOM! BOX™

WELCOME TO WANDERLAND, September 2019. Published by BOOM! Box, a division of Boom Entertainment, Inc. Welcome to Wanderland is ™ & © 2019 Jacqueline Ball. Originally published in single magazine form as WELCOME TO WANDERLAND No. 1-4. ™ & © 2018, 2019 Jacqueline Ball. All rights reserved. BOOM! Box™ and the BOOM! Box logo are trademarks of Boom Entertainment, Inc., registered in various countries and categories. All characters, events, and institutions depicted herein are fictional. Any similarity between any of the names, characters, persons, events, and/or institutions in this publication to actual names, characters, and persons, whether living or dead, events, and/or institutions is unintended and purely coincidental. BOOM! Box does not read or accept unsolicited submissions of ideas, stories, or artwork.

BOOM! Studios, 5670 Wilshire Boulevard, Suite 400, Los Angeles, CA 90036-5679. Printed in China. First Printing.

ISBN: 978-1-68415-472-2, eISBN: 978-1-64144-589-4

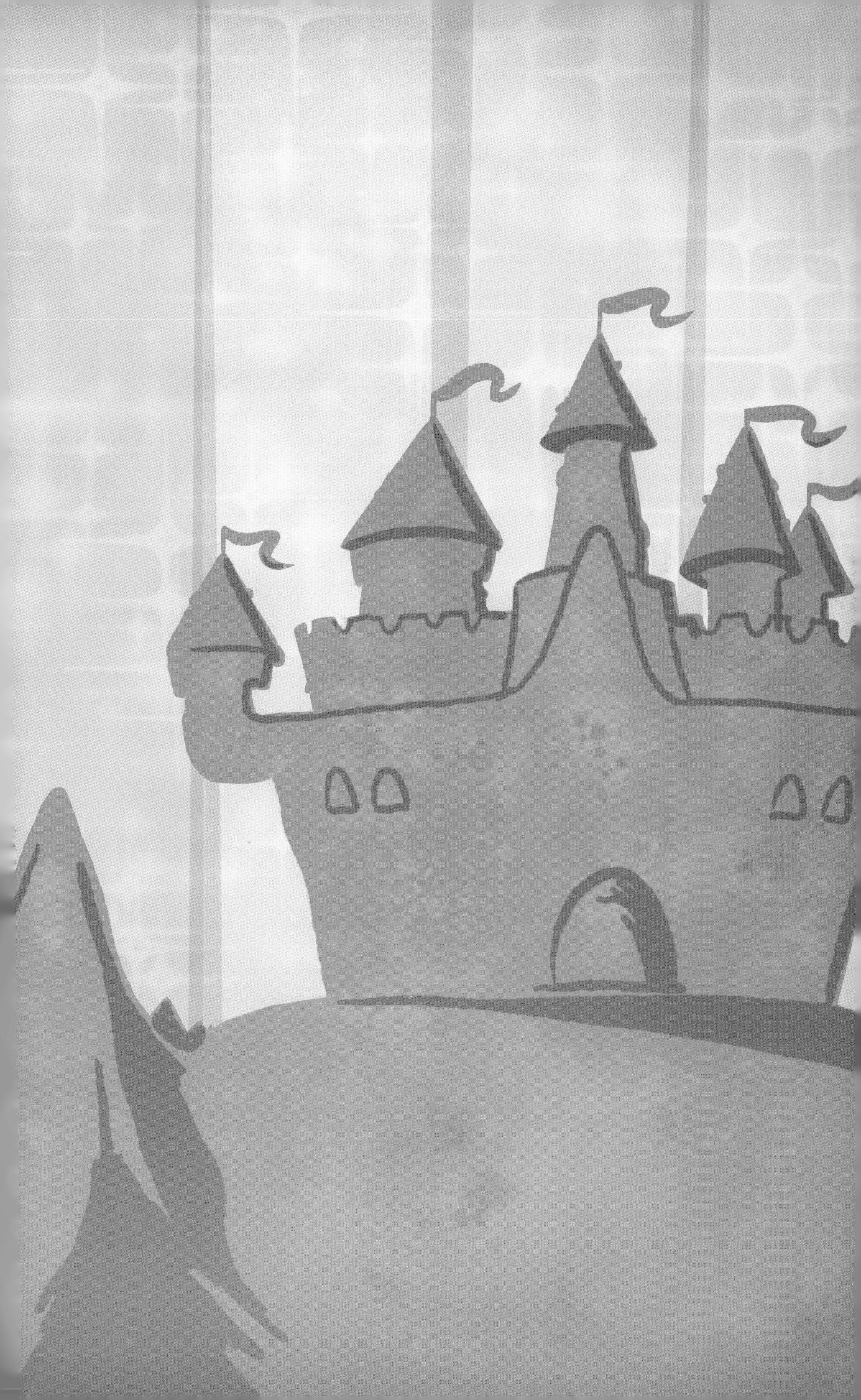

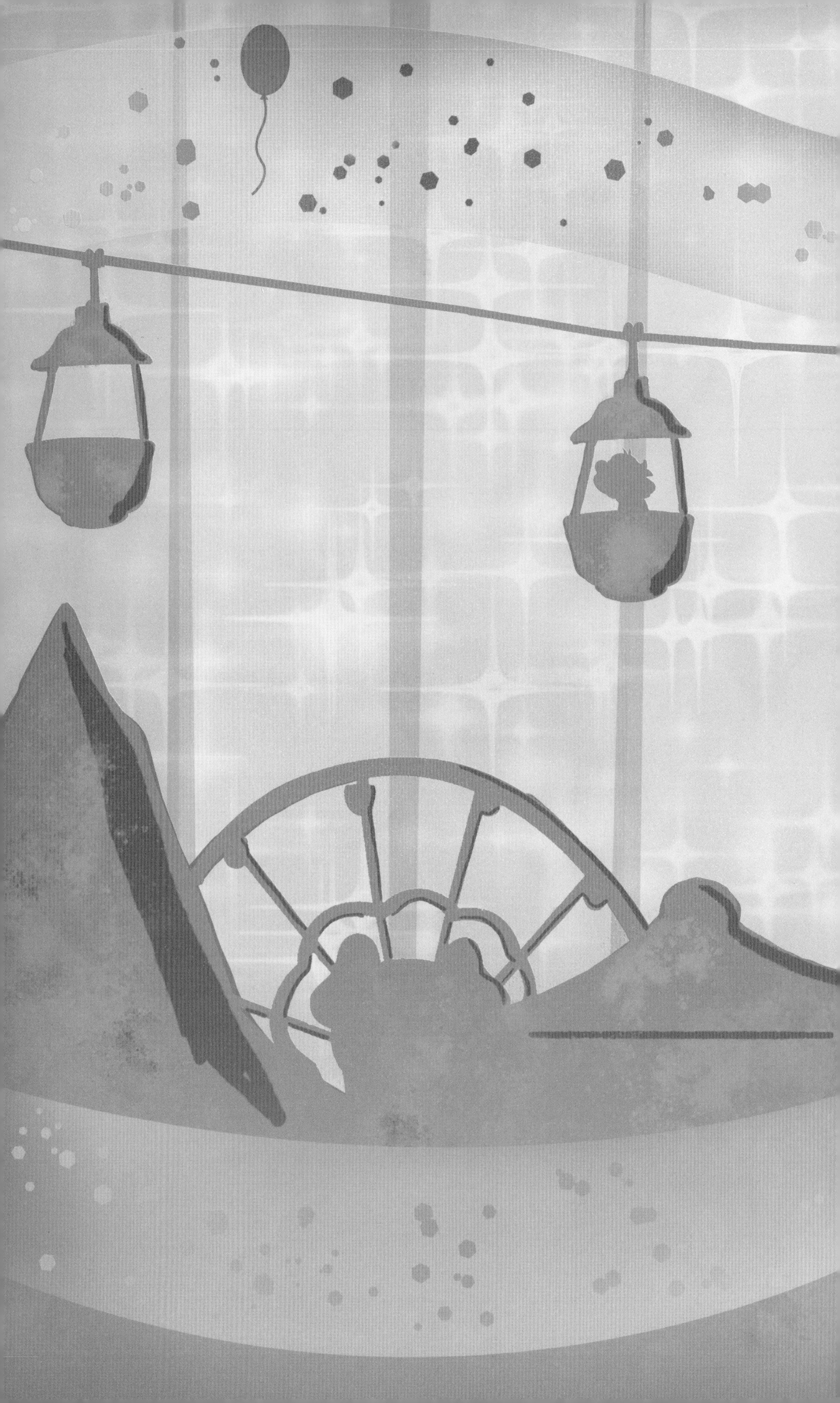

Welcome to WANDERLAND

Created & Written by
Jackie Ball

Illustrated by
**Maddi Gonzalez &
Mollie Rose** (Chapter 4)

Inked by
Raven Warner (Chapter 3)
with Ilaria Catalani & Tasha Neva (Chapter 3)

Colored by
Nimali Abeyratne
with Cathy Le (Chapters 2 & 4),
Maarta Laiho & Cristina Rose Chua (Chapter 2),
Rebecca Nalty & Kieran Quigley (Chapter 3)

Lettered by
Ed Dukeshire
with Deron Bennett (Chapter 2)

Consultation on Chapter 4 by Mey Rude.

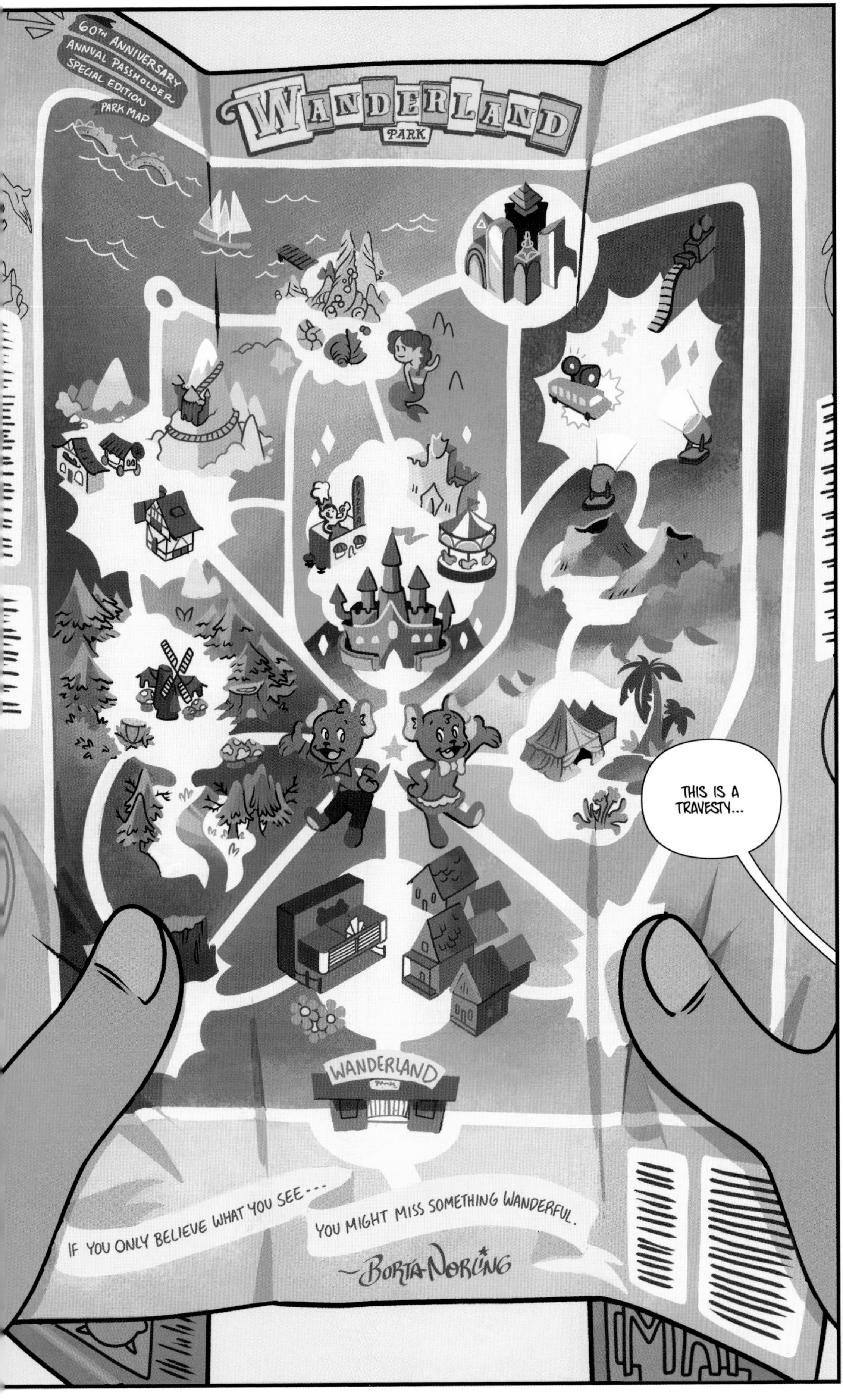
60TH ANNIVERSARY
ANNUAL PASSHOLDER
SPECIAL EDITION
PARK MAP
WANDERLAND
PARK
WANDERLAND
THIS IS A TRAVESTY...
IF YOU ONLY BELIEVE WHAT YOU SEE---
YOU MIGHT MISS SOMETHING WANDERFUL.
~BORTA-NORLING

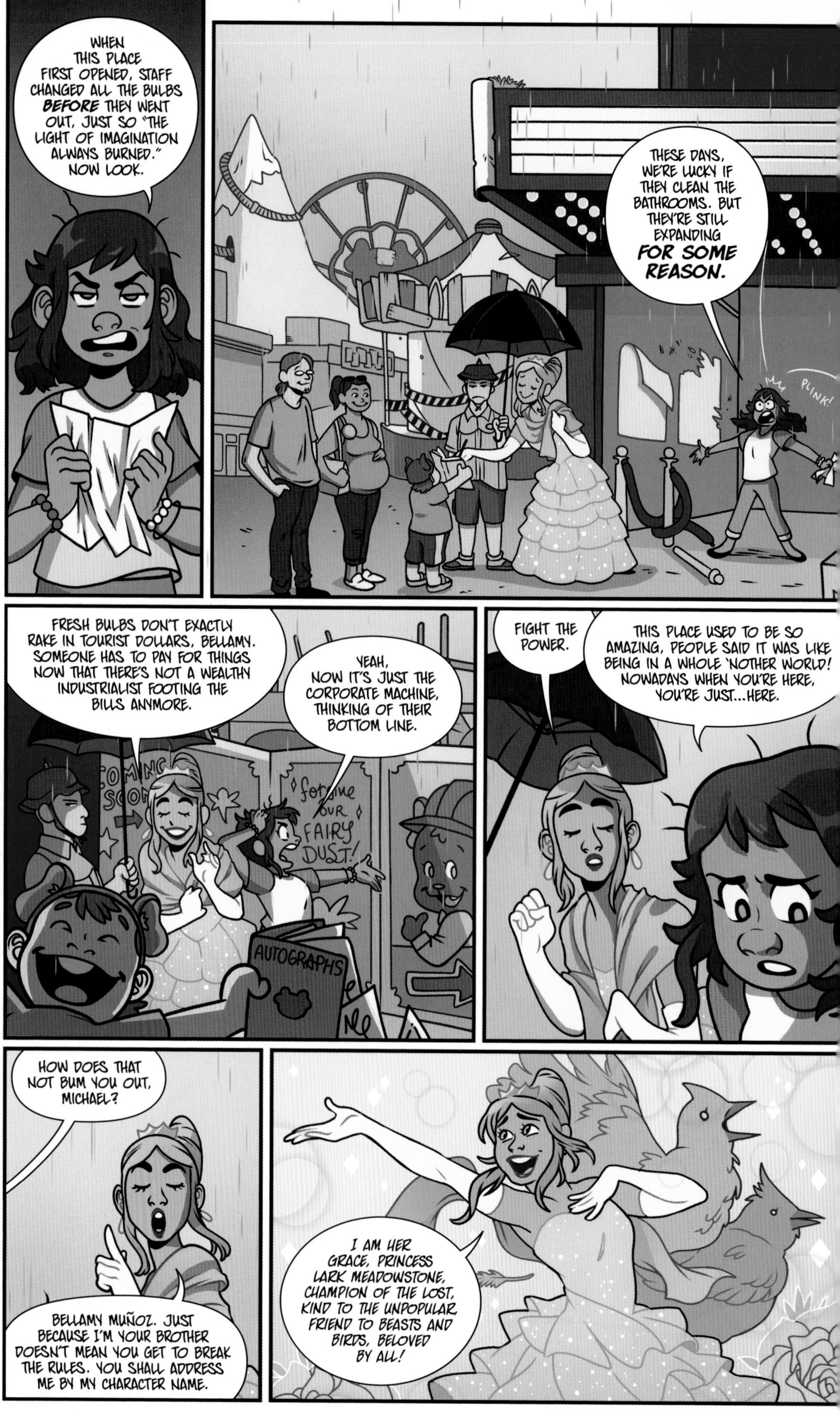
WHEN THIS PLACE FIRST OPENED, STAFF CHANGED ALL THE BULBS *BEFORE* THEY WENT OUT, JUST SO "THE LIGHT OF IMAGINATION ALWAYS BURNED." NOW LOOK.
THESE DAYS, WE'RE LUCKY IF THEY CLEAN THE BATHROOMS. BUT THEY'RE STILL EXPANDING **FOR SOME REASON.**
PLINK!
FRESH BULBS DON'T EXACTLY RAKE IN TOURIST DOLLARS, BELLAMY. SOMEONE HAS TO PAY FOR THINGS NOW THAT THERE'S NOT A WEALTHY INDUSTRIALIST FOOTING THE BILLS ANYMORE.
YEAH, NOW IT'S JUST THE CORPORATE MACHINE, THINKING OF THEIR BOTTOM LINE.
forgive our FAIRY DUST!
AUTOGRAPHS
FIGHT THE POWER.
THIS PLACE USED TO BE SO AMAZING, PEOPLE SAID IT WAS LIKE BEING IN A WHOLE 'NOTHER WORLD! NOWADAYS WHEN YOU'RE HERE, YOU'RE JUST...HERE.
HOW DOES THAT NOT BUM YOU OUT, MICHAEL?
BELLAMY MUÑOZ. JUST BECAUSE I'M YOUR BROTHER DOESN'T MEAN YOU GET TO BREAK THE RULES. YOU SHALL ADDRESS ME BY MY CHARACTER NAME.
I AM HER GRACE, PRINCESS LARK MEADOWSTONE, CHAMPION OF THE LOST, KIND TO THE UNPOPULAR, FRIEND TO BEASTS AND BIRDS, BELOVED BY ALL!

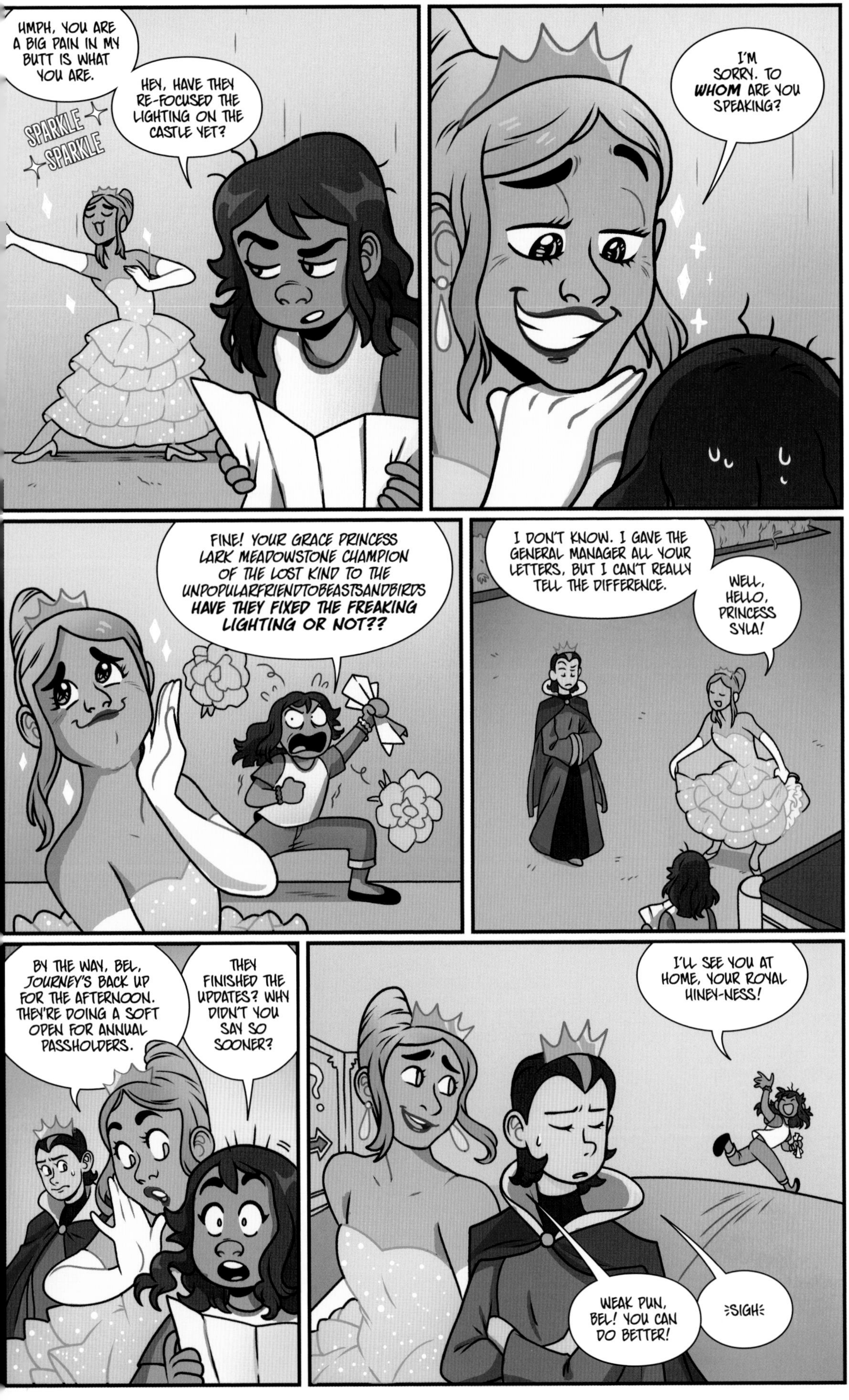
HUMPH, YOU ARE A BIG PAIN IN MY BUTT IS WHAT YOU ARE.
HEY, HAVE THEY RE-FOCUSED THE LIGHTING ON THE CASTLE YET?
SPARKLE SPARKLE
I'M SORRY. TO WHOM ARE YOU SPEAKING?
FINE! YOUR GRACE PRINCESS LARK MEADOWSTONE CHAMPION OF THE LOST KIND TO THE UNPOPULARFRIENDTOBEASTSANDBIRDS HAVE THEY FIXED THE FREAKING LIGHTING OR NOT??
I DON'T KNOW. I GAVE THE GENERAL MANAGER ALL YOUR LETTERS, BUT I CAN'T REALLY TELL THE DIFFERENCE.
WELL, HELLO, PRINCESS SYLA!
BY THE WAY, BEL, JOURNEY'S BACK UP FOR THE AFTERNOON. THEY'RE DOING A SOFT OPEN FOR ANNUAL PASSHOLDERS.
THEY FINISHED THE UPDATES? WHY DIDN'T YOU SAY SO SOONER?
I'LL SEE YOU AT HOME, YOUR ROYAL HINEY-NESS!
WEAK PUN, BEL! YOU CAN DO BETTER!
SIGH

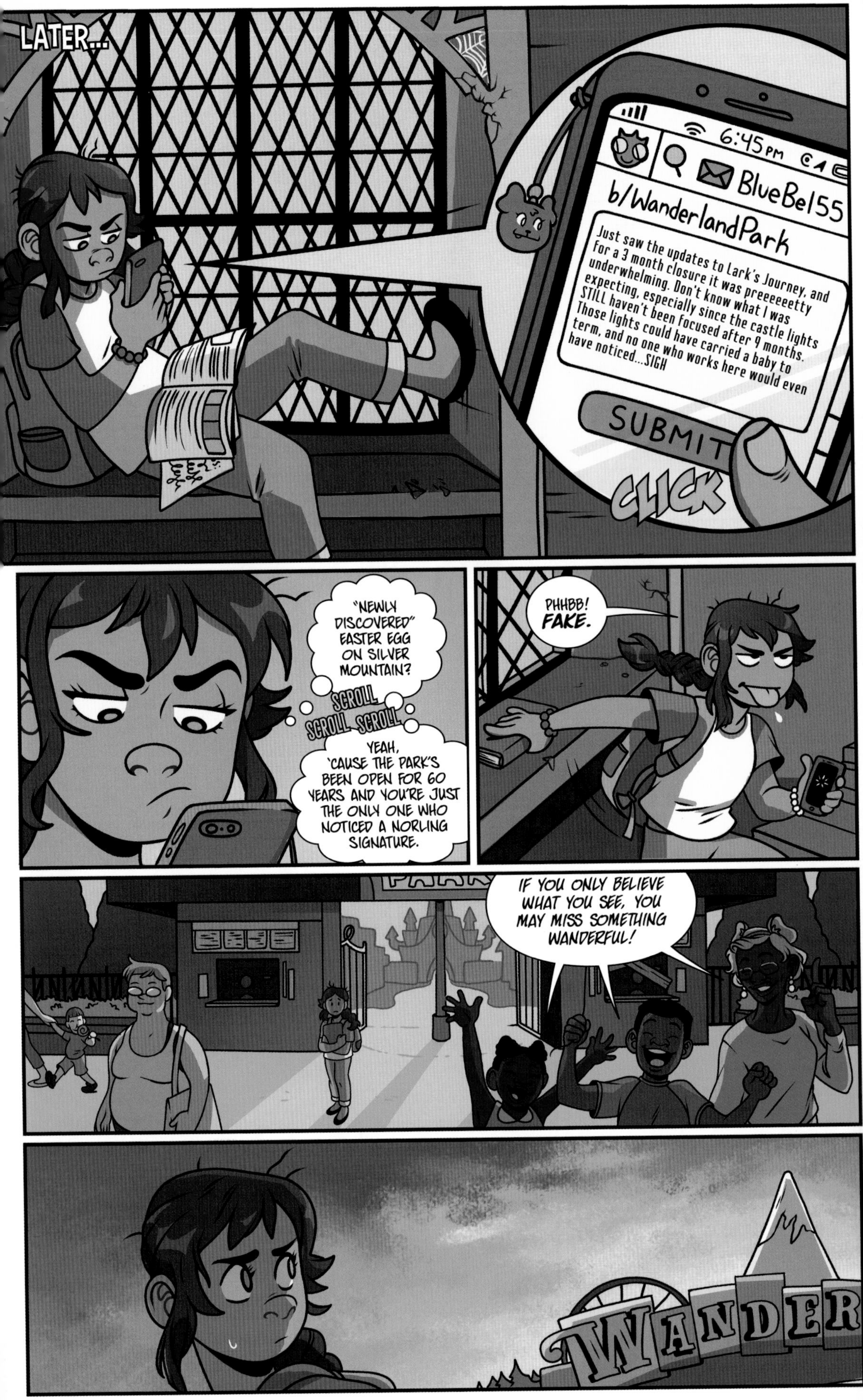
LATER...
6:45PM
BlueBel55
b/WanderlandPark
Just saw the updates to Lark's Journey, and for a 3 month closure it was preeeeetty underwhelming. Don't know what I was expecting, especially since the castle lights STILL haven't been focused after 9 months. Those lights could have carried a baby to term, and no one who works here would even have noticed...SIGH
SUBMIT
CLICK
"NEWLY DISCOVERED" EASTER EGG ON SILVER MOUNTAIN?
SCROLL SCROLL SCROLL
YEAH, 'CAUSE THE PARK'S BEEN OPEN FOR 60 YEARS AND YOU'RE JUST THE ONLY ONE WHO NOTICED A NORLING SIGNATURE.
PHHBB! FAKE.
IF YOU ONLY BELIEVE WHAT YOU SEE, YOU MAY MISS SOMETHING WANDERFUL!
WANDER

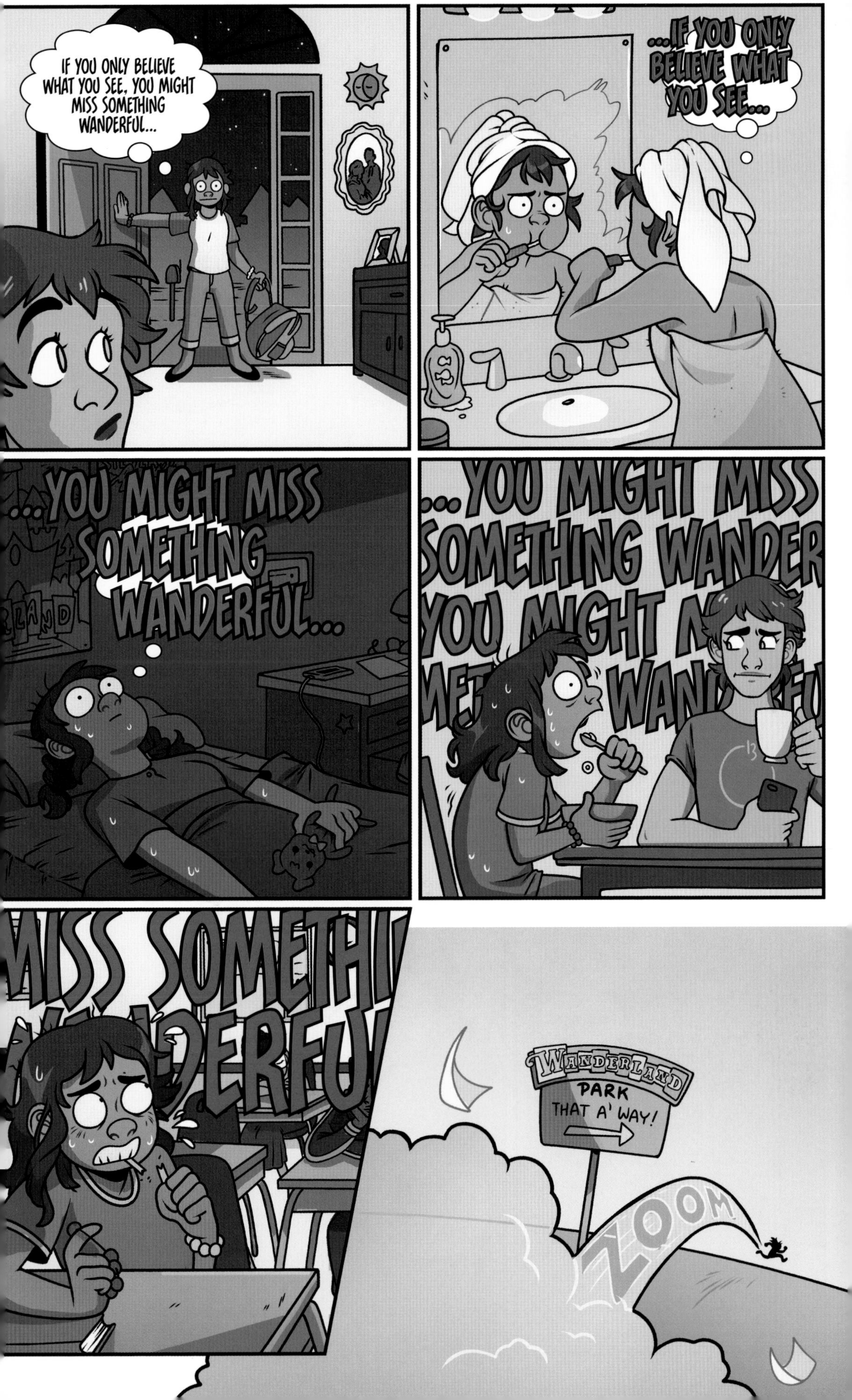
IF YOU ONLY BELIEVE WHAT YOU SEE, YOU MIGHT MISS SOMETHING WANDERFUL...
...IF YOU ONLY BELIEVE WHAT YOU SEE...
...YOU MIGHT MISS SOMETHING WANDERFUL...
...YOU MIGHT MISS SOMETHING WANDER
YOU MIGHT
WAN
MISS SOMETH
DERFU
WANDERLAND
PARK
THAT A' WAY!
ZOOM

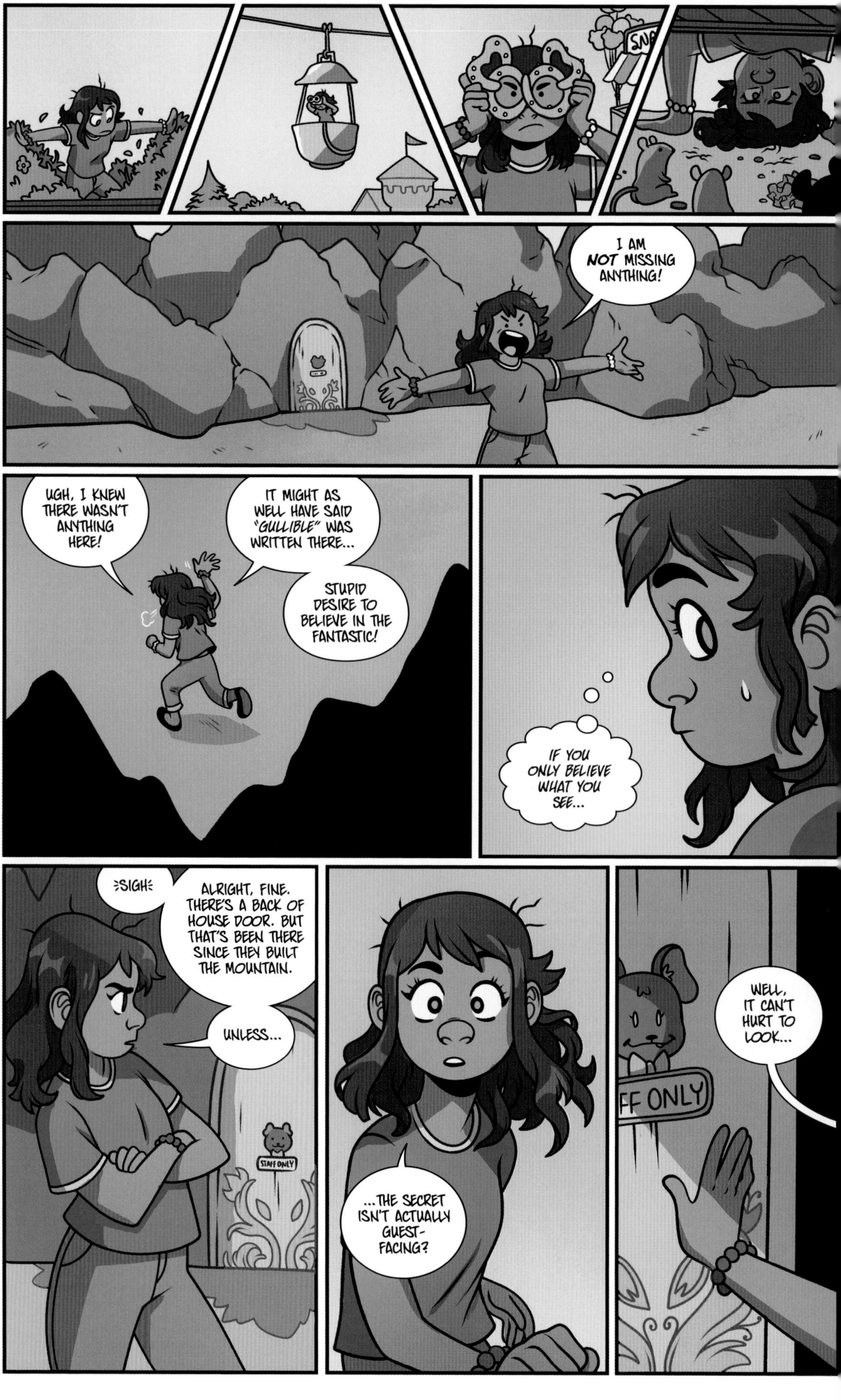

SNA
I AM **NOT** MISSING ANYTHING!
UGH, I KNEW THERE WASN'T ANYTHING HERE!
IT MIGHT AS WELL HAVE SAID *"GULLIBLE"* WAS WRITTEN THERE...
STUPID DESIRE TO BELIEVE IN THE FANTASTIC!
IF YOU ONLY BELIEVE WHAT YOU SEE...
⁝SIGH⁝
ALRIGHT, FINE. THERE'S A BACK OF HOUSE DOOR. BUT THAT'S BEEN THERE SINCE THEY BUILT THE MOUNTAIN.
UNLESS...
STAFF ONLY
...THE SECRET ISN'T ACTUALLY GUEST-FACING?
FF ONLY
WELL, IT CAN'T HURT TO LOOK...

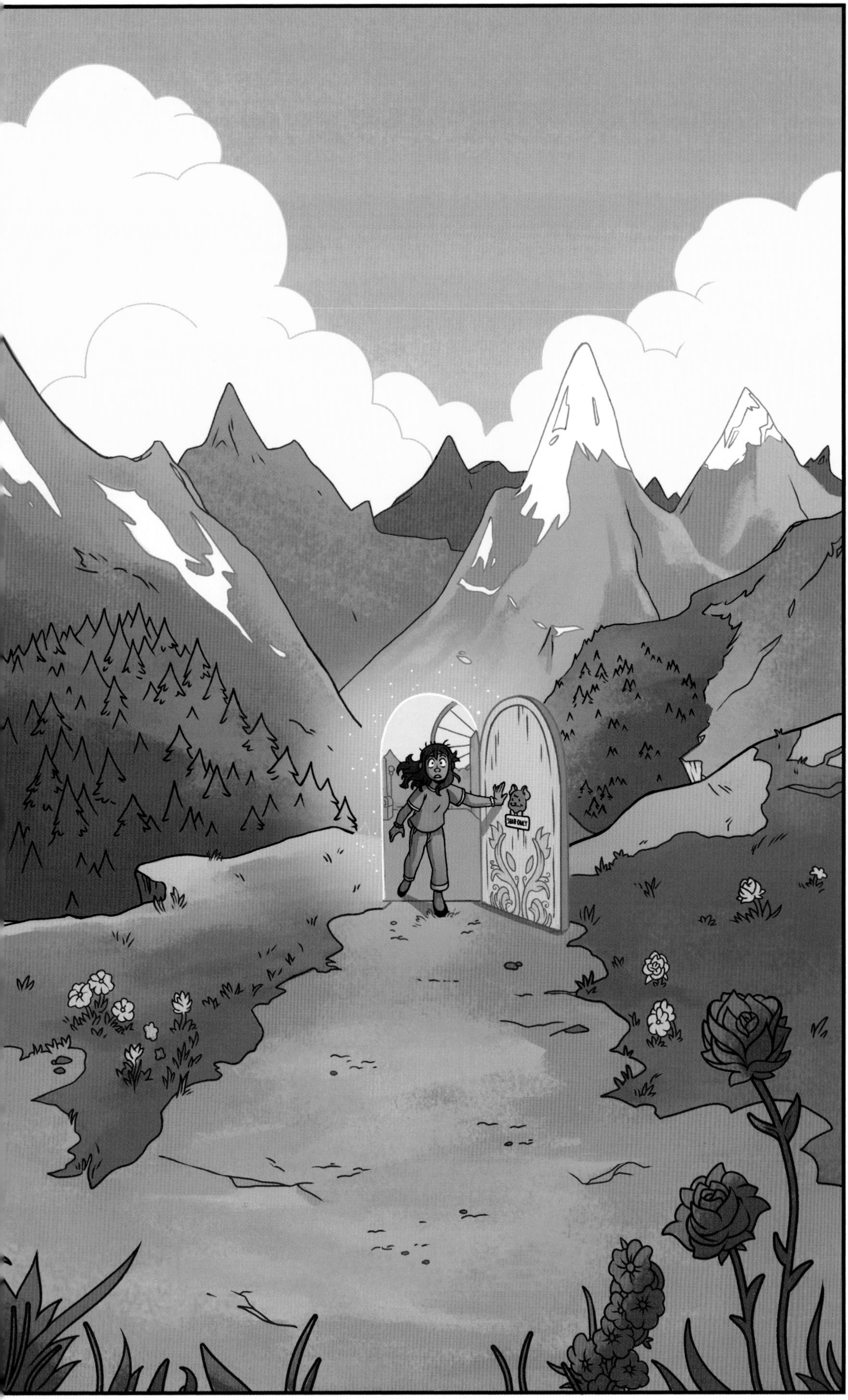

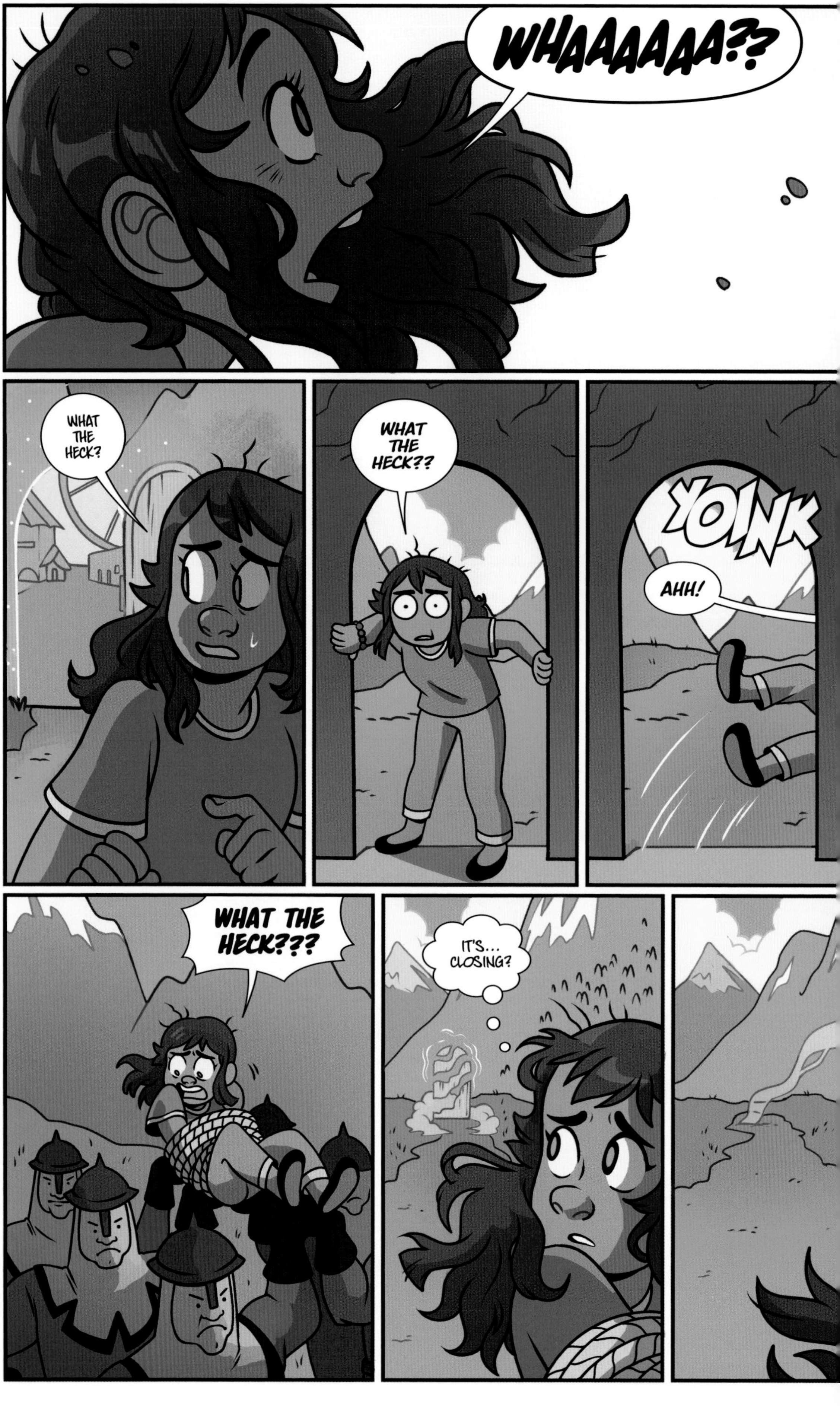
WHAAAAAA??
WHAT THE HECK?
WHAT THE HECK??
YOINK
AHH!
WHAT THE HECK???
IT'S... CLOSING?

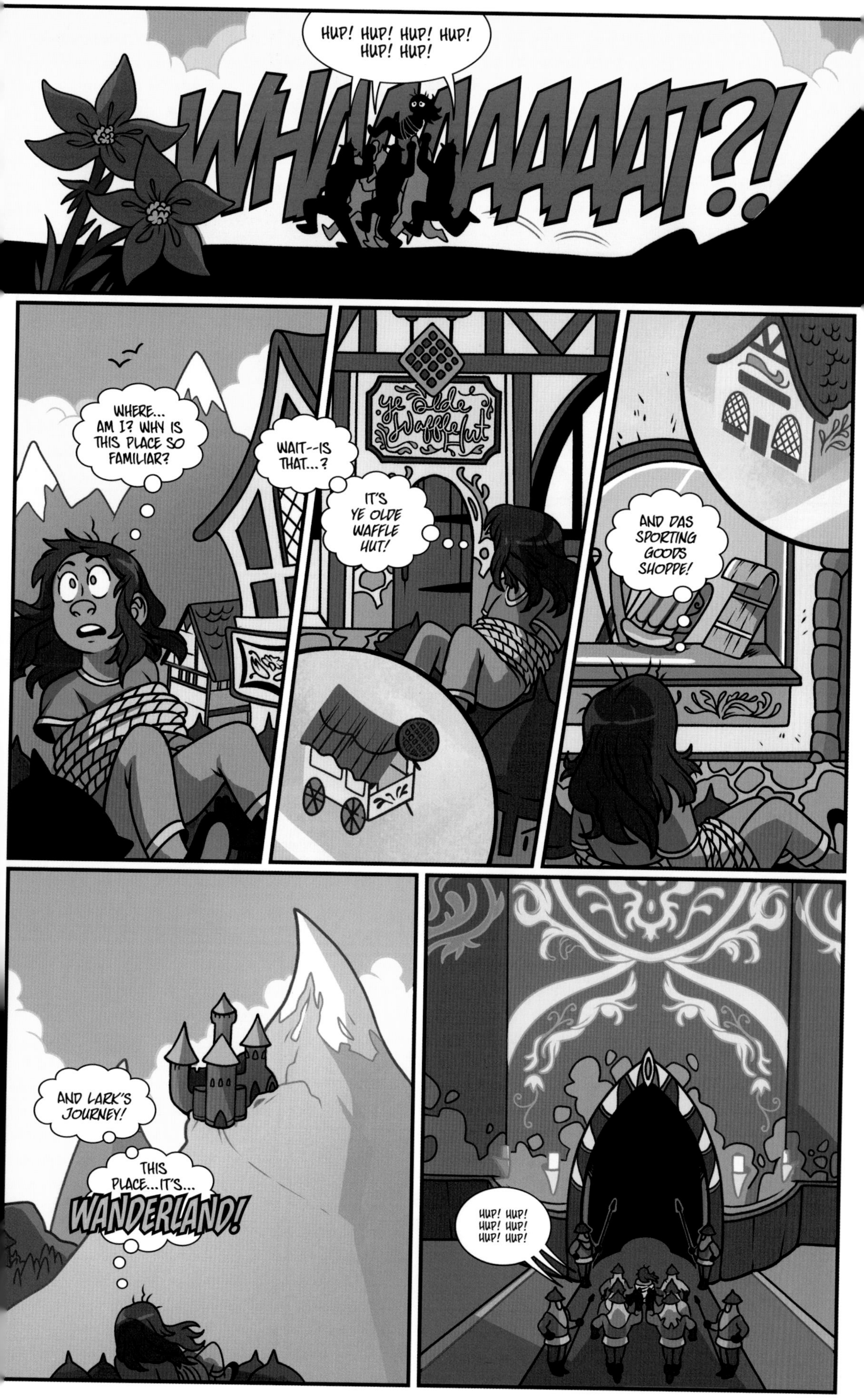
HUP! HUP! HUP! HUP! HUP! HUP!
WHAAAAAAT?!
WHERE... AM I? WHY IS THIS PLACE SO FAMILIAR?
WAIT--IS THAT...?
ye olde Waffle Hut
IT'S YE OLDE WAFFLE HUT!
AND DAS SPORTING GOODS SHOPPE!
AND LARK'S JOURNEY!
THIS PLACE...IT'S... WANDERLAND!
HUP! HUP! HUP! HUP! HUP! HUP!

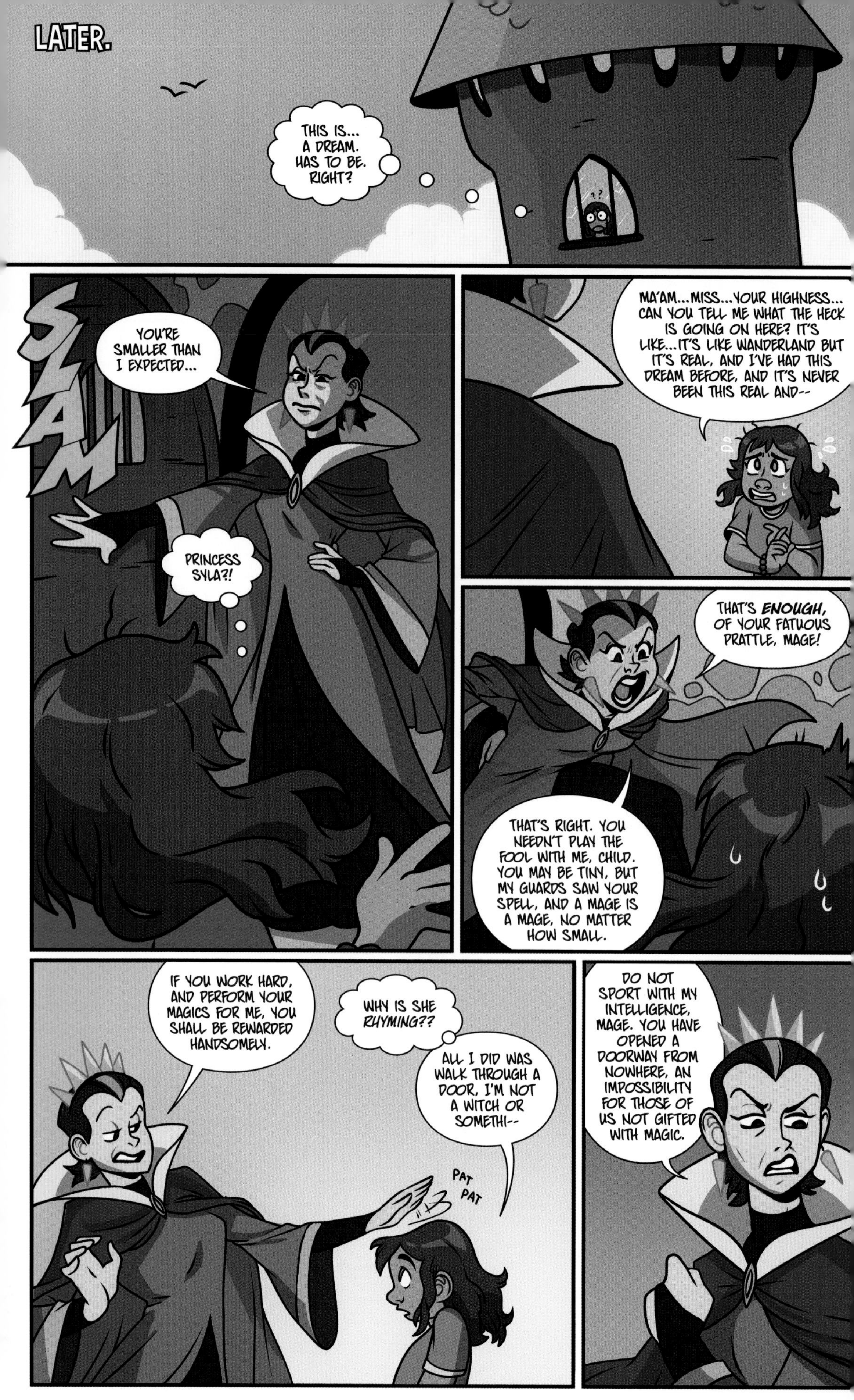
LATER.
THIS IS... A DREAM. HAS TO BE. RIGHT?
SLAM
YOU'RE SMALLER THAN I EXPECTED...
PRINCESS SYLA?!
MA'AM...MISS...YOUR HIGHNESS... CAN YOU TELL ME WHAT THE HECK IS GOING ON HERE? IT'S LIKE...IT'S LIKE WANDERLAND BUT IT'S REAL, AND I'VE HAD THIS DREAM BEFORE, AND IT'S NEVER BEEN THIS REAL AND--
THAT'S **ENOUGH,** OF YOUR FATUOUS PRATTLE, MAGE!
THAT'S RIGHT. YOU NEEDN'T PLAY THE FOOL WITH ME, CHILD. YOU MAY BE TINY, BUT MY GUARDS SAW YOUR SPELL, AND A MAGE IS A MAGE, NO MATTER HOW SMALL.
IF YOU WORK HARD, AND PERFORM YOUR MAGICS FOR ME, YOU SHALL BE REWARDED HANDSOMELY.
WHY IS SHE RHYMING??
ALL I DID WAS WALK THROUGH A DOOR, I'M NOT A WITCH OR SOMETHI--
PAT PAT
DO NOT SPORT WITH MY INTELLIGENCE, MAGE. YOU HAVE OPENED A DOORWAY FROM NOWHERE, AN IMPOSSIBILITY FOR THOSE OF US NOT GIFTED WITH MAGIC.

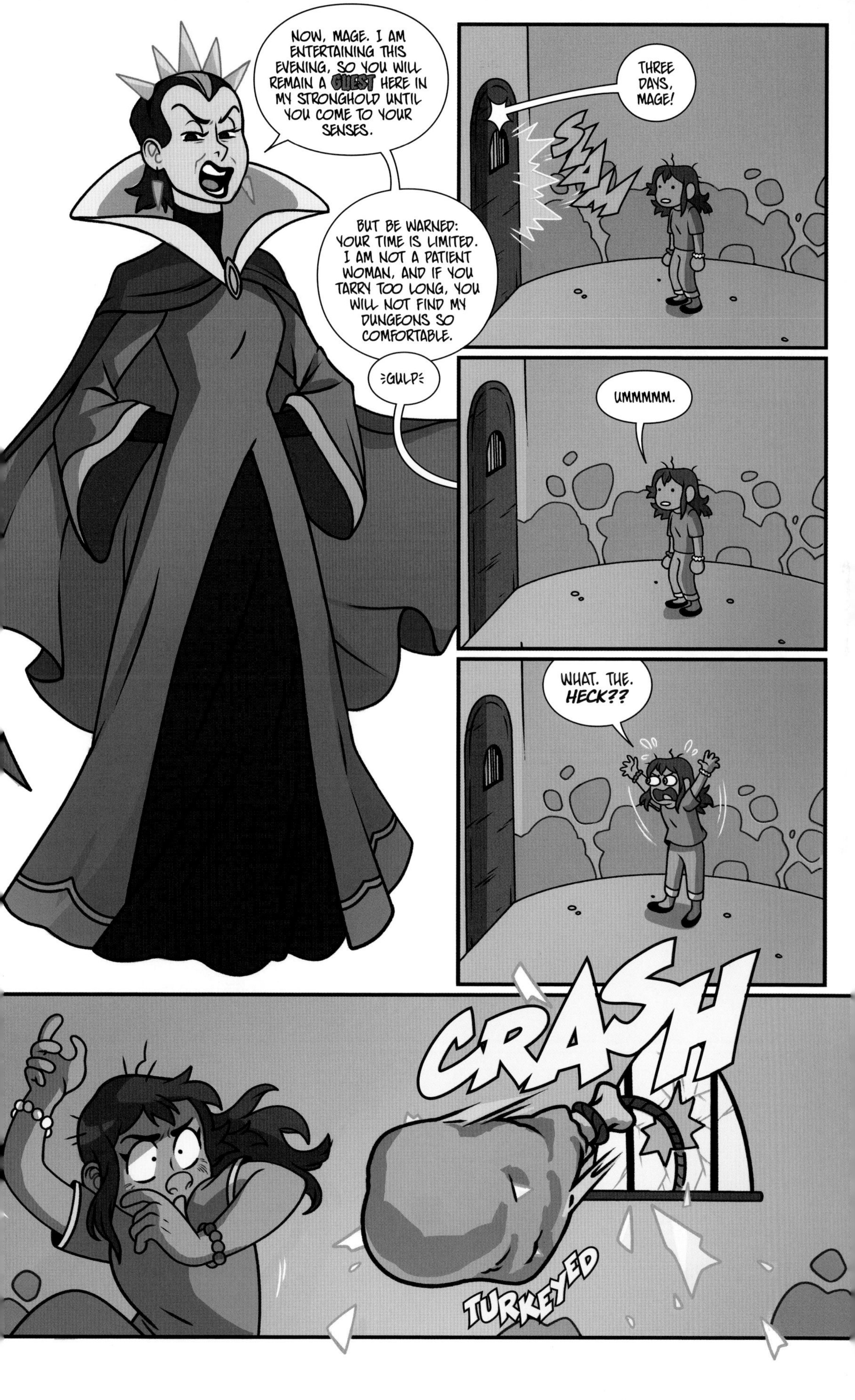
NOW, MAGE. I AM ENTERTAINING THIS EVENING, SO YOU WILL REMAIN A GUEST HERE IN MY STRONGHOLD UNTIL YOU COME TO YOUR SENSES.
BUT BE WARNED: YOUR TIME IS LIMITED. I AM NOT A PATIENT WOMAN, AND IF YOU TARRY TOO LONG, YOU WILL NOT FIND MY DUNGEONS SO COMFORTABLE.
GULP
THREE DAYS, MAGE!
SLAM
UMMMMM.
WHAT. THE. HECK??
CRASH
TURKEYED

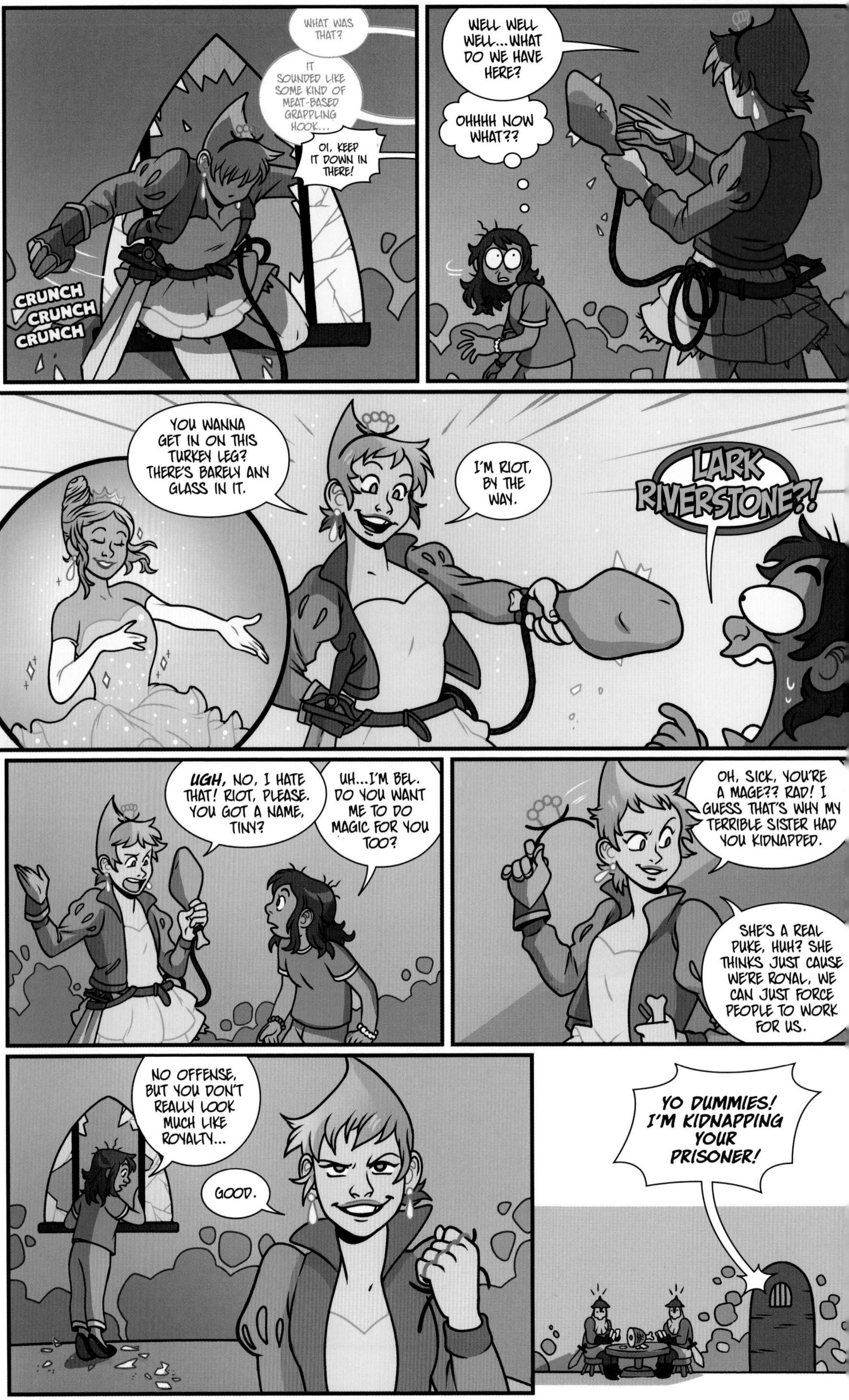
WHAT WAS THAT?
IT SOUNDED LIKE SOME KIND OF MEAT-BASED GRAPPLING HOOK...
OI, KEEP IT DOWN IN THERE!
CRUNCH CRUNCH CRUNCH
WELL WELL WELL...WHAT DO WE HAVE HERE?
OHHHH NOW WHAT??
YOU WANNA GET IN ON THIS TURKEY LEG? THERE'S BARELY ANY GLASS IN IT.
I'M RIOT, BY THE WAY.
LARK RIVERSTONE?!
UGH, NO, I HATE THAT! RIOT, PLEASE. YOU GOT A NAME, TINY?
UH...I'M BEL. DO YOU WANT ME TO DO MAGIC FOR YOU TOO?
OH, SICK, YOU'RE A MAGE?? RAD! I GUESS THAT'S WHY MY TERRIBLE SISTER HAD YOU KIDNAPPED.
SHE'S A REAL PUKE, HUH? SHE THINKS JUST CAUSE WE'RE ROYAL, WE CAN JUST FORCE PEOPLE TO WORK FOR US.
NO OFFENSE, BUT YOU DON'T REALLY LOOK MUCH LIKE ROYALTY...
GOOD.
YO DUMMIES! I'M KIDNAPPING YOUR PRISONER!

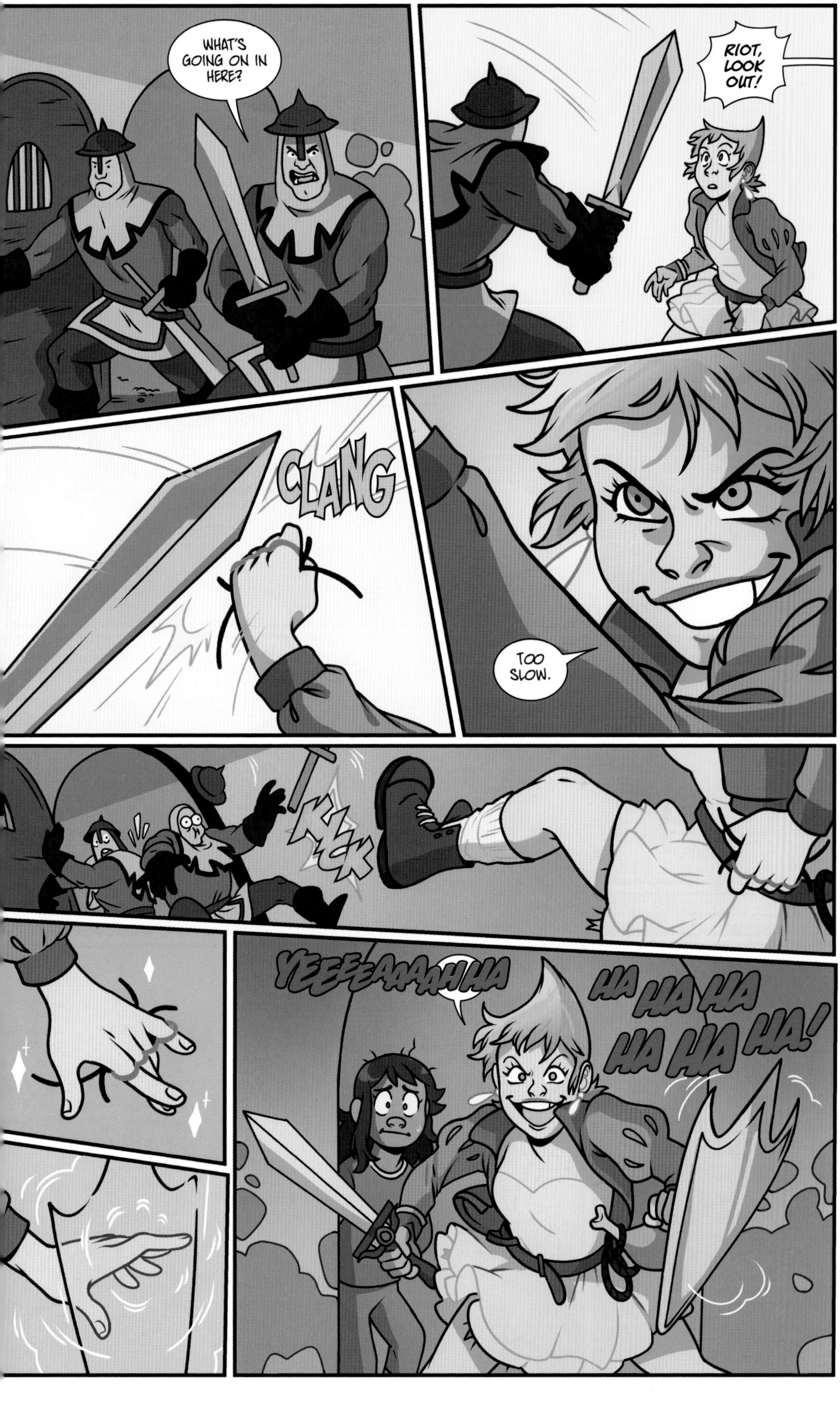
WHAT'S GOING ON IN HERE?
RIOT, LOOK OUT!
CLANG
TOO SLOW.
KLICK
YEEEEAAAAHHA
HA HA HA HA HA HA!

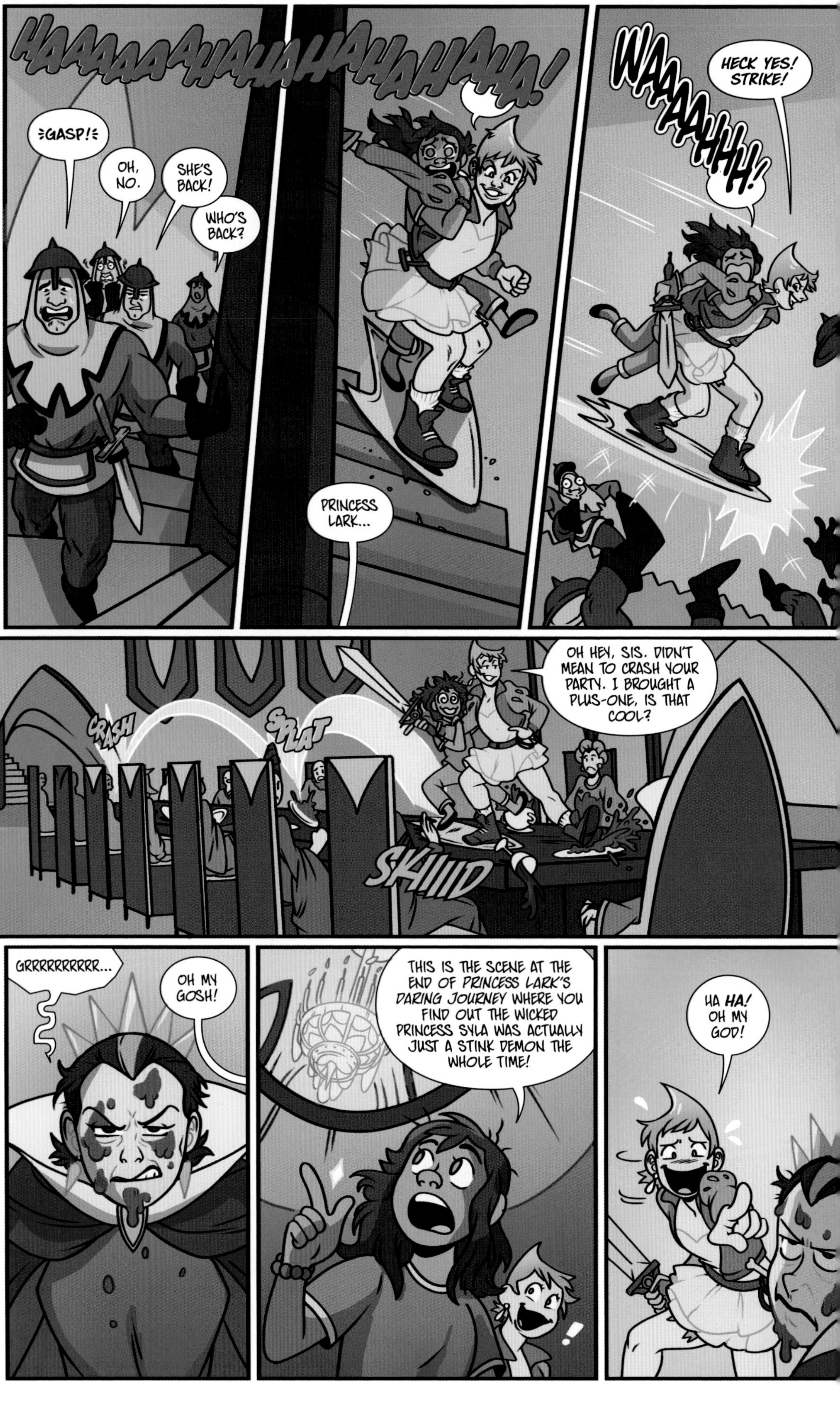

HAAAAAAHAHAHAHAHAHAHA!
¡GASP!¡
OH, NO.
SHE'S BACK!
WHO'S BACK?
PRINCESS LARK...
WAAAAAHHH!
HECK YES! STRIKE!
CRASH
SPLAT
SKIIID
OH HEY, SIS. DIDN'T MEAN TO CRASH YOUR PARTY. I BROUGHT A PLUS-ONE, IS THAT COOL?
GRRRRRRRRR...
OH MY GOSH!
THIS IS THE SCENE AT THE END OF PRINCESS LARK'S DARING JOURNEY WHERE YOU FIND OUT THE WICKED PRINCESS SYLA WAS ACTUALLY JUST A STINK DEMON THE WHOLE TIME!
HA HA! OH MY GOD!

STINK DEMON, I LOVE IT! SOLID BURN, B!

SYLA, DO YOU GET IT? IT'S CAUSE YOU SMELL BAD, BUT ALSO YOU HAVE A TERRIBLE PERSONALITY!

SAY WHATEVER YOU WANT "RIOT". CHAMPION OF THE UNPOPULAR.

BUT YOU AND I BOTH KNOW THE ONLY REASON YOU'RE EVEN HERE IS BECAUSE NO ONE ELSE IN THIS WHOLE KINGDOM EVEN REMEMBERS YOU EXIST.

DANG!

WHISPER...

WHISPER...

OOOOOOOH!

=GASP!=

WHISPER...

WHISPER...

TEE HEE!

TEE HEE!

WHISPER

OOOOO

DANG!

TEE HEE!

WHISPER...

TEE HEE

TCHT.

YOU'RE PATHE--

AAGGHH!

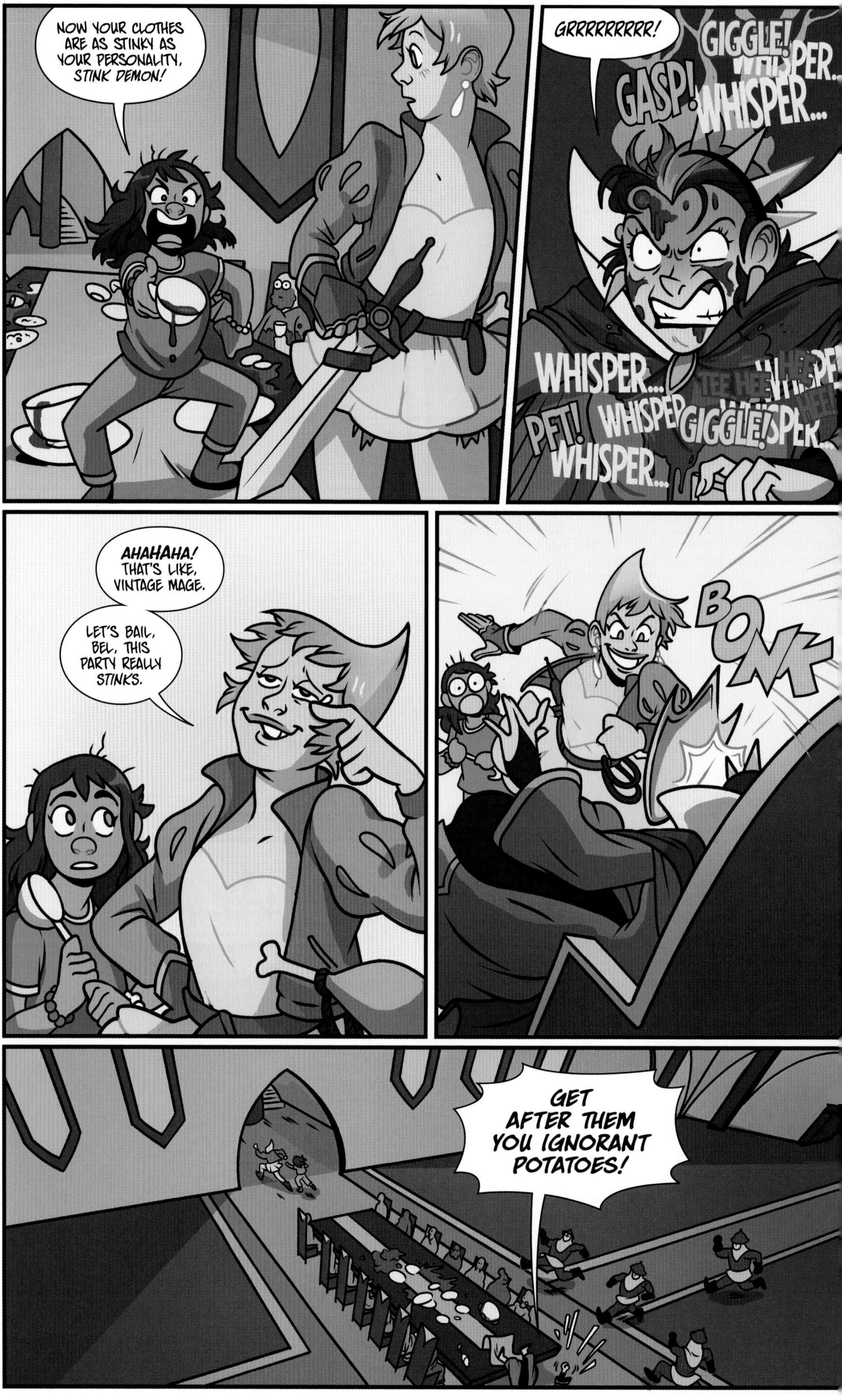
NOW YOUR CLOTHES ARE AS STINKY AS YOUR PERSONALITY, STINK DEMON!
GRRRRRRRRR!
GIGGLE!
WHISPER...
GASP!
WHISPER...
WHISPER...
TEE HEE
WHISPER
HEE!
PFT!
WHISPER
GIGGLE!
WHISPER...
WHISPER...
AHAHAHA! THAT'S LIKE, VINTAGE MAGE.
LET'S BAIL, BEL, THIS PARTY REALLY STINKS.
BONK
GET AFTER THEM YOU IGNORANT POTATOES!

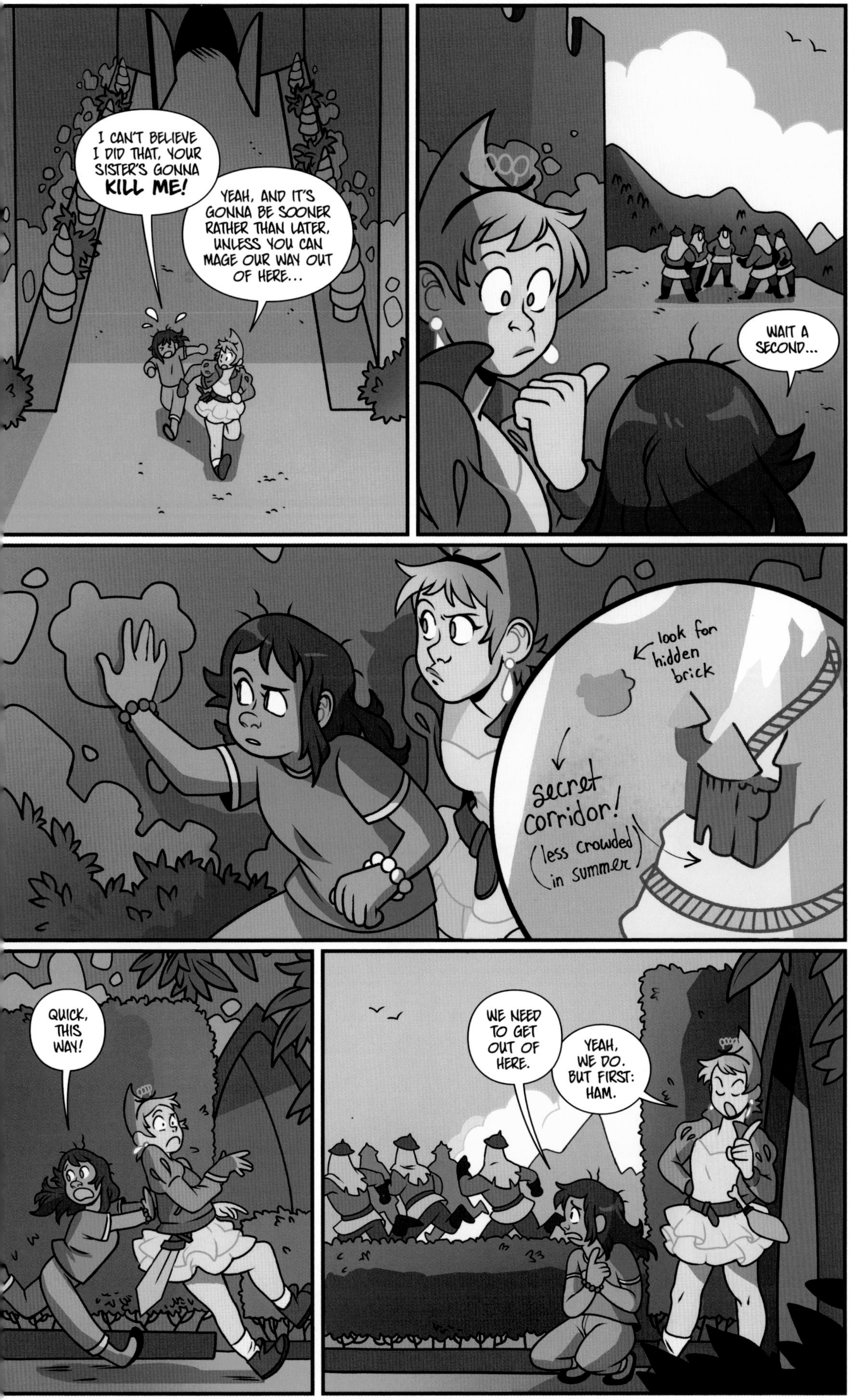
I CAN'T BELIEVE I DID THAT, YOUR SISTER'S GONNA KILL ME!
YEAH, AND IT'S GONNA BE SOONER RATHER THAN LATER, UNLESS YOU CAN MAGE OUR WAY OUT OF HERE...
WAIT A SECOND...
look for hidden brick
secret corridor!
(less crowded in summer)
QUICK, THIS WAY!
WE NEED TO GET OUT OF HERE.
YEAH, WE DO. BUT FIRST: HAM.

ham haus

OH, YOU KNOW US, PRINCESS. HAM HAUS IS NO SUPPORTER OF YOUR SISTER'S TAKING OVER THE KEEP.

DON'T HAVE ANY EXTRA ROOMS FOR THE NIGHT, BUT YOU CAN STAY WARM NEAR THE FIRE.

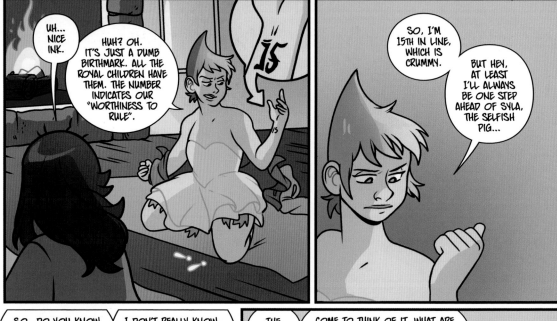

UH... NICE INK.

HUH? OH. IT'S JUST A DUMB BIRTHMARK. ALL THE ROYAL CHILDREN HAVE THEM. THE NUMBER INDICATES OUR "WORTHINESS TO RULE".

SO, I'M 15TH IN LINE, WHICH IS CRUMMY.

BUT HEY, AT LEAST I'LL ALWAYS BE ONE STEP AHEAD OF SYLA, THE SELFISH PIG...

SO...DO YOU KNOW ANYTHING ABOUT WHAT MAGES ARE SUPPOSED TO DO? MAYBE I COULD USE MAGIC TO GET BACK TO MY WORLD...

I DON'T REALLY KNOW. IT'S GOT SOMETHING TO DO WITH...BUILDING STUFF, I GUESS? BET YOU COULD FIND SOME INFO IN THE PALACE ARCHIVES...

THE PALACE.

COME TO THINK OF IT, WHAT ARE YOU DOING HANGING AROUND SYLA'S DUMPY FORTRESS, ANYWAY? I THOUGHT YOU'D *LIVE* IN THE PALACE...

UGH. NO...

I JUST STARTED MY "INTERNSHIP."

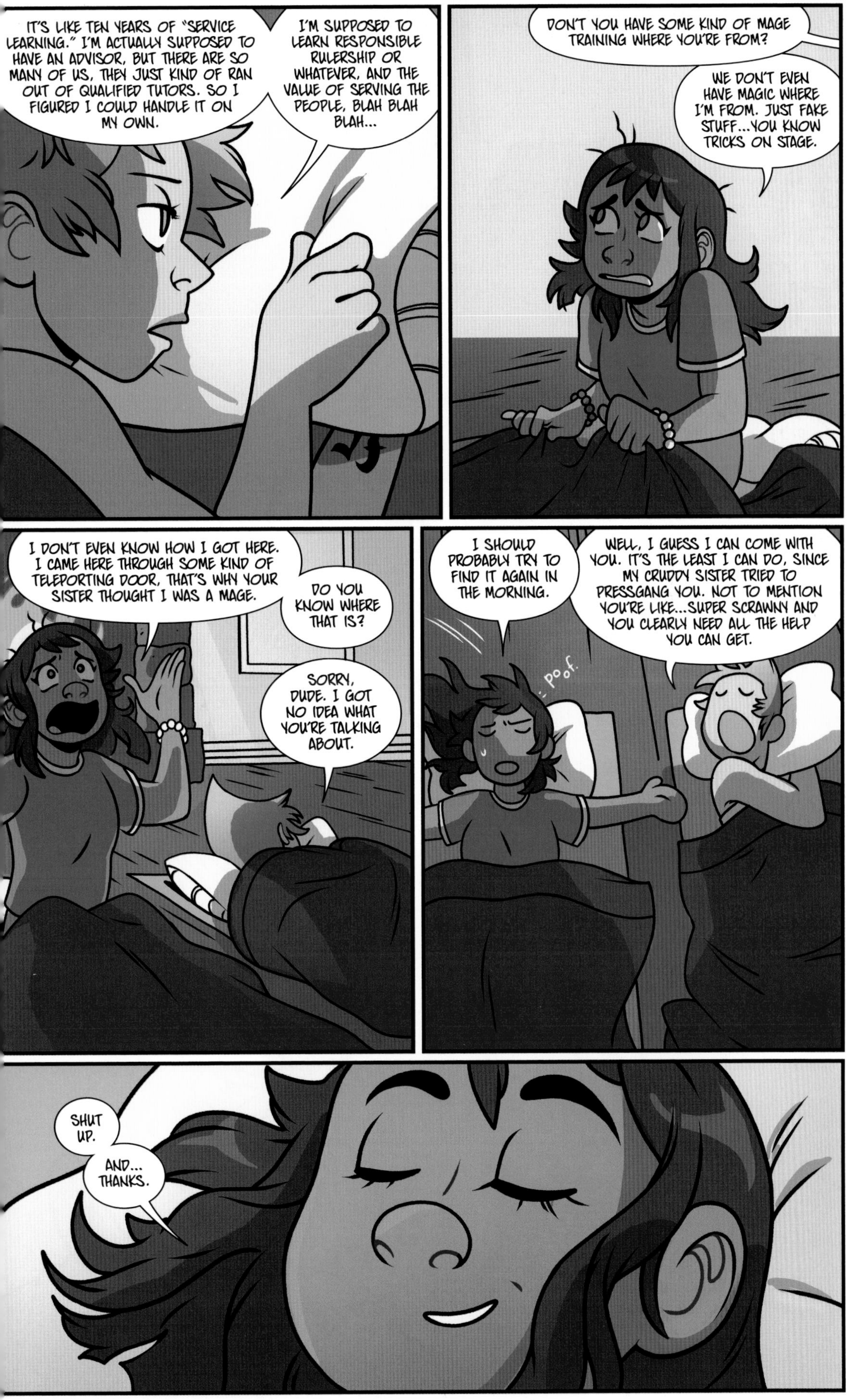
IT'S LIKE TEN YEARS OF "SERVICE LEARNING." I'M ACTUALLY SUPPOSED TO HAVE AN ADVISOR, BUT THERE ARE SO MANY OF US, THEY JUST KIND OF RAN OUT OF QUALIFIED TUTORS. SO I FIGURED I COULD HANDLE IT ON MY OWN.
I'M SUPPOSED TO LEARN RESPONSIBLE RULERSHIP OR WHATEVER, AND THE VALUE OF SERVING THE PEOPLE, BLAH BLAH BLAH...
DON'T YOU HAVE SOME KIND OF MAGE TRAINING WHERE YOU'RE FROM?
WE DON'T EVEN HAVE MAGIC WHERE I'M FROM. JUST FAKE STUFF...YOU KNOW TRICKS ON STAGE.
I DON'T EVEN KNOW HOW I GOT HERE. I CAME HERE THROUGH SOME KIND OF TELEPORTING DOOR, THAT'S WHY YOUR SISTER THOUGHT I WAS A MAGE.
DO YOU KNOW WHERE THAT IS?
SORRY, DUDE. I GOT NO IDEA WHAT YOU'RE TALKING ABOUT.
I SHOULD PROBABLY TRY TO FIND IT AGAIN IN THE MORNING.
poof.
WELL, I GUESS I CAN COME WITH YOU. IT'S THE LEAST I CAN DO, SINCE MY CRUDDY SISTER TRIED TO PRESSGANG YOU. NOT TO MENTION YOU'RE LIKE...SUPER SCRAWNY AND YOU CLEARLY NEED ALL THE HELP YOU CAN GET.
SHUT UP.
AND... THANKS.

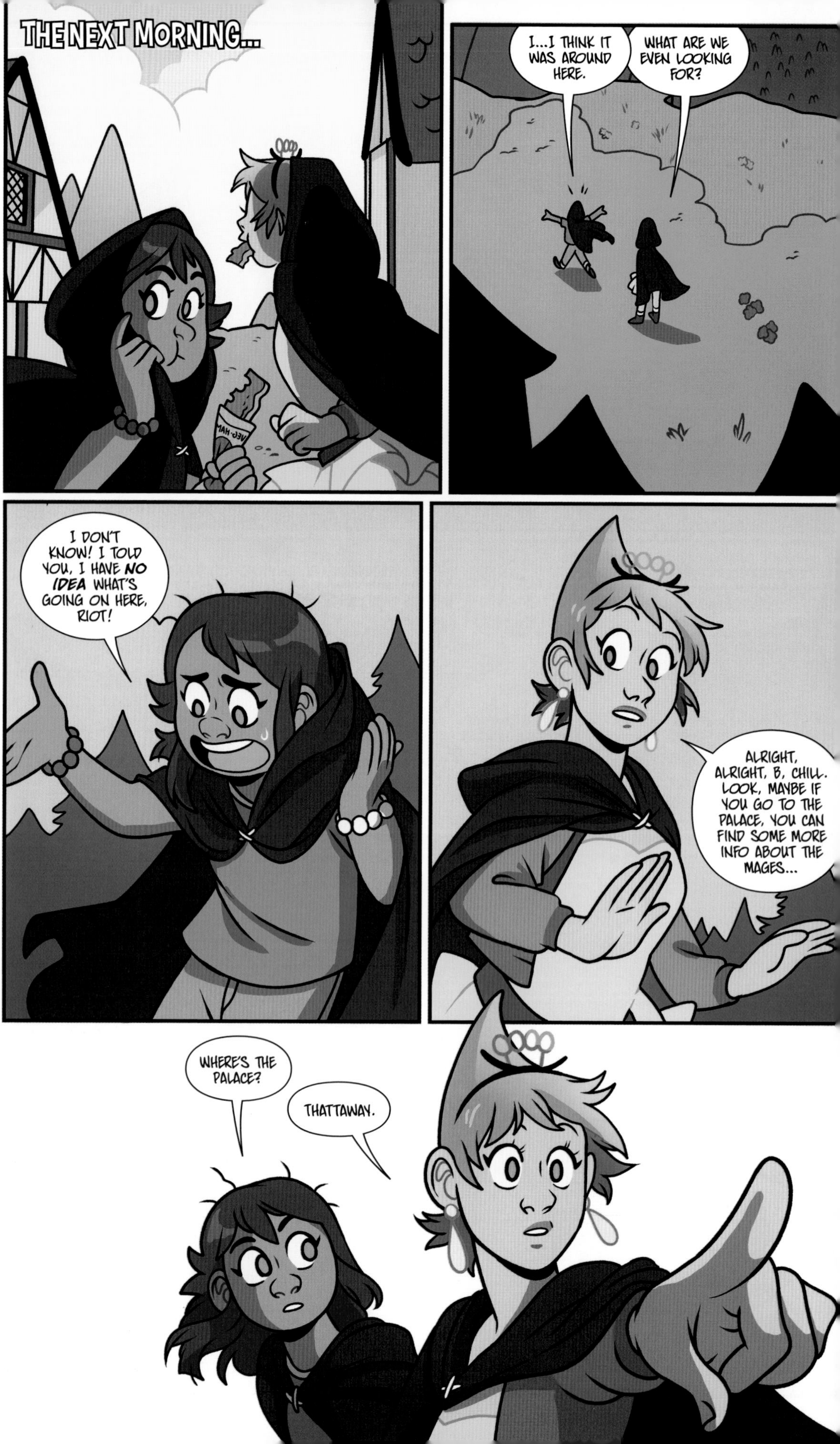
THE NEXT MORNING...
I...I THINK IT WAS AROUND HERE.
WHAT ARE WE EVEN LOOKING FOR?
I DON'T KNOW! I TOLD YOU, I HAVE NO IDEA WHAT'S GOING ON HERE, RIOT!
ALRIGHT, ALRIGHT, B, CHILL. LOOK, MAYBE IF YOU GO TO THE PALACE, YOU CAN FIND SOME MORE INFO ABOUT THE MAGES...
WHERE'S THE PALACE?
THATTAWAY.

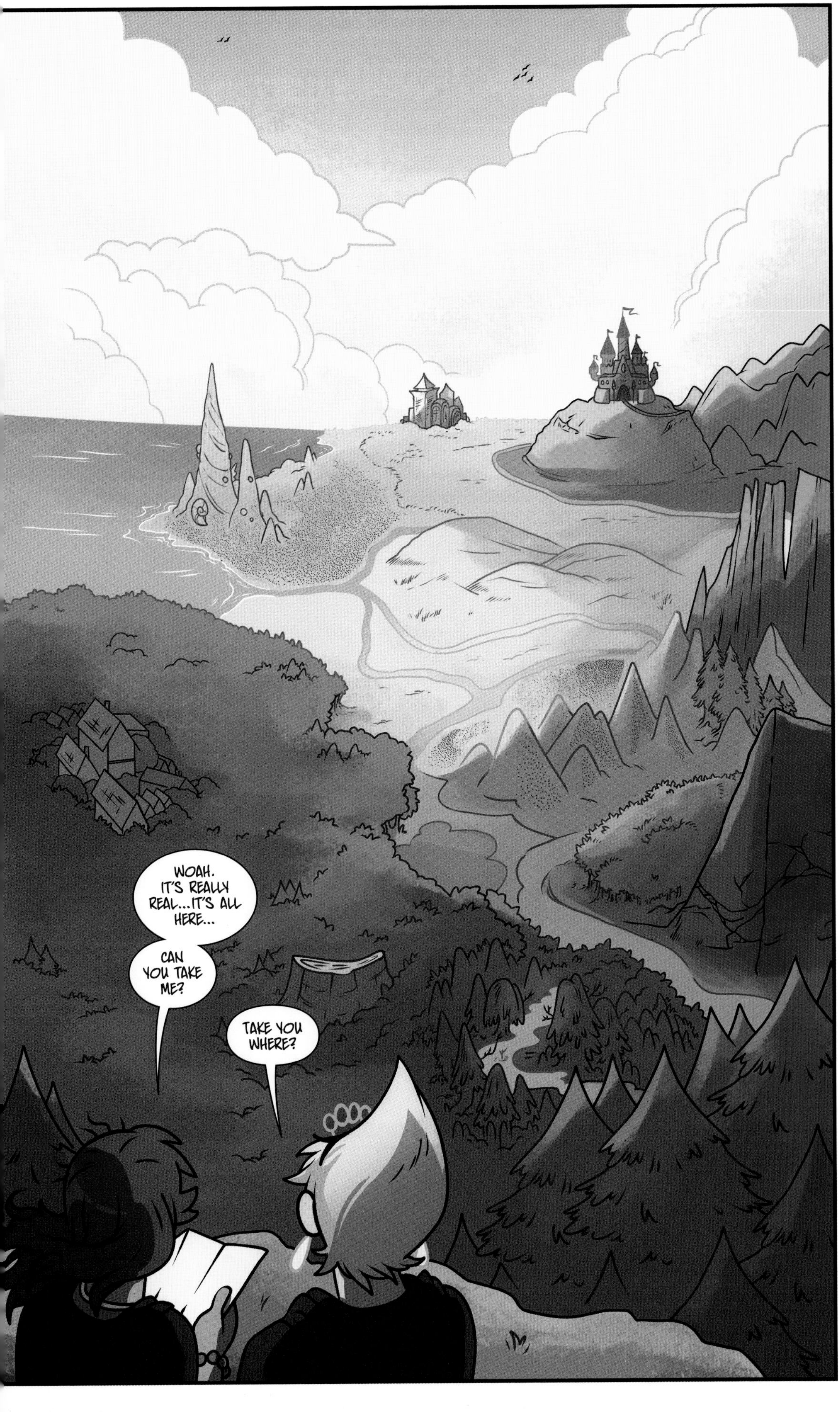
WOAH. IT'S REALLY REAL...IT'S ALL HERE...
CAN YOU TAKE ME?
TAKE YOU WHERE?

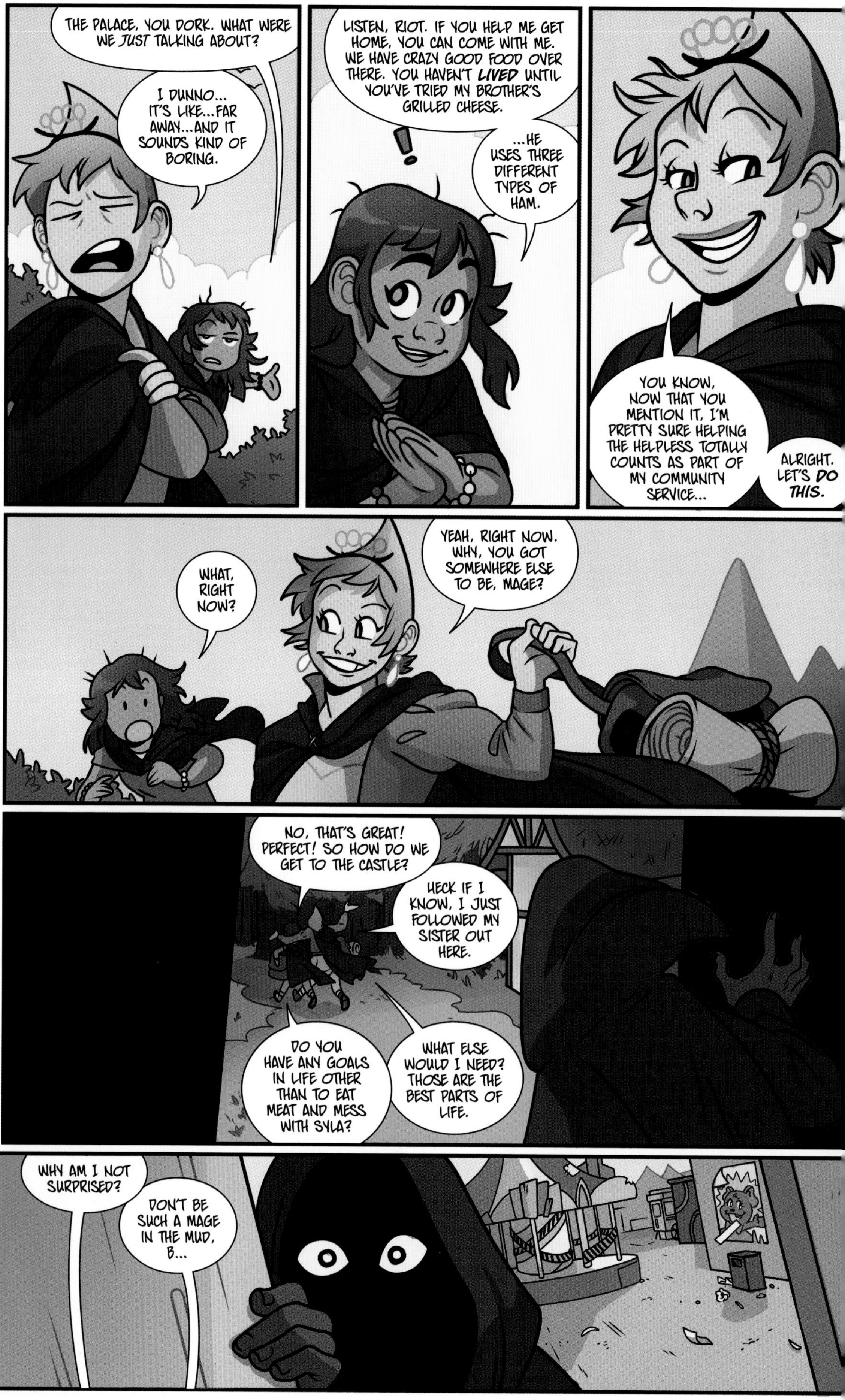
THE PALACE, YOU DORK. WHAT WERE WE *JUST* TALKING ABOUT?
I DUNNO... IT'S LIKE...FAR AWAY...AND IT SOUNDS KIND OF BORING.
LISTEN, RIOT. IF YOU HELP ME GET HOME, YOU CAN COME WITH ME. WE HAVE CRAZY GOOD FOOD OVER THERE. YOU HAVEN'T ***LIVED*** UNTIL YOU'VE TRIED MY BROTHER'S GRILLED CHEESE.
...HE USES THREE DIFFERENT TYPES OF HAM.
YOU KNOW, NOW THAT YOU MENTION IT, I'M PRETTY SURE HELPING THE HELPLESS TOTALLY COUNTS AS PART OF MY COMMUNITY SERVICE...
ALRIGHT. LET'S ***DO THIS.***
WHAT, RIGHT NOW?
YEAH, RIGHT NOW. WHY, YOU GOT SOMEWHERE ELSE TO BE, MAGE?
NO, THAT'S GREAT! PERFECT! SO HOW DO WE GET TO THE CASTLE?
HECK IF I KNOW, I JUST FOLLOWED MY SISTER OUT HERE.
DO YOU HAVE ANY GOALS IN LIFE OTHER THAN TO EAT MEAT AND MESS WITH SYLA?
WHAT ELSE WOULD I NEED? THOSE ARE THE BEST PARTS OF LIFE.
WHY AM I NOT SURPRISED?
DON'T BE SUCH A MAGE IN THE MUD, B...

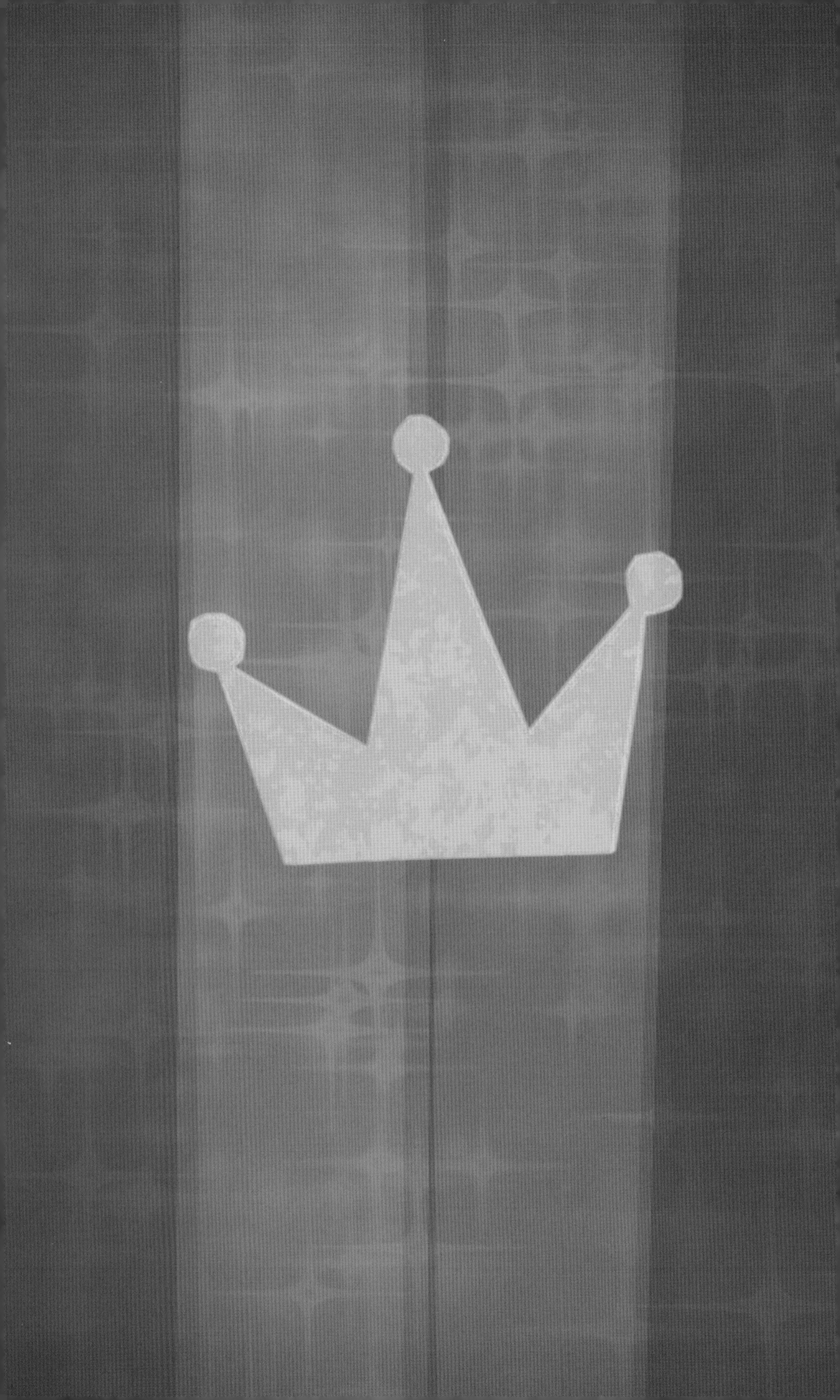

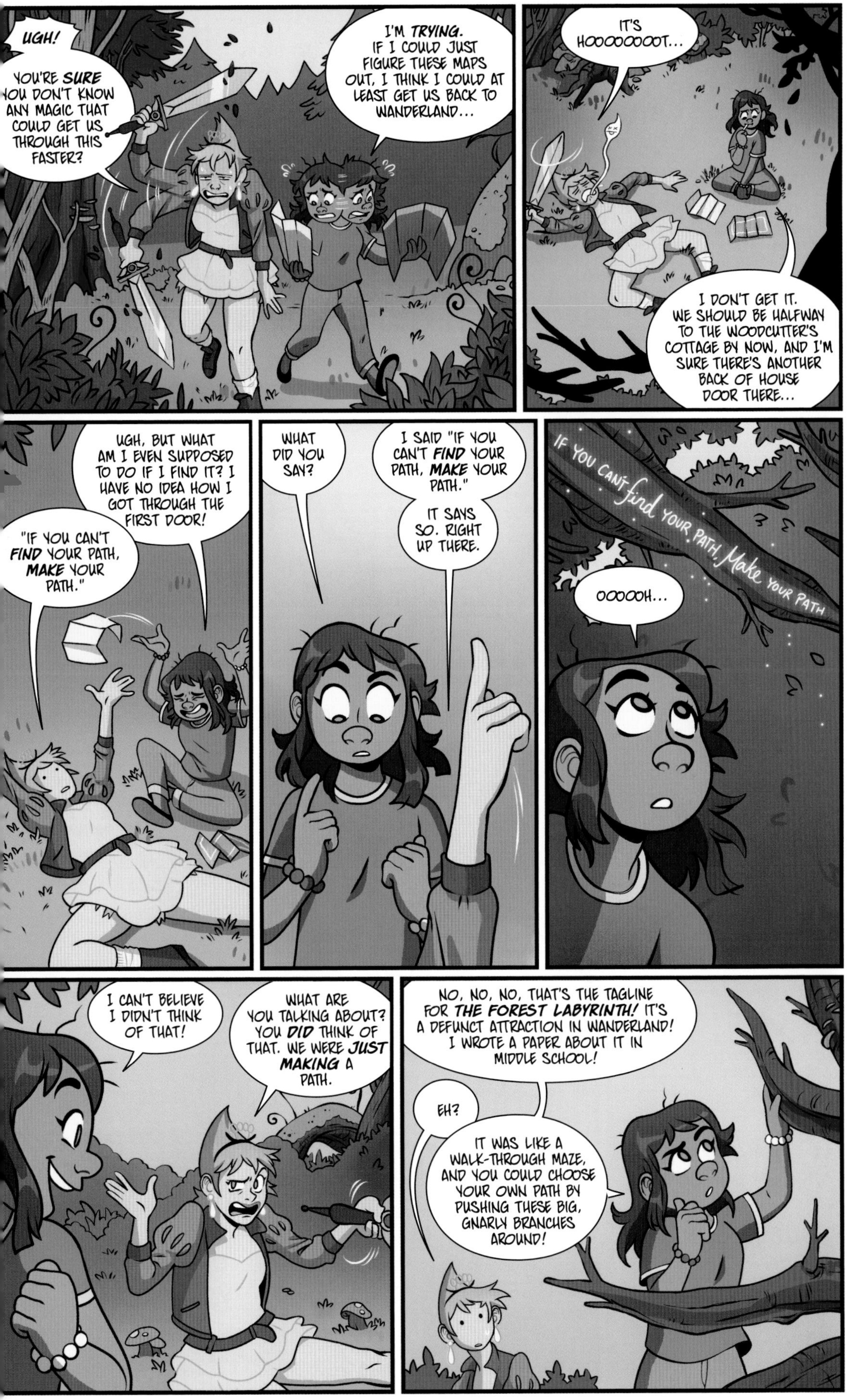
UGH!
YOU'RE SURE YOU DON'T KNOW ANY MAGIC THAT COULD GET US THROUGH THIS FASTER?
I'M TRYING. IF I COULD JUST FIGURE THESE MAPS OUT, I THINK I COULD AT LEAST GET US BACK TO WANDERLAND...
IT'S HOOOOOOOOT...
I DON'T GET IT. WE SHOULD BE HALFWAY TO THE WOODCUTTER'S COTTAGE BY NOW, AND I'M SURE THERE'S ANOTHER BACK OF HOUSE DOOR THERE...
UGH, BUT WHAT AM I EVEN SUPPOSED TO DO IF I FIND IT? I HAVE NO IDEA HOW I GOT THROUGH THE FIRST DOOR!
"IF YOU CAN'T FIND YOUR PATH, MAKE YOUR PATH."
WHAT DID YOU SAY?
I SAID "IF YOU CAN'T FIND YOUR PATH, MAKE YOUR PATH."
IT SAYS SO. RIGHT UP THERE.
IF YOU CAN'T find YOUR PATH, Make YOUR PATH
OOOOOH...
I CAN'T BELIEVE I DIDN'T THINK OF THAT!
WHAT ARE YOU TALKING ABOUT? YOU DID THINK OF THAT. WE WERE JUST MAKING A PATH.
NO, NO, NO, THAT'S THE TAGLINE FOR THE FOREST LABYRINTH! IT'S A DEFUNCT ATTRACTION IN WANDERLAND! I WROTE A PAPER ABOUT IT IN MIDDLE SCHOOL!
EH?
IT WAS LIKE A WALK-THROUGH MAZE, AND YOU COULD CHOOSE YOUR OWN PATH BY PUSHING THESE BIG, GNARLY BRANCHES AROUND!

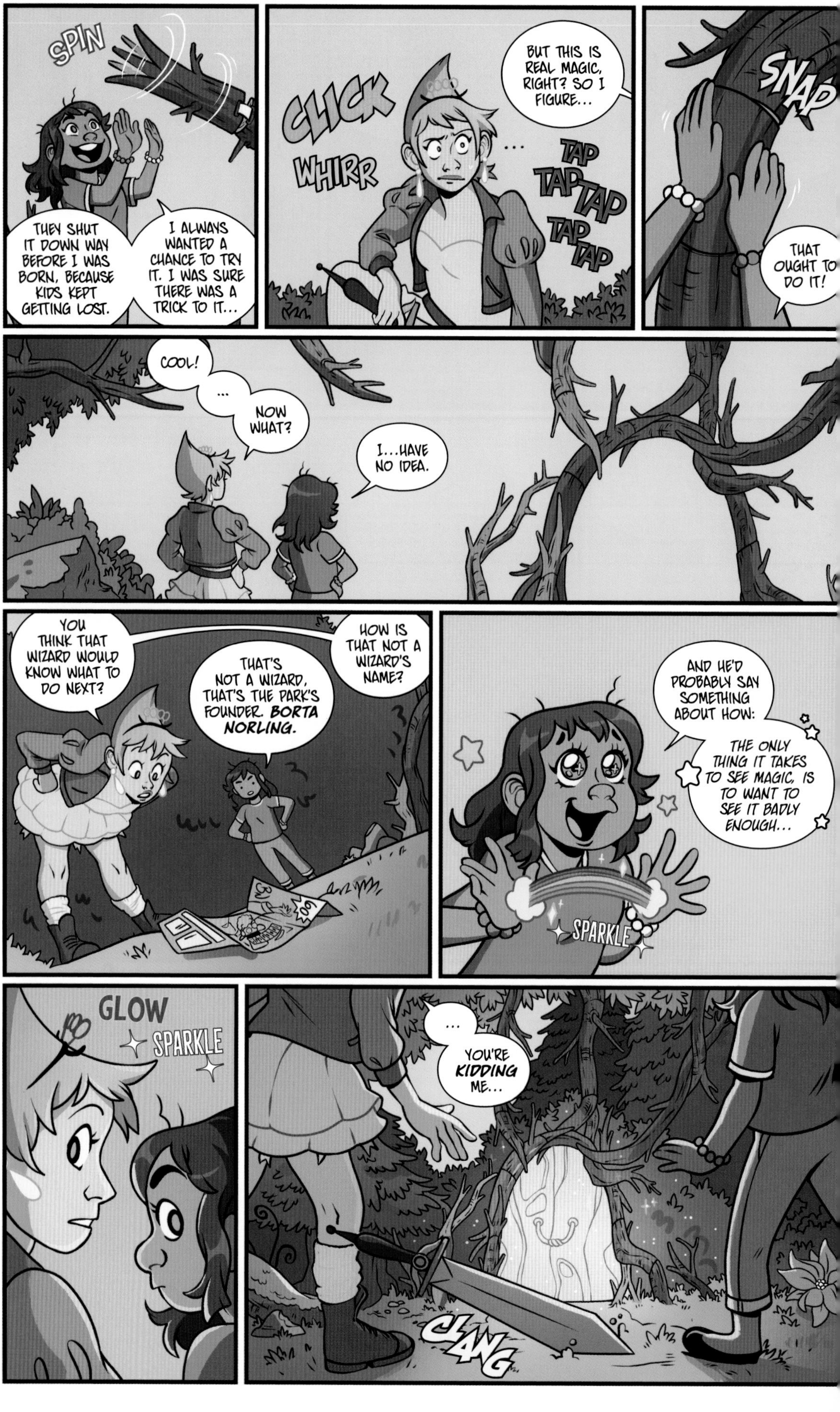
SPIN
THEY SHUT IT DOWN WAY BEFORE I WAS BORN, BECAUSE KIDS KEPT GETTING LOST.
I ALWAYS WANTED A CHANCE TO TRY IT. I WAS SURE THERE WAS A TRICK TO IT...
CLICK
WHIRR
...
BUT THIS IS REAL MAGIC, RIGHT? SO I FIGURE...
TAP TAP TAP TAP TAP
SNAP
THAT OUGHT TO DO IT!
COOL!
...
NOW WHAT?
I...HAVE NO IDEA.
YOU THINK THAT WIZARD WOULD KNOW WHAT TO DO NEXT?
THAT'S NOT A WIZARD, THAT'S THE PARK'S FOUNDER. **BORTA NORLING.**
HOW IS THAT NOT A WIZARD'S NAME?
AND HE'D PROBABLY SAY SOMETHING ABOUT HOW:
THE ONLY THING IT TAKES TO SEE MAGIC, IS TO WANT TO SEE IT BADLY ENOUGH...
SPARKLE
GLOW
SPARKLE
...
YOU'RE **KIDDING** ME...
CLANG

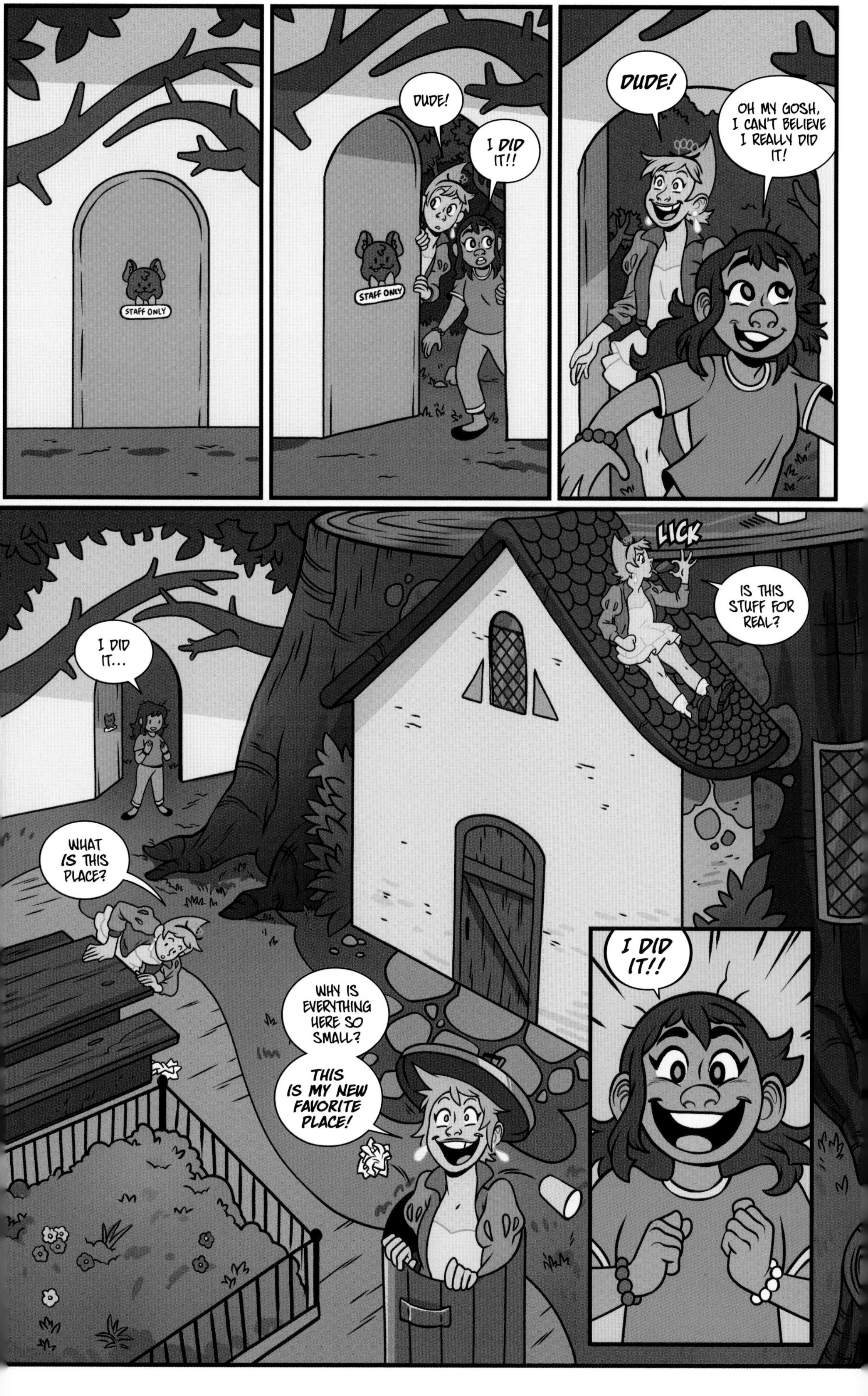
STAFF ONLY
DUDE!
I DID IT!!
STAFF ONLY
DUDE!
OH MY GOSH, I CAN'T BELIEVE I REALLY DID IT!
I DID IT...
LICK
IS THIS STUFF FOR REAL?
WHAT IS THIS PLACE?
WHY IS EVERYTHING HERE SO SMALL?
THIS IS MY NEW FAVORITE PLACE!
I DID IT!!

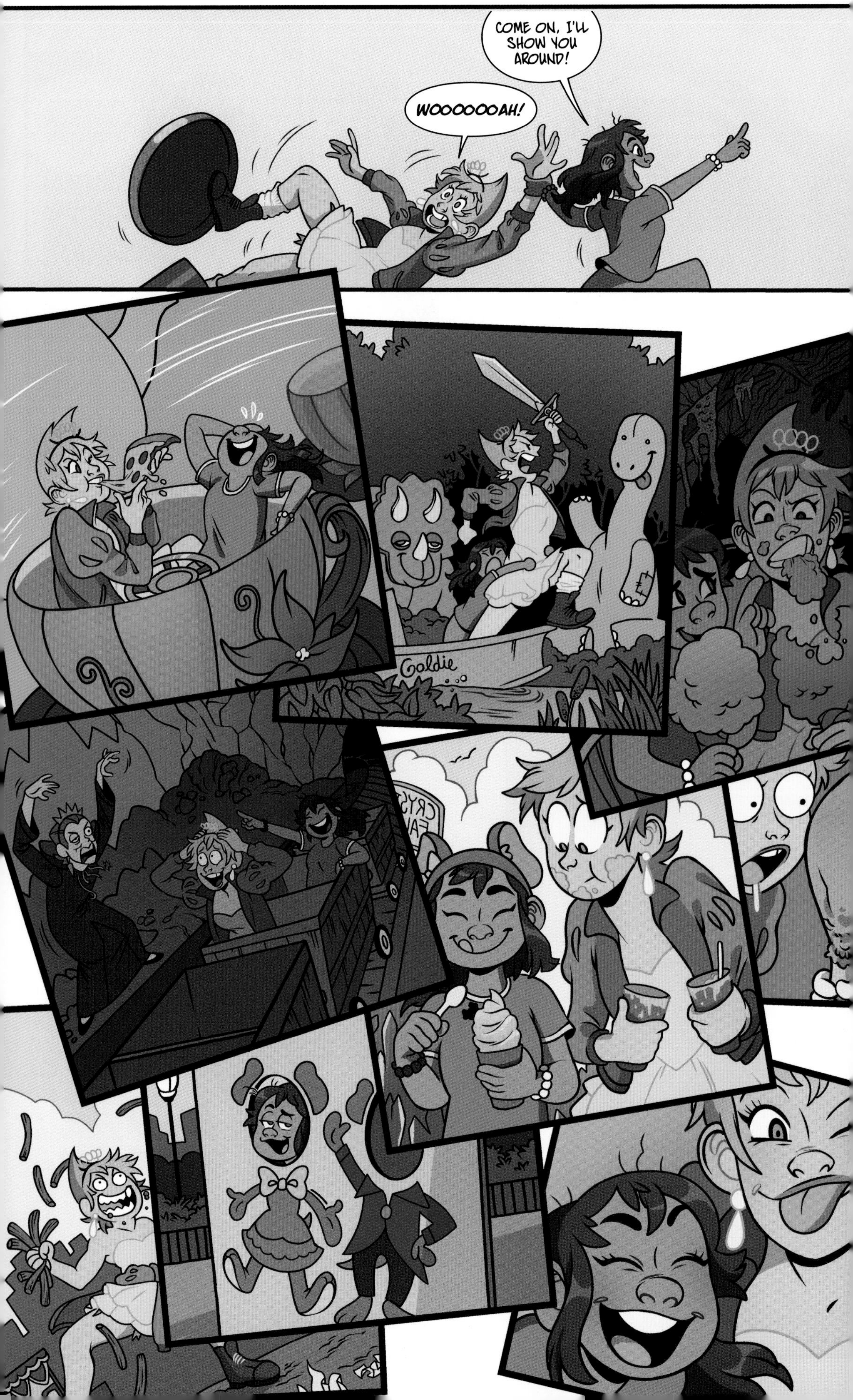
WOOOOOOAH!
COME ON, I'LL SHOW YOU AROUND!
Goldie

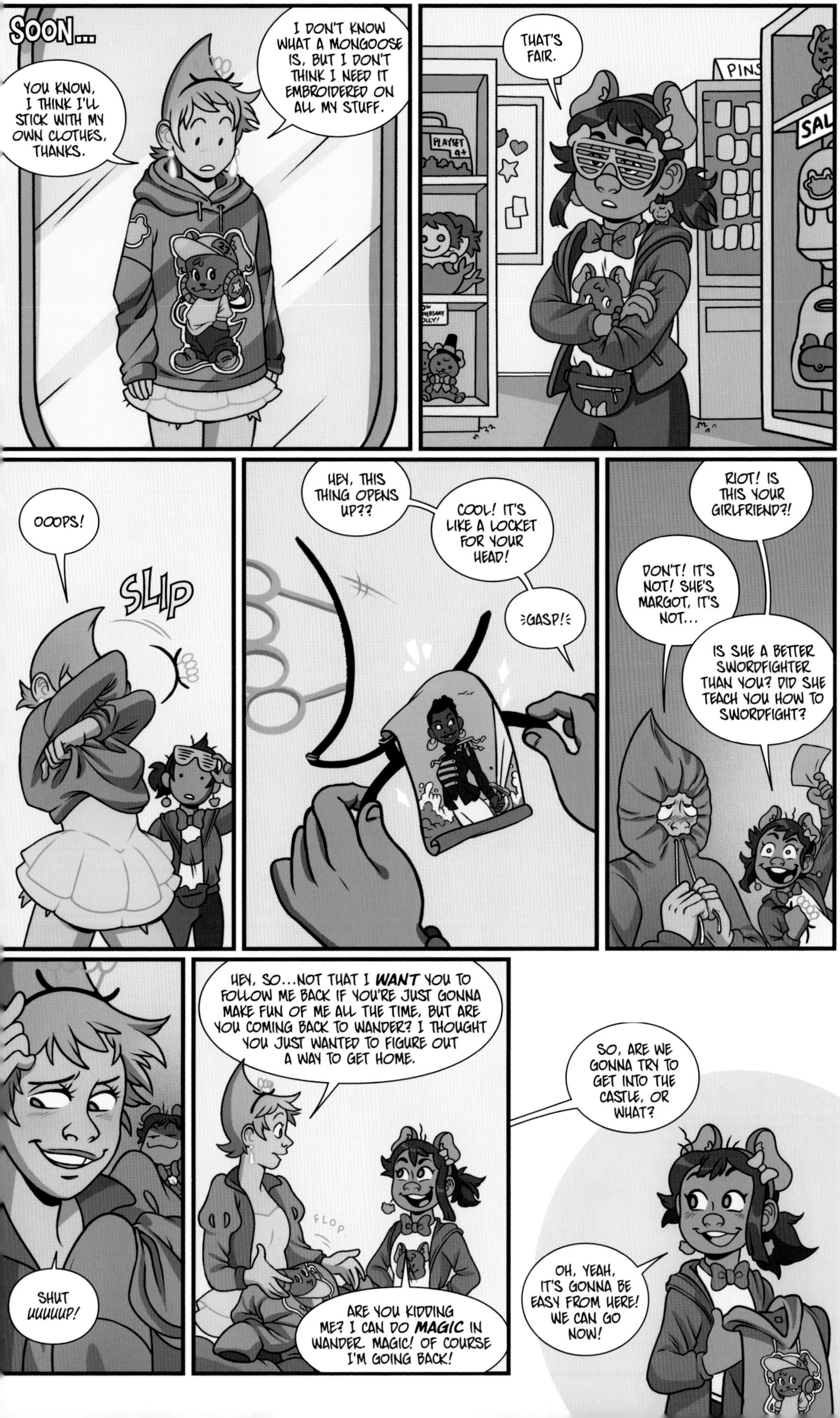

SOON...
YOU KNOW, I THINK I'LL STICK WITH MY OWN CLOTHES, THANKS.
I DON'T KNOW WHAT A MONGOOSE IS, BUT I DON'T THINK I NEED IT EMBROIDERED ON ALL MY STUFF.
THAT'S FAIR.
PINS
PLAYSET 4+
OOOPS!
SLIP
HEY, THIS THING OPENS UP??
COOL! IT'S LIKE A LOCKET FOR YOUR HEAD!
GASP!
RIOT! IS THIS YOUR GIRLFRIEND?!
DON'T! IT'S NOT! SHE'S MARGOT, IT'S NOT...
IS SHE A BETTER SWORDFIGHTER THAN YOU? DID SHE TEACH YOU HOW TO SWORDFIGHT?
SHUT UUUUUP!
HEY, SO...NOT THAT I WANT YOU TO FOLLOW ME BACK IF YOU'RE JUST GONNA MAKE FUN OF ME ALL THE TIME, BUT ARE YOU COMING BACK TO WANDER? I THOUGHT YOU JUST WANTED TO FIGURE OUT A WAY TO GET HOME.
FLOP
ARE YOU KIDDING ME? I CAN DO MAGIC IN WANDER. MAGIC! OF COURSE I'M GOING BACK!
SO, ARE WE GONNA TRY TO GET INTO THE CASTLE, OR WHAT?
OH, YEAH, IT'S GONNA BE EASY FROM HERE! WE CAN GO NOW!

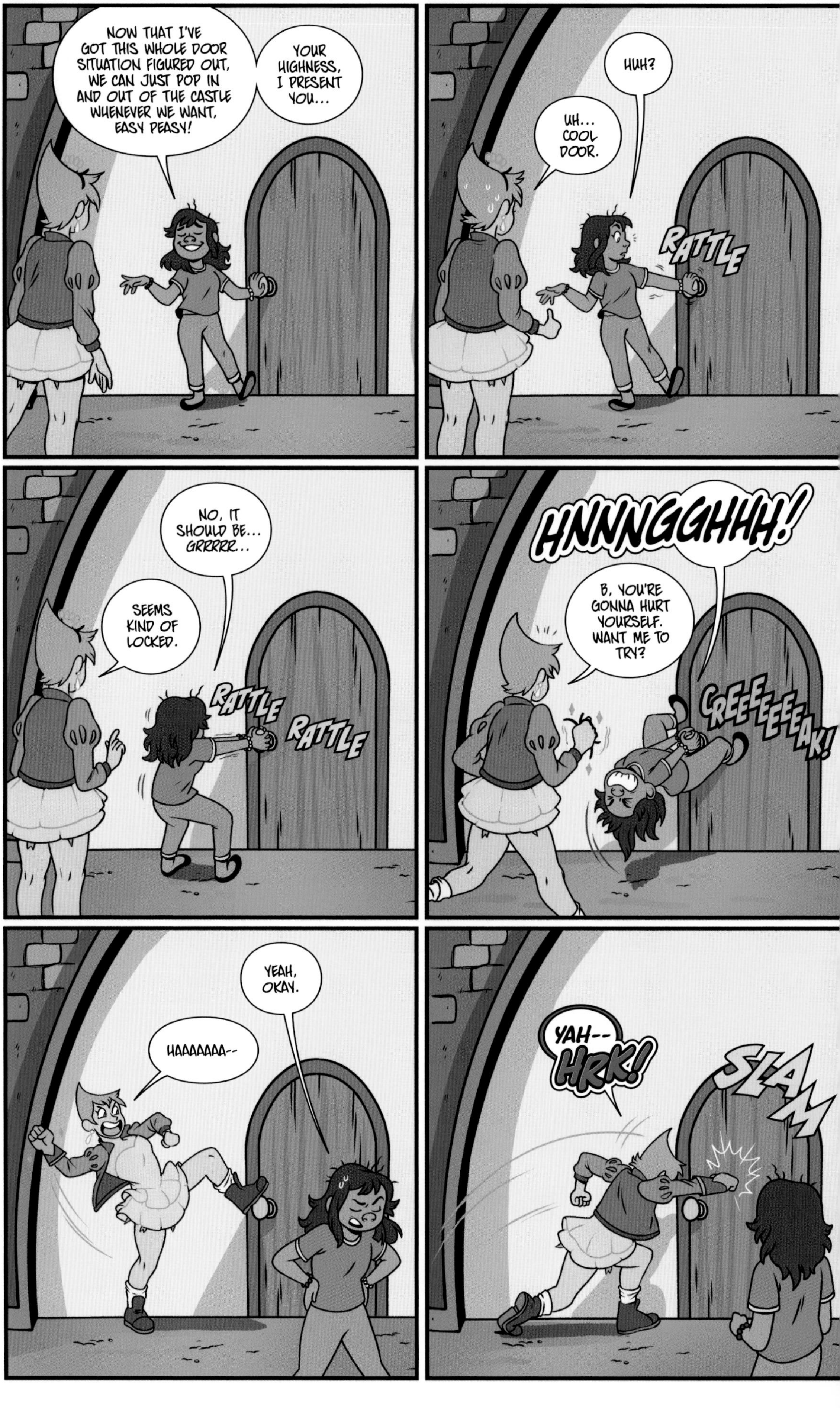
NOW THAT I'VE GOT THIS WHOLE DOOR SITUATION FIGURED OUT, WE CAN JUST POP IN AND OUT OF THE CASTLE WHENEVER WE WANT, EASY PEASY!
YOUR HIGHNESS, I PRESENT YOU...
HUH?
UH... COOL DOOR.
RATTLE
NO, IT SHOULD BE... GRRRRR...
SEEMS KIND OF LOCKED.
RATTLE
RATTLE
HNNNGGHHH!
B, YOU'RE GONNA HURT YOURSELF. WANT ME TO TRY?
CREEEEEEEAK!
YEAH, OKAY.
HAAAAAAA--
YAH--
HRK!
SLAM

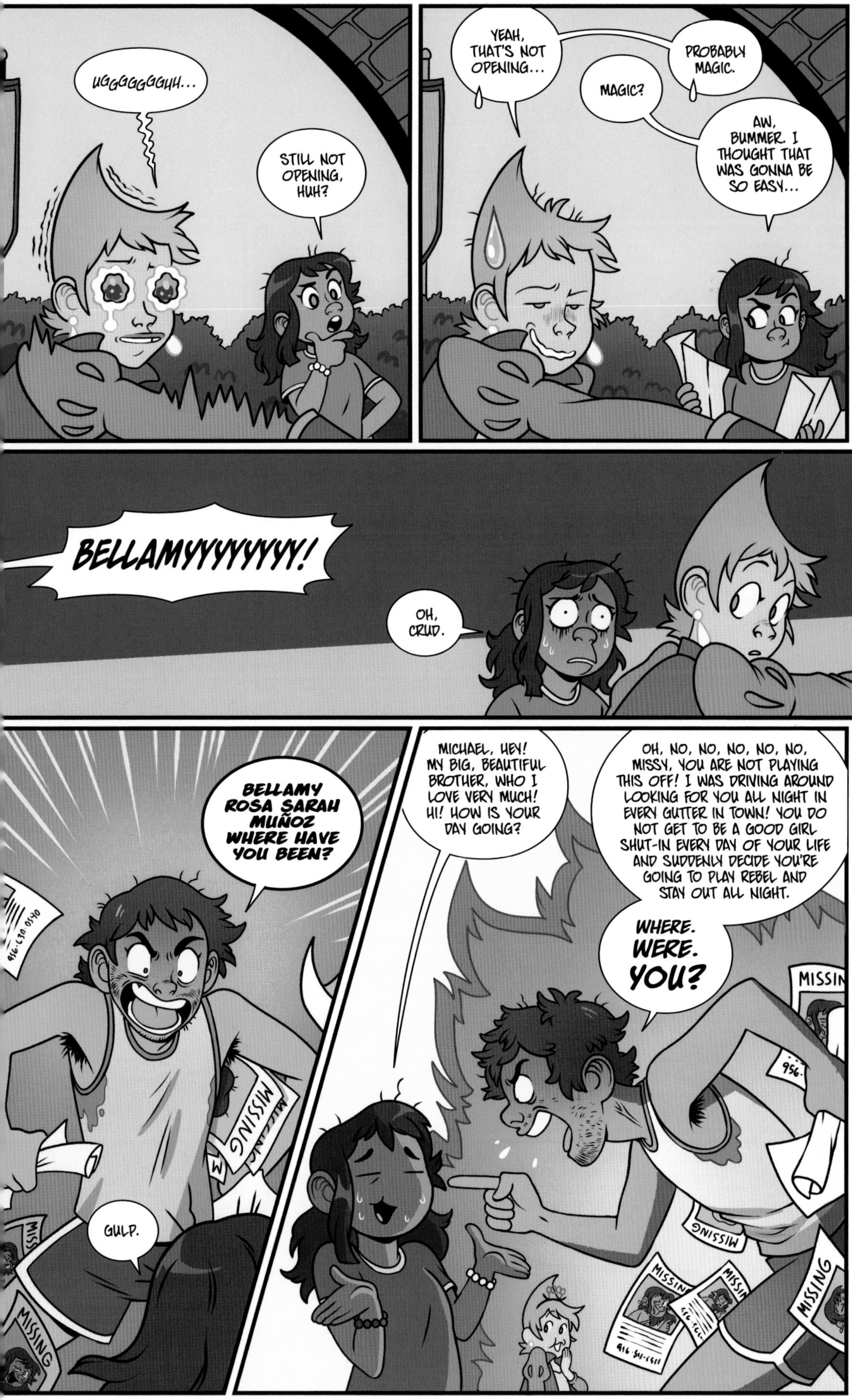
UGGGGGGGHH...
STILL NOT OPENING, HUH?
YEAH, THAT'S NOT OPENING...
PROBABLY MAGIC.
MAGIC?
AW, BUMMER. I THOUGHT THAT WAS GONNA BE SO EASY...
BELLAMYYYYYYY!
OH, CRUD.
BELLAMY ROSA SARAH MUÑOZ WHERE HAVE YOU BEEN?
GULP.
MISSING
MICHAEL, HEY! MY BIG, BEAUTIFUL BROTHER, WHO I LOVE VERY MUCH! HI! HOW IS YOUR DAY GOING?
OH, NO, NO, NO, NO, NO, MISSY, YOU ARE NOT PLAYING THIS OFF! I WAS DRIVING AROUND LOOKING FOR YOU ALL NIGHT IN EVERY GUTTER IN TOWN! YOU DO NOT GET TO BE A GOOD GIRL SHUT-IN EVERY DAY OF YOUR LIFE AND SUDDENLY DECIDE YOU'RE GOING TO PLAY REBEL AND STAY OUT ALL NIGHT.
WHERE. WERE. YOU?
MISSING

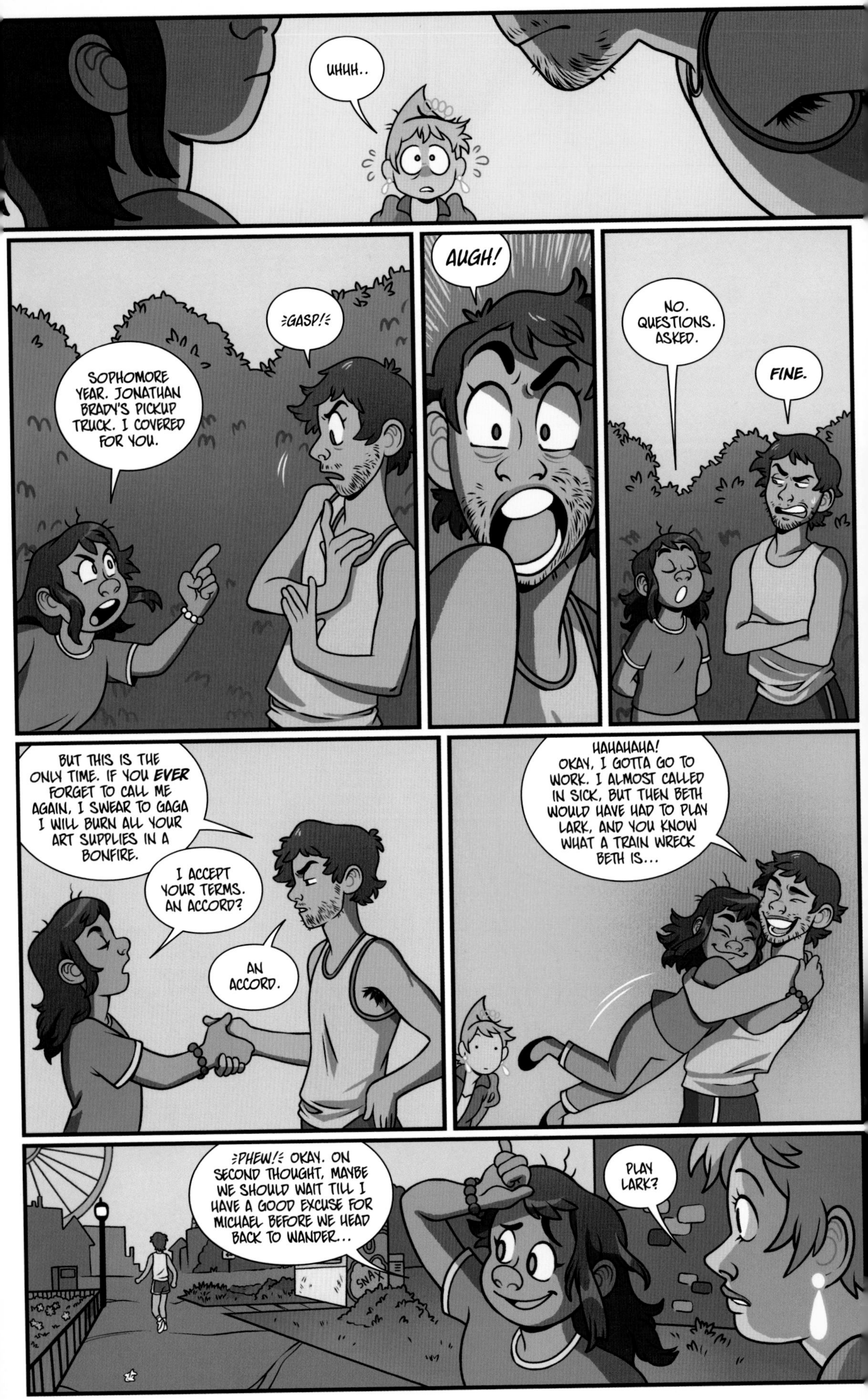
UHHH..
SOPHOMORE YEAR. JONATHAN BRADY'S PICKUP TRUCK. I COVERED FOR YOU.
GASP!
AUGH!
NO. QUESTIONS. ASKED.
FINE.
BUT THIS IS THE ONLY TIME. IF YOU **EVER** FORGET TO CALL ME AGAIN, I SWEAR TO GAGA I WILL BURN ALL YOUR ART SUPPLIES IN A BONFIRE.
I ACCEPT YOUR TERMS. AN ACCORD?
AN ACCORD.
HAHAHAHA! OKAY, I GOTTA GO TO WORK. I ALMOST CALLED IN SICK, BUT THEN BETH WOULD HAVE HAD TO PLAY LARK, AND YOU KNOW WHAT A TRAIN WRECK BETH IS...
PHEW! OKAY. ON SECOND THOUGHT, MAYBE WE SHOULD WAIT TILL I HAVE A GOOD EXCUSE FOR MICHAEL BEFORE WE HEAD BACK TO WANDER...
PLAY LARK?
SNAX

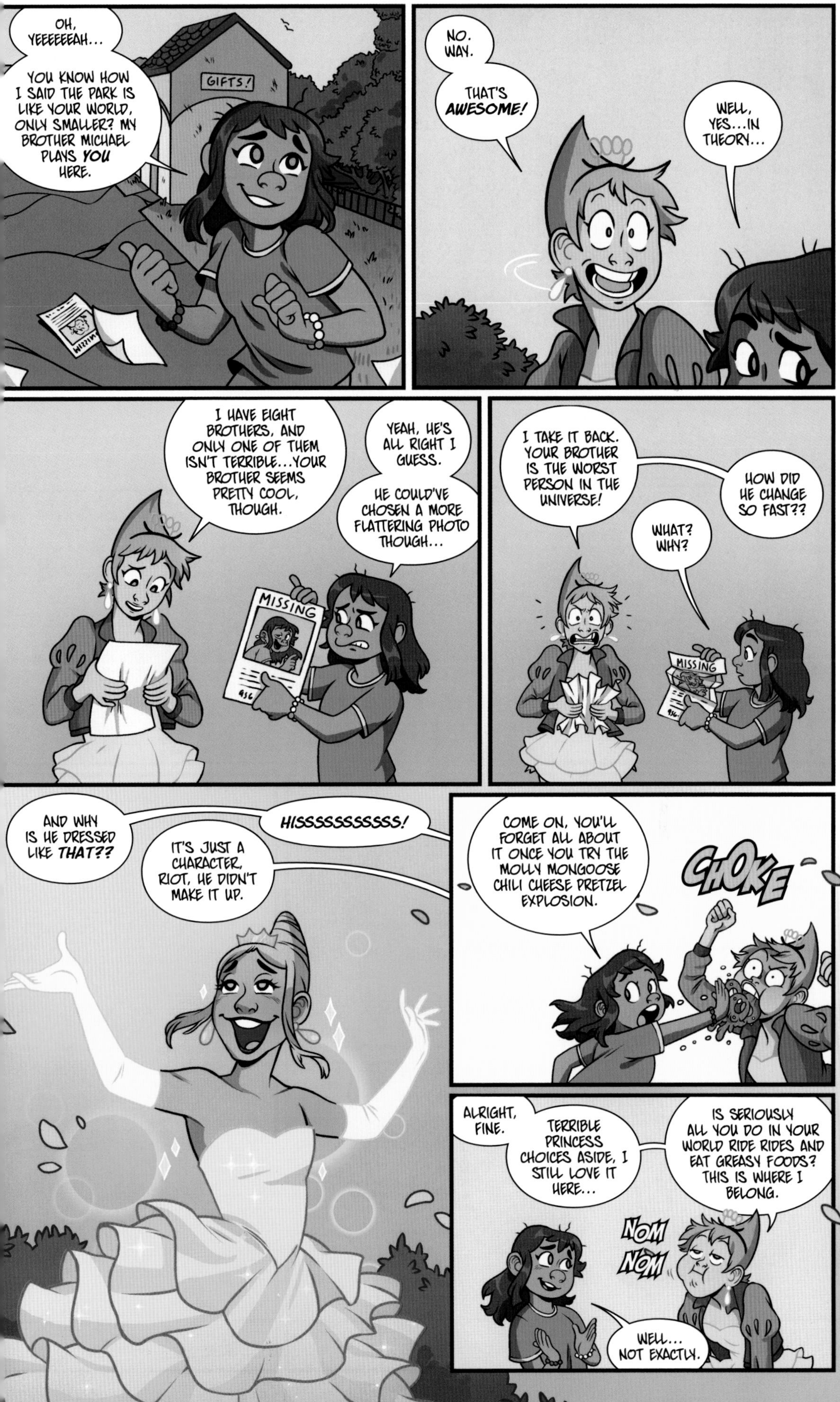
OH, YEEEEEEAH...
YOU KNOW HOW I SAID THE PARK IS LIKE YOUR WORLD, ONLY SMALLER? MY BROTHER MICHAEL PLAYS *YOU* HERE.
GIFTS!
NO. WAY.
THAT'S *AWESOME!*
WELL, YES...IN THEORY...
I HAVE EIGHT BROTHERS, AND ONLY ONE OF THEM ISN'T TERRIBLE...YOUR BROTHER SEEMS PRETTY COOL, THOUGH.
YEAH, HE'S ALL RIGHT I GUESS.
HE COULD'VE CHOSEN A MORE FLATTERING PHOTO THOUGH...
MISSING
I TAKE IT BACK. YOUR BROTHER IS THE WORST PERSON IN THE UNIVERSE!
HOW DID HE CHANGE SO FAST??
WHAT? WHY?
MISSING
AND WHY IS HE DRESSED LIKE *THAT??*
HISSSSSSSSSSS!
IT'S JUST A CHARACTER, RIOT, HE DIDN'T MAKE IT UP.
COME ON, YOU'LL FORGET ALL ABOUT IT ONCE YOU TRY THE MOLLY MONGOOSE CHILI CHEESE PRETZEL EXPLOSION.
CHOKE
ALRIGHT, FINE.
TERRIBLE PRINCESS CHOICES ASIDE, I STILL LOVE IT HERE...
IS SERIOUSLY ALL YOU DO IN YOUR WORLD RIDE RIDES AND EAT GREASY FOODS? THIS IS WHERE I BELONG.
NOM NOM
WELL... NOT EXACTLY.

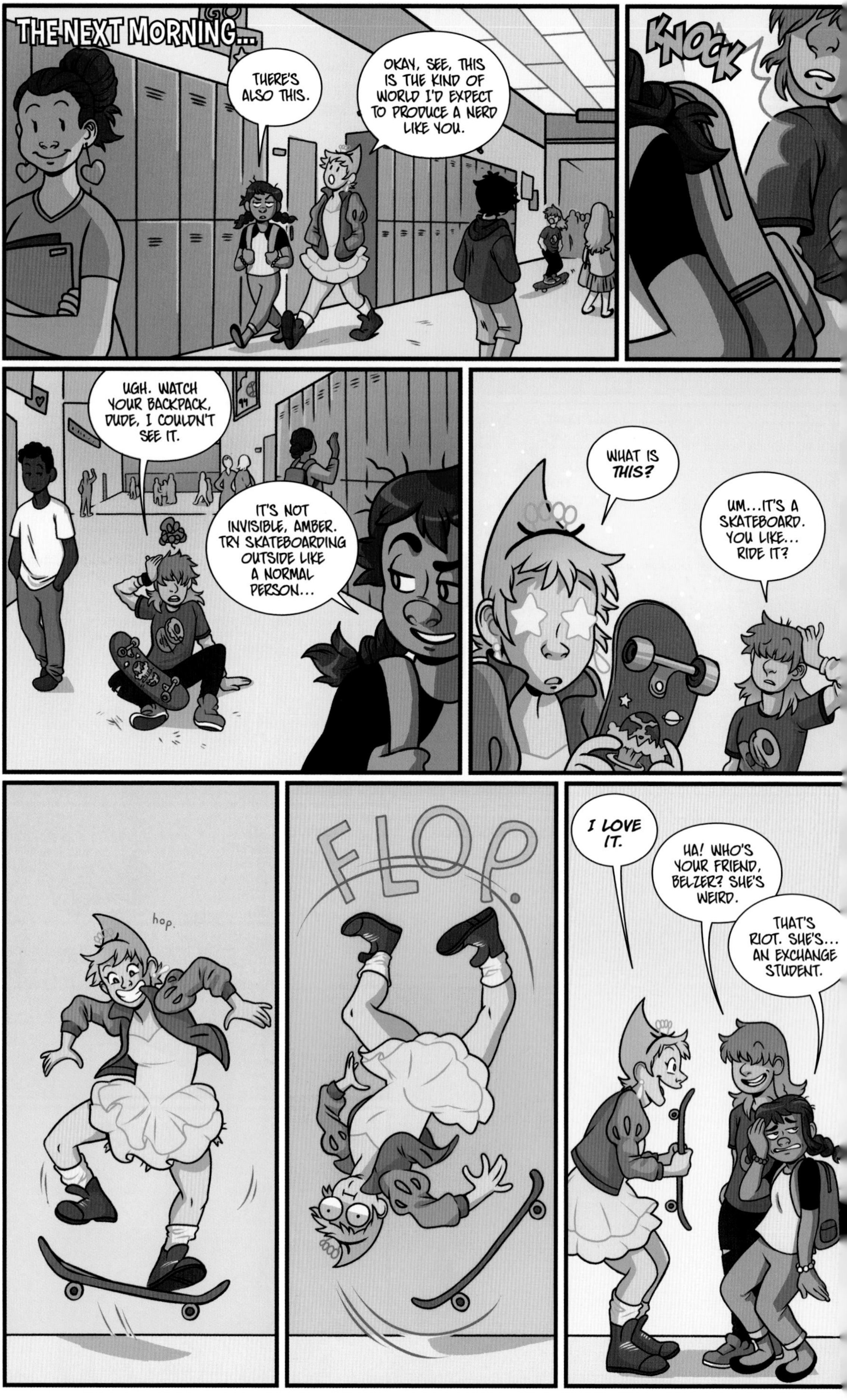

THE NEXT MORNING...
THERE'S ALSO THIS.
OKAY, SEE, THIS IS THE KIND OF WORLD I'D EXPECT TO PRODUCE A NERD LIKE YOU.
KNOCK
UGH. WATCH YOUR BACKPACK, DUDE, I COULDN'T SEE IT.
IT'S NOT INVISIBLE, AMBER. TRY SKATEBOARDING OUTSIDE LIKE A NORMAL PERSON...
WHAT IS THIS?
UM...IT'S A SKATEBOARD. YOU LIKE... RIDE IT?
hop.
FLOP.
I LOVE IT.
HA! WHO'S YOUR FRIEND, BELZER? SHE'S WEIRD.
THAT'S RIOT. SHE'S... AN EXCHANGE STUDENT.

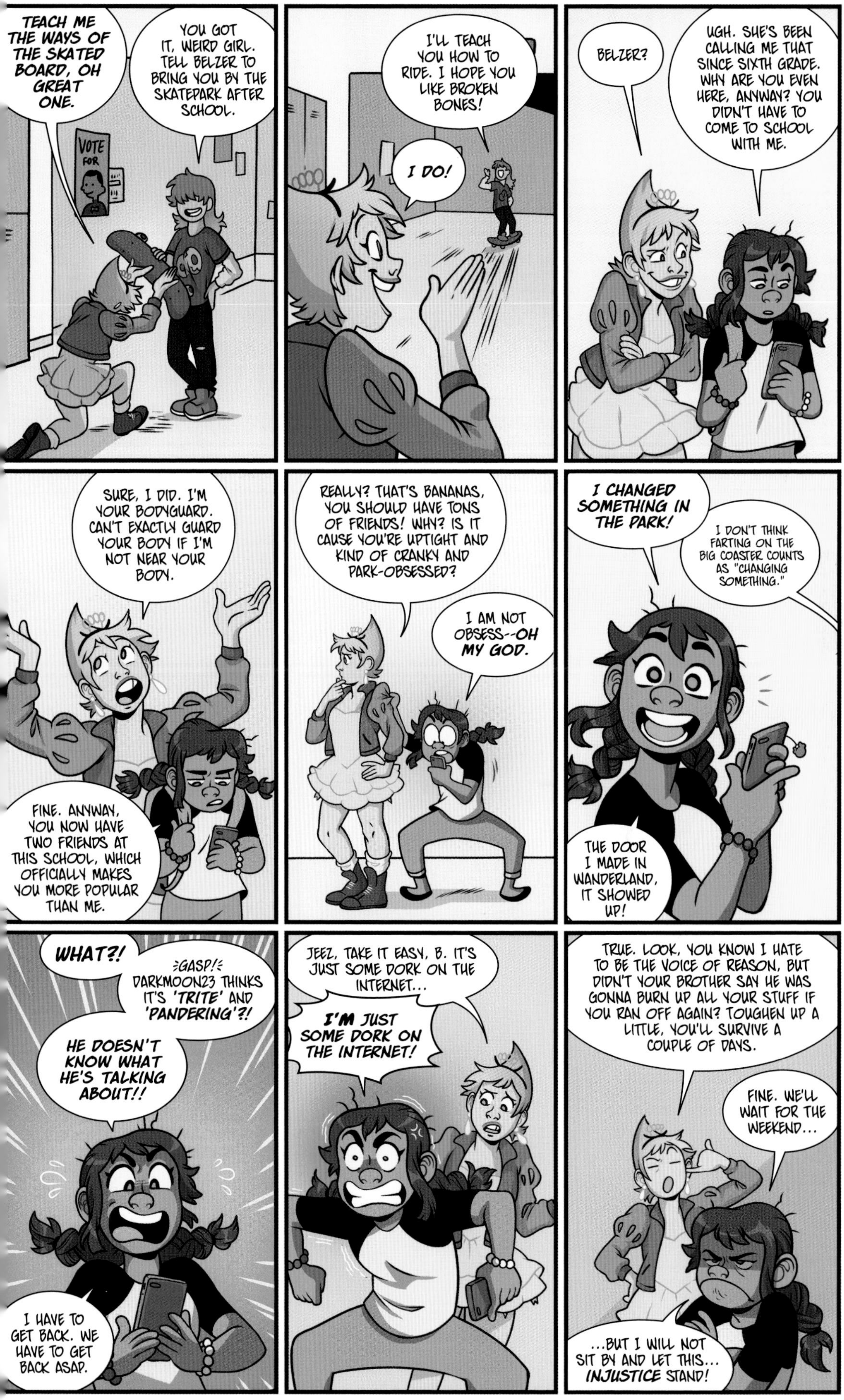

TEACH ME THE WAYS OF THE SKATED BOARD, OH GREAT ONE.
YOU GOT IT, WEIRD GIRL. TELL BELZER TO BRING YOU BY THE SKATEPARK AFTER SCHOOL.
VOTE FOR
I'LL TEACH YOU HOW TO RIDE. I HOPE YOU LIKE BROKEN BONES!
I DO!
BELZER?
UGH. SHE'S BEEN CALLING ME THAT SINCE SIXTH GRADE. WHY ARE YOU EVEN HERE, ANYWAY? YOU DIDN'T HAVE TO COME TO SCHOOL WITH ME.
SURE, I DID. I'M YOUR BODYGUARD. CAN'T EXACTLY GUARD YOUR BODY IF I'M NOT NEAR YOUR BODY.
FINE. ANYWAY, YOU NOW HAVE TWO FRIENDS AT THIS SCHOOL, WHICH OFFICIALLY MAKES YOU MORE POPULAR THAN ME.
REALLY? THAT'S BANANAS, YOU SHOULD HAVE TONS OF FRIENDS! WHY? IS IT CAUSE YOU'RE UPTIGHT AND KIND OF CRANKY AND PARK-OBSESSED?
I AM NOT OBSESS--OH MY GOD.
I CHANGED SOMETHING IN THE PARK!
I DON'T THINK FARTING ON THE BIG COASTER COUNTS AS "CHANGING SOMETHING."
THE DOOR I MADE IN WANDERLAND, IT SHOWED UP!
WHAT?!
GASP! DARKMOON23 THINKS IT'S 'TRITE' AND 'PANDERING'?!
HE DOESN'T KNOW WHAT HE'S TALKING ABOUT!!
I HAVE TO GET BACK. WE HAVE TO GET BACK ASAP.
JEEZ, TAKE IT EASY, B. IT'S JUST SOME DORK ON THE INTERNET...
I'M JUST SOME DORK ON THE INTERNET!
TRUE. LOOK, YOU KNOW I HATE TO BE THE VOICE OF REASON, BUT DIDN'T YOUR BROTHER SAY HE WAS GONNA BURN UP ALL YOUR STUFF IF YOU RAN OFF AGAIN? TOUGHEN UP A LITTLE, YOU'LL SURVIVE A COUPLE OF DAYS.
FINE. WE'LL WAIT FOR THE WEEKEND...
...BUT I WILL NOT SIT BY AND LET THIS... INJUSTICE STAND!

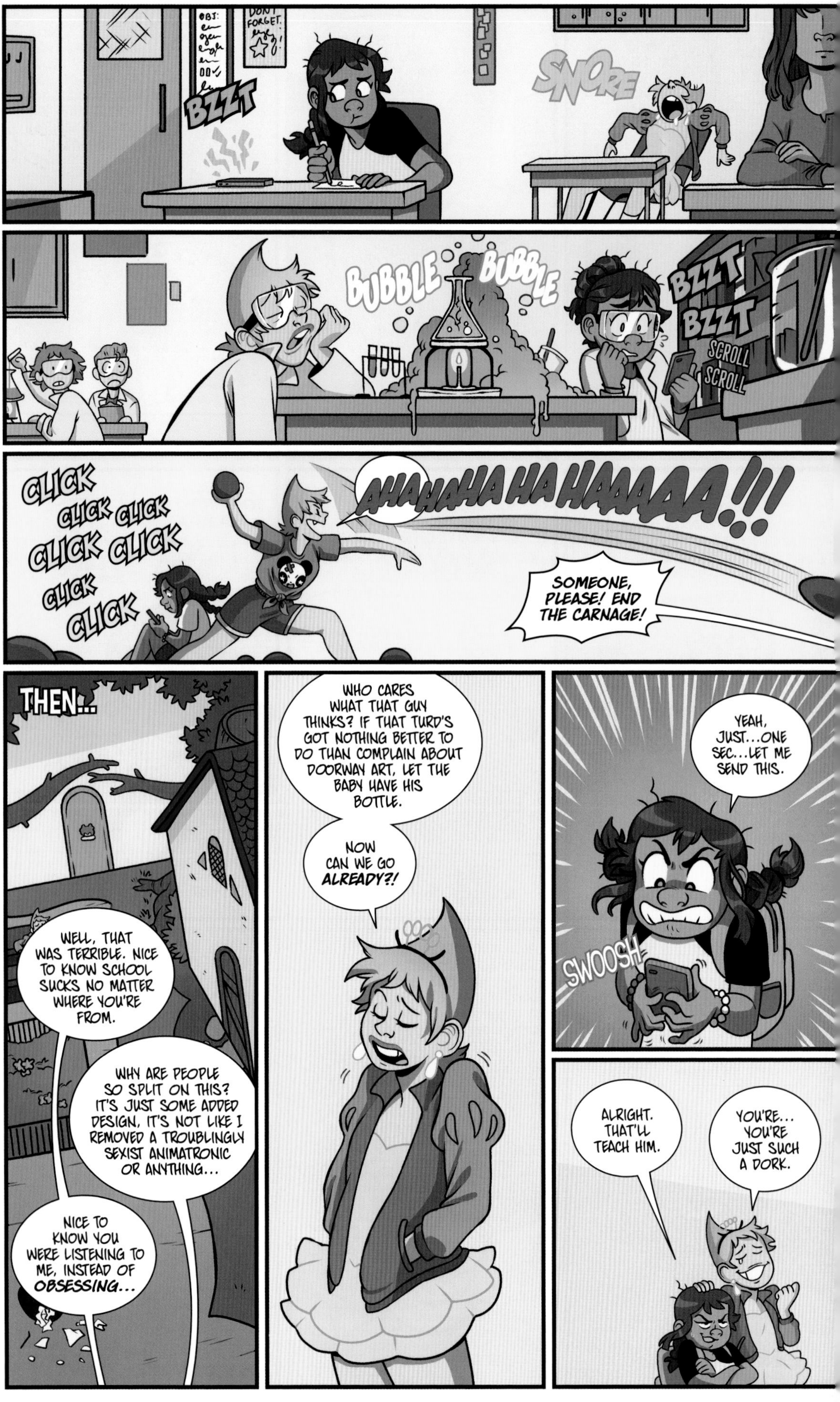
OBJ:
DON'T FORGET.
BZZT
SNORE
BUBBLE
BUBBLE
BZZT
BZZT
SCROLL
SCROLL
CLICK
CLICK CLICK
CLICK CLICK
CLICK
CLICK
AHAHAHA HA HAAAAAA!!!
SOMEONE, PLEASE! END THE CARNAGE!
THEN...
WELL, THAT WAS TERRIBLE. NICE TO KNOW SCHOOL SUCKS NO MATTER WHERE YOU'RE FROM.
WHY ARE PEOPLE SO SPLIT ON THIS? IT'S JUST SOME ADDED DESIGN, IT'S NOT LIKE I REMOVED A TROUBLINGLY SEXIST ANIMATRONIC OR ANYTHING...
NICE TO KNOW YOU WERE LISTENING TO ME, INSTEAD OF OBSESSING...
WHO CARES WHAT THAT GUY THINKS? IF THAT TURD'S GOT NOTHING BETTER TO DO THAN COMPLAIN ABOUT DOORWAY ART, LET THE BABY HAVE HIS BOTTLE.
NOW CAN WE GO ALREADY?!
YEAH, JUST...ONE SEC...LET ME SEND THIS.
SWOOSH
ALRIGHT. THAT'LL TEACH HIM.
YOU'RE... YOU'RE JUST SUCH A DORK.

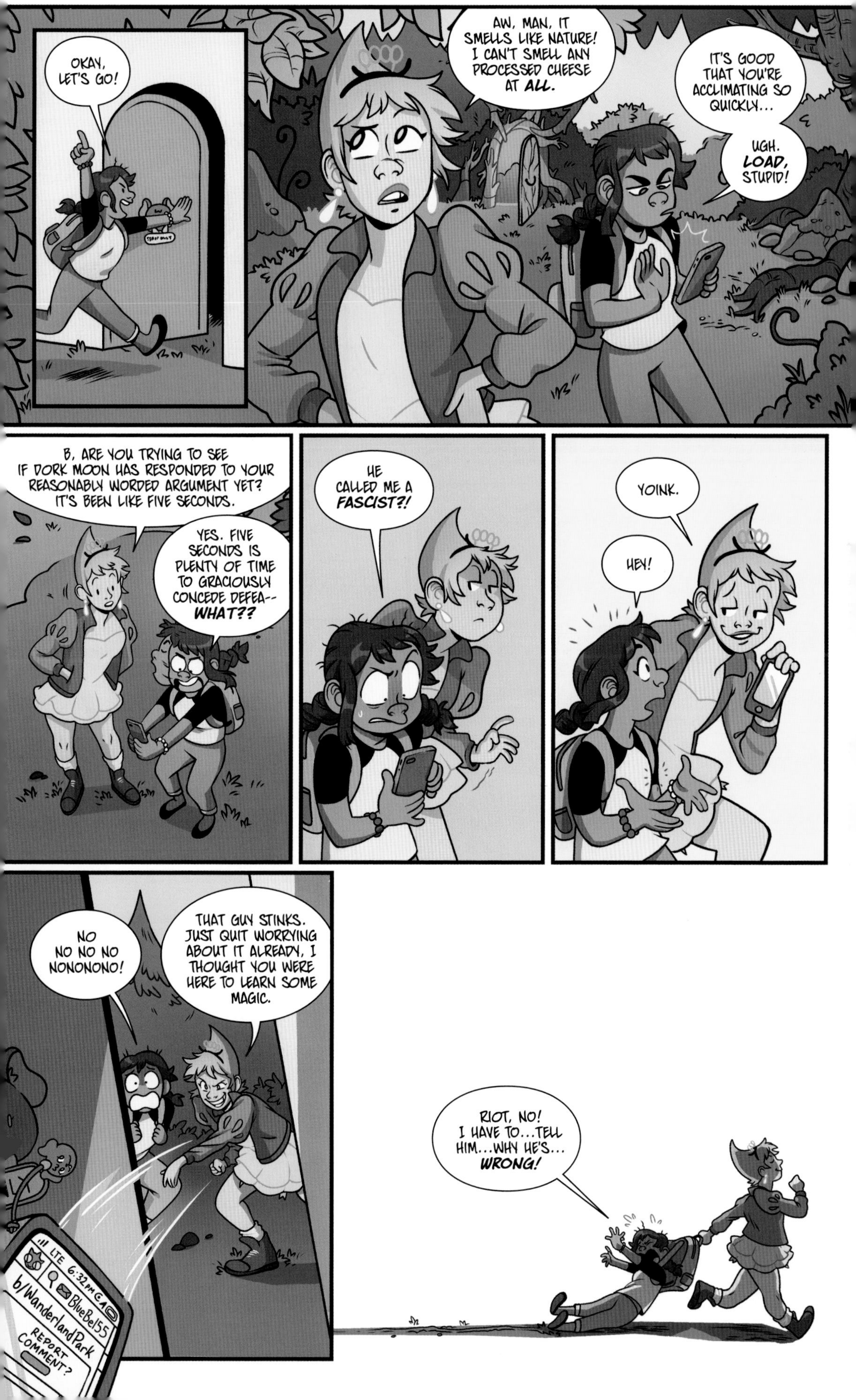
OKAY, LET'S GO!
AW, MAN, IT SMELLS LIKE NATURE! I CAN'T SMELL ANY PROCESSED CHEESE AT **ALL**.
IT'S GOOD THAT YOU'RE ACCLIMATING SO QUICKLY...
UGH. **LOAD,** STUPID!
B, ARE YOU TRYING TO SEE IF DORK MOON HAS RESPONDED TO YOUR REASONABLY WORDED ARGUMENT YET? IT'S BEEN LIKE FIVE SECONDS.
YES. FIVE SECONDS IS PLENTY OF TIME TO GRACIOUSLY CONCEDE DEFEA-- **WHAT??**
HE CALLED ME A ***FASCIST?!***
YOINK.
HEY!
NO NO NO NO NONONONO!
THAT GUY STINKS. JUST QUIT WORRYING ABOUT IT ALREADY, I THOUGHT YOU WERE HERE TO LEARN SOME MAGIC.
LTE 6:32PM
BlueBel55
b/WanderlandPark
REPORT COMMENT?
RIOT, NO! I HAVE TO...TELL HIM...WHY HE'S... ***WRONG!***

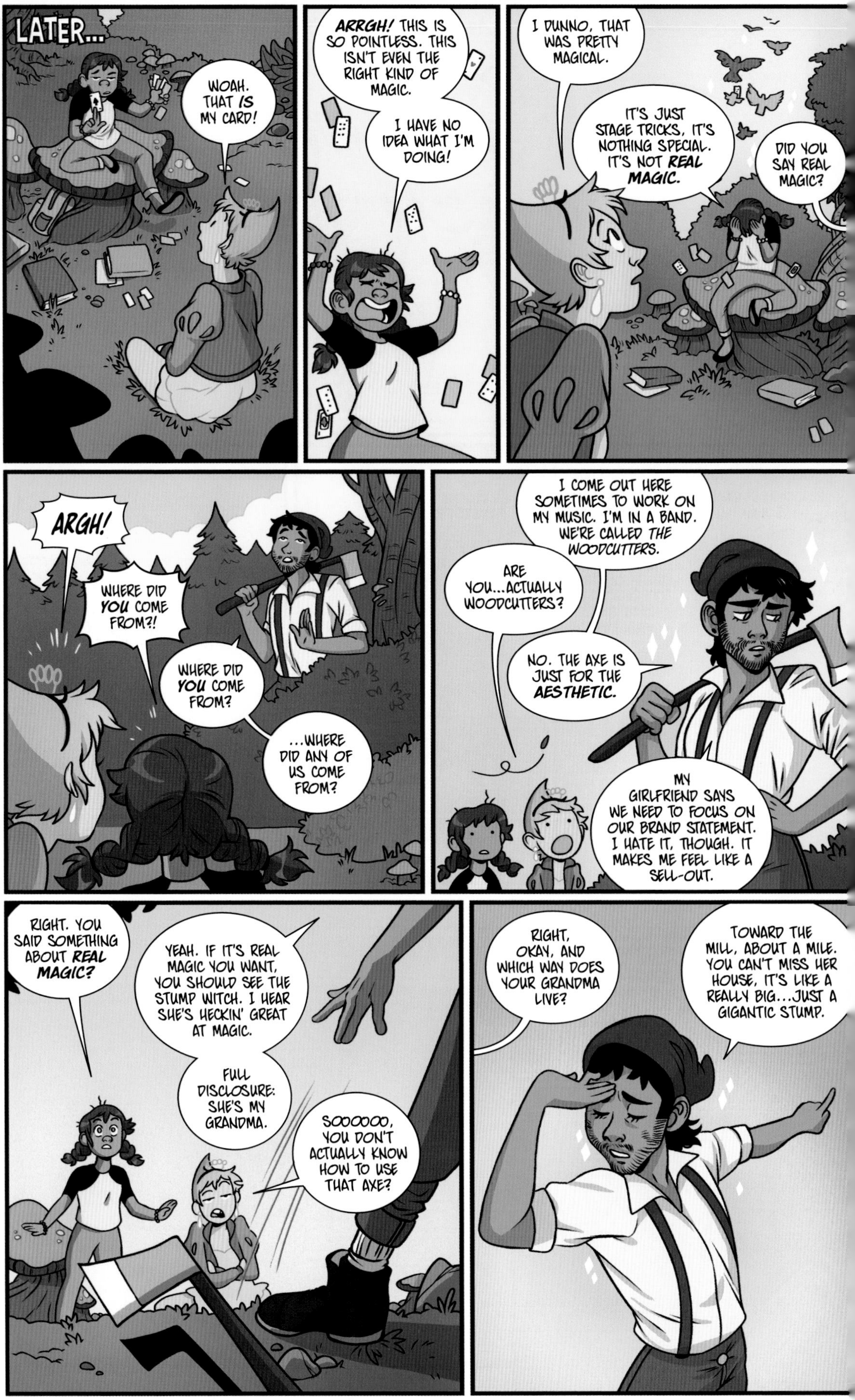
LATER...
WOAH. THAT *IS* MY CARD!
ARRGH! THIS IS SO POINTLESS. THIS ISN'T EVEN THE RIGHT KIND OF MAGIC.
I HAVE NO IDEA WHAT I'M DOING!
I DUNNO, THAT WAS PRETTY MAGICAL.
IT'S JUST STAGE TRICKS, IT'S NOTHING SPECIAL. IT'S NOT ***REAL MAGIC.***
DID YOU SAY REAL MAGIC?
ARGH!
WHERE DID ***YOU*** COME FROM?!
WHERE DID ***YOU*** COME FROM?
...WHERE DID ANY OF US COME FROM?
I COME OUT HERE SOMETIMES TO WORK ON MY MUSIC. I'M IN A BAND. WE'RE CALLED *THE WOODCUTTERS.*
ARE YOU...ACTUALLY WOODCUTTERS?
NO. THE AXE IS JUST FOR THE ***AESTHETIC.***
MY GIRLFRIEND SAYS WE NEED TO FOCUS ON OUR BRAND STATEMENT. I HATE IT, THOUGH. IT MAKES ME FEEL LIKE A SELL-OUT.
RIGHT. YOU SAID SOMETHING ABOUT ***REAL MAGIC?***
YEAH. IF IT'S REAL MAGIC YOU WANT, YOU SHOULD SEE THE STUMP WITCH. I HEAR SHE'S HECKIN' GREAT AT MAGIC.
FULL DISCLOSURE: SHE'S MY GRANDMA.
SOOOOOO, YOU DON'T ACTUALLY KNOW HOW TO USE THAT AXE?
RIGHT, OKAY, AND WHICH WAY DOES YOUR GRANDMA LIVE?
TOWARD THE MILL, ABOUT A MILE. YOU CAN'T MISS HER HOUSE, IT'S LIKE A REALLY BIG...JUST A GIGANTIC STUMP.

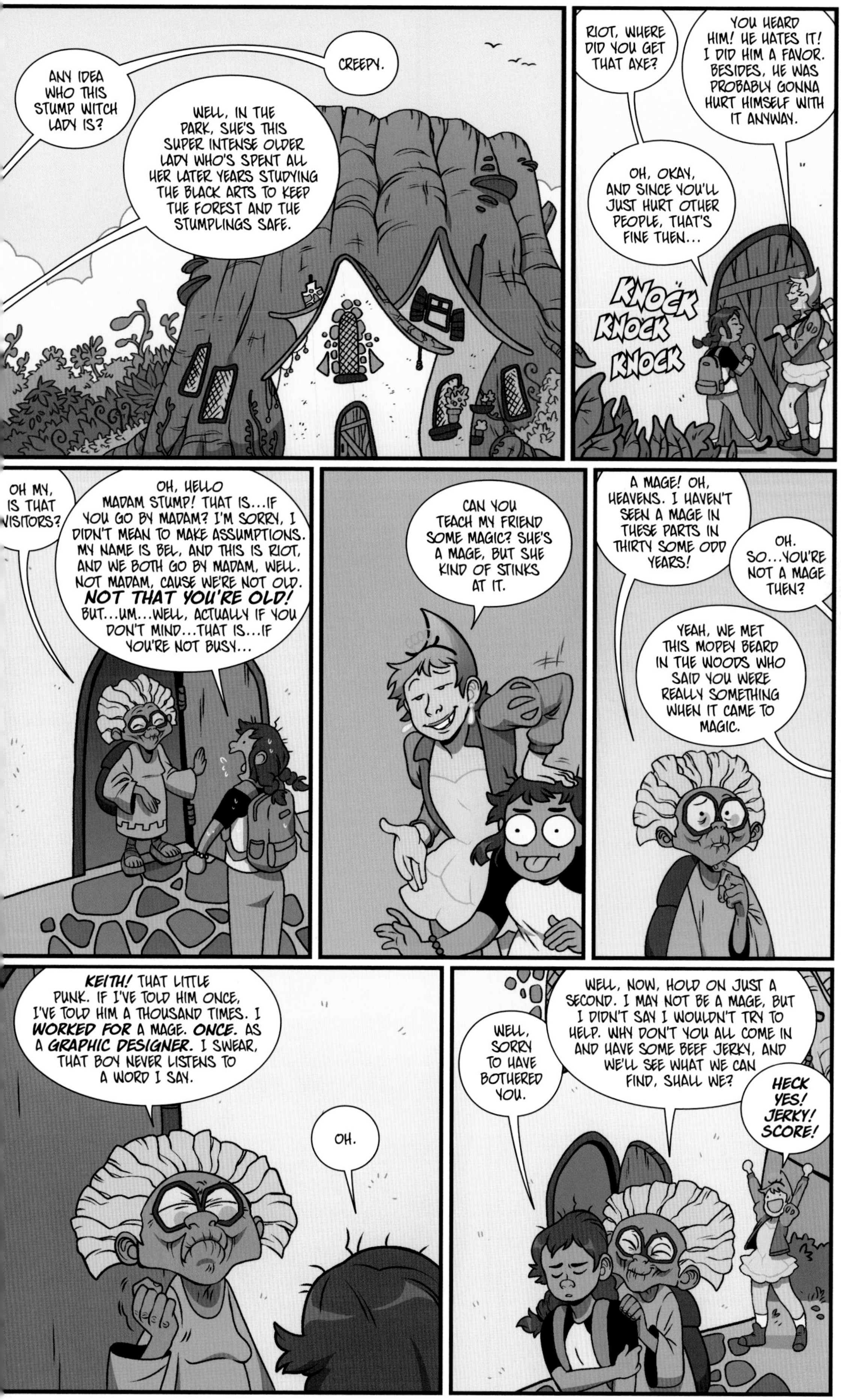
ANY IDEA WHO THIS STUMP WITCH LADY IS?
CREEPY.
WELL, IN THE PARK, SHE'S THIS SUPER INTENSE OLDER LADY WHO'S SPENT ALL HER LATER YEARS STUDYING THE BLACK ARTS TO KEEP THE FOREST AND THE STUMPLINGS SAFE.
RIOT, WHERE DID YOU GET THAT AXE?
YOU HEARD HIM! HE HATES IT! I DID HIM A FAVOR. BESIDES, HE WAS PROBABLY GONNA HURT HIMSELF WITH IT ANYWAY.
OH, OKAY, AND SINCE YOU'LL JUST HURT OTHER PEOPLE, THAT'S FINE THEN...
KNOCK KNOCK KNOCK
OH MY, IS THAT VISITORS?
OH, HELLO MADAM STUMP! THAT IS...IF YOU GO BY MADAM? I'M SORRY, I DIDN'T MEAN TO MAKE ASSUMPTIONS. MY NAME IS BEL, AND THIS IS RIOT, AND WE BOTH GO BY MADAM, WELL. NOT MADAM, CAUSE WE'RE NOT OLD. NOT THAT YOU'RE OLD! BUT...UM...WELL, ACTUALLY IF YOU DON'T MIND...THAT IS...IF YOU'RE NOT BUSY...
CAN YOU TEACH MY FRIEND SOME MAGIC? SHE'S A MAGE, BUT SHE KIND OF STINKS AT IT.
A MAGE! OH, HEAVENS. I HAVEN'T SEEN A MAGE IN THESE PARTS IN THIRTY SOME ODD YEARS!
OH. SO...YOU'RE NOT A MAGE THEN?
YEAH, WE MET THIS MOPEY BEARD IN THE WOODS WHO SAID YOU WERE REALLY SOMETHING WHEN IT CAME TO MAGIC.
KEITH! THAT LITTLE PUNK. IF I'VE TOLD HIM ONCE, I'VE TOLD HIM A THOUSAND TIMES. I WORKED FOR A MAGE. ONCE. AS A GRAPHIC DESIGNER. I SWEAR, THAT BOY NEVER LISTENS TO A WORD I SAY.
OH.
WELL, SORRY TO HAVE BOTHERED YOU.
WELL, NOW, HOLD ON JUST A SECOND. I MAY NOT BE A MAGE, BUT I DIDN'T SAY I WOULDN'T TRY TO HELP. WHY DON'T YOU ALL COME IN AND HAVE SOME BEEF JERKY, AND WE'LL SEE WHAT WE CAN FIND, SHALL WE?
HECK YES! JERKY! SCORE!

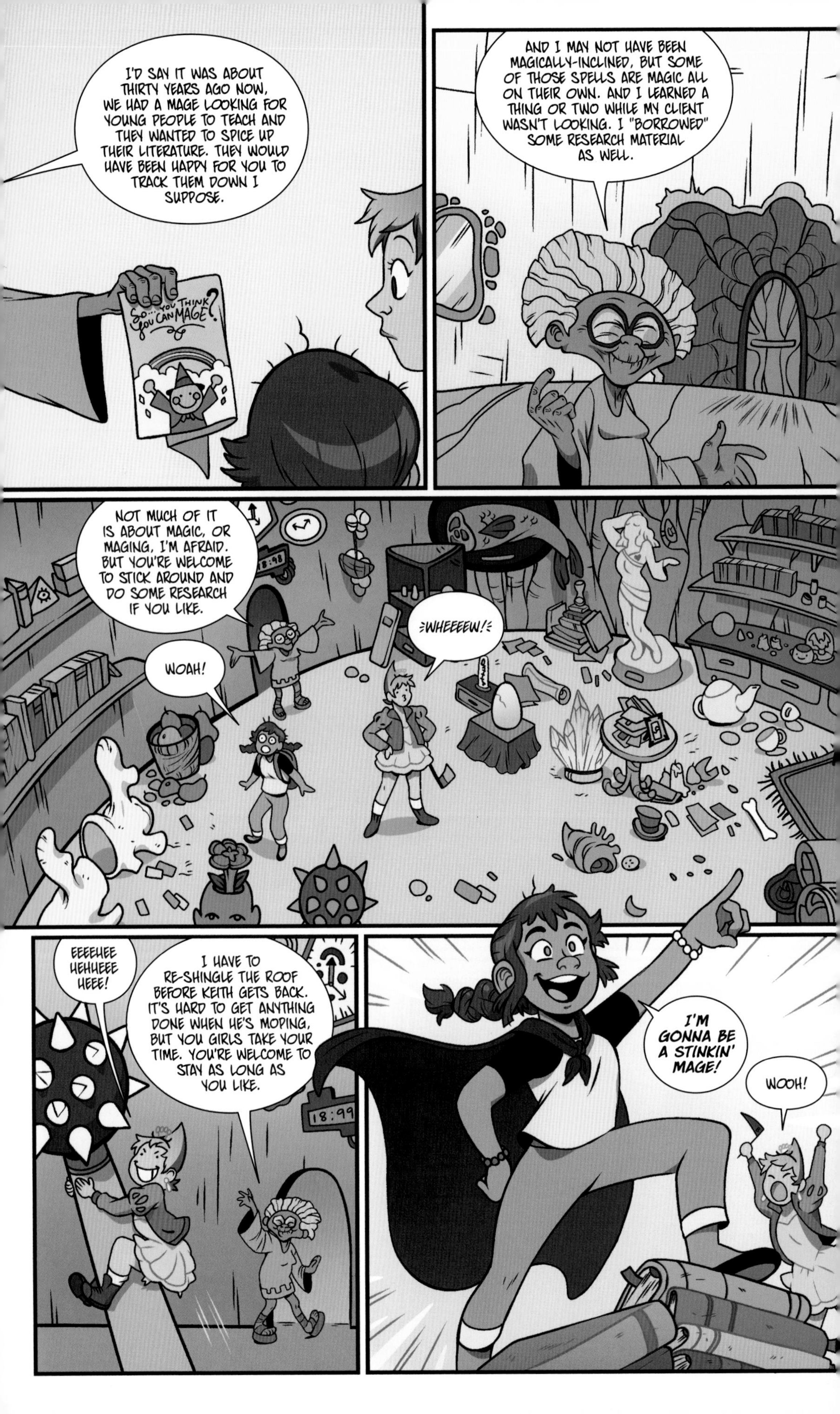
I'D SAY IT WAS ABOUT THIRTY YEARS AGO NOW, WE HAD A MAGE LOOKING FOR YOUNG PEOPLE TO TEACH AND THEY WANTED TO SPICE UP THEIR LITERATURE. THEY WOULD HAVE BEEN HAPPY FOR YOU TO TRACK THEM DOWN I SUPPOSE.
SO... YOU THINK YOU CAN MAGE?
AND I MAY NOT HAVE BEEN MAGICALLY-INCLINED, BUT SOME OF THOSE SPELLS ARE MAGIC ALL ON THEIR OWN. AND I LEARNED A THING OR TWO WHILE MY CLIENT WASN'T LOOKING. I "BORROWED" SOME RESEARCH MATERIAL AS WELL.
NOT MUCH OF IT IS ABOUT MAGIC, OR MAGING, I'M AFRAID. BUT YOU'RE WELCOME TO STICK AROUND AND DO SOME RESEARCH IF YOU LIKE.
18:98
WOAH!
WHEEEEW!
EEEEHEE HEHHEEE HEEE!
I HAVE TO RE-SHINGLE THE ROOF BEFORE KEITH GETS BACK. IT'S HARD TO GET ANYTHING DONE WHEN HE'S MOPING, BUT YOU GIRLS TAKE YOUR TIME. YOU'RE WELCOME TO STAY AS LONG AS YOU LIKE.
18:99
I'M GONNA BE A STINKIN' MAGE!
WOOH!

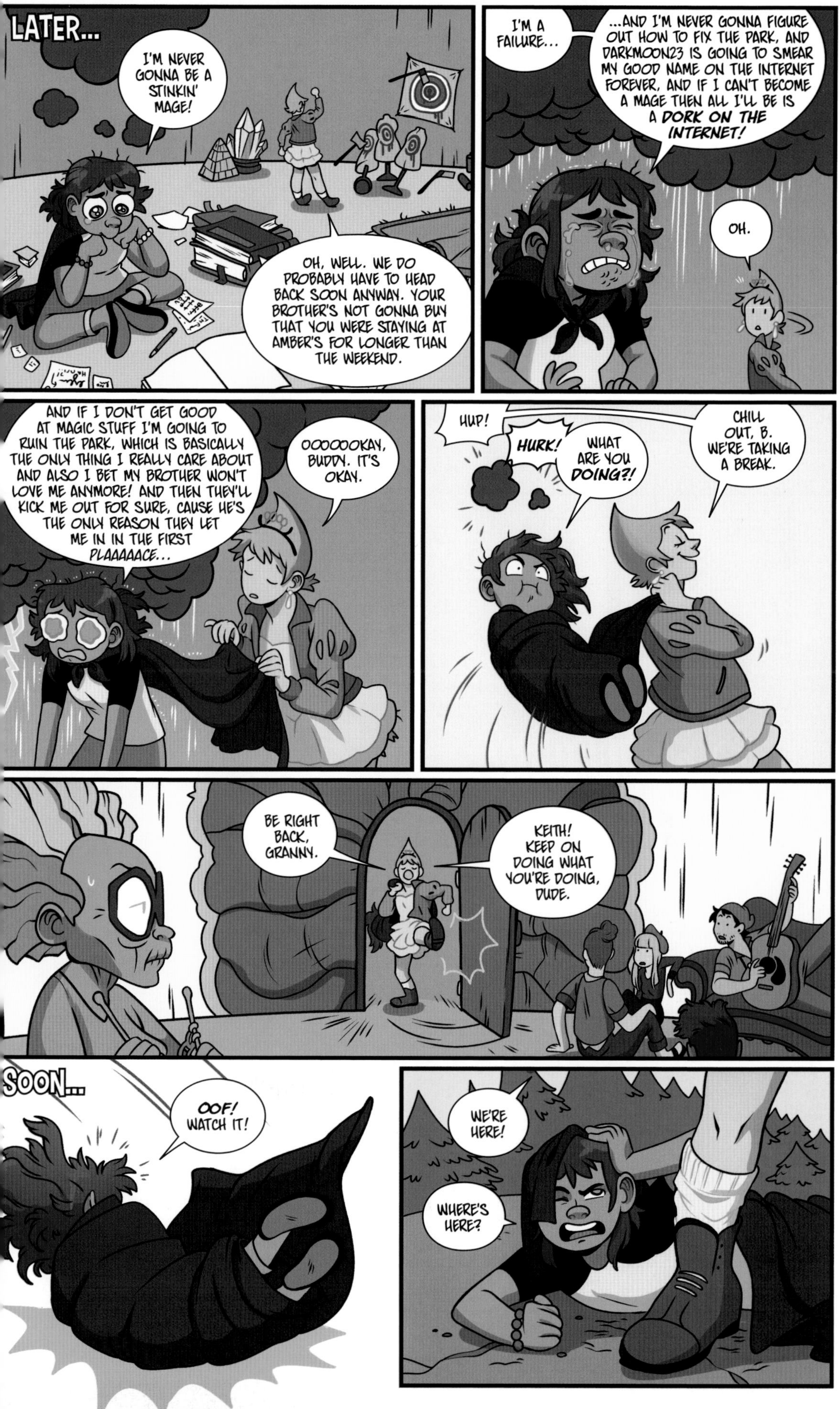
LATER...
I'M NEVER GONNA BE A STINKIN' MAGE!
OH, WELL. WE DO PROBABLY HAVE TO HEAD BACK SOON ANYWAY. YOUR BROTHER'S NOT GONNA BUY THAT YOU WERE STAYING AT AMBER'S FOR LONGER THAN THE WEEKEND.
I'M A FAILURE...
...AND I'M NEVER GONNA FIGURE OUT HOW TO FIX THE PARK, AND DARKMOON23 IS GOING TO SMEAR MY GOOD NAME ON THE INTERNET FOREVER, AND IF I CAN'T BECOME A MAGE THEN ALL I'LL BE IS A DORK ON THE INTERNET!
OH.
AND IF I DON'T GET GOOD AT MAGIC STUFF I'M GOING TO RUIN THE PARK, WHICH IS BASICALLY THE ONLY THING I REALLY CARE ABOUT AND ALSO I BET MY BROTHER WON'T LOVE ME ANYMORE! AND THEN THEY'LL KICK ME OUT FOR SURE, CAUSE HE'S THE ONLY REASON THEY LET ME IN IN THE FIRST PLAAAAACE...
OOOOOOKAY, BUDDY. IT'S OKAY.
HUP!
HURK!
WHAT ARE YOU DOING?!
CHILL OUT, B. WE'RE TAKING A BREAK.
BE RIGHT BACK, GRANNY.
KEITH! KEEP ON DOING WHAT YOU'RE DOING, DUDE.
SOON...
OOF! WATCH IT!
WE'RE HERE!
WHERE'S HERE?

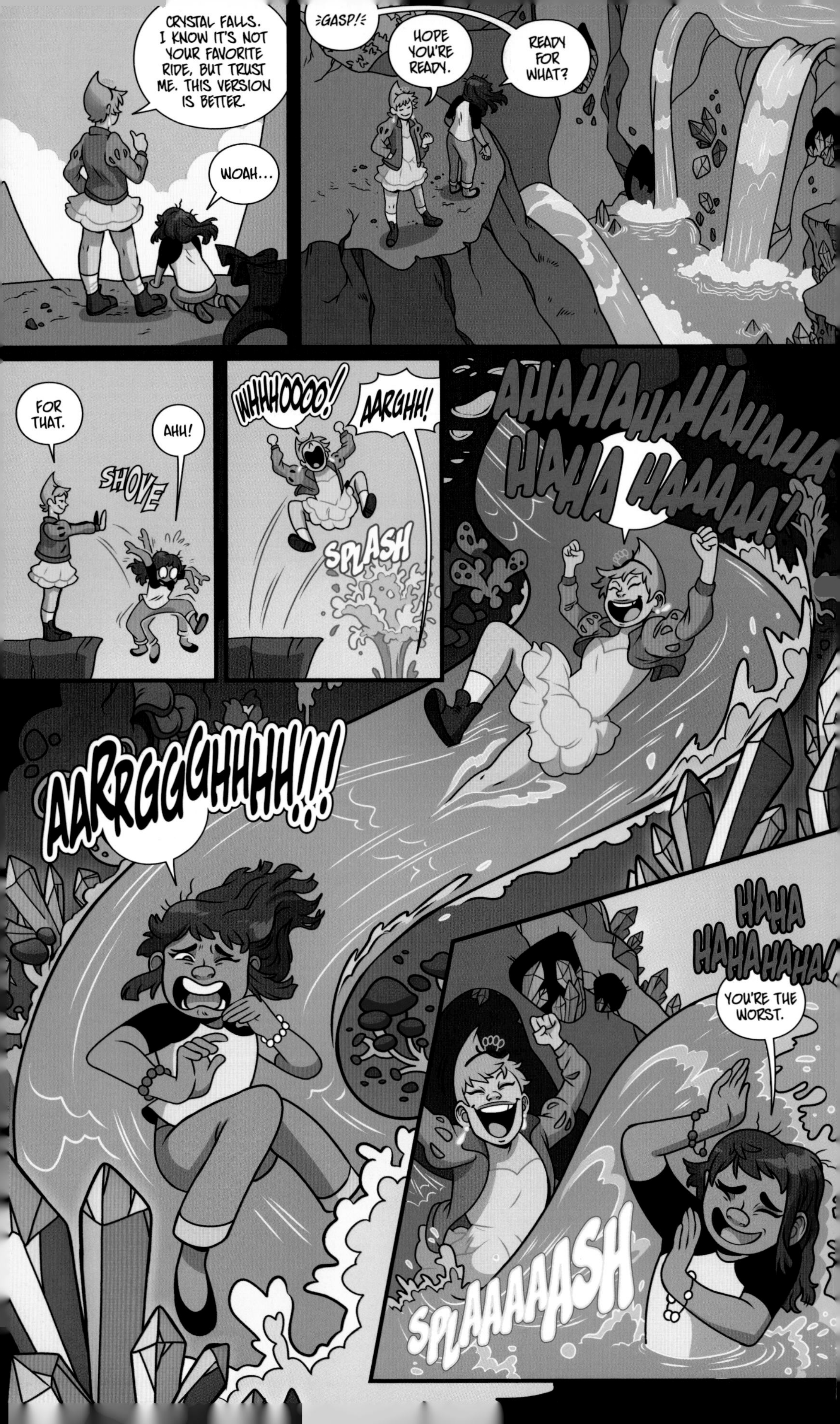
CRYSTAL FALLS. I KNOW IT'S NOT YOUR FAVORITE RIDE, BUT TRUST ME. THIS VERSION IS BETTER.
WOAH...
GASP!
HOPE YOU'RE READY.
READY FOR WHAT?
FOR THAT.
AHH!
SHOVE
WHHHOOOO!
AARGHH!
SPLASH
AHAHAHAHAHAHAHAHA HAHA HAAAAAA!
AARRGGGHHHH!!!
HAHA HAHAHAHA!
YOU'RE THE WORST.
SPLAAAAASH

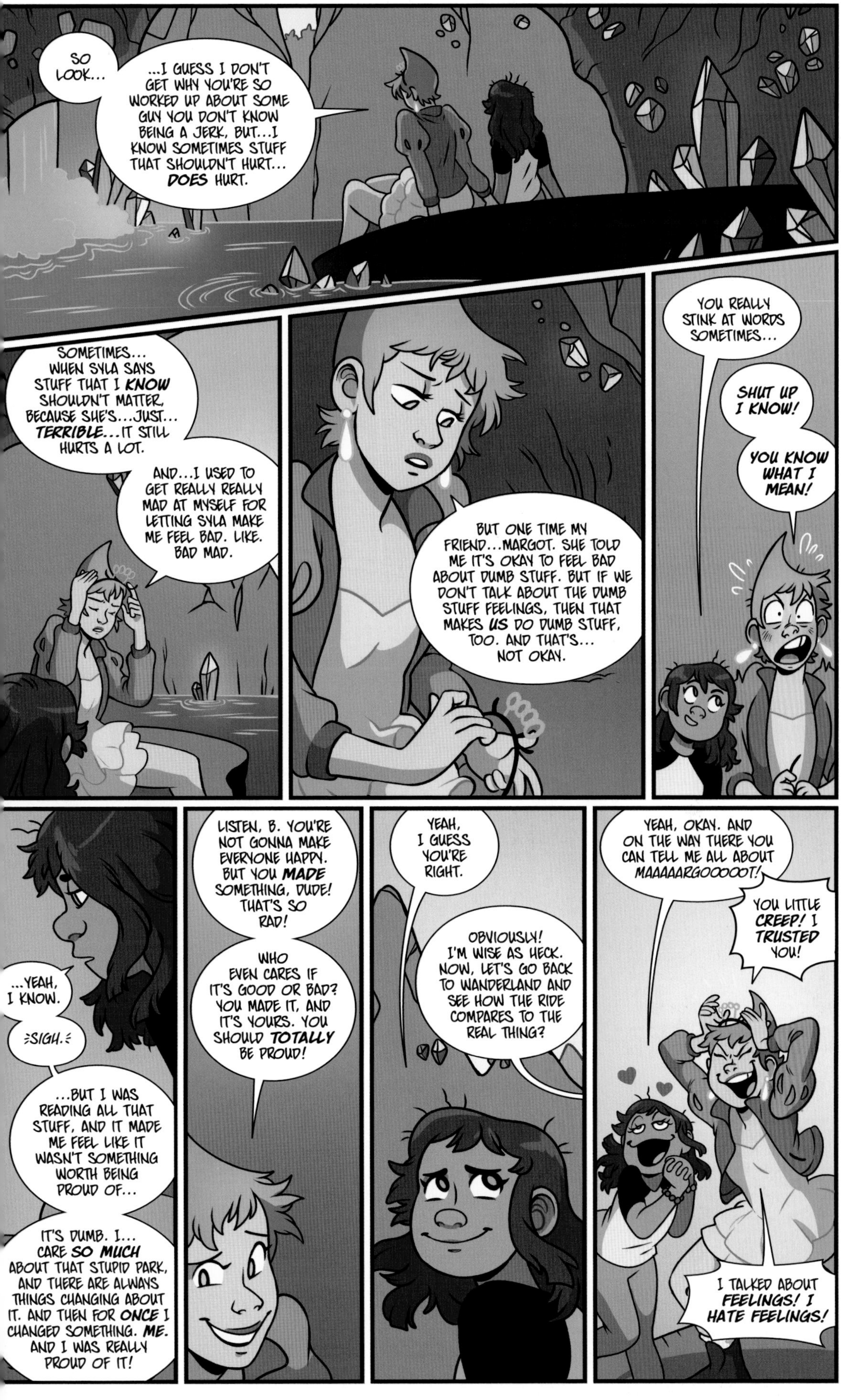
SO LOOK...
...I GUESS I DON'T GET WHY YOU'RE SO WORKED UP ABOUT SOME GUY YOU DON'T KNOW BEING A JERK, BUT...I KNOW SOMETIMES STUFF THAT SHOULDN'T HURT... DOES HURT.
SOMETIMES... WHEN SYLA SAYS STUFF THAT I KNOW SHOULDN'T MATTER, BECAUSE SHE'S...JUST... TERRIBLE...IT STILL HURTS A LOT.
AND...I USED TO GET REALLY REALLY MAD AT MYSELF FOR LETTING SYLA MAKE ME FEEL BAD. LIKE. BAD MAD.
BUT ONE TIME MY FRIEND...MARGOT. SHE TOLD ME IT'S OKAY TO FEEL BAD ABOUT DUMB STUFF. BUT IF WE DON'T TALK ABOUT THE DUMB STUFF FEELINGS, THEN THAT MAKES US DO DUMB STUFF, TOO. AND THAT'S... NOT OKAY.
YOU REALLY STINK AT WORDS SOMETIMES...
SHUT UP I KNOW!
YOU KNOW WHAT I MEAN!
...YEAH, I KNOW.
SIGH.
...BUT I WAS READING ALL THAT STUFF, AND IT MADE ME FEEL LIKE IT WASN'T SOMETHING WORTH BEING PROUD OF...
IT'S DUMB. I... CARE SO MUCH ABOUT THAT STUPID PARK, AND THERE ARE ALWAYS THINGS CHANGING ABOUT IT. AND THEN FOR ONCE I CHANGED SOMETHING. ME. AND I WAS REALLY PROUD OF IT!
LISTEN, B. YOU'RE NOT GONNA MAKE EVERYONE HAPPY. BUT YOU MADE SOMETHING, DUDE! THAT'S SO RAD!
WHO EVEN CARES IF IT'S GOOD OR BAD? YOU MADE IT, AND IT'S YOURS. YOU SHOULD TOTALLY BE PROUD!
YEAH, I GUESS YOU'RE RIGHT.
OBVIOUSLY! I'M WISE AS HECK. NOW, LET'S GO BACK TO WANDERLAND AND SEE HOW THE RIDE COMPARES TO THE REAL THING?
YEAH, OKAY. AND ON THE WAY THERE YOU CAN TELL ME ALL ABOUT MAAAAARGOOOOOT!
YOU LITTLE CREEP! I TRUSTED YOU!
I TALKED ABOUT FEELINGS! I HATE FEELINGS!

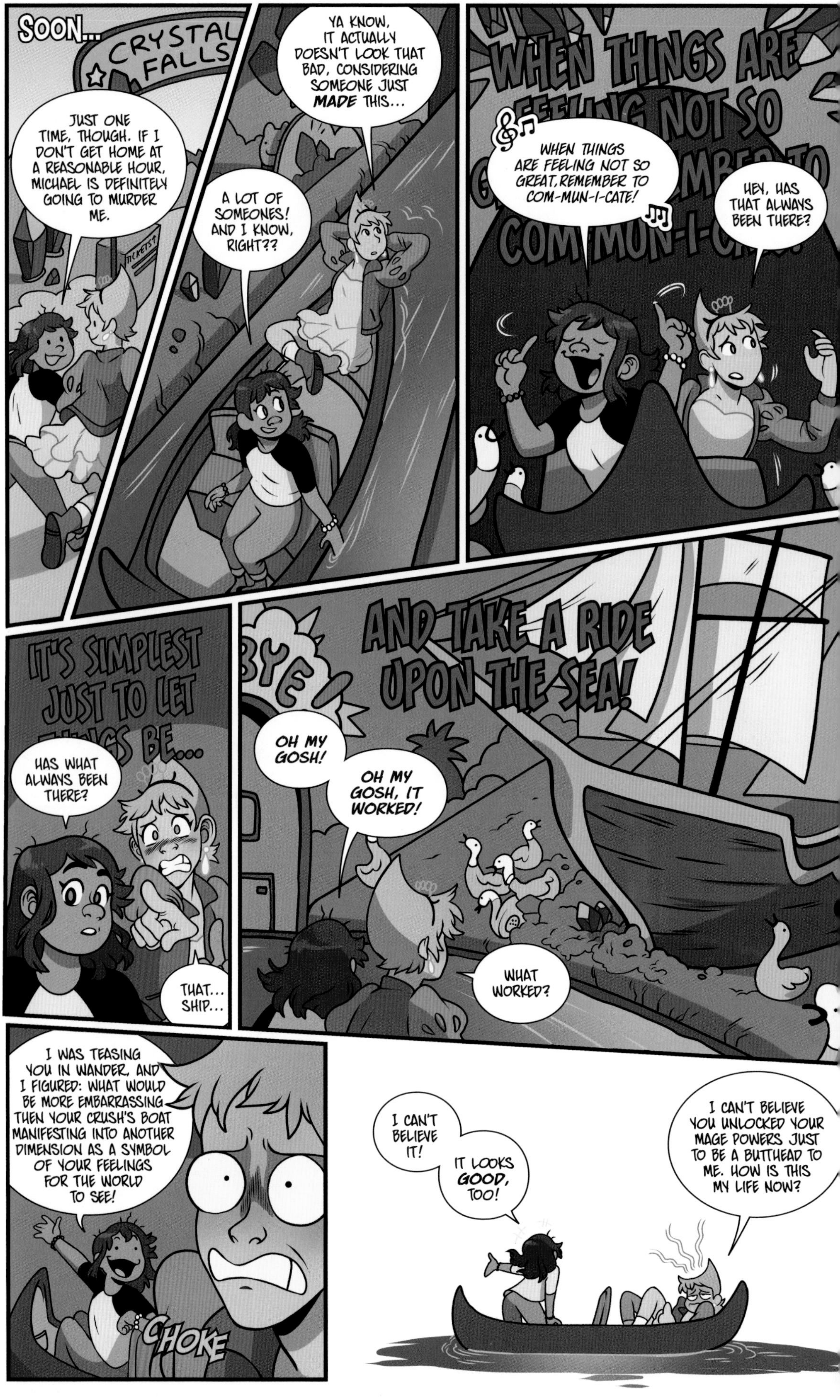
SOON...
CRYSTAL FALLS
TICKETS
JUST ONE TIME, THOUGH. IF I DON'T GET HOME AT A REASONABLE HOUR, MICHAEL IS DEFINITELY GOING TO MURDER ME.
YA KNOW, IT ACTUALLY DOESN'T LOOK THAT BAD, CONSIDERING SOMEONE JUST MADE THIS...
A LOT OF SOMEONES! AND I KNOW, RIGHT??
WHEN THINGS ARE FEELING NOT SO GREAT, REMEMBER TO COM-MUN-I-CATE!
WHEN THINGS ARE FEELING NOT SO GREAT, REMEMBER TO COM-MUN-I-CATE!
HEY, HAS THAT ALWAYS BEEN THERE?
IT'S SIMPLEST JUST TO LET THINGS BE...
HAS WHAT ALWAYS BEEN THERE?
THAT... SHIP...
BYE!
AND TAKE A RIDE UPON THE SEA!
OH MY GOSH!
OH MY GOSH, IT WORKED!
WHAT WORKED?
I WAS TEASING YOU IN WANDER, AND I FIGURED: WHAT WOULD BE MORE EMBARRASSING THEN YOUR CRUSH'S BOAT MANIFESTING INTO ANOTHER DIMENSION AS A SYMBOL OF YOUR FEELINGS FOR THE WORLD TO SEE!
CHOKE
I CAN'T BELIEVE IT!
IT LOOKS GOOD, TOO!
I CAN'T BELIEVE YOU UNLOCKED YOUR MAGE POWERS JUST TO BE A BUTTHEAD TO ME. HOW IS THIS MY LIFE NOW?

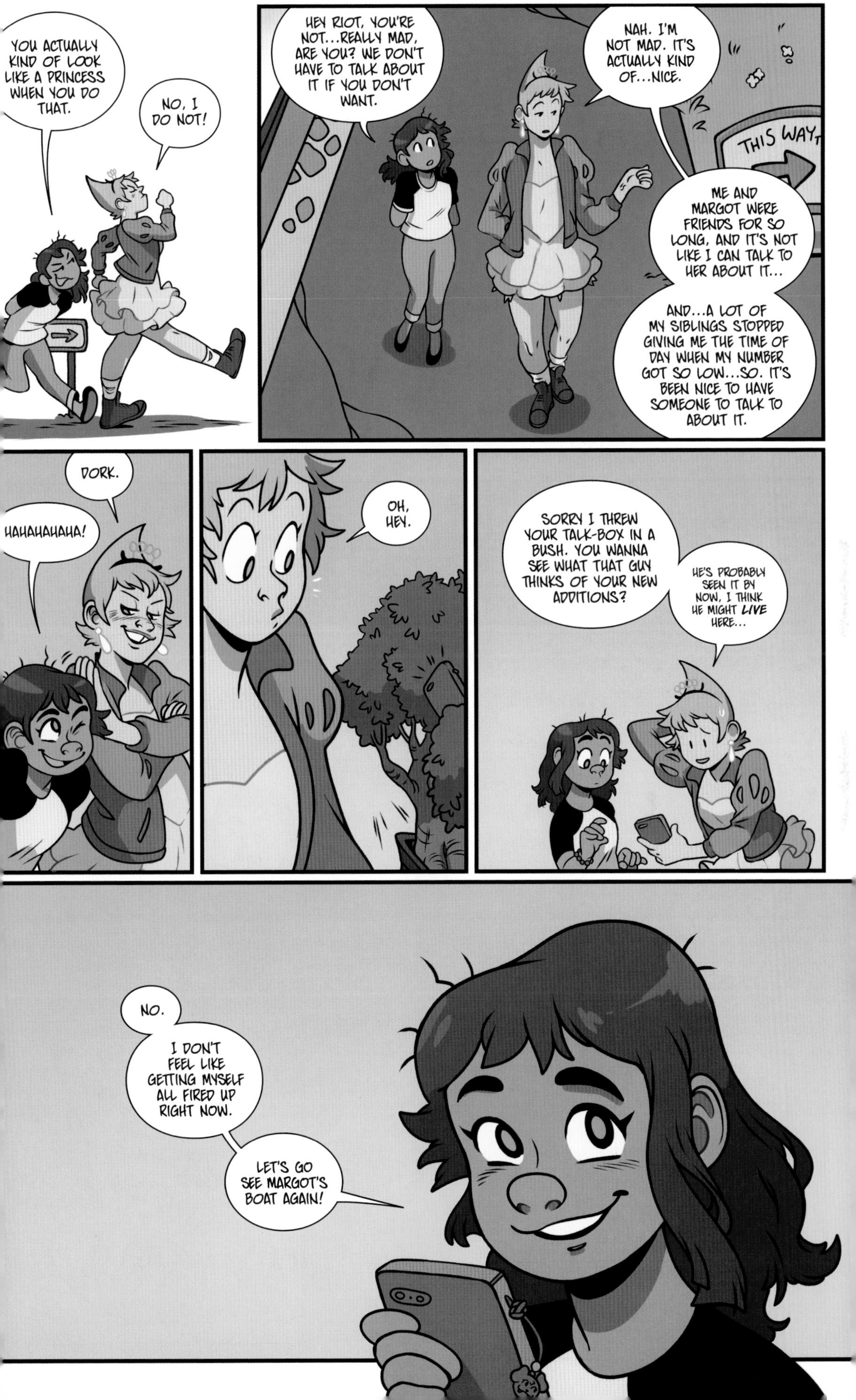

YOU ACTUALLY KIND OF LOOK LIKE A PRINCESS WHEN YOU DO THAT.
NO, I DO NOT!
HEY RIOT, YOU'RE NOT...REALLY MAD, ARE YOU? WE DON'T HAVE TO TALK ABOUT IT IF YOU DON'T WANT.
NAH. I'M NOT MAD. IT'S ACTUALLY KIND OF...NICE.
THIS WAY
ME AND MARGOT WERE FRIENDS FOR SO LONG, AND IT'S NOT LIKE I CAN TALK TO HER ABOUT IT...
AND...A LOT OF MY SIBLINGS STOPPED GIVING ME THE TIME OF DAY WHEN MY NUMBER GOT SO LOW...SO. IT'S BEEN NICE TO HAVE SOMEONE TO TALK TO ABOUT IT.
DORK.
HAHAHAHAHA!
OH, HEY.
SORRY I THREW YOUR TALK-BOX IN A BUSH. YOU WANNA SEE WHAT THAT GUY THINKS OF YOUR NEW ADDITIONS?
HE'S PROBABLY SEEN IT BY NOW, I THINK HE MIGHT *LIVE* HERE...
NO.
I DON'T FEEL LIKE GETTING MYSELF ALL FIRED UP RIGHT NOW.
LET'S GO SEE MARGOT'S BOAT AGAIN!

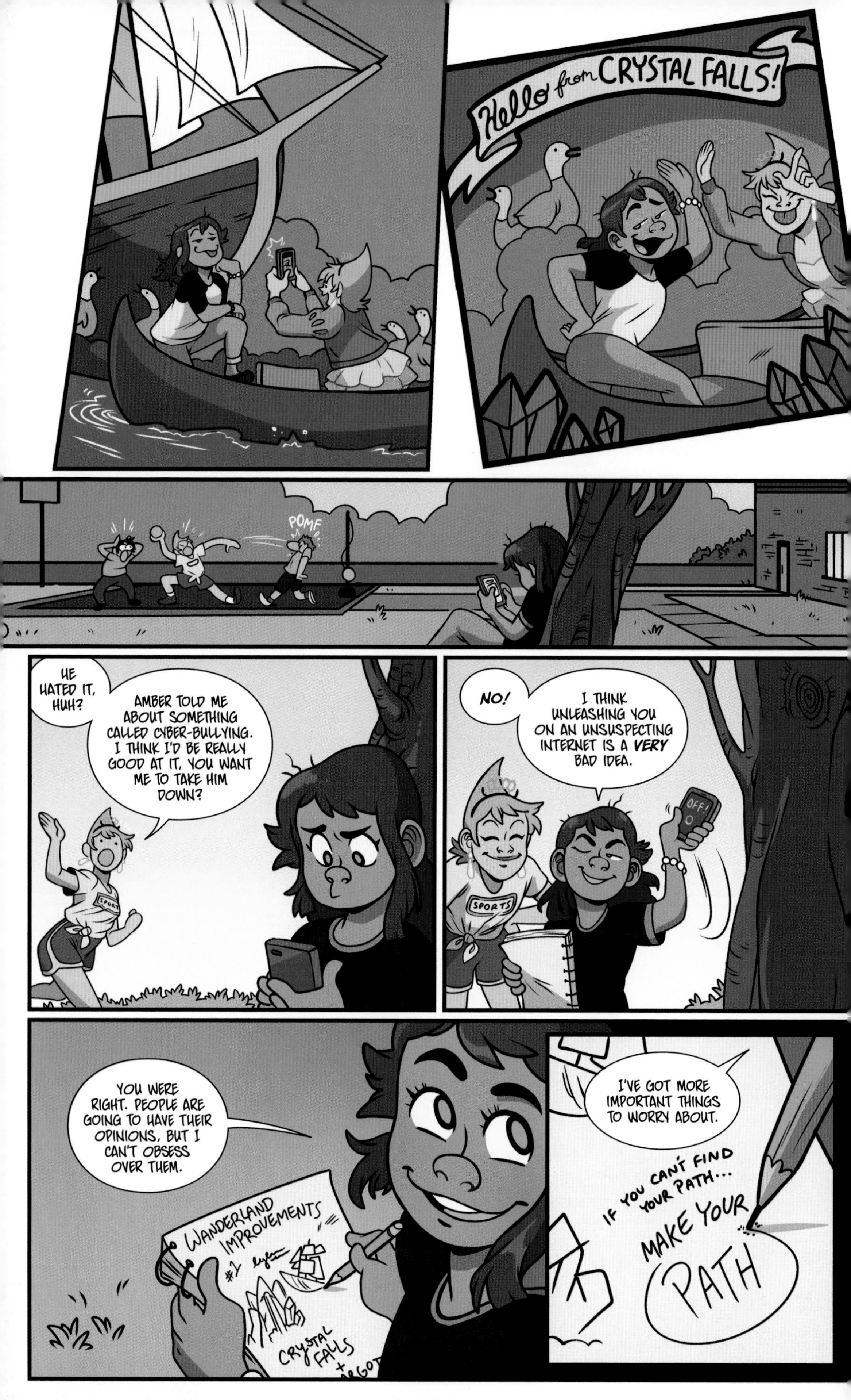

Hello from CRYSTAL FALLS!
POMF
HE HATED IT, HUH?
AMBER TOLD ME ABOUT SOMETHING CALLED CYBER-BULLYING. I THINK I'D BE REALLY GOOD AT IT, YOU WANT ME TO TAKE HIM DOWN?
SPORTS
NO!
I THINK UNLEASHING YOU ON AN UNSUSPECTING INTERNET IS A VERY BAD IDEA.
OFF!
SPORTS
YOU WERE RIGHT. PEOPLE ARE GOING TO HAVE THEIR OPINIONS, BUT I CAN'T OBSESS OVER THEM.
WANDERLAND IMPROVEMENTS
#1
CRYSTAL FALLS +
I'VE GOT MORE IMPORTANT THINGS TO WORRY ABOUT.
IF YOU CAN'T FIND YOUR PATH...
MAKE YOUR PATH

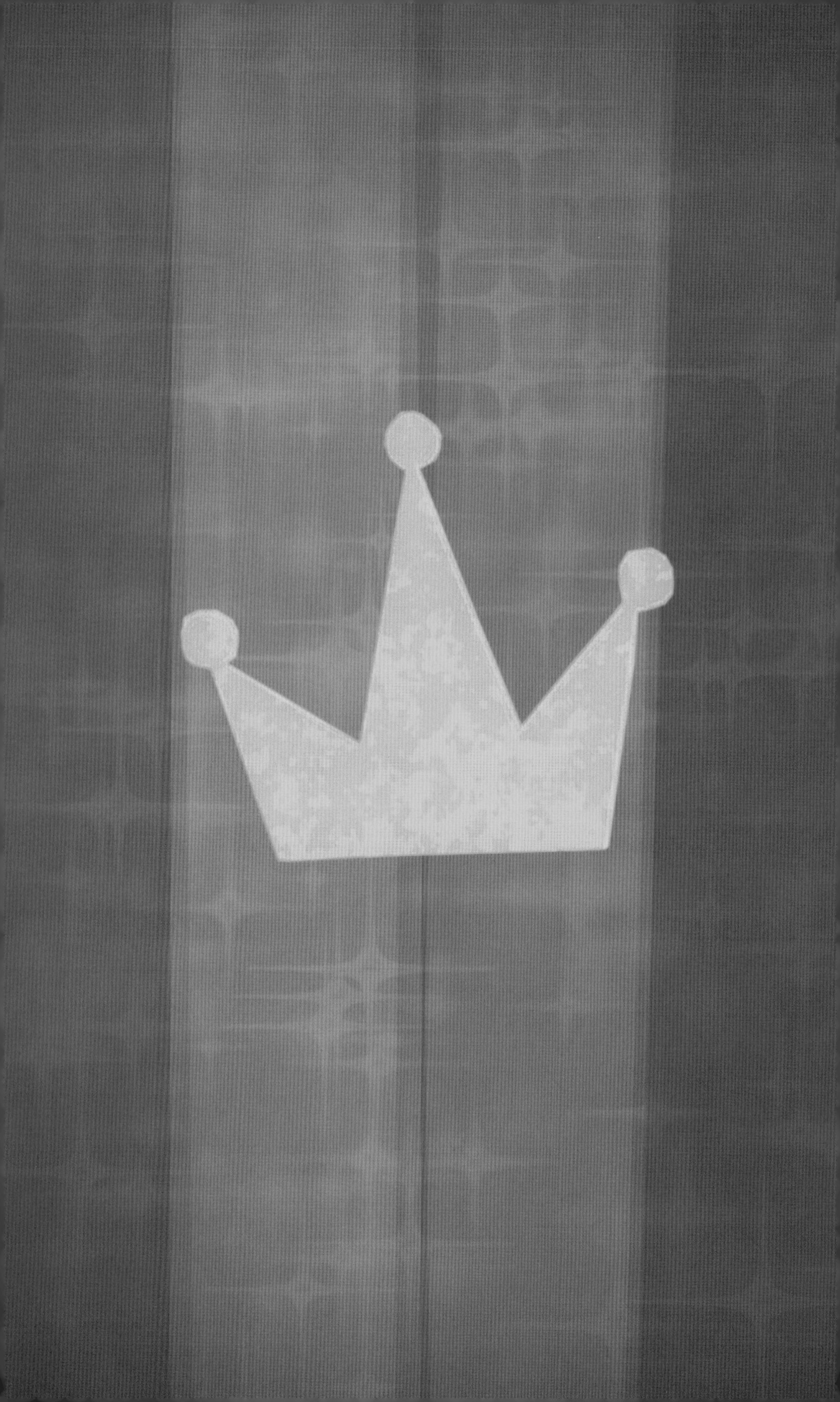

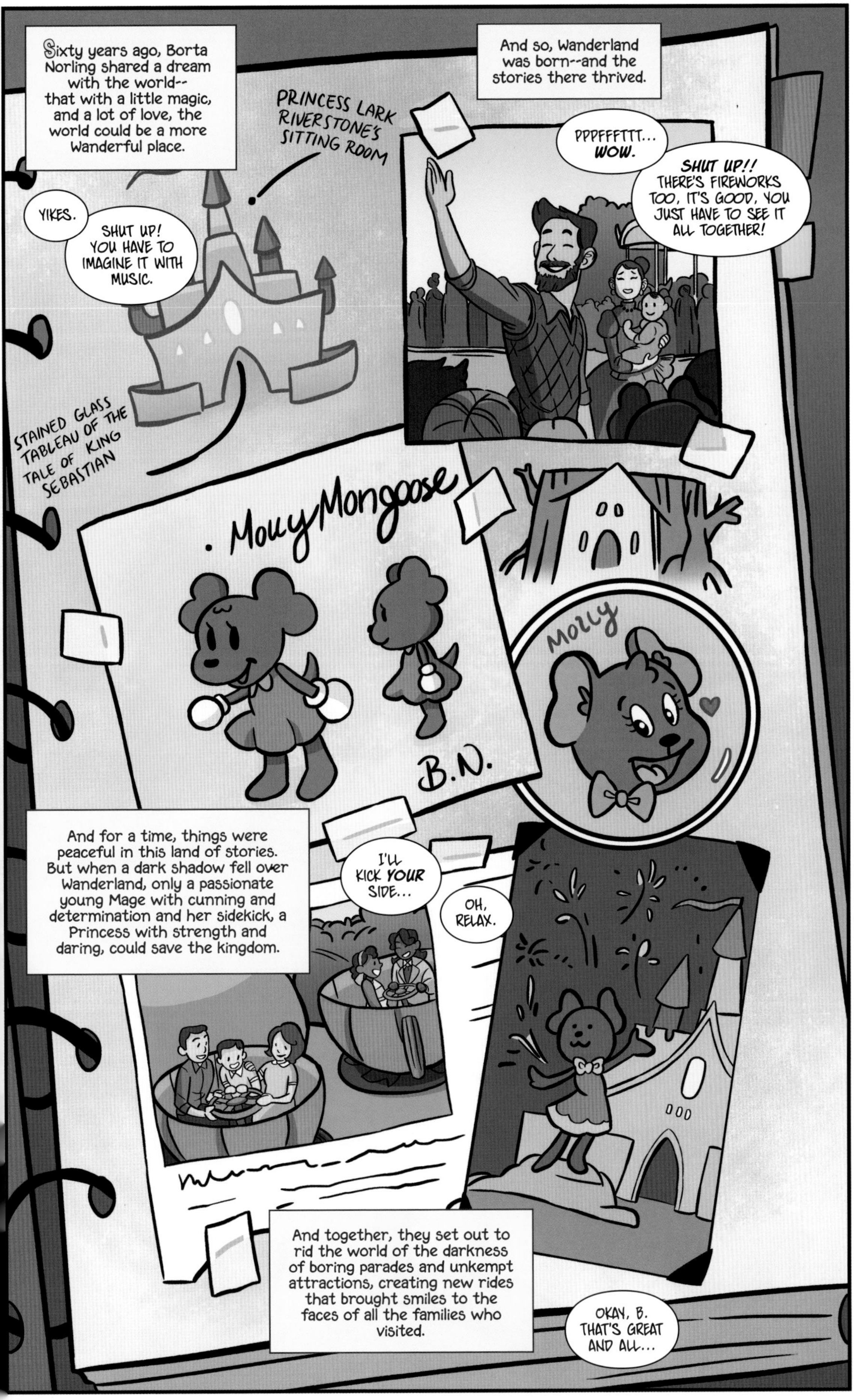
Sixty years ago, Borta Norling shared a dream with the world--that with a little magic, and a lot of love, the world could be a more Wanderful place.
PRINCESS LARK RIVERSTONE'S SITTING ROOM
YIKES.
SHUT UP! YOU HAVE TO IMAGINE IT WITH MUSIC.
STAINED GLASS TABLEAU OF THE TALE OF KING SEBASTIAN
And so, Wanderland was born--and the stories there thrived.
PPPFFFTTT... WOW.
SHUT UP!! THERE'S FIREWORKS TOO, IT'S GOOD, YOU JUST HAVE TO SEE IT ALL TOGETHER!
Molly Mongoose
B.N.
MOLLY
And for a time, things were peaceful in this land of stories. But when a dark shadow fell over Wanderland, only a passionate young Mage with cunning and determination and her sidekick, a Princess with strength and daring, could save the kingdom.
I'LL KICK YOUR SIDE...
OH, RELAX.
And together, they set out to rid the world of the darkness of boring parades and unkempt attractions, creating new rides that brought smiles to the faces of all the families who visited.
OKAY, B. THAT'S GREAT AND ALL...

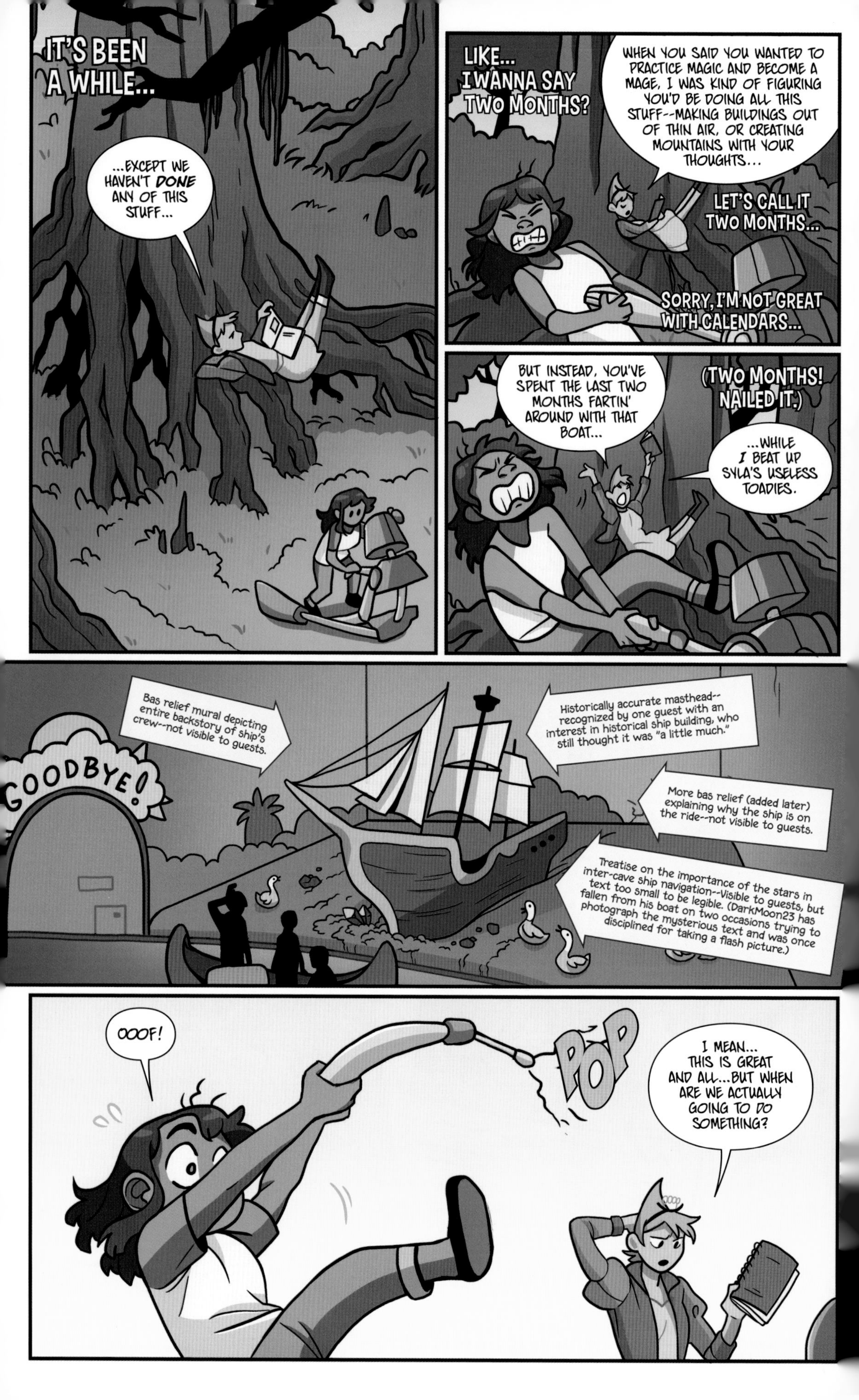
IT'S BEEN A WHILE...
...EXCEPT WE HAVEN'T DONE ANY OF THIS STUFF...
LIKE... I WANNA SAY TWO MONTHS?
WHEN YOU SAID YOU WANTED TO PRACTICE MAGIC AND BECOME A MAGE, I WAS KIND OF FIGURING YOU'D BE DOING ALL THIS STUFF--MAKING BUILDINGS OUT OF THIN AIR, OR CREATING MOUNTAINS WITH YOUR THOUGHTS...
LET'S CALL IT TWO MONTHS...
SORRY, I'M NOT GREAT WITH CALENDARS...
BUT INSTEAD, YOU'VE SPENT THE LAST TWO MONTHS FARTIN' AROUND WITH THAT BOAT...
(TWO MONTHS! NAILED IT.)
...WHILE I BEAT UP SYLA'S USELESS TOADIES.
Bas relief mural depicting entire backstory of ship's crew--not visible to guests.
GOODBYE!
Historically accurate masthead--recognized by one guest with an interest in historical ship building, who still thought it was "a little much."
More bas relief (added later) explaining why the ship is on the ride--not visible to guests.
Treatise on the importance of the stars in inter-cave ship navigation--Visible to guests, but text too small to be legible. (DarkMoon23 has fallen from his boat on two occasions trying to photograph the mysterious text and was once disciplined for taking a flash picture.)
OOOF!
POP
I MEAN... THIS IS GREAT AND ALL...BUT WHEN ARE WE ACTUALLY GOING TO DO SOMETHING?

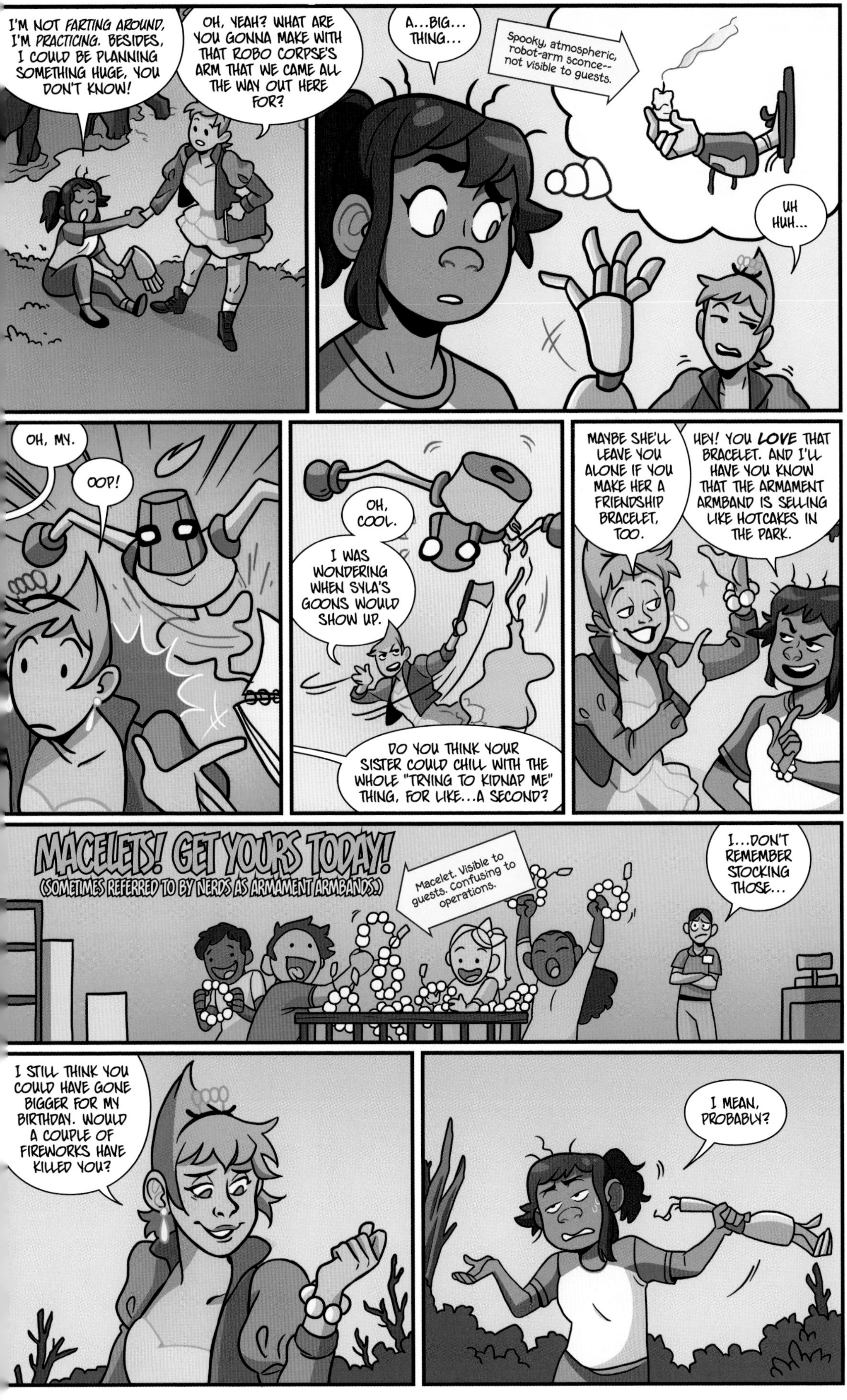

I'M NOT FARTING AROUND, I'M PRACTICING. BESIDES, I COULD BE PLANNING SOMETHING HUGE, YOU DON'T KNOW!
OH, YEAH? WHAT ARE YOU GONNA MAKE WITH THAT ROBO CORPSE'S ARM THAT WE CAME ALL THE WAY OUT HERE FOR?
A...BIG... THING...
Spooky, atmospheric, robot-arm sconce-- not visible to guests.
UH HUH...
OH, MY.
OOP!
OH, COOL.
I WAS WONDERING WHEN SYLA'S GOONS WOULD SHOW UP.
DO YOU THINK YOUR SISTER COULD CHILL WITH THE WHOLE "TRYING TO KIDNAP ME" THING, FOR LIKE...A SECOND?
MAYBE SHE'LL LEAVE YOU ALONE IF YOU MAKE HER A FRIENDSHIP BRACELET, TOO.
HEY! YOU LOVE THAT BRACELET. AND I'LL HAVE YOU KNOW THAT THE ARMAMENT ARMBAND IS SELLING LIKE HOTCAKES IN THE PARK.
MACELETS! GET YOURS TODAY!
(SOMETIMES REFERRED TO BY NERDS AS ARMAMENT ARMBANDS.)
Macelet. Visible to guests. Confusing to operations.
I...DON'T REMEMBER STOCKING THOSE...
I STILL THINK YOU COULD HAVE GONE BIGGER FOR MY BIRTHDAY. WOULD A COUPLE OF FIREWORKS HAVE KILLED YOU?
I MEAN, PROBABLY?

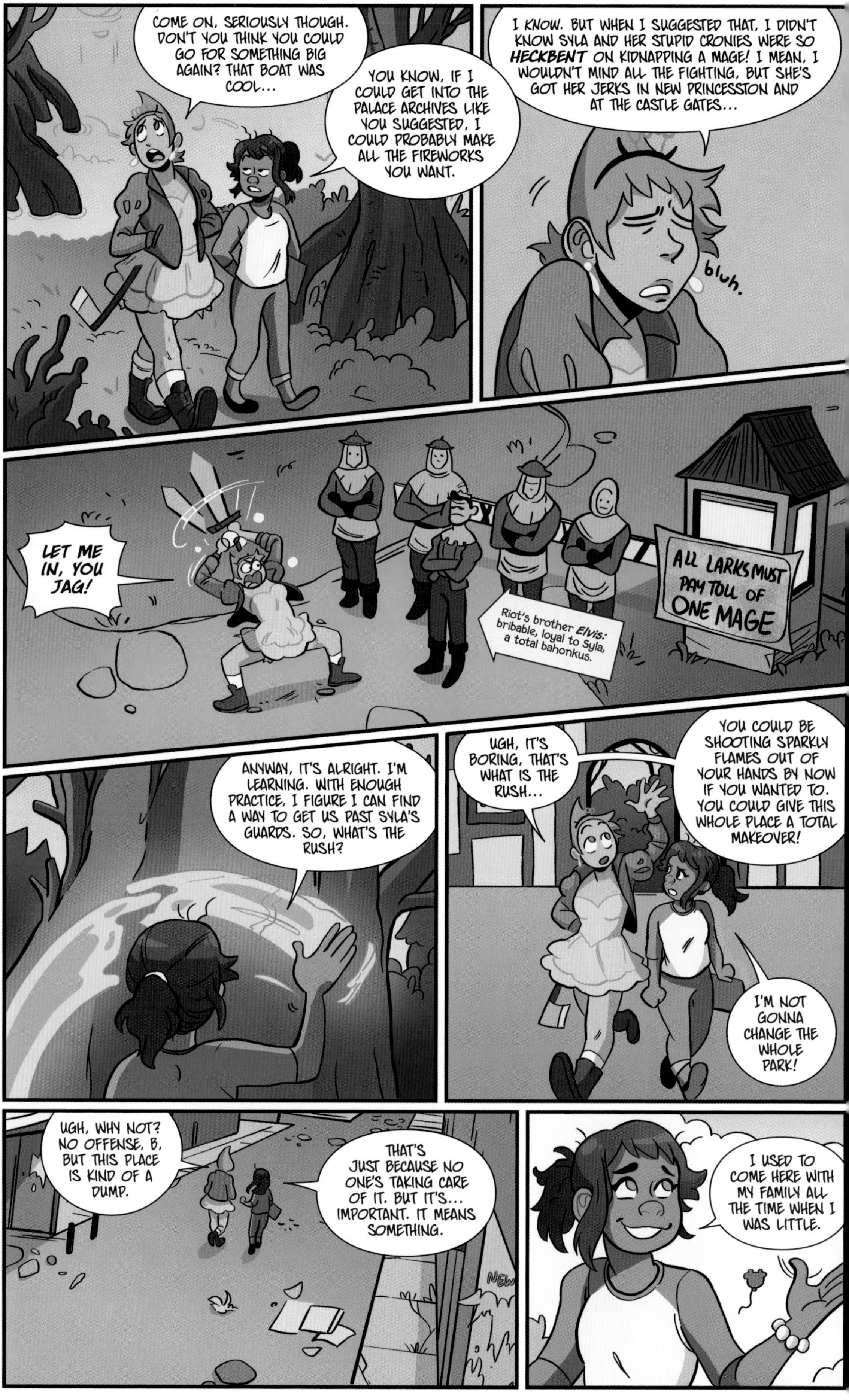

COME ON, SERIOUSLY THOUGH. DON'T YOU THINK YOU COULD GO FOR SOMETHING BIG AGAIN? THAT BOAT WAS COOL...
YOU KNOW, IF I COULD GET INTO THE PALACE ARCHIVES LIKE YOU SUGGESTED, I COULD PROBABLY MAKE ALL THE FIREWORKS YOU WANT.
I KNOW. BUT WHEN I SUGGESTED THAT, I DIDN'T KNOW SYLA AND HER STUPID CRONIES WERE SO HECKBENT ON KIDNAPPING A MAGE! I MEAN, I WOULDN'T MIND ALL THE FIGHTING, BUT SHE'S GOT HER JERKS IN NEW PRINCESSTON AND AT THE CASTLE GATES...
bluh.
LET ME IN, YOU JAG!
Riot's brother Elvis: bribable, loyal to Syla, a total bahonkus.
ALL LARKS MUST PAY TOLL OF ONE MAGE
ANYWAY, IT'S ALRIGHT. I'M LEARNING. WITH ENOUGH PRACTICE, I FIGURE I CAN FIND A WAY TO GET US PAST SYLA'S GUARDS. SO, WHAT'S THE RUSH?
UGH, IT'S BORING, THAT'S WHAT IS THE RUSH...
YOU COULD BE SHOOTING SPARKLY FLAMES OUT OF YOUR HANDS BY NOW IF YOU WANTED TO. YOU COULD GIVE THIS WHOLE PLACE A TOTAL MAKEOVER!
I'M NOT GONNA CHANGE THE WHOLE PARK!
UGH, WHY NOT? NO OFFENSE, B, BUT THIS PLACE IS KIND OF A DUMP.
THAT'S JUST BECAUSE NO ONE'S TAKING CARE OF IT. BUT IT'S... IMPORTANT. IT MEANS SOMETHING.
NEW
I USED TO COME HERE WITH MY FAMILY ALL THE TIME WHEN I WAS LITTLE.

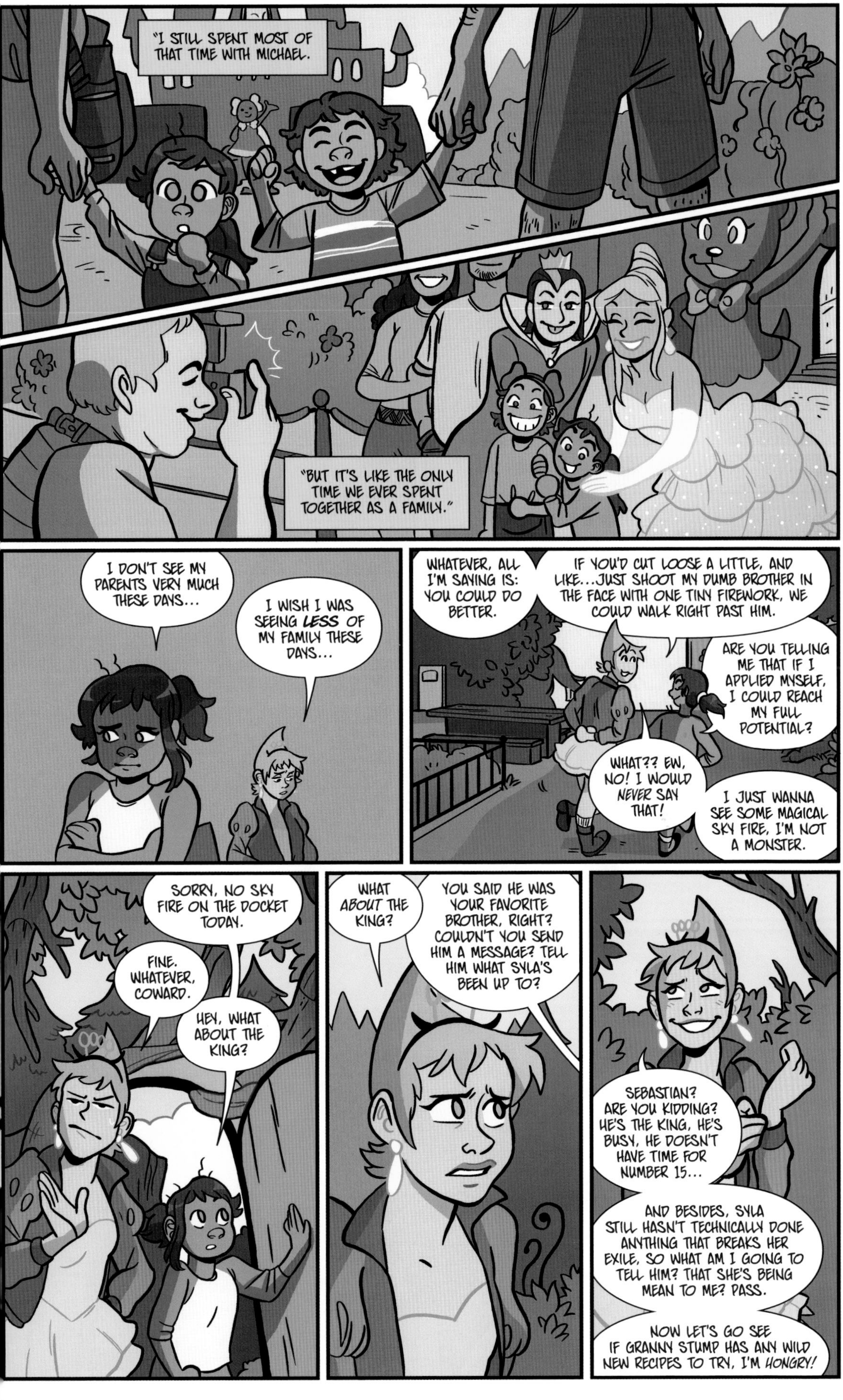
"I STILL SPENT MOST OF THAT TIME WITH MICHAEL.
"BUT IT'S LIKE THE ONLY TIME WE EVER SPENT TOGETHER AS A FAMILY."
I DON'T SEE MY PARENTS VERY MUCH THESE DAYS...
I WISH I WAS SEEING LESS OF MY FAMILY THESE DAYS...
WHATEVER, ALL I'M SAYING IS: YOU COULD DO BETTER.
IF YOU'D CUT LOOSE A LITTLE, AND LIKE...JUST SHOOT MY DUMB BROTHER IN THE FACE WITH ONE TINY FIREWORK, WE COULD WALK RIGHT PAST HIM.
ARE YOU TELLING ME THAT IF I APPLIED MYSELF, I COULD REACH MY FULL POTENTIAL?
WHAT?? EW, NO! I WOULD NEVER SAY THAT!
I JUST WANNA SEE SOME MAGICAL SKY FIRE, I'M NOT A MONSTER.
SORRY, NO SKY FIRE ON THE DOCKET TODAY.
FINE. WHATEVER, COWARD.
HEY, WHAT ABOUT THE KING?
WHAT ABOUT THE KING?
YOU SAID HE WAS YOUR FAVORITE BROTHER, RIGHT? COULDN'T YOU SEND HIM A MESSAGE? TELL HIM WHAT SYLA'S BEEN UP TO?
SEBASTIAN? ARE YOU KIDDING? HE'S THE KING, HE'S BUSY, HE DOESN'T HAVE TIME FOR NUMBER 15...
AND BESIDES, SYLA STILL HASN'T TECHNICALLY DONE ANYTHING THAT BREAKS HER EXILE, SO WHAT AM I GOING TO TELL HIM? THAT SHE'S BEING MEAN TO ME? PASS.
NOW LET'S GO SEE IF GRANNY STUMP HAS ANY WILD NEW RECIPES TO TRY, I'M HONGRY!

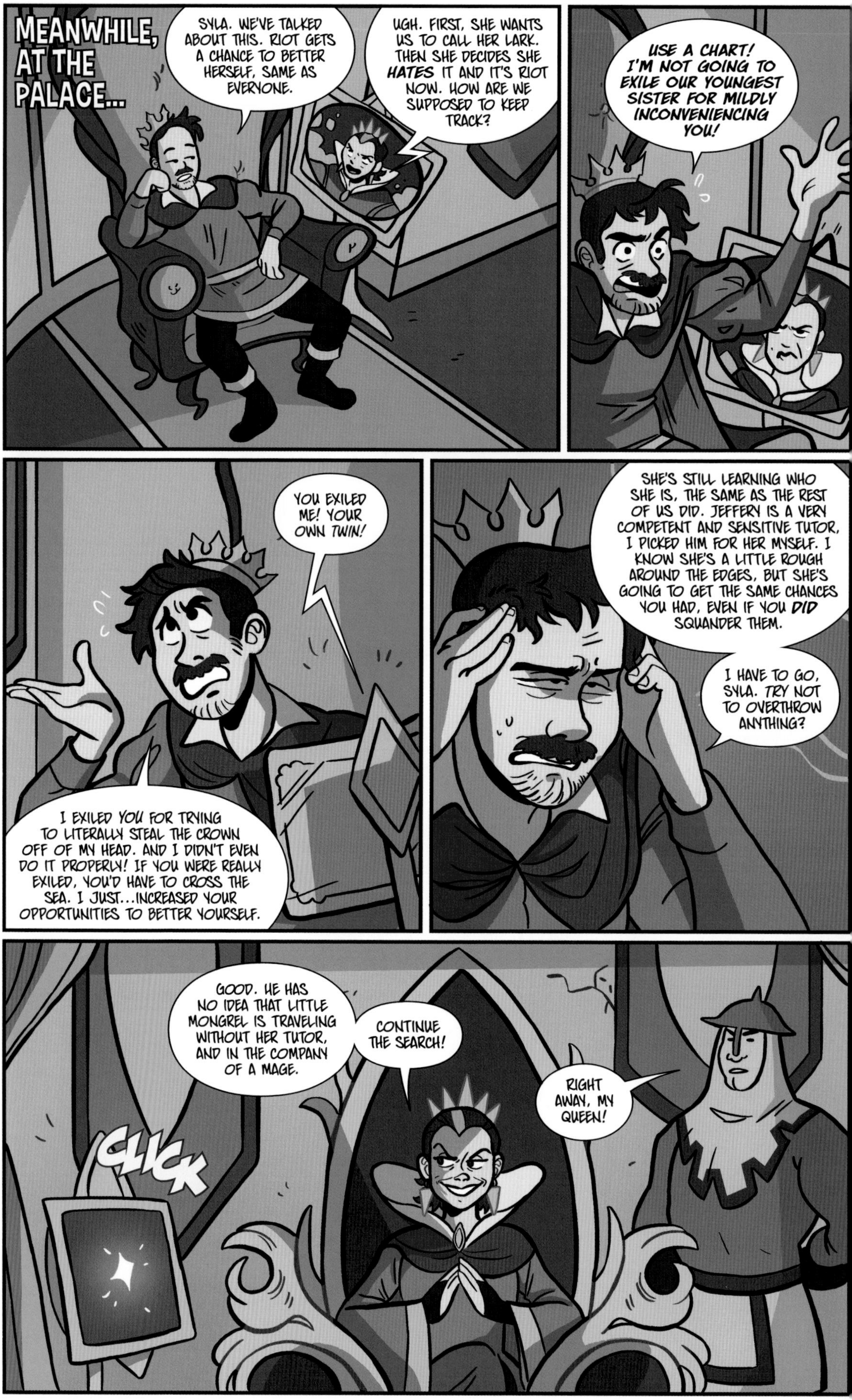
MEANWHILE, AT THE PALACE...
SYLA. WE'VE TALKED ABOUT THIS. RIOT GETS A CHANCE TO BETTER HERSELF, SAME AS EVERYONE.
UGH. FIRST, SHE WANTS US TO CALL HER LARK. THEN SHE DECIDES SHE HATES IT AND IT'S RIOT NOW. HOW ARE WE SUPPOSED TO KEEP TRACK?
USE A CHART! I'M NOT GOING TO EXILE OUR YOUNGEST SISTER FOR MILDLY INCONVENIENCING YOU!
YOU EXILED ME! YOUR OWN TWIN!
I EXILED YOU FOR TRYING TO LITERALLY STEAL THE CROWN OFF OF MY HEAD. AND I DIDN'T EVEN DO IT PROPERLY! IF YOU WERE REALLY EXILED, YOU'D HAVE TO CROSS THE SEA. I JUST...INCREASED YOUR OPPORTUNITIES TO BETTER YOURSELF.
SHE'S STILL LEARNING WHO SHE IS, THE SAME AS THE REST OF US DID. JEFFERY IS A VERY COMPETENT AND SENSITIVE TUTOR, I PICKED HIM FOR HER MYSELF. I KNOW SHE'S A LITTLE ROUGH AROUND THE EDGES, BUT SHE'S GOING TO GET THE SAME CHANCES YOU HAD, EVEN IF YOU DID SQUANDER THEM.
I HAVE TO GO, SYLA. TRY NOT TO OVERTHROW ANYTHING?
CLICK
GOOD. HE HAS NO IDEA THAT LITTLE MONGREL IS TRAVELING WITHOUT HER TUTOR, AND IN THE COMPANY OF A MAGE.
CONTINUE THE SEARCH!
RIGHT AWAY, MY QUEEN!

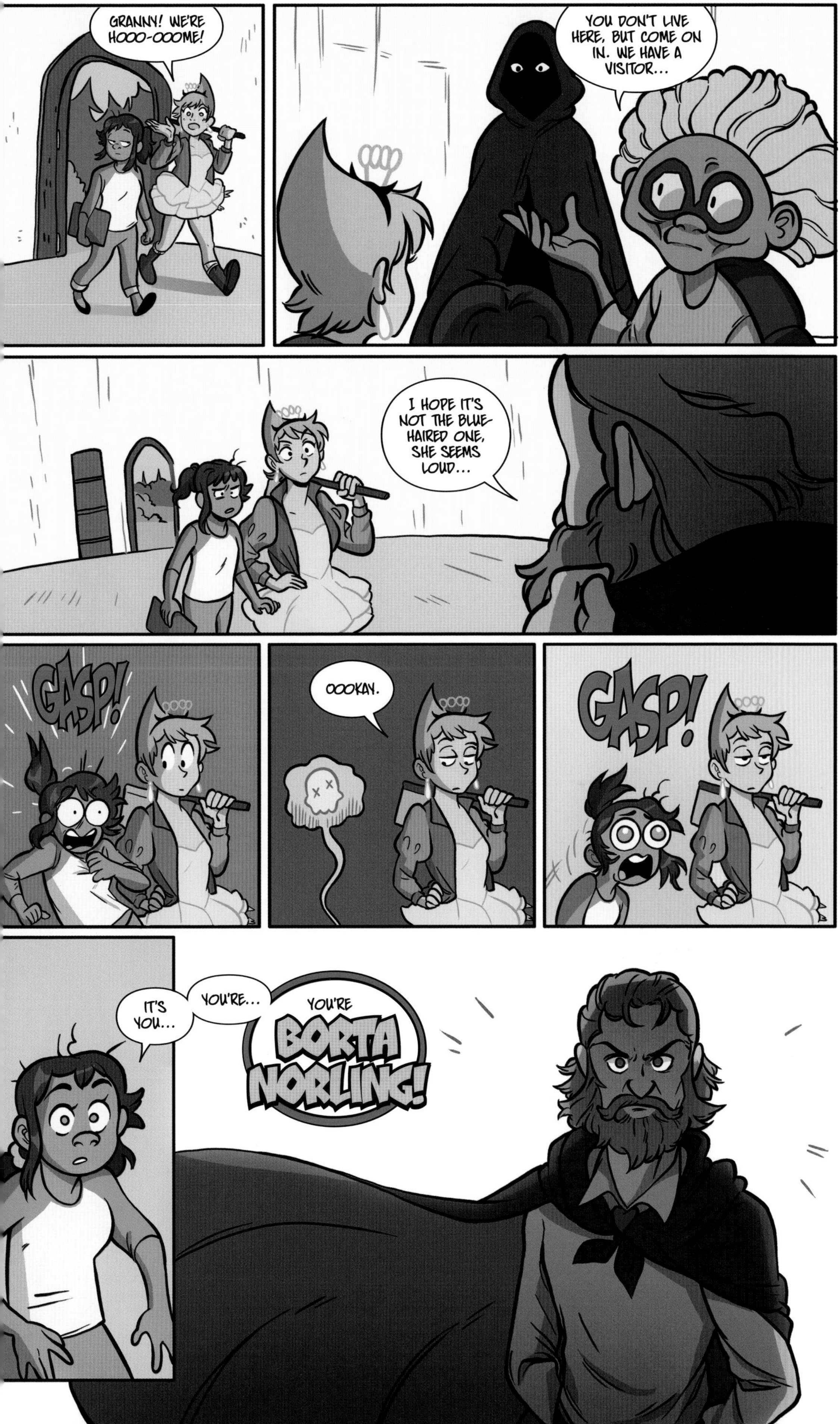

GRANNY! WE'RE HOOO-OOOME!
YOU DON'T LIVE HERE, BUT COME ON IN. WE HAVE A VISITOR...
I HOPE IT'S NOT THE BLUE-HAIRED ONE, SHE SEEMS LOUD...
GASP!
OOOKAY.
GASP!
IT'S YOU...
YOU'RE...
YOU'RE
BORTA NORLING!

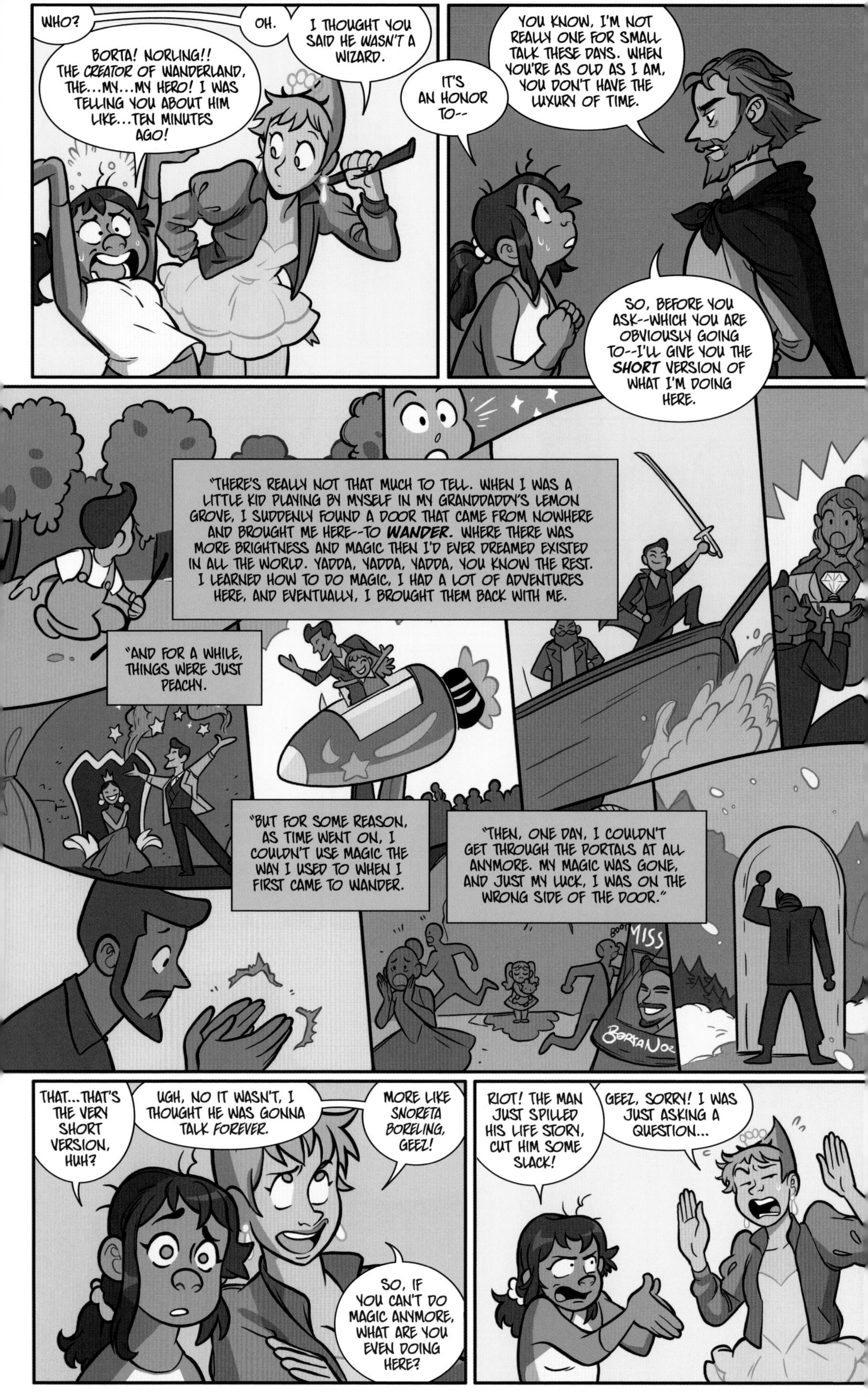
WHO?
BORTA! NORLING!! THE CREATOR OF WANDERLAND, THE...MY...MY HERO! I WAS TELLING YOU ABOUT HIM LIKE...TEN MINUTES AGO!
OH.
I THOUGHT YOU SAID HE WASN'T A WIZARD.
IT'S AN HONOR TO--
YOU KNOW, I'M NOT REALLY ONE FOR SMALL TALK THESE DAYS. WHEN YOU'RE AS OLD AS I AM, YOU DON'T HAVE THE LUXURY OF TIME.
SO, BEFORE YOU ASK--WHICH YOU ARE OBVIOUSLY GOING TO--I'LL GIVE YOU THE **SHORT** VERSION OF WHAT I'M DOING HERE.
"THERE'S REALLY NOT THAT MUCH TO TELL. WHEN I WAS A LITTLE KID PLAYING BY MYSELF IN MY GRANDDADDY'S LEMON GROVE, I SUDDENLY FOUND A DOOR THAT CAME FROM NOWHERE AND BROUGHT ME HERE--TO ***WANDER.*** WHERE THERE WAS MORE BRIGHTNESS AND MAGIC THEN I'D EVER DREAMED EXISTED IN ALL THE WORLD. YADDA, YADDA, YADDA, YOU KNOW THE REST. I LEARNED HOW TO DO MAGIC, I HAD A LOT OF ADVENTURES HERE, AND EVENTUALLY, I BROUGHT THEM BACK WITH ME.
"AND FOR A WHILE, THINGS WERE JUST PEACHY.
"BUT FOR SOME REASON, AS TIME WENT ON, I COULDN'T USE MAGIC THE WAY I USED TO WHEN I FIRST CAME TO WANDER.
"THEN, ONE DAY, I COULDN'T GET THROUGH THE PORTALS AT ALL ANYMORE. MY MAGIC WAS GONE, AND JUST MY LUCK, I WAS ON THE WRONG SIDE OF THE DOOR."
BOOT
MISS
BORTA NOR
THAT...THAT'S THE VERY SHORT VERSION, HUH?
UGH, NO IT WASN'T, I THOUGHT HE WAS GONNA TALK FOREVER.
MORE LIKE SNORETA BORELING, GEEZ!
SO, IF YOU CAN'T DO MAGIC ANYMORE, WHAT ARE YOU EVEN DOING HERE?
RIOT! THE MAN JUST SPILLED HIS LIFE STORY, CUT HIM SOME SLACK!
GEEZ, SORRY! I WAS JUST ASKING A QUESTION...

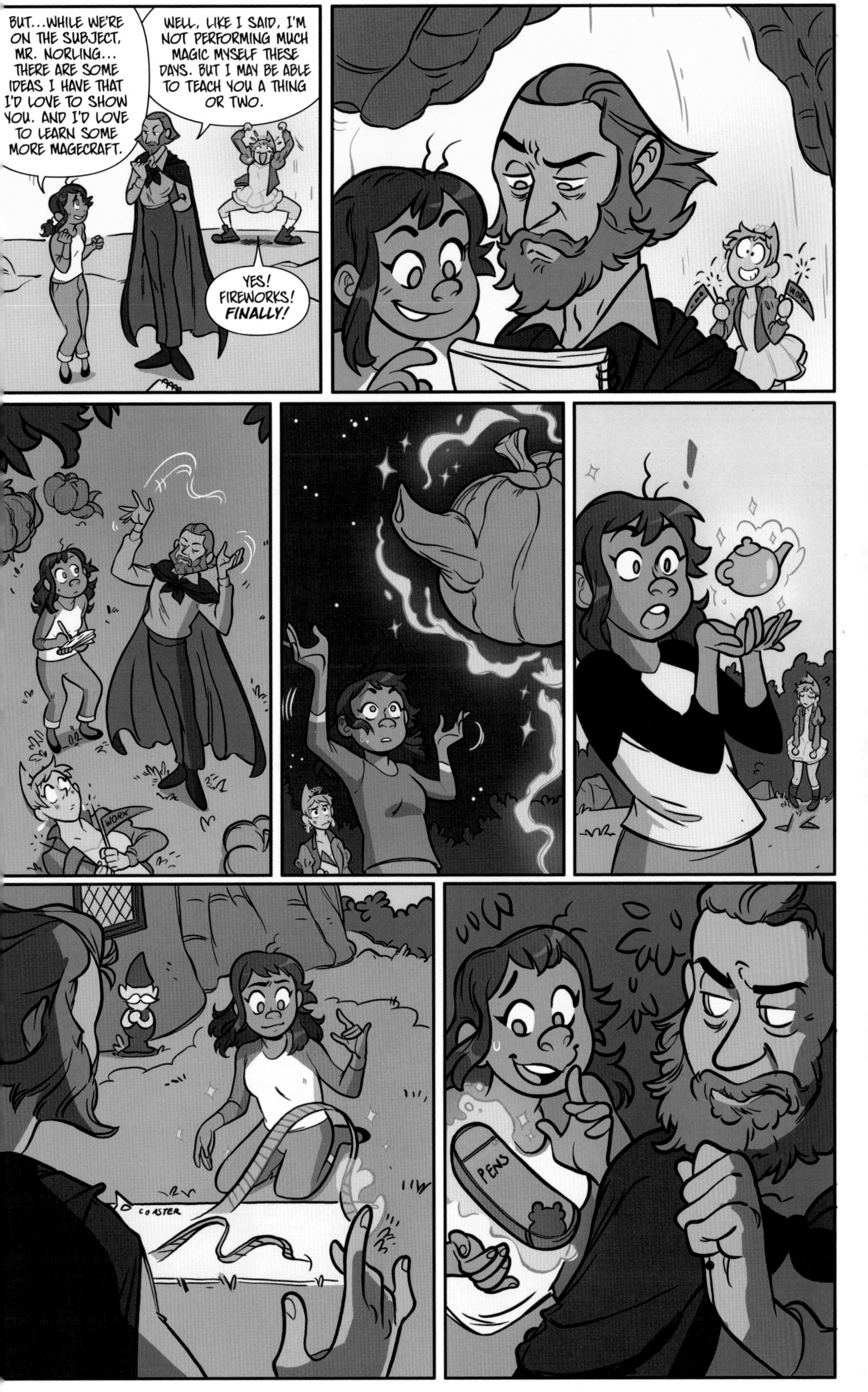

BUT...WHILE WE'RE ON THE SUBJECT, MR. NORLING... THERE ARE SOME IDEAS I HAVE THAT I'D LOVE TO SHOW YOU. AND I'D LOVE TO LEARN SOME MORE MAGECRAFT.
WELL, LIKE I SAID, I'M NOT PERFORMING MUCH MAGIC MYSELF THESE DAYS. BUT I MAY BE ABLE TO TEACH YOU A THING OR TWO.
YES! FIREWORKS! FINALLY!
WORX
WORX
!
COASTER
PENS

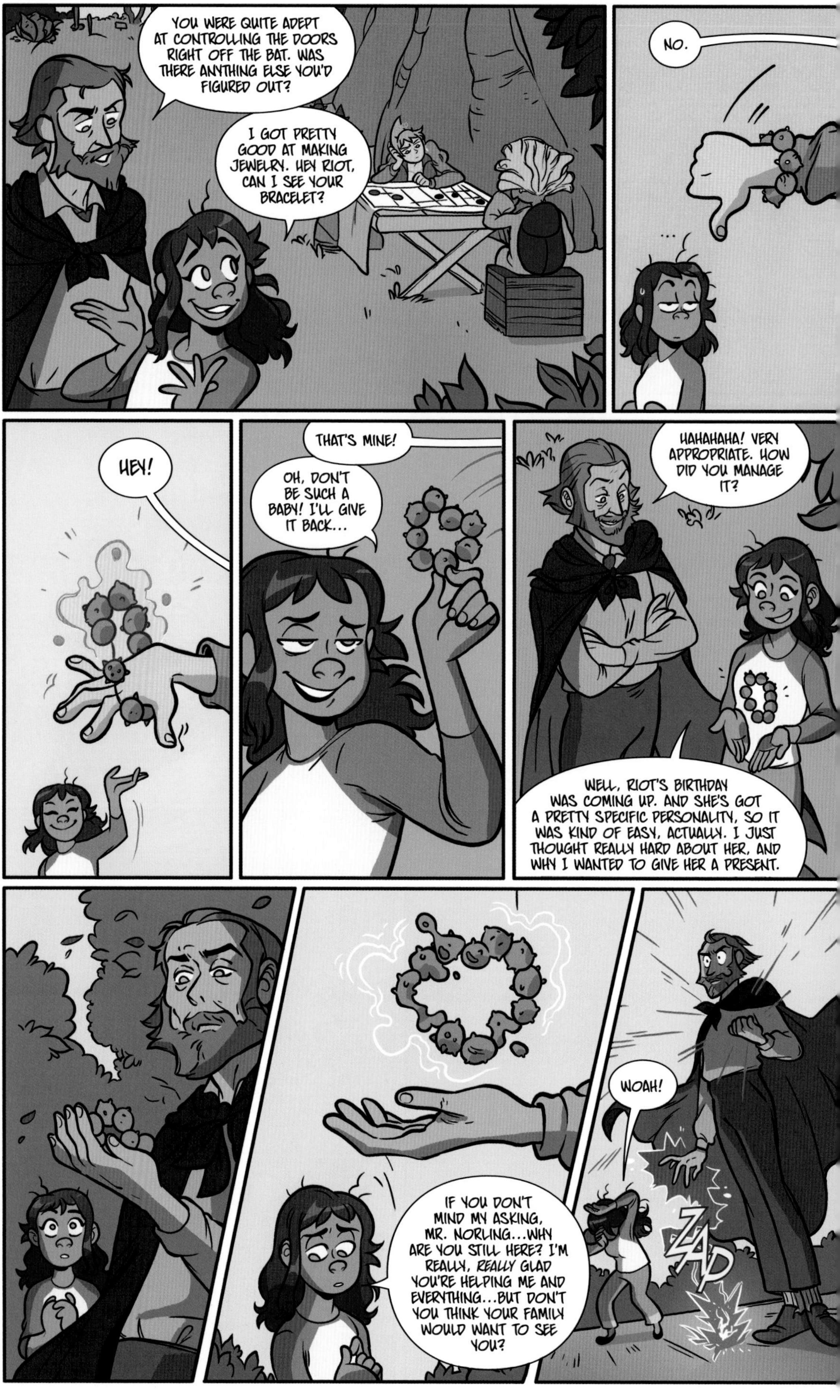

YOU WERE QUITE ADEPT AT CONTROLLING THE DOORS RIGHT OFF THE BAT. WAS THERE ANYTHING ELSE YOU'D FIGURED OUT?
I GOT PRETTY GOOD AT MAKING JEWELRY. HEY RIOT, CAN I SEE YOUR BRACELET?
NO.
...
HEY!
THAT'S MINE!
OH, DON'T BE SUCH A BABY! I'LL GIVE IT BACK...
HAHAHAHA! VERY APPROPRIATE. HOW DID YOU MANAGE IT?
WELL, RIOT'S BIRTHDAY WAS COMING UP. AND SHE'S GOT A PRETTY SPECIFIC PERSONALITY, SO IT WAS KIND OF EASY, ACTUALLY. I JUST THOUGHT REALLY HARD ABOUT HER, AND WHY I WANTED TO GIVE HER A PRESENT.
IF YOU DON'T MIND MY ASKING, MR. NORLING...WHY ARE YOU STILL HERE? I'M REALLY, REALLY GLAD YOU'RE HELPING ME AND EVERYTHING...BUT DON'T YOU THINK YOUR FAMILY WOULD WANT TO SEE YOU?
WOAH!
ZAP

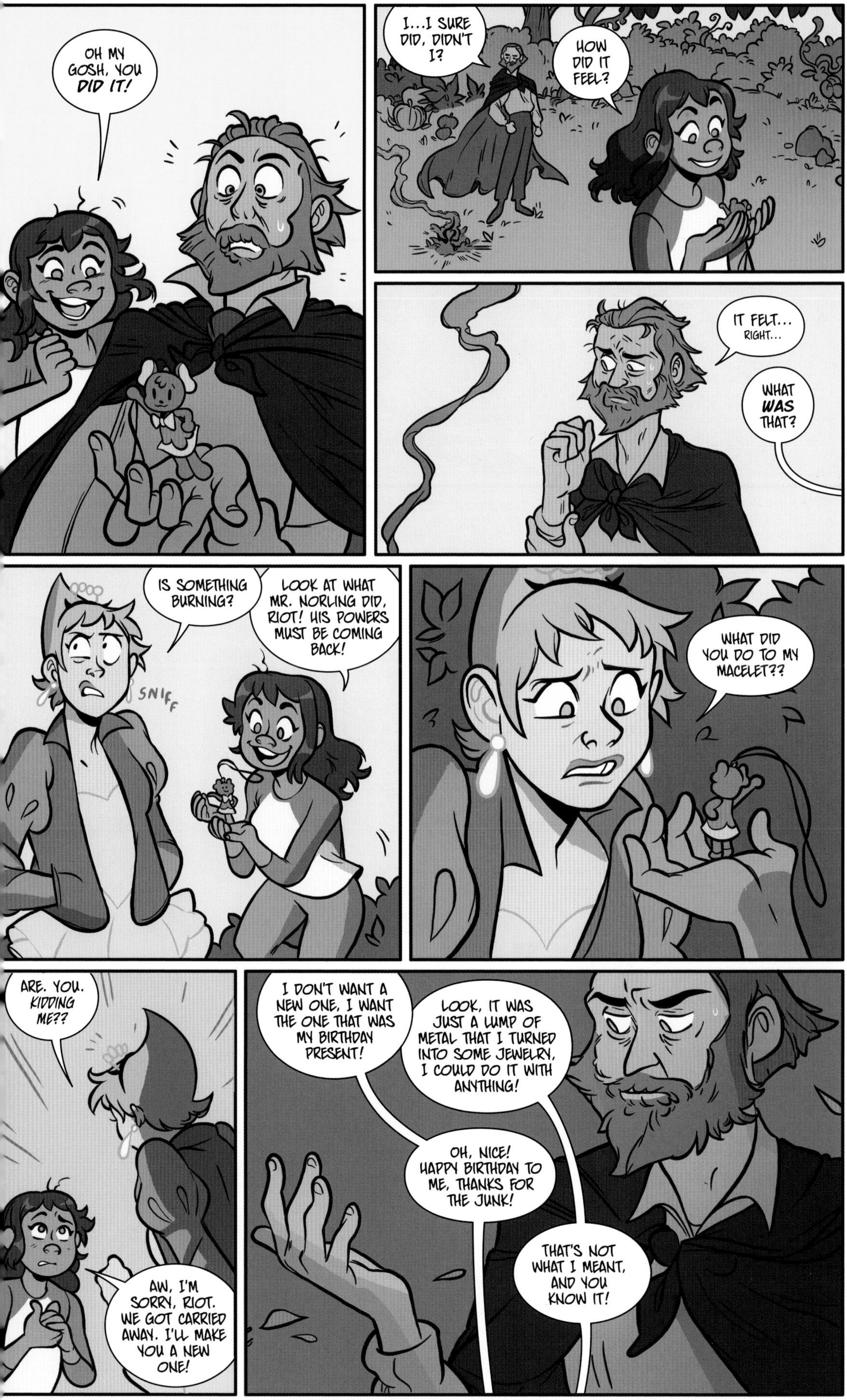
OH MY GOSH, YOU *DID IT!*
I...I SURE DID, DIDN'T I?
HOW DID IT FEEL?
IT FELT... RIGHT...
WHAT *WAS* THAT?
IS SOMETHING BURNING?
SNIFF
LOOK AT WHAT MR. NORLING DID, RIOT! HIS POWERS MUST BE COMING BACK!
WHAT DID YOU DO TO MY MACELET??
ARE. YOU. KIDDING ME??
AW, I'M SORRY, RIOT. WE GOT CARRIED AWAY. I'LL MAKE YOU A NEW ONE!
I DON'T WANT A NEW ONE, I WANT THE ONE THAT WAS MY BIRTHDAY PRESENT!
LOOK, IT WAS JUST A LUMP OF METAL THAT I TURNED INTO SOME JEWELRY, I COULD DO IT WITH ANYTHING!
OH, NICE! HAPPY BIRTHDAY TO ME, THANKS FOR THE JUNK!
THAT'S NOT WHAT I MEANT, AND YOU KNOW IT!

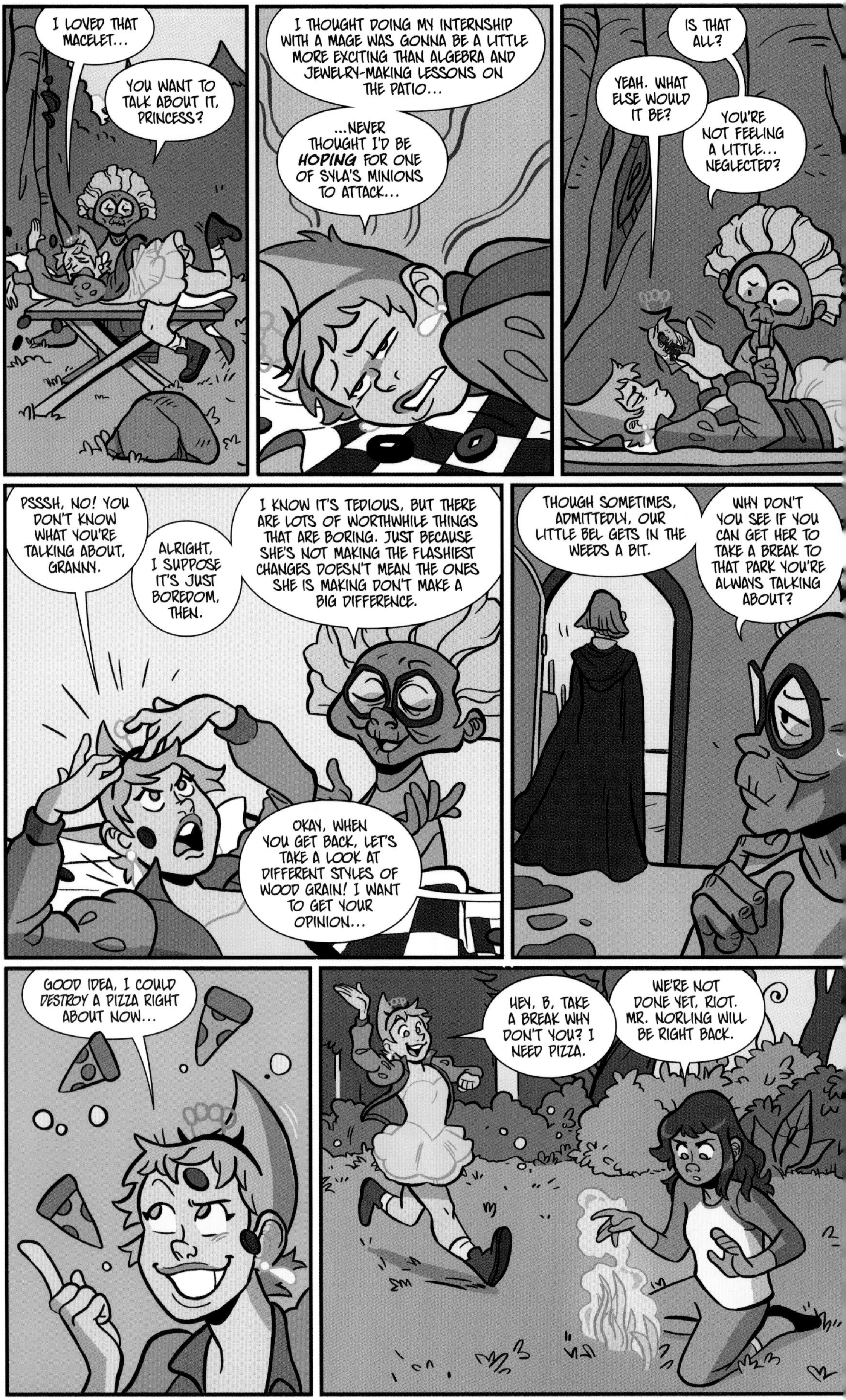
I LOVED THAT MACELET...
YOU WANT TO TALK ABOUT IT, PRINCESS?
I THOUGHT DOING MY INTERNSHIP WITH A MAGE WAS GONNA BE A LITTLE MORE EXCITING THAN ALGEBRA AND JEWELRY-MAKING LESSONS ON THE PATIO...
...NEVER THOUGHT I'D BE HOPING FOR ONE OF SYLA'S MINIONS TO ATTACK...
IS THAT ALL?
YEAH. WHAT ELSE WOULD IT BE?
YOU'RE NOT FEELING A LITTLE... NEGLECTED?
PSSSH, NO! YOU DON'T KNOW WHAT YOU'RE TALKING ABOUT, GRANNY.
ALRIGHT, I SUPPOSE IT'S JUST BOREDOM, THEN.
I KNOW IT'S TEDIOUS, BUT THERE ARE LOTS OF WORTHWHILE THINGS THAT ARE BORING. JUST BECAUSE SHE'S NOT MAKING THE FLASHIEST CHANGES DOESN'T MEAN THE ONES SHE IS MAKING DON'T MAKE A BIG DIFFERENCE.
OKAY, WHEN YOU GET BACK, LET'S TAKE A LOOK AT DIFFERENT STYLES OF WOOD GRAIN! I WANT TO GET YOUR OPINION...
THOUGH SOMETIMES, ADMITTEDLY, OUR LITTLE BEL GETS IN THE WEEDS A BIT.
WHY DON'T YOU SEE IF YOU CAN GET HER TO TAKE A BREAK TO THAT PARK YOU'RE ALWAYS TALKING ABOUT?
GOOD IDEA, I COULD DESTROY A PIZZA RIGHT ABOUT NOW...
HEY, B, TAKE A BREAK WHY DON'T YOU? I NEED PIZZA.
WE'RE NOT DONE YET, RIOT. MR. NORLING WILL BE RIGHT BACK.

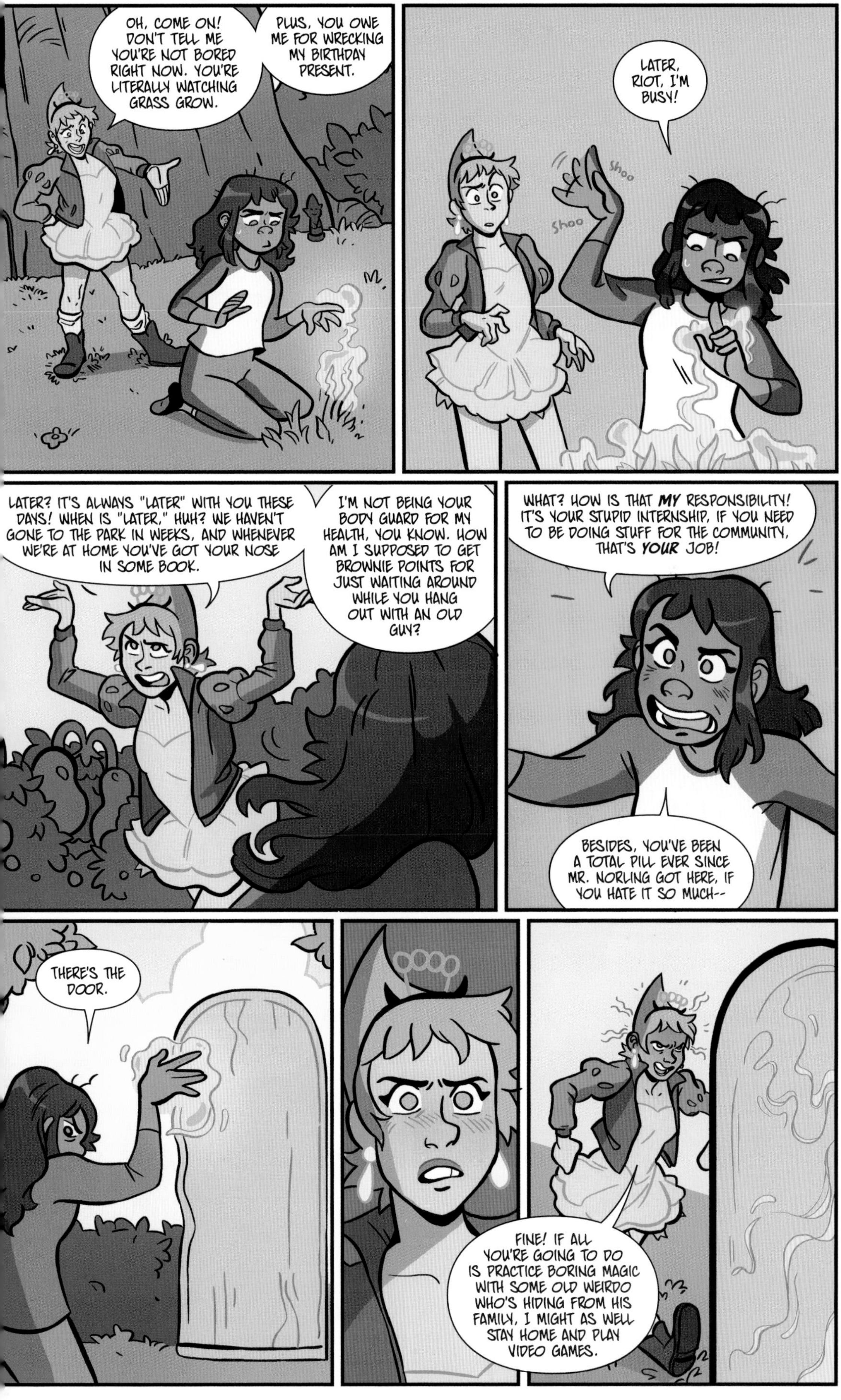

OH, COME ON! DON'T TELL ME YOU'RE NOT BORED RIGHT NOW. YOU'RE LITERALLY WATCHING GRASS GROW.
PLUS, YOU OWE ME FOR WRECKING MY BIRTHDAY PRESENT.
LATER, RIOT, I'M BUSY!
Shoo
Shoo
LATER? IT'S ALWAYS "LATER" WITH YOU THESE DAYS! WHEN IS "LATER," HUH? WE HAVEN'T GONE TO THE PARK IN WEEKS, AND WHENEVER WE'RE AT HOME YOU'VE GOT YOUR NOSE IN SOME BOOK.
I'M NOT BEING YOUR BODY GUARD FOR MY HEALTH, YOU KNOW. HOW AM I SUPPOSED TO GET BROWNIE POINTS FOR JUST WAITING AROUND WHILE YOU HANG OUT WITH AN OLD GUY?
WHAT? HOW IS THAT **MY** RESPONSIBILITY! IT'S YOUR STUPID INTERNSHIP, IF YOU NEED TO BE DOING STUFF FOR THE COMMUNITY, THAT'S **YOUR** JOB!
BESIDES, YOU'VE BEEN A TOTAL PILL EVER SINCE MR. NORLING GOT HERE, IF YOU HATE IT SO MUCH--
THERE'S THE DOOR.
FINE! IF ALL YOU'RE GOING TO DO IS PRACTICE BORING MAGIC WITH SOME OLD WEIRDO WHO'S HIDING FROM HIS FAMILY, I MIGHT AS WELL STAY HOME AND PLAY VIDEO GAMES.

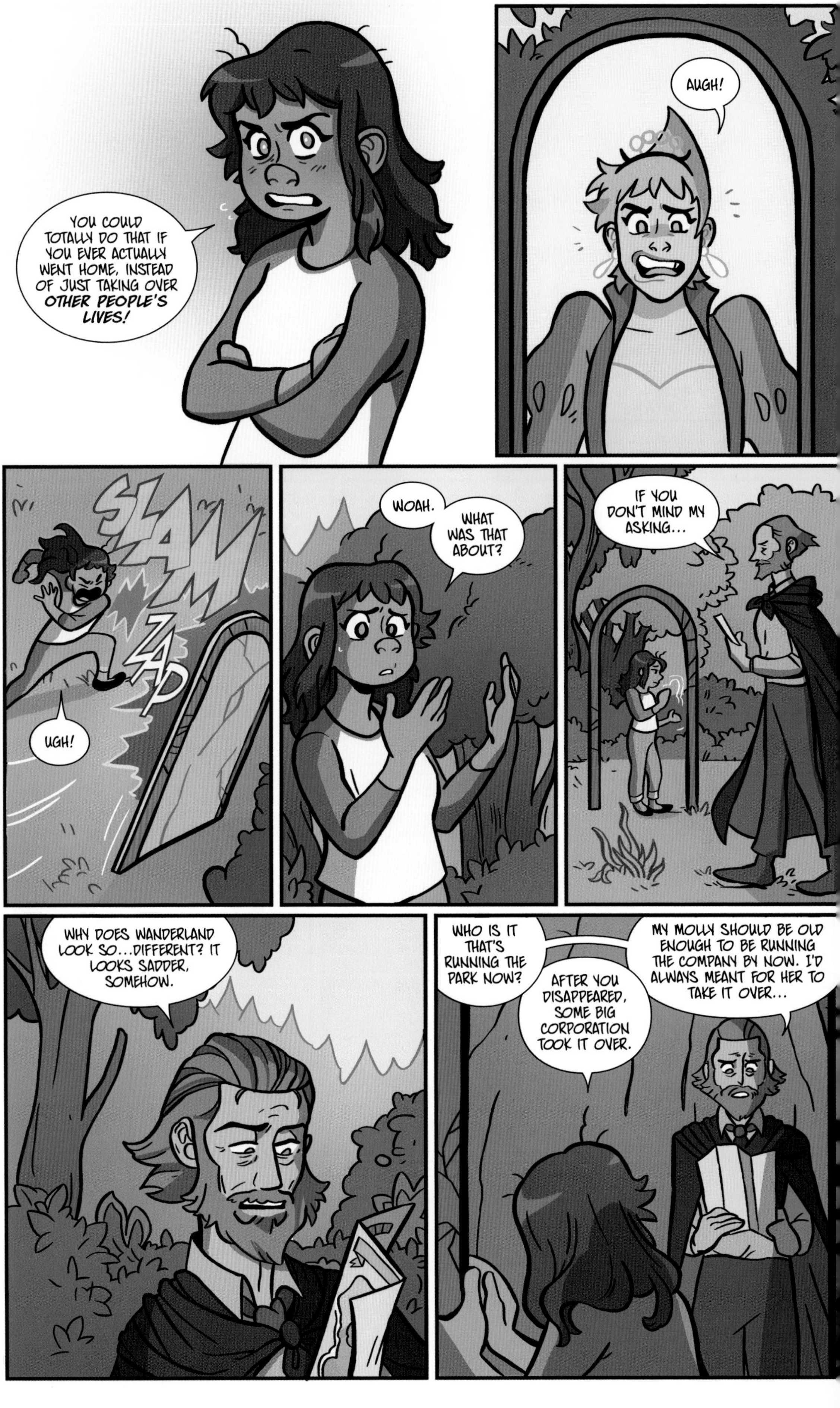
YOU COULD TOTALLY DO THAT IF YOU EVER ACTUALLY WENT HOME, INSTEAD OF JUST TAKING OVER OTHER PEOPLE'S LIVES!
AUGH!
SLAM
ZAP
UGH!
WOAH.
WHAT WAS THAT ABOUT?
IF YOU DON'T MIND MY ASKING...
WHY DOES WANDERLAND LOOK SO...DIFFERENT? IT LOOKS SADDER, SOMEHOW.
WHO IS IT THAT'S RUNNING THE PARK NOW?
AFTER YOU DISAPPEARED, SOME BIG CORPORATION TOOK IT OVER.
MY MOLLY SHOULD BE OLD ENOUGH TO BE RUNNING THE COMPANY BY NOW. I'D ALWAYS MEANT FOR HER TO TAKE IT OVER...

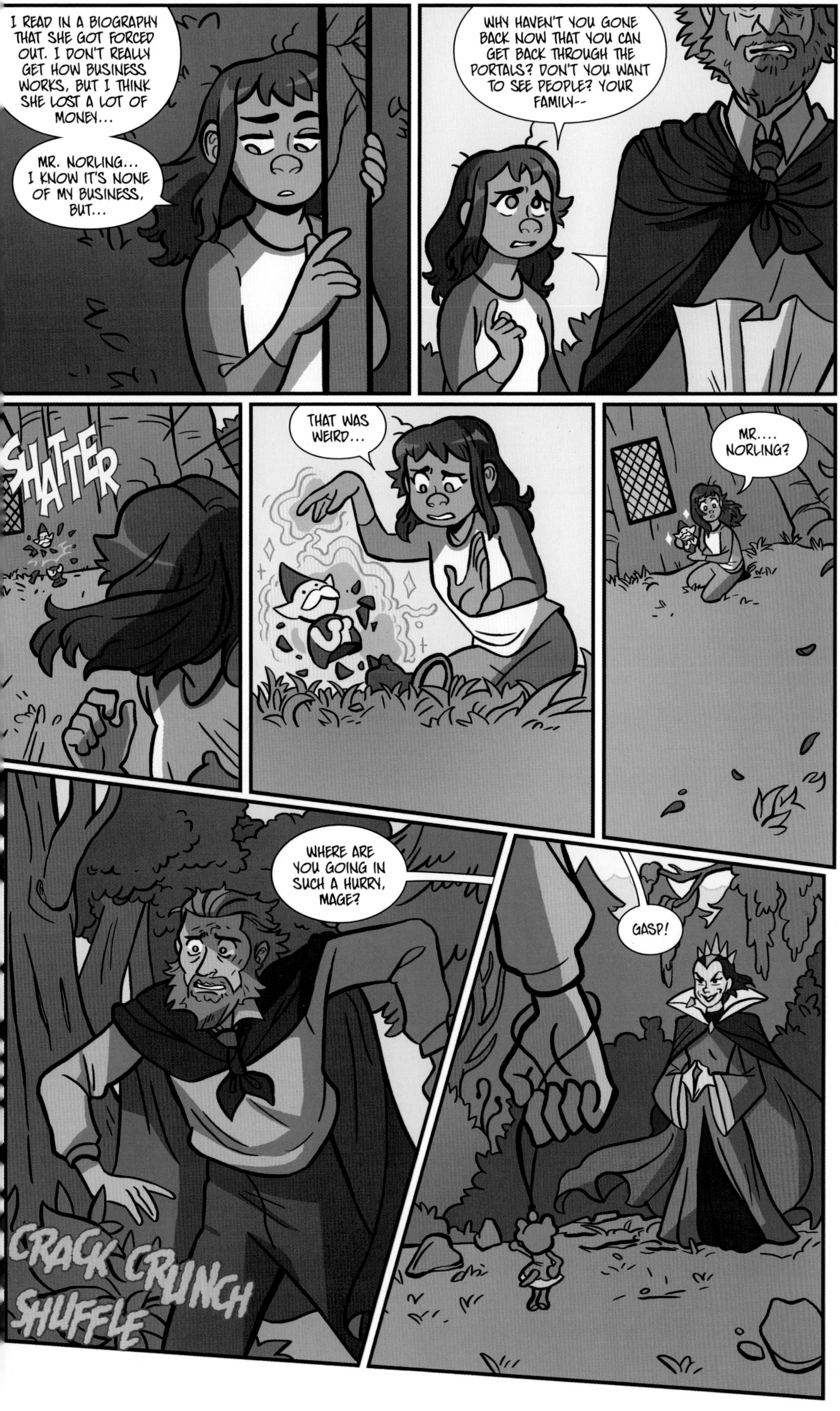
I READ IN A BIOGRAPHY THAT SHE GOT FORCED OUT. I DON'T REALLY GET HOW BUSINESS WORKS, BUT I THINK SHE LOST A LOT OF MONEY...
MR. NORLING... I KNOW IT'S NONE OF MY BUSINESS, BUT...
WHY HAVEN'T YOU GONE BACK NOW THAT YOU CAN GET BACK THROUGH THE PORTALS? DON'T YOU WANT TO SEE PEOPLE? YOUR FAMILY--
SHATTER
THAT WAS WEIRD...
MR.... NORLING?
WHERE ARE YOU GOING IN SUCH A HURRY, MAGE?
CRACK CRUNCH
SHUFFLE
GASP!

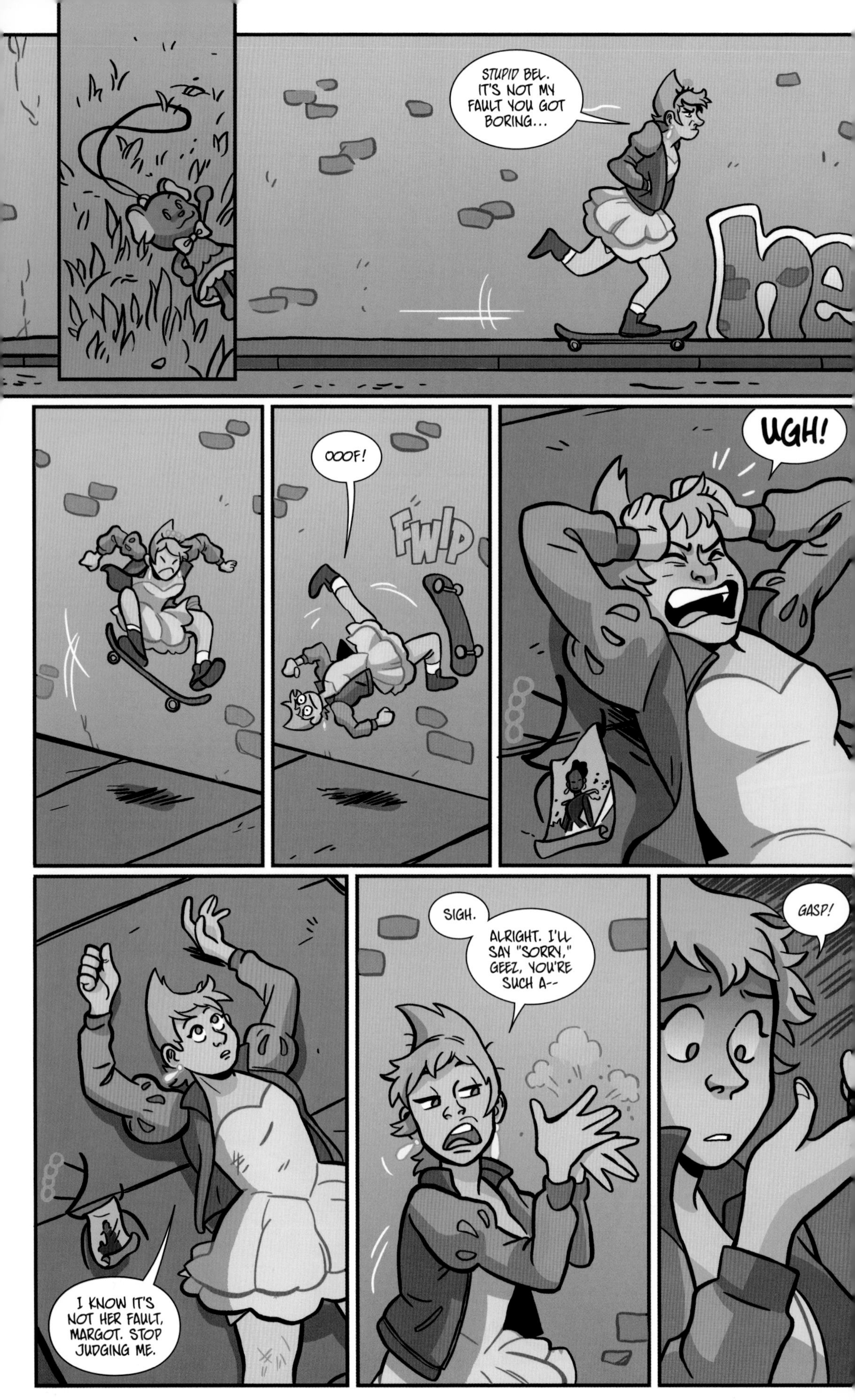
STUPID BEL. IT'S NOT MY FAULT YOU GOT BORING...
OOOF!
FWIP
UGH!
I KNOW IT'S NOT HER FAULT, MARGOT. STOP JUDGING ME.
SIGH.
ALRIGHT. I'LL SAY "SORRY," GEEZ, YOU'RE SUCH A--
GASP!

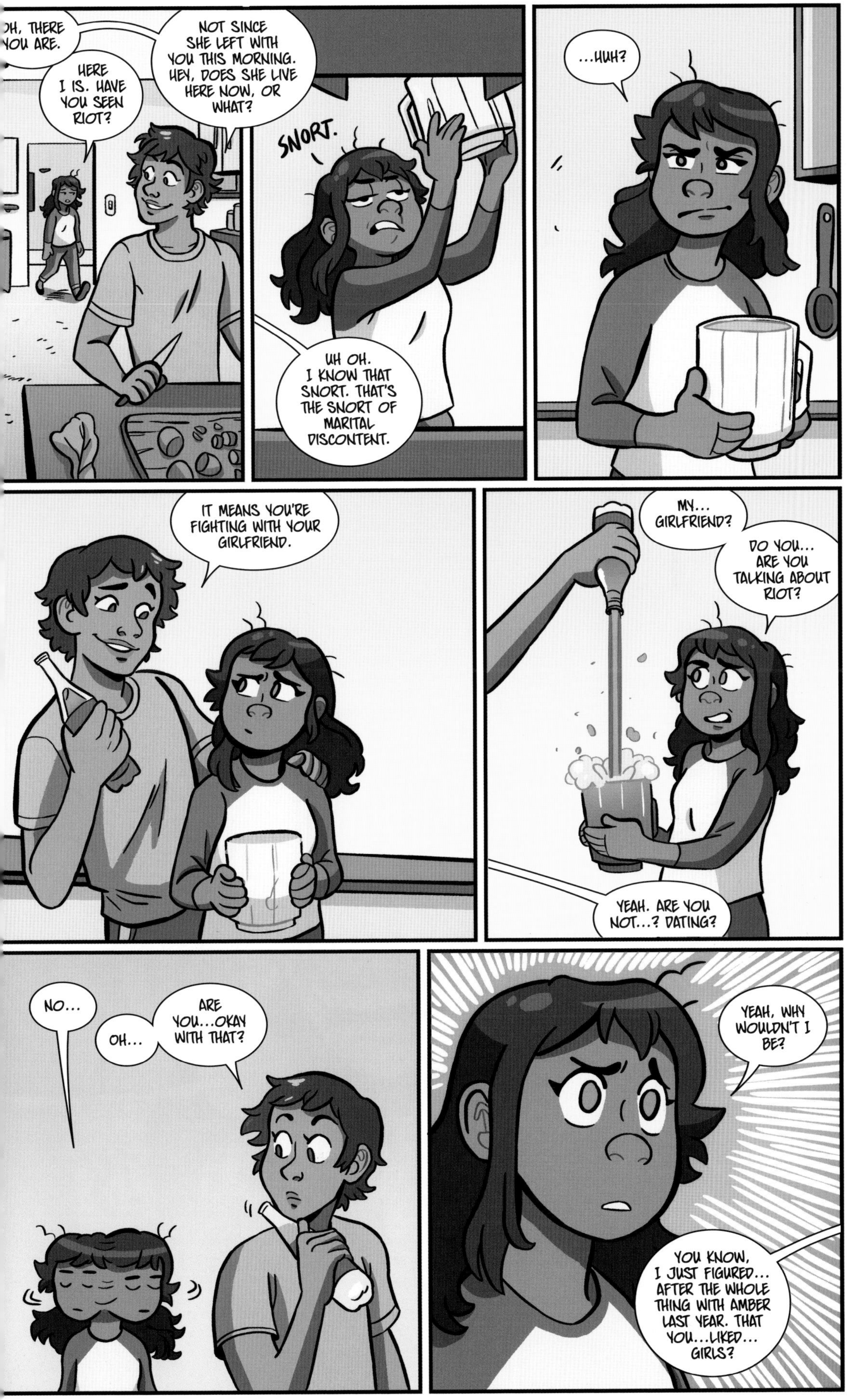

OH, THERE YOU ARE.
HERE I IS. HAVE YOU SEEN RIOT?
NOT SINCE SHE LEFT WITH YOU THIS MORNING. HEY, DOES SHE LIVE HERE NOW, OR WHAT?
SNORT.
UH OH. I KNOW THAT SNORT. THAT'S THE SNORT OF MARITAL DISCONTENT.
...HUH?
IT MEANS YOU'RE FIGHTING WITH YOUR GIRLFRIEND.
MY... GIRLFRIEND?
DO YOU... ARE YOU TALKING ABOUT RIOT?
YEAH. ARE YOU NOT...? DATING?
NO...
OH...
ARE YOU...OKAY WITH THAT?
YEAH, WHY WOULDN'T I BE?
YOU KNOW, I JUST FIGURED... AFTER THE WHOLE THING WITH AMBER LAST YEAR. THAT YOU...LIKED... GIRLS?

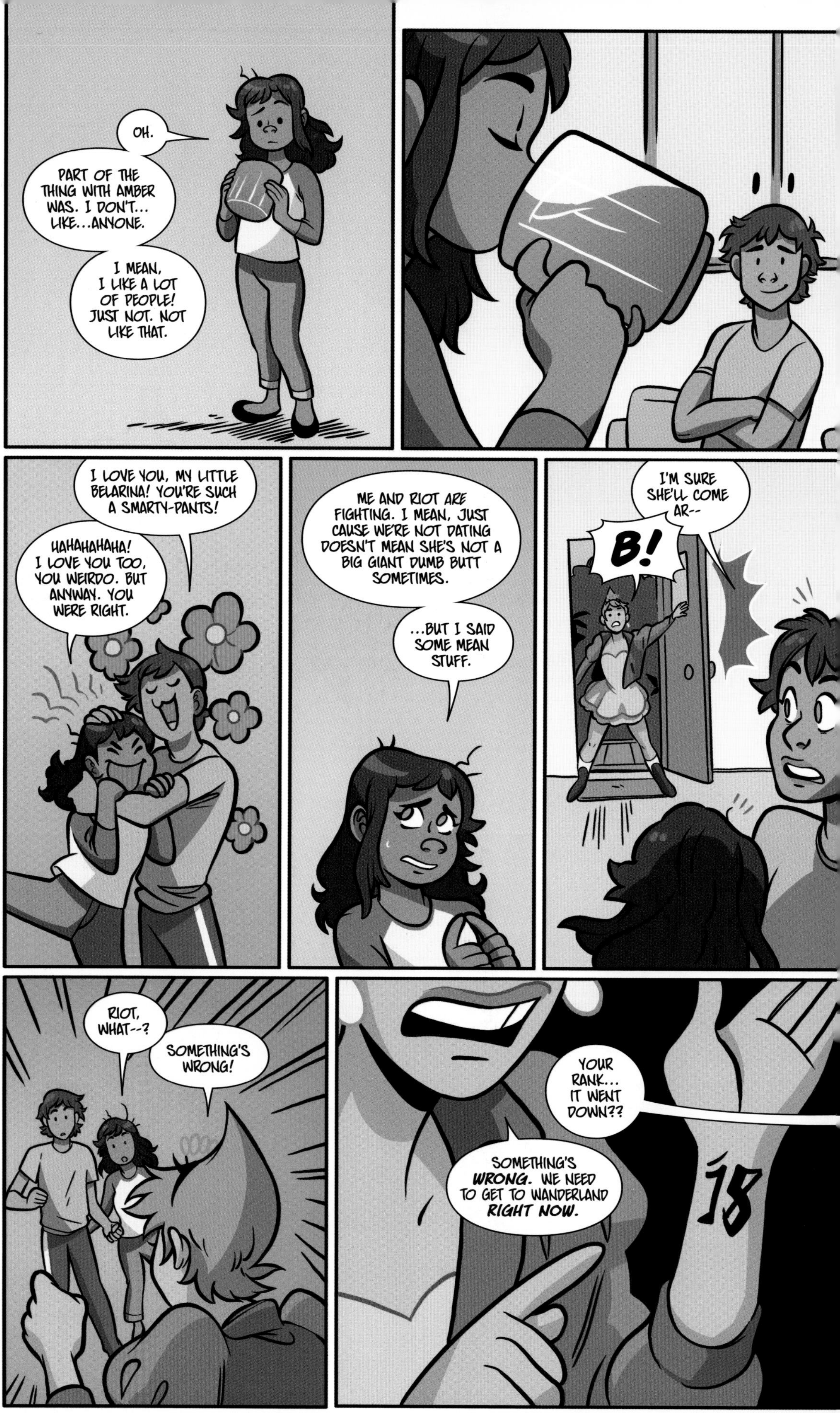

OH.
PART OF THE THING WITH AMBER WAS. I DON'T... LIKE...ANYONE.
I MEAN, I LIKE A LOT OF PEOPLE! JUST NOT. NOT LIKE THAT.
I LOVE YOU, MY LITTLE BELARINA! YOU'RE SUCH A SMARTY-PANTS!
HAHAHAHAHA! I LOVE YOU TOO, YOU WEIRDO. BUT ANYWAY. YOU WERE RIGHT.
ME AND RIOT ARE FIGHTING. I MEAN, JUST CAUSE WE'RE NOT DATING DOESN'T MEAN SHE'S NOT A BIG GIANT DUMB BUTT SOMETIMES.
...BUT I SAID SOME MEAN STUFF.
I'M SURE SHE'LL COME AR--
B!
RIOT, WHAT--?
SOMETHING'S WRONG!
YOUR RANK... IT WENT DOWN??
SOMETHING'S **WRONG.** WE NEED TO GET TO WANDERLAND **RIGHT NOW.**
18

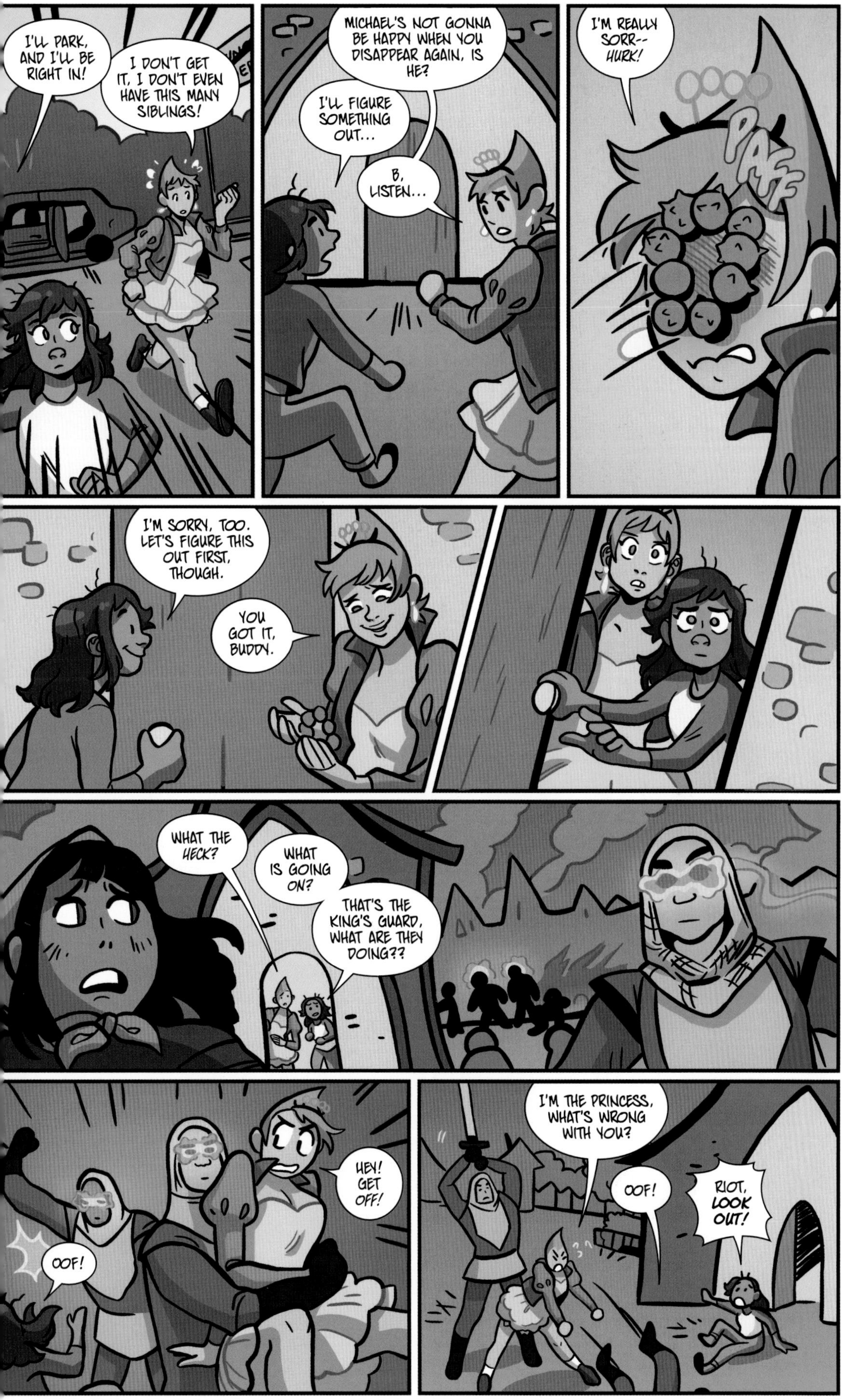

I'LL PARK, AND I'LL BE RIGHT IN!
I DON'T GET IT, I DON'T EVEN HAVE THIS MANY SIBLINGS!
MICHAEL'S NOT GONNA BE HAPPY WHEN YOU DISAPPEAR AGAIN, IS HE?
I'LL FIGURE SOMETHING OUT...
B, LISTEN...
I'M REALLY SORR-- HURK!
PAFF
I'M SORRY, TOO. LET'S FIGURE THIS OUT FIRST, THOUGH.
YOU GOT IT, BUDDY.
WHAT THE HECK?
WHAT IS GOING ON?
THAT'S THE KING'S GUARD, WHAT ARE THEY DOING??
HEY! GET OFF!
OOF!
I'M THE PRINCESS, WHAT'S WRONG WITH YOU?
OOF!
RIOT, LOOK OUT!

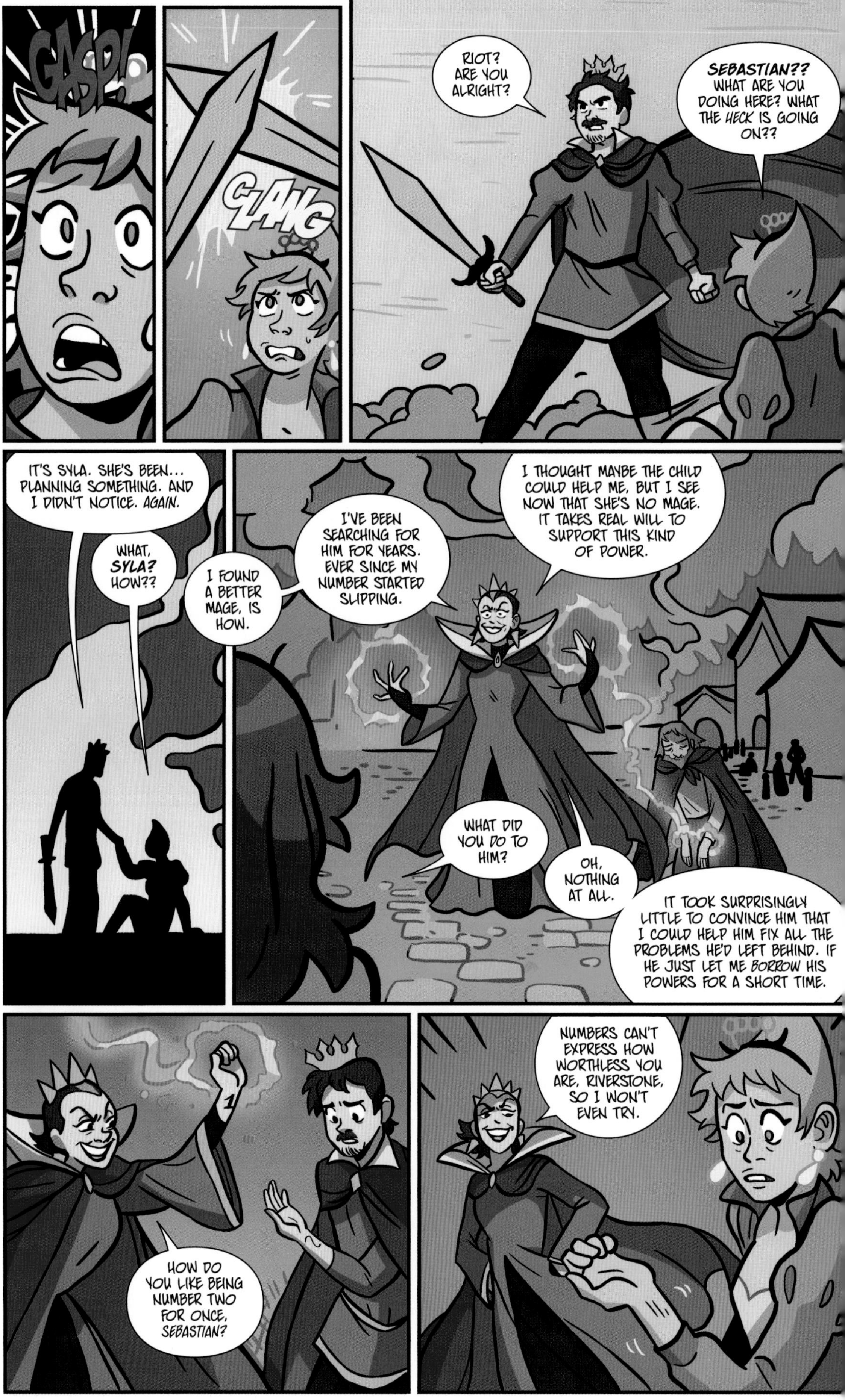
GASP!
CLANG
RIOT? ARE YOU ALRIGHT?
SEBASTIAN?? WHAT ARE YOU DOING HERE? WHAT THE HECK IS GOING ON??
IT'S SYLA. SHE'S BEEN... PLANNING SOMETHING. AND I DIDN'T NOTICE. AGAIN.
WHAT, SYLA? HOW??
I FOUND A BETTER MAGE, IS HOW.
I'VE BEEN SEARCHING FOR HIM FOR YEARS. EVER SINCE MY NUMBER STARTED SLIPPING.
I THOUGHT MAYBE THE CHILD COULD HELP ME, BUT I SEE NOW THAT SHE'S NO MAGE. IT TAKES REAL WILL TO SUPPORT THIS KIND OF POWER.
WHAT DID YOU DO TO HIM?
OH, NOTHING AT ALL.
IT TOOK SURPRISINGLY LITTLE TO CONVINCE HIM THAT I COULD HELP HIM FIX ALL THE PROBLEMS HE'D LEFT BEHIND. IF HE JUST LET ME BORROW HIS POWERS FOR A SHORT TIME.
HOW DO YOU LIKE BEING NUMBER TWO FOR ONCE, SEBASTIAN?
NUMBERS CAN'T EXPRESS HOW WORTHLESS YOU ARE, RIVERSTONE, SO I WON'T EVEN TRY.

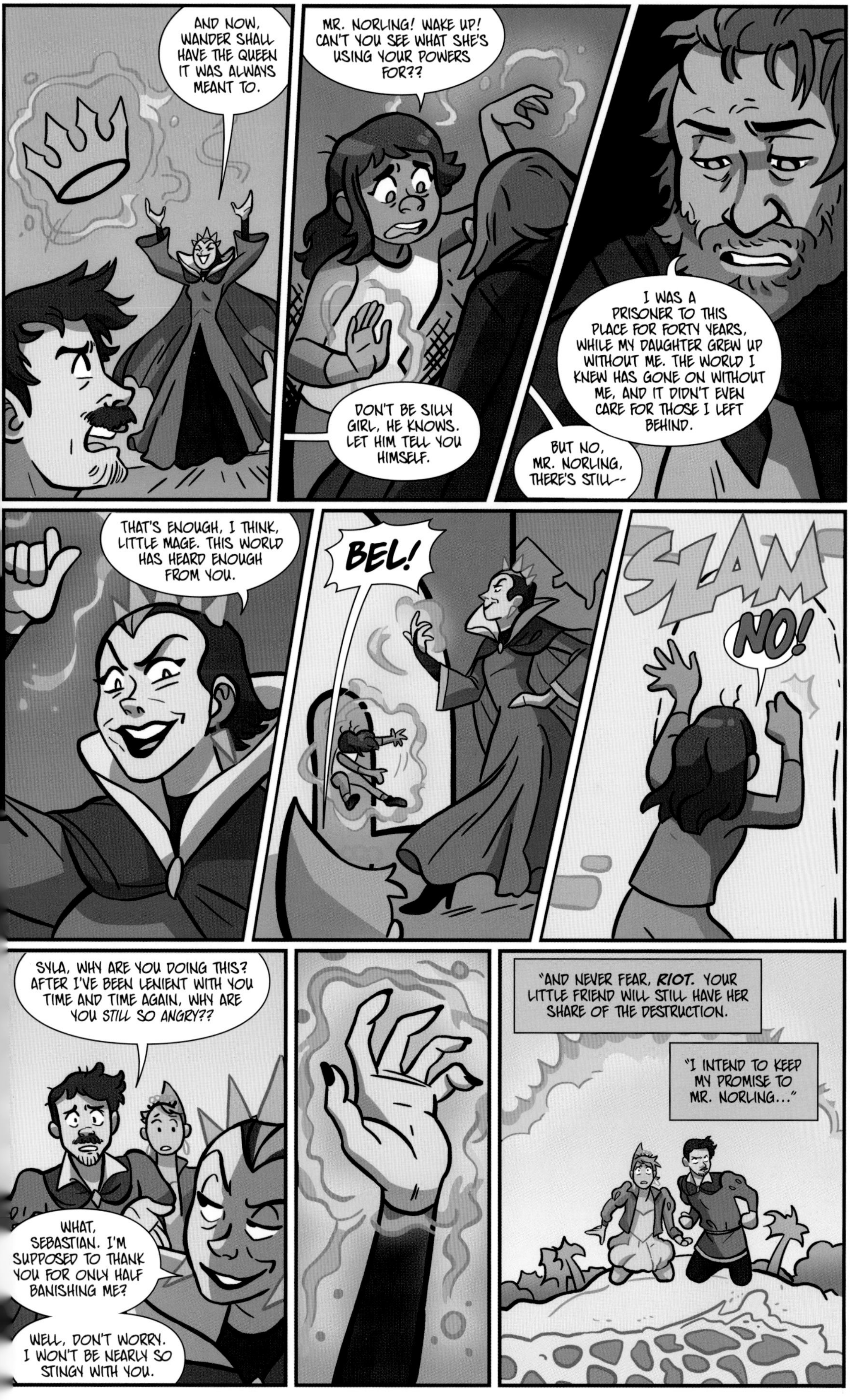
AND NOW, WANDER SHALL HAVE THE QUEEN IT WAS ALWAYS MEANT TO.
MR. NORLING! WAKE UP! CAN'T YOU SEE WHAT SHE'S USING YOUR POWERS FOR??
DON'T BE SILLY GIRL, HE KNOWS. LET HIM TELL YOU HIMSELF.
I WAS A PRISONER TO THIS PLACE FOR FORTY YEARS, WHILE MY DAUGHTER GREW UP WITHOUT ME. THE WORLD I KNEW HAS GONE ON WITHOUT ME, AND IT DIDN'T EVEN CARE FOR THOSE I LEFT BEHIND.
BUT NO, MR. NORLING, THERE'S STILL--
THAT'S ENOUGH, I THINK, LITTLE MAGE. THIS WORLD HAS HEARD ENOUGH FROM YOU.
BEL!
SLAM
NO!
SYLA, WHY ARE YOU DOING THIS? AFTER I'VE BEEN LENIENT WITH YOU TIME AND TIME AGAIN, WHY ARE YOU STILL SO ANGRY??
WHAT, SEBASTIAN. I'M SUPPOSED TO THANK YOU FOR ONLY HALF BANISHING ME?
WELL, DON'T WORRY. I WON'T BE NEARLY SO STINGY WITH YOU.
"AND NEVER FEAR, RIOT. YOUR LITTLE FRIEND WILL STILL HAVE HER SHARE OF THE DESTRUCTION.
"I INTEND TO KEEP MY PROMISE TO MR. NORLING..."

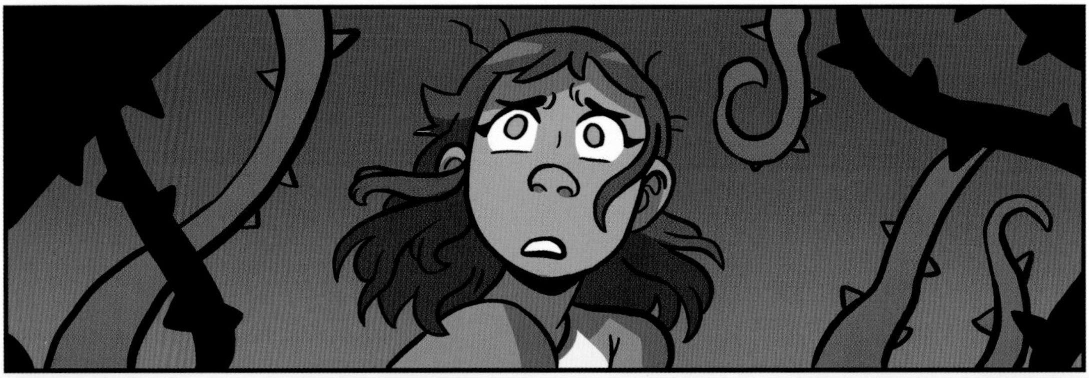

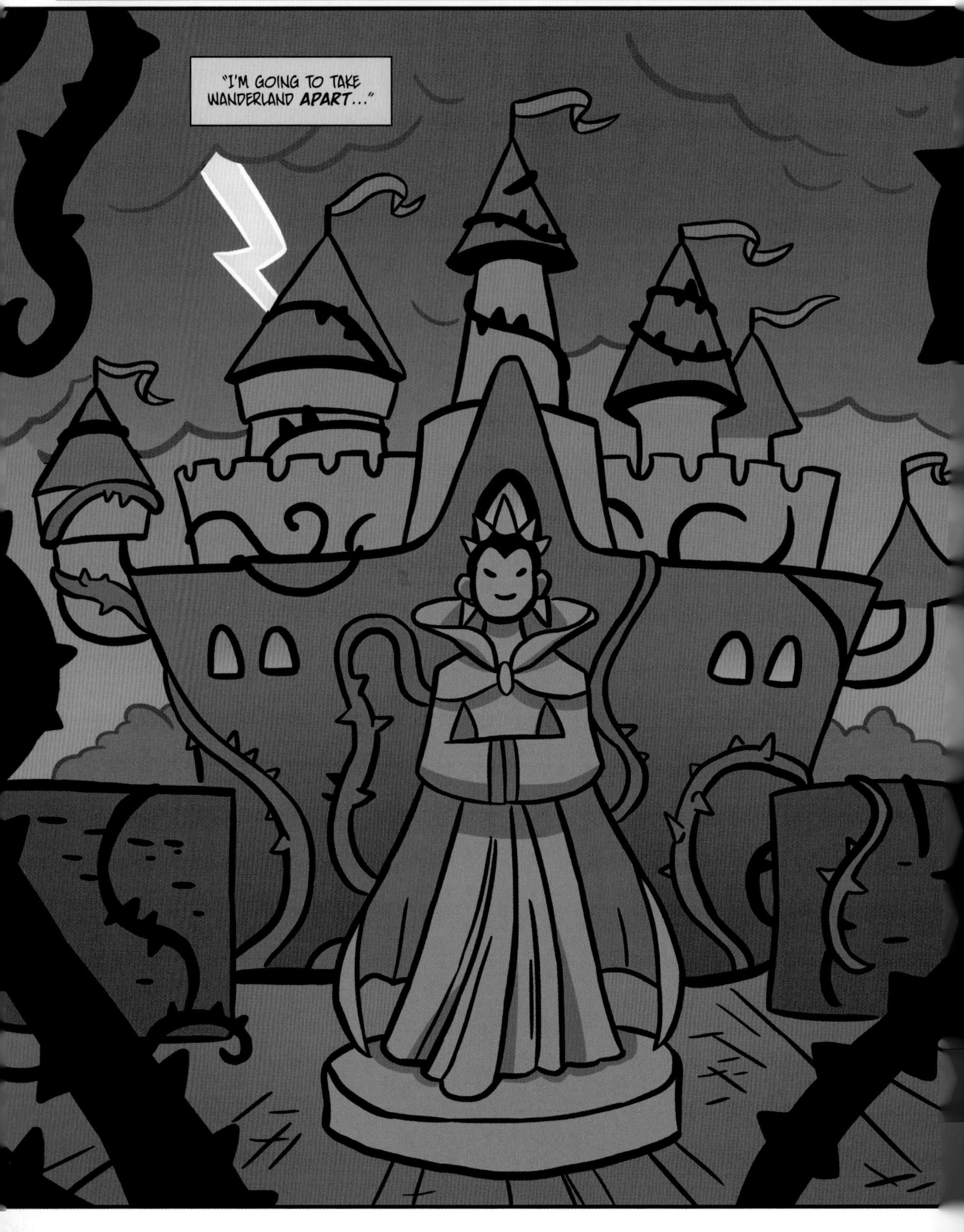
"I'M GOING TO TAKE WANDERLAND **APART**..."

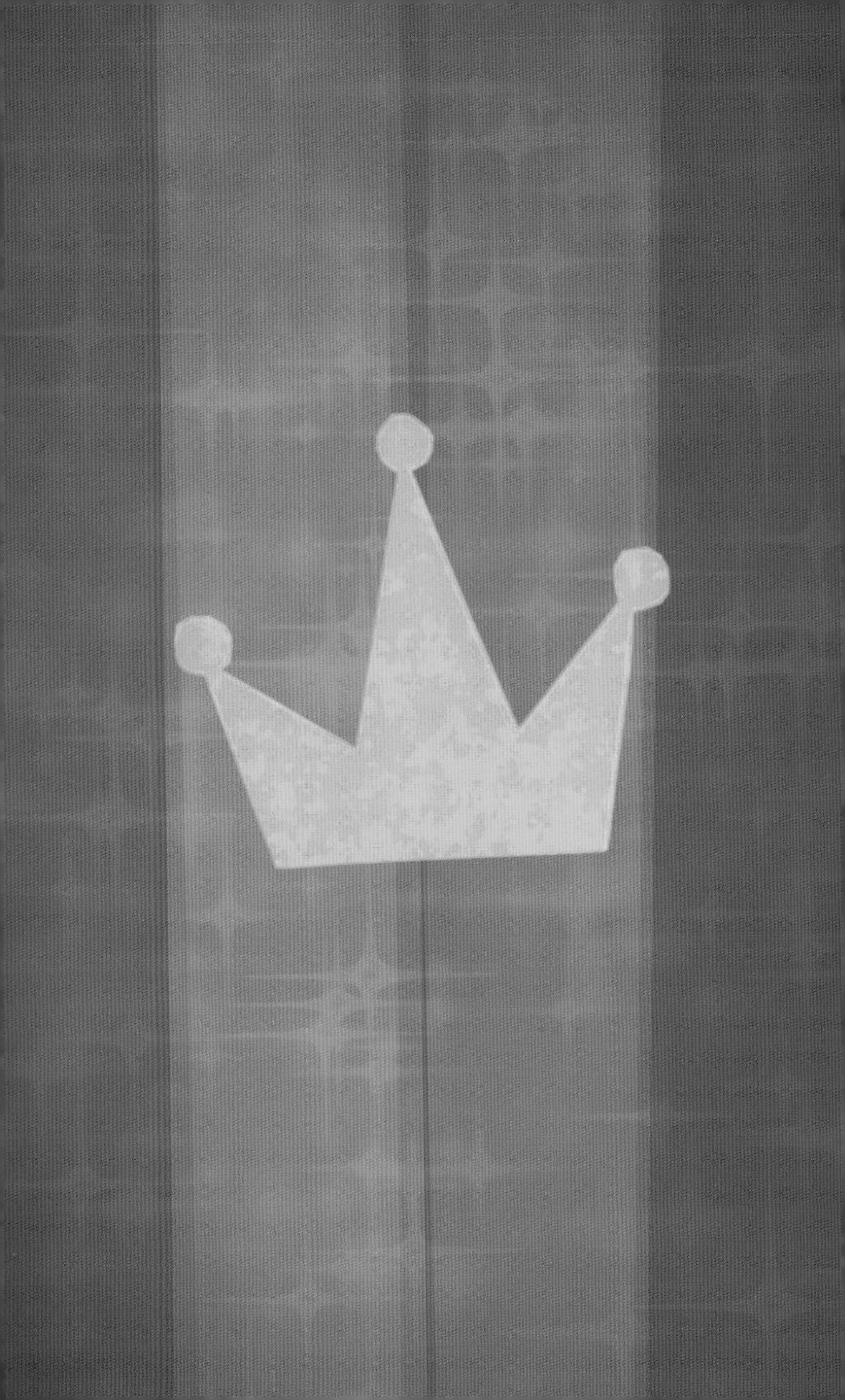

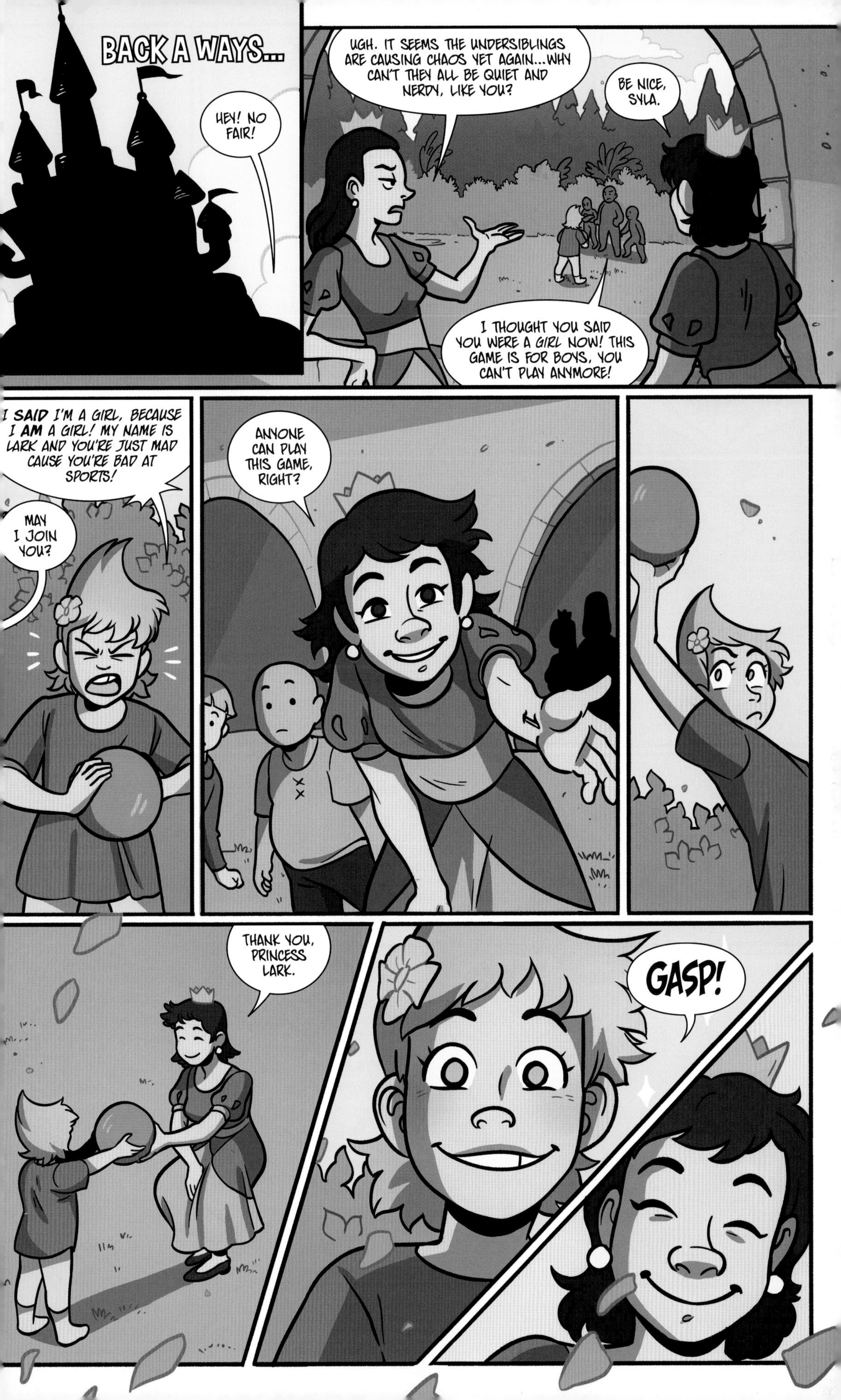

BACK A WAYS...
HEY! NO FAIR!
UGH. IT SEEMS THE UNDERSIBLINGS ARE CAUSING CHAOS YET AGAIN...WHY CAN'T THEY ALL BE QUIET AND NERDY, LIKE YOU?
BE NICE, SYLA.
I THOUGHT YOU SAID YOU WERE A GIRL NOW! THIS GAME IS FOR BOYS, YOU CAN'T PLAY ANYMORE!
I SAID I'M A GIRL, BECAUSE I AM A GIRL! MY NAME IS LARK AND YOU'RE JUST MAD CAUSE YOU'RE BAD AT SPORTS!
MAY I JOIN YOU?
ANYONE CAN PLAY THIS GAME, RIGHT?
THANK YOU, PRINCESS LARK.
GASP!

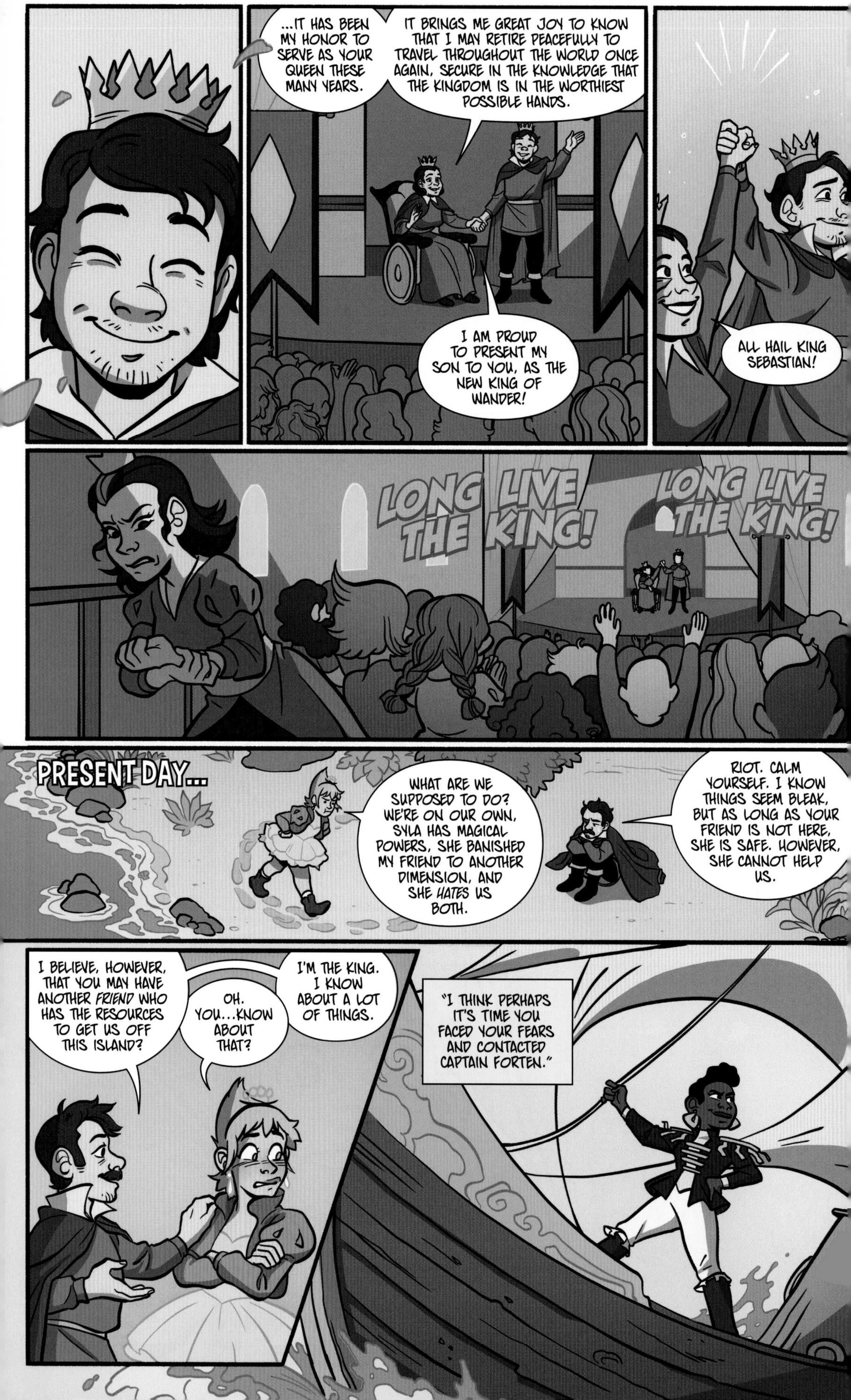
...IT HAS BEEN MY HONOR TO SERVE AS YOUR QUEEN THESE MANY YEARS.
IT BRINGS ME GREAT JOY TO KNOW THAT I MAY RETIRE PEACEFULLY TO TRAVEL THROUGHOUT THE WORLD ONCE AGAIN, SECURE IN THE KNOWLEDGE THAT THE KINGDOM IS IN THE WORTHIEST POSSIBLE HANDS.
I AM PROUD TO PRESENT MY SON TO YOU, AS THE NEW KING OF WANDER!
ALL HAIL KING SEBASTIAN!
LONG LIVE THE KING!
LONG LIVE THE KING!
PRESENT DAY...
WHAT ARE WE SUPPOSED TO DO? WE'RE ON OUR OWN, SYLA HAS MAGICAL POWERS, SHE BANISHED MY FRIEND TO ANOTHER DIMENSION, AND SHE *HATES* US BOTH.
RIOT. CALM YOURSELF. I KNOW THINGS SEEM BLEAK, BUT AS LONG AS YOUR FRIEND IS NOT HERE, SHE IS SAFE. HOWEVER, SHE CANNOT HELP US.
I BELIEVE, HOWEVER, THAT YOU MAY HAVE ANOTHER *FRIEND* WHO HAS THE RESOURCES TO GET US OFF THIS ISLAND?
OH. YOU...KNOW ABOUT THAT?
I'M THE KING. I KNOW ABOUT A LOT OF THINGS.
"I THINK PERHAPS IT'S TIME YOU FACED YOUR FEARS AND CONTACTED CAPTAIN FORTEN."

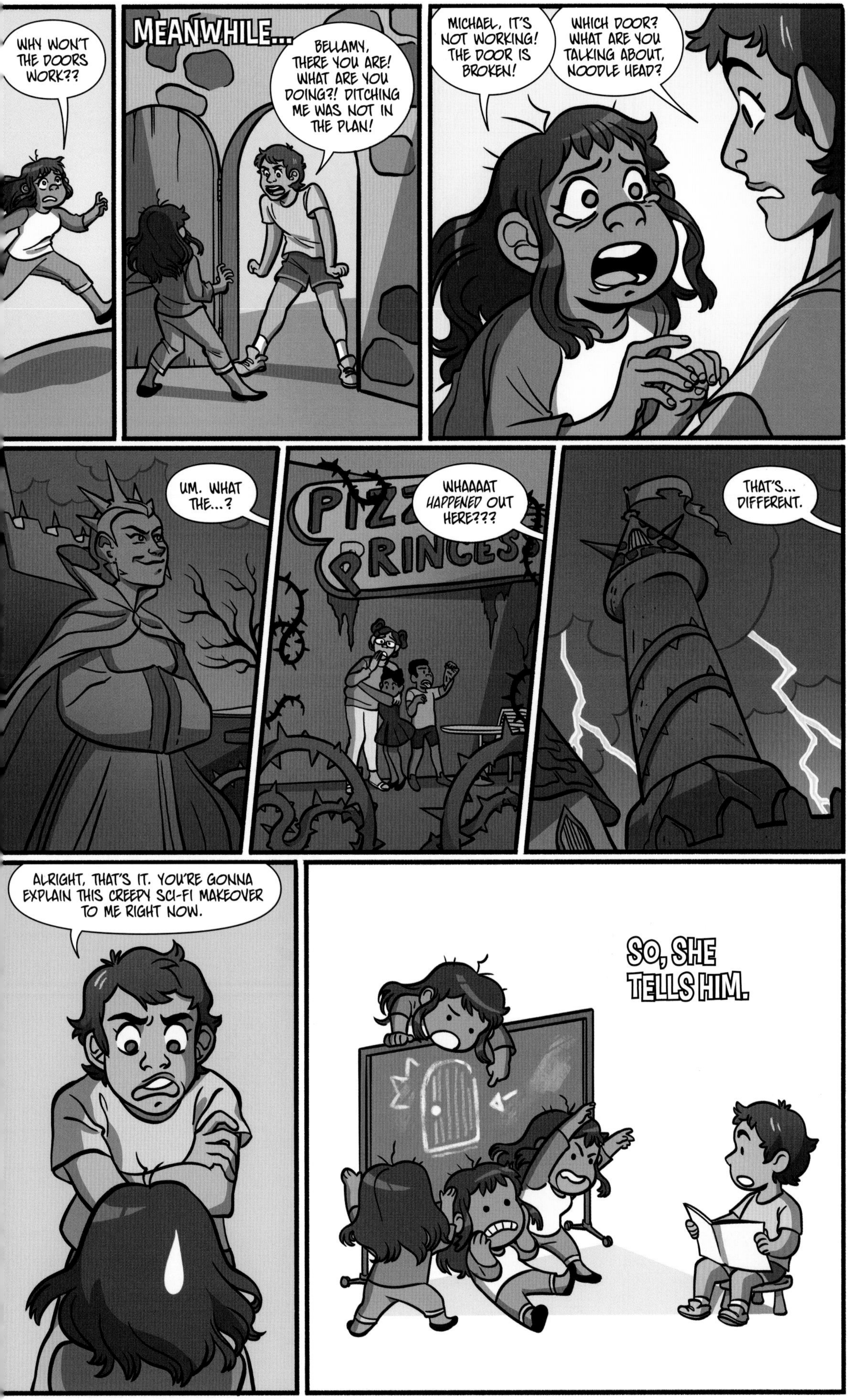
WHY WON'T THE DOORS WORK??
MEANWHILE...
BELLAMY, THERE YOU ARE! WHAT ARE YOU DOING?! DITCHING ME WAS NOT IN THE PLAN!
MICHAEL, IT'S NOT WORKING! THE DOOR IS BROKEN!
WHICH DOOR? WHAT ARE YOU TALKING ABOUT, NOODLE HEAD?
UM. WHAT THE...?
PIZZ PRINCESS
WHAAAAT HAPPENED OUT HERE???
THAT'S... DIFFERENT.
ALRIGHT, THAT'S IT. YOU'RE GONNA EXPLAIN THIS CREEPY SCI-FI MAKEOVER TO ME RIGHT NOW.
SO, SHE TELLS HIM.

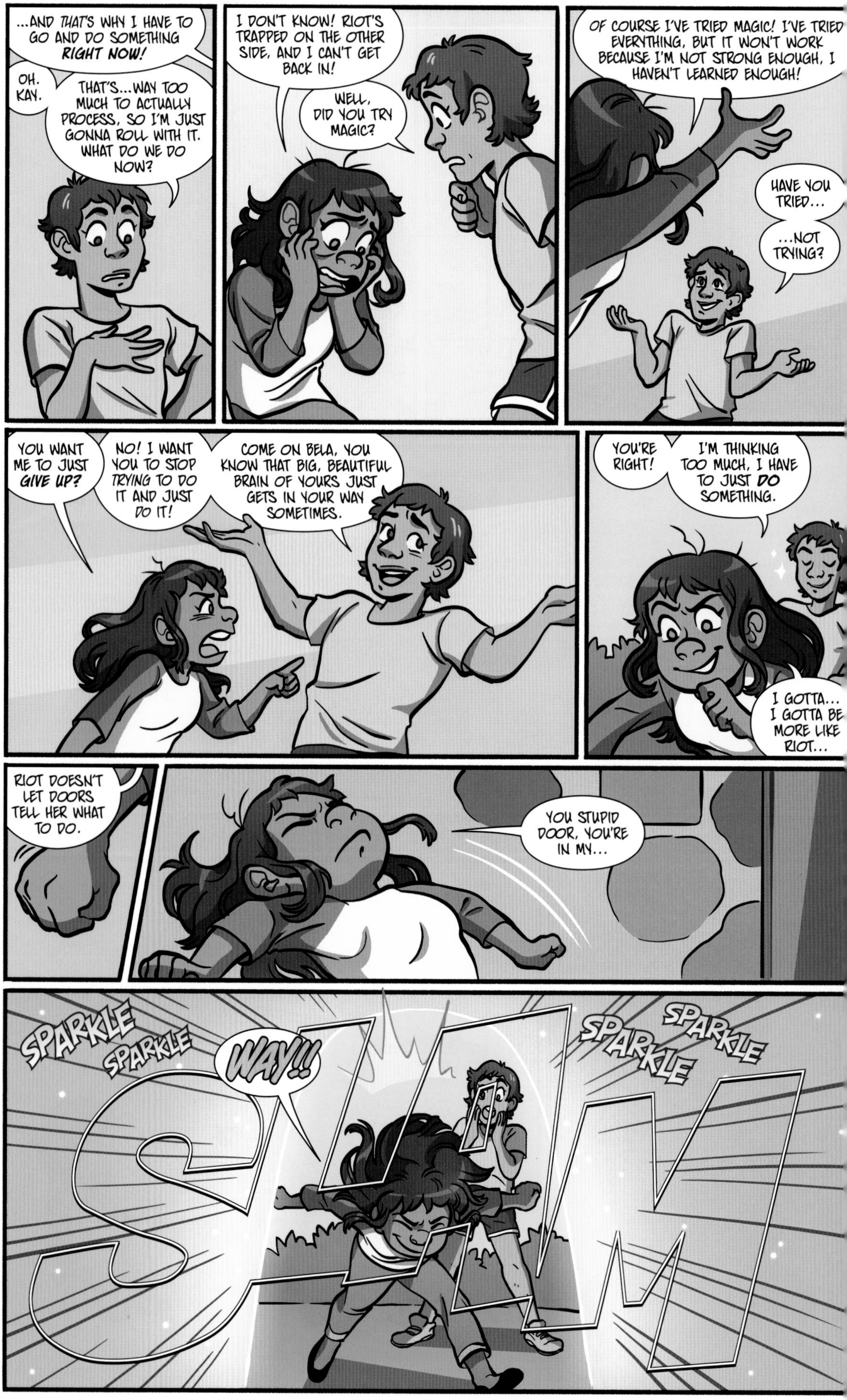

...AND THAT'S WHY I HAVE TO GO AND DO SOMETHING RIGHT NOW!
OH. KAY.
THAT'S...WAY TOO MUCH TO ACTUALLY PROCESS, SO I'M JUST GONNA ROLL WITH IT. WHAT DO WE DO NOW?
I DON'T KNOW! RIOT'S TRAPPED ON THE OTHER SIDE, AND I CAN'T GET BACK IN!
WELL, DID YOU TRY MAGIC?
OF COURSE I'VE TRIED MAGIC! I'VE TRIED EVERYTHING, BUT IT WON'T WORK BECAUSE I'M NOT STRONG ENOUGH, I HAVEN'T LEARNED ENOUGH!
HAVE YOU TRIED...
...NOT TRYING?
YOU WANT ME TO JUST GIVE UP?
NO! I WANT YOU TO STOP TRYING TO DO IT AND JUST DO IT!
COME ON BELA, YOU KNOW THAT BIG, BEAUTIFUL BRAIN OF YOURS JUST GETS IN YOUR WAY SOMETIMES.
YOU'RE RIGHT!
I'M THINKING TOO MUCH, I HAVE TO JUST DO SOMETHING.
I GOTTA... I GOTTA BE MORE LIKE RIOT...
RIOT DOESN'T LET DOORS TELL HER WHAT TO DO.
YOU STUPID DOOR, YOU'RE IN MY...
SPARKLE
SPARKLE
WAY!!
SPARKLE
SPARKLE
SLAM

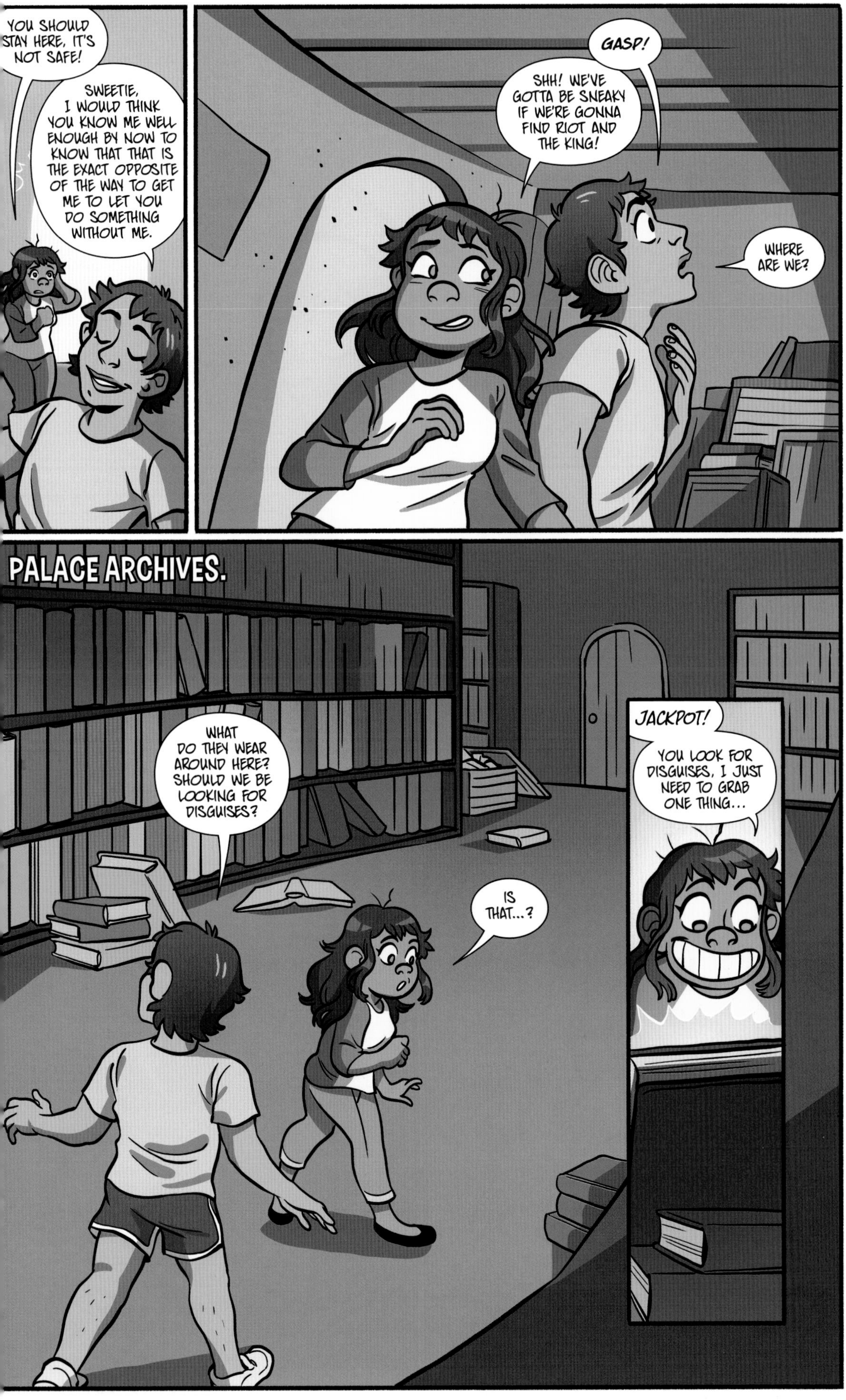

YOU SHOULD STAY HERE, IT'S NOT SAFE!
SWEETIE, I WOULD THINK YOU KNOW ME WELL ENOUGH BY NOW TO KNOW THAT THAT IS THE EXACT OPPOSITE OF THE WAY TO GET ME TO LET YOU DO SOMETHING WITHOUT ME.
GASP!
SHH! WE'VE GOTTA BE SNEAKY IF WE'RE GONNA FIND RIOT AND THE KING!
WHERE ARE WE?
PALACE ARCHIVES.
WHAT DO THEY WEAR AROUND HERE? SHOULD WE BE LOOKING FOR DISGUISES?
IS THAT...?
JACKPOT!
YOU LOOK FOR DISGUISES, I JUST NEED TO GRAB ONE THING...

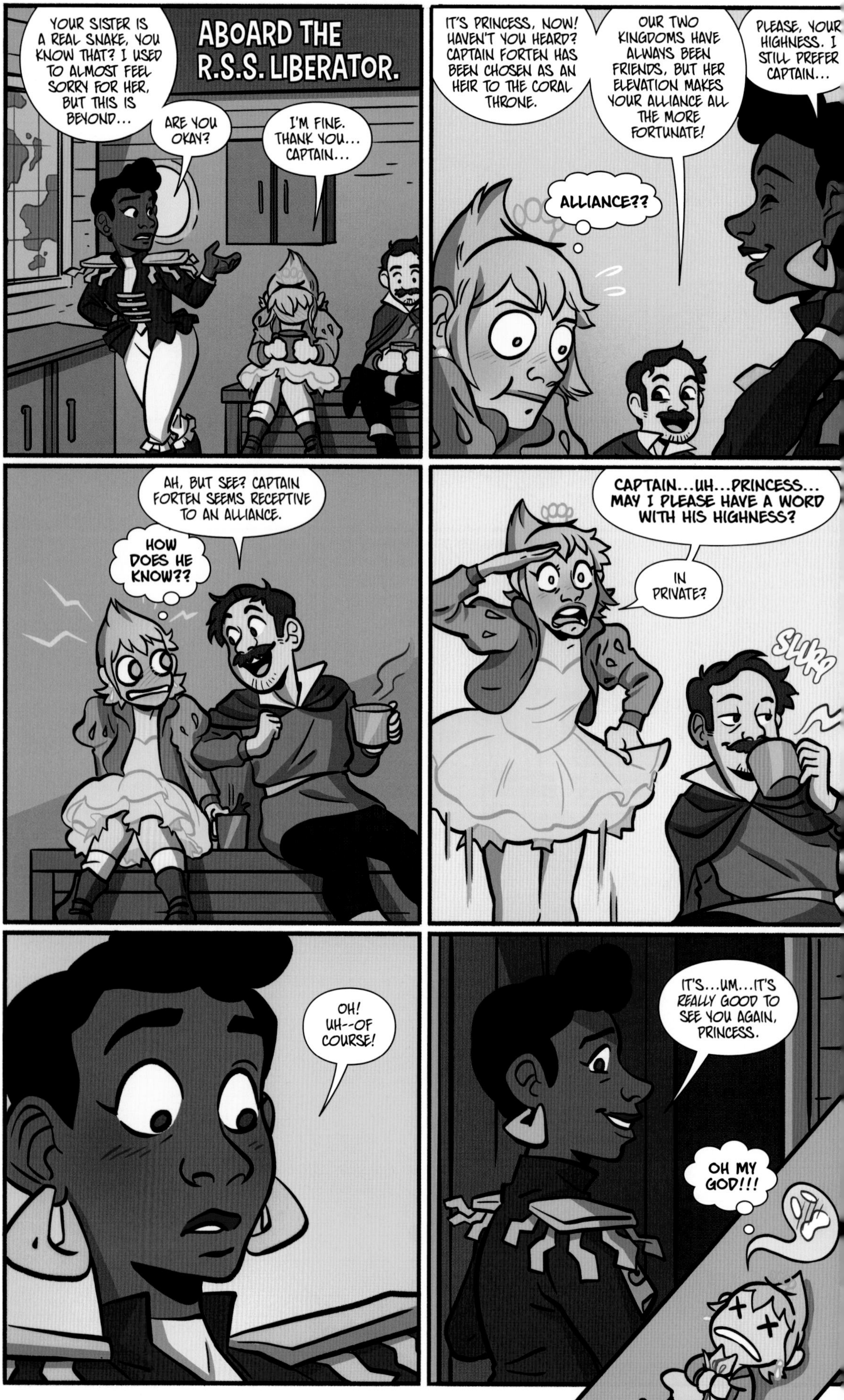
ABOARD THE R.S.S. LIBERATOR.
YOUR SISTER IS A REAL SNAKE, YOU KNOW THAT? I USED TO ALMOST FEEL SORRY FOR HER, BUT THIS IS BEYOND...
ARE YOU OKAY?
I'M FINE. THANK YOU... CAPTAIN...
IT'S PRINCESS, NOW! HAVEN'T YOU HEARD? CAPTAIN FORTEN HAS BEEN CHOSEN AS AN HEIR TO THE CORAL THRONE.
OUR TWO KINGDOMS HAVE ALWAYS BEEN FRIENDS, BUT HER ELEVATION MAKES YOUR ALLIANCE ALL THE MORE FORTUNATE!
PLEASE, YOUR HIGHNESS. I STILL PREFER CAPTAIN...
ALLIANCE??
AH, BUT SEE? CAPTAIN FORTEN SEEMS RECEPTIVE TO AN ALLIANCE.
HOW DOES HE KNOW??
CAPTAIN...UH...PRINCESS... MAY I PLEASE HAVE A WORD WITH HIS HIGHNESS?
IN PRIVATE?
SLURP
OH! UH--OF COURSE!
IT'S...UM...IT'S REALLY GOOD TO SEE YOU AGAIN, PRINCESS.
OH MY GOD!!!

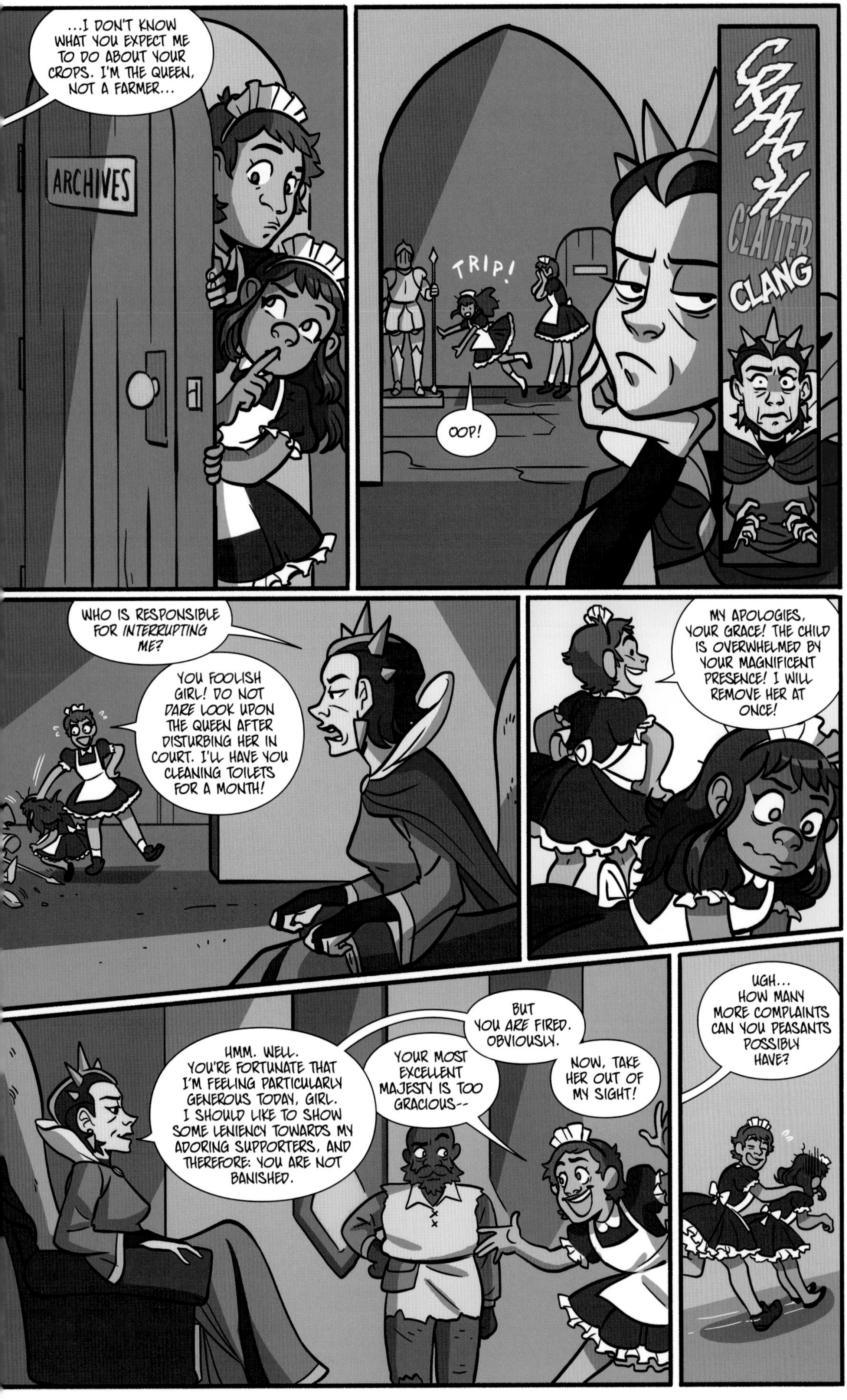

...I DON'T KNOW WHAT YOU EXPECT ME TO DO ABOUT YOUR CROPS. I'M THE QUEEN, NOT A FARMER...
ARCHIVES
CRASH
CLATTER
CLANG
TRIP!
OOP!
WHO IS RESPONSIBLE FOR INTERRUPTING ME?
YOU FOOLISH GIRL! DO NOT DARE LOOK UPON THE QUEEN AFTER DISTURBING HER IN COURT. I'LL HAVE YOU CLEANING TOILETS FOR A MONTH!
MY APOLOGIES, YOUR GRACE! THE CHILD IS OVERWHELMED BY YOUR MAGNIFICENT PRESENCE! I WILL REMOVE HER AT ONCE!
HMM. WELL. YOU'RE FORTUNATE THAT I'M FEELING PARTICULARLY GENEROUS TODAY, GIRL. I SHOULD LIKE TO SHOW SOME LENIENCY TOWARDS MY ADORING SUPPORTERS, AND THEREFORE: YOU ARE NOT BANISHED.
YOUR MOST EXCELLENT MAJESTY IS TOO GRACIOUS--
BUT YOU ARE FIRED. OBVIOUSLY.
NOW, TAKE HER OUT OF MY SIGHT!
UGH... HOW MANY MORE COMPLAINTS CAN YOU PEASANTS POSSIBLY HAVE?

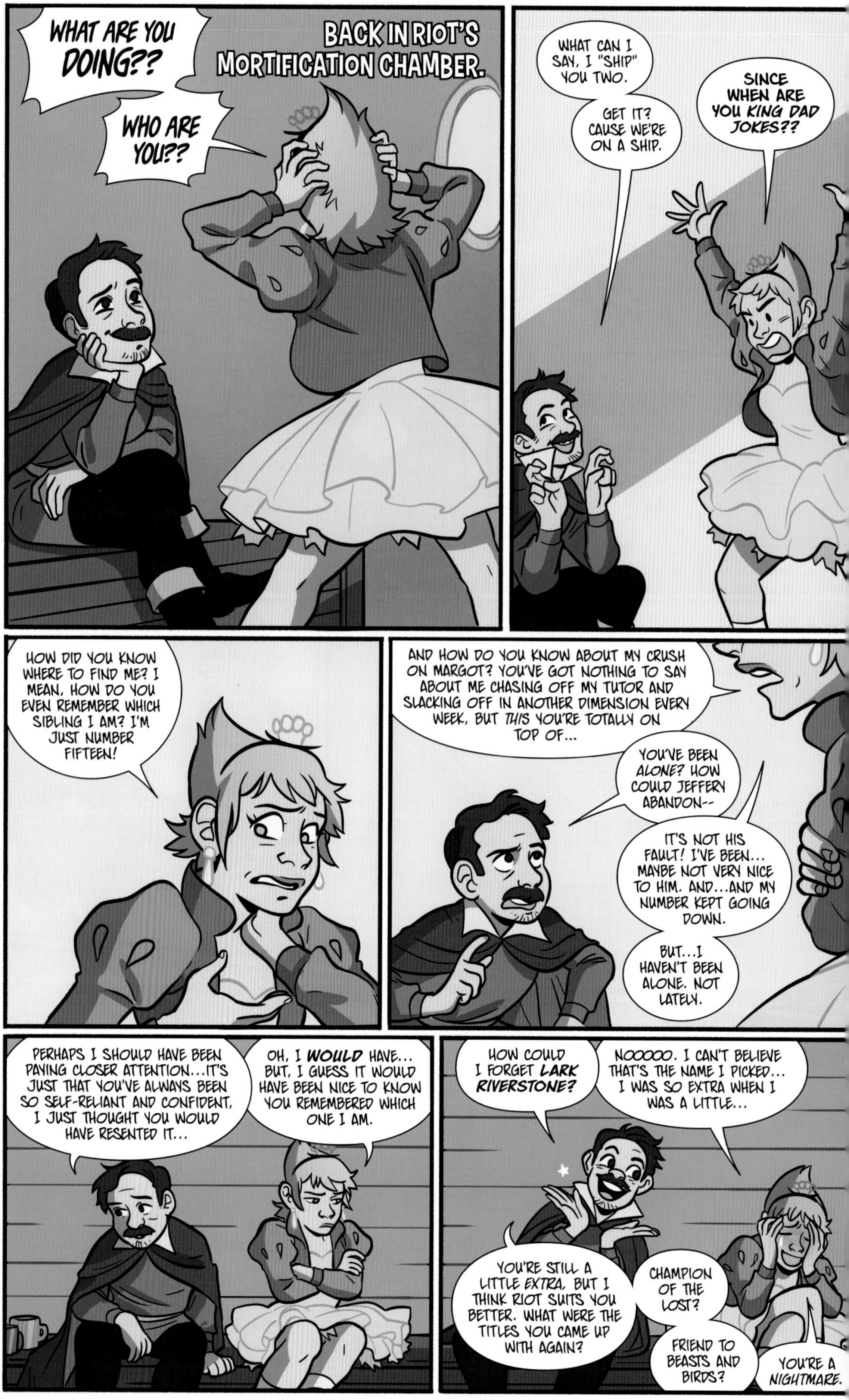
BACK IN RIOT'S MORTIFICATION CHAMBER.
WHAT ARE YOU DOING??
WHO ARE YOU??
WHAT CAN I SAY, I "SHIP" YOU TWO.
GET IT? CAUSE WE'RE ON A SHIP.
SINCE WHEN ARE YOU KING DAD JOKES??
HOW DID YOU KNOW WHERE TO FIND ME? I MEAN, HOW DO YOU EVEN REMEMBER WHICH SIBLING I AM? I'M JUST NUMBER FIFTEEN!
AND HOW DO YOU KNOW ABOUT MY CRUSH ON MARGOT? YOU'VE GOT NOTHING TO SAY ABOUT ME CHASING OFF MY TUTOR AND SLACKING OFF IN ANOTHER DIMENSION EVERY WEEK, BUT THIS YOU'RE TOTALLY ON TOP OF...
YOU'VE BEEN ALONE? HOW COULD JEFFERY ABANDON--
IT'S NOT HIS FAULT! I'VE BEEN... MAYBE NOT VERY NICE TO HIM. AND...AND MY NUMBER KEPT GOING DOWN.
BUT...I HAVEN'T BEEN ALONE. NOT LATELY.
PERHAPS I SHOULD HAVE BEEN PAYING CLOSER ATTENTION...IT'S JUST THAT YOU'VE ALWAYS BEEN SO SELF-RELIANT AND CONFIDENT, I JUST THOUGHT YOU WOULD HAVE RESENTED IT...
OH, I WOULD HAVE... BUT, I GUESS IT WOULD HAVE BEEN NICE TO KNOW YOU REMEMBERED WHICH ONE I AM.
HOW COULD I FORGET LARK RIVERSTONE?
NOOOOO. I CAN'T BELIEVE THAT'S THE NAME I PICKED... I WAS SO EXTRA WHEN I WAS A LITTLE...
YOU'RE STILL A LITTLE EXTRA, BUT I THINK RIOT SUITS YOU BETTER. WHAT WERE THE TITLES YOU CAME UP WITH AGAIN?
CHAMPION OF THE LOST?
FRIEND TO BEASTS AND BIRDS?
YOU'RE A NIGHTMARE.

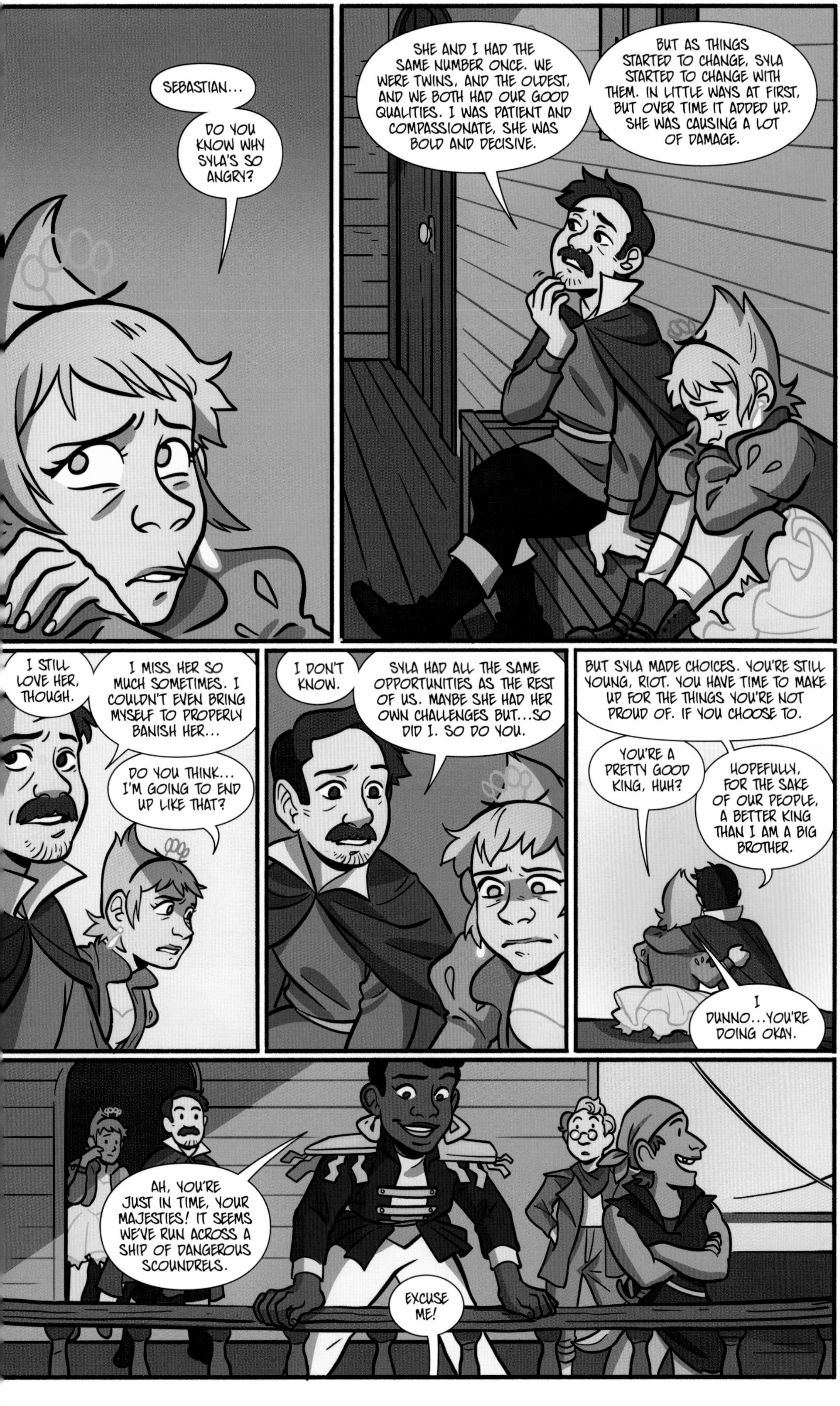
SEBASTIAN...
DO YOU KNOW WHY SYLA'S SO ANGRY?
SHE AND I HAD THE SAME NUMBER ONCE. WE WERE TWINS, AND THE OLDEST, AND WE BOTH HAD OUR GOOD QUALITIES. I WAS PATIENT AND COMPASSIONATE, SHE WAS BOLD AND DECISIVE.
BUT AS THINGS STARTED TO CHANGE, SYLA STARTED TO CHANGE WITH THEM. IN LITTLE WAYS AT FIRST, BUT OVER TIME IT ADDED UP. SHE WAS CAUSING A LOT OF DAMAGE.
I STILL LOVE HER, THOUGH.
I MISS HER SO MUCH SOMETIMES. I COULDN'T EVEN BRING MYSELF TO PROPERLY BANISH HER...
DO YOU THINK... I'M GOING TO END UP LIKE THAT?
I DON'T KNOW.
SYLA HAD ALL THE SAME OPPORTUNITIES AS THE REST OF US. MAYBE SHE HAD HER OWN CHALLENGES BUT...SO DID I. SO DO YOU.
BUT SYLA MADE CHOICES. YOU'RE STILL YOUNG, RIOT. YOU HAVE TIME TO MAKE UP FOR THE THINGS YOU'RE NOT PROUD OF. IF YOU CHOOSE TO.
YOU'RE A PRETTY GOOD KING, HUH?
HOPEFULLY, FOR THE SAKE OF OUR PEOPLE, A BETTER KING THAN I AM A BIG BROTHER.
I DUNNO...YOU'RE DOING OKAY.
AH, YOU'RE JUST IN TIME, YOUR MAJESTIES! IT SEEMS WE'VE RUN ACROSS A SHIP OF DANGEROUS SCOUNDRELS.
EXCUSE ME!

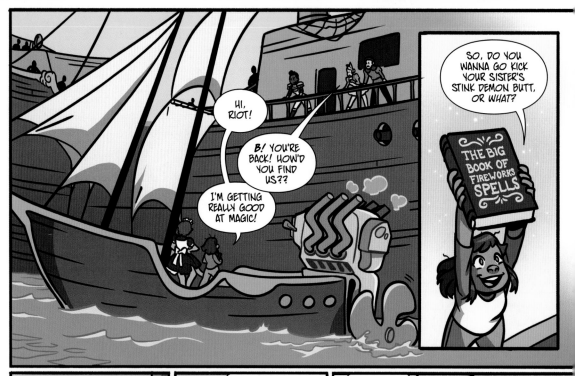

HI, RIOT!

B! YOU'RE BACK! HOW'D YOU FIND US??

I'M GETTING REALLY GOOD AT MAGIC!

SO, DO YOU WANNA GO KICK YOUR SISTER'S STINK DEMON BUTT, OR WHAT?

THE BIG BOOK OF FIREWORKS SPELLS

HECK YEAH, I DO! WHOOO!

SPLASH

I HATE TO SAY IT, BUT YOUR SHIP DOES LOOK FASTER...

HAMMOND! YOU HAVE THE SHIP. BLAZE, NICHOLS-- WITH ME!

AYE, CAPTAIN!

AYE, CAPTAIN!

GO GET 'ER, CAPTAIN!

RIOT, GET OFF! YOU'RE ALL GROSS!

SO, WHAT'S THE PLAN? WE CAN'T TAKE A SHIP ALL THE WAY TO THE PALACE.

OH, DOES THE MAGIC BOAT NOT GO ON LAND?

I HAD AN IDEA ABOUT THAT.

THERE'S AN ISLAND NOT FAR FROM HERE. BEFORE THE...CURRENT RESIDENTS TOOK OWNERSHIP, IT WAS A VACATION SPOT FOR THE ROYAL FAMILY.

THERE'S A TRAIN THERE THAT STILL OPERATES, AND IT TRAVELS DIRECTLY TO NEW PRINCESSTON.

BUT I WARN YOU, THIS TRIP WILL NOT BE PLEASANT...

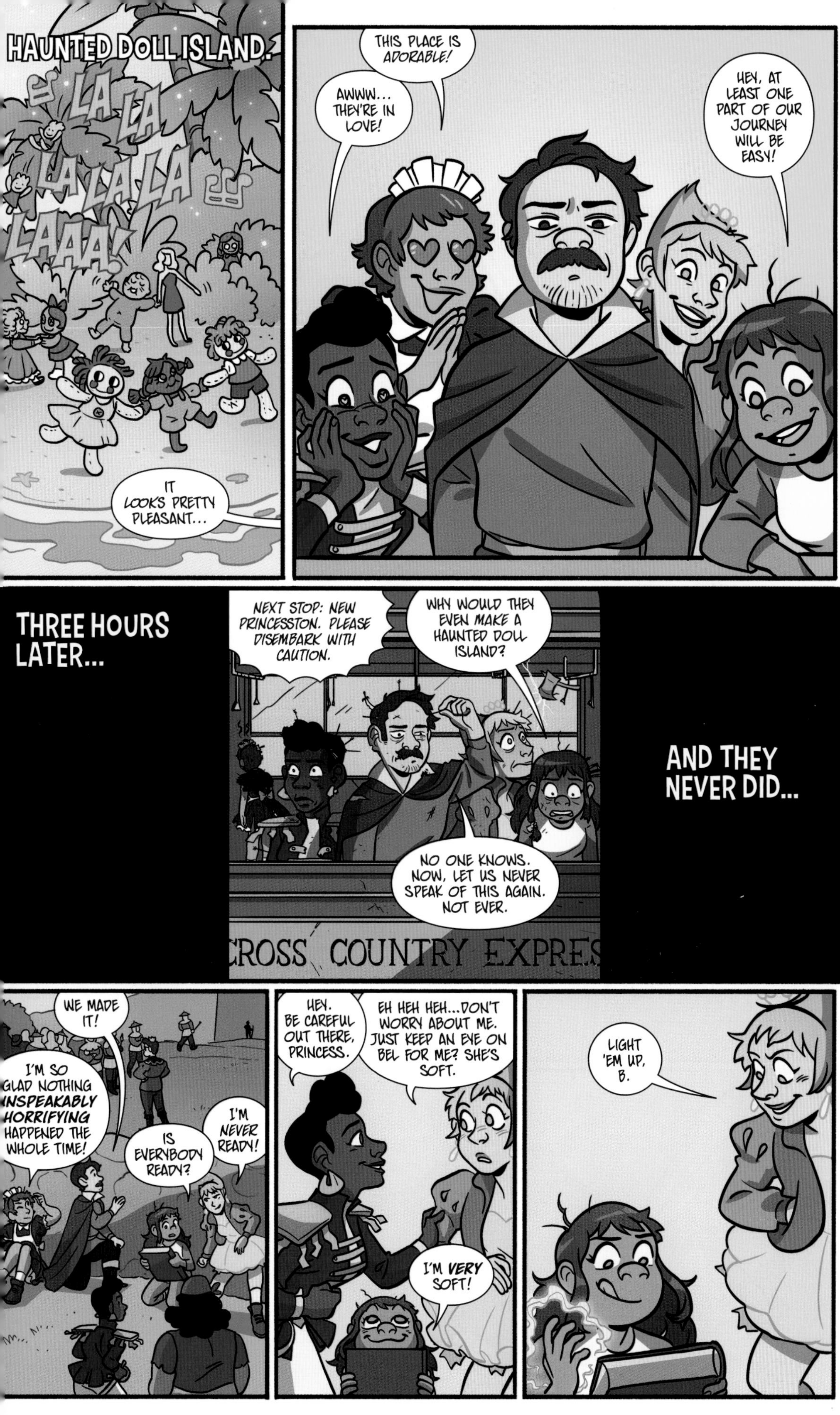

HAUNTED DOLL ISLAND.
LA LA LA LA LA LAAA!
IT LOOKS PRETTY PLEASANT...
AWWW... THEY'RE IN LOVE!
THIS PLACE IS ADORABLE!
HEY, AT LEAST ONE PART OF OUR JOURNEY WILL BE EASY!
THREE HOURS LATER...
NEXT STOP: NEW PRINCESSTON. PLEASE DISEMBARK WITH CAUTION.
WHY WOULD THEY EVEN MAKE A HAUNTED DOLL ISLAND?
NO ONE KNOWS. NOW, LET US NEVER SPEAK OF THIS AGAIN. NOT EVER.
CROSS COUNTRY EXPRES
AND THEY NEVER DID...
WE MADE IT!
I'M SO GLAD NOTHING UNSPEAKABLY HORRIFYING HAPPENED THE WHOLE TIME!
IS EVERYBODY READY?
I'M NEVER READY!
HEY. BE CAREFUL OUT THERE, PRINCESS.
EH HEH HEH...DON'T WORRY ABOUT ME. JUST KEEP AN EYE ON BEL FOR ME? SHE'S SOFT.
I'M VERY SOFT!
LIGHT 'EM UP, B.

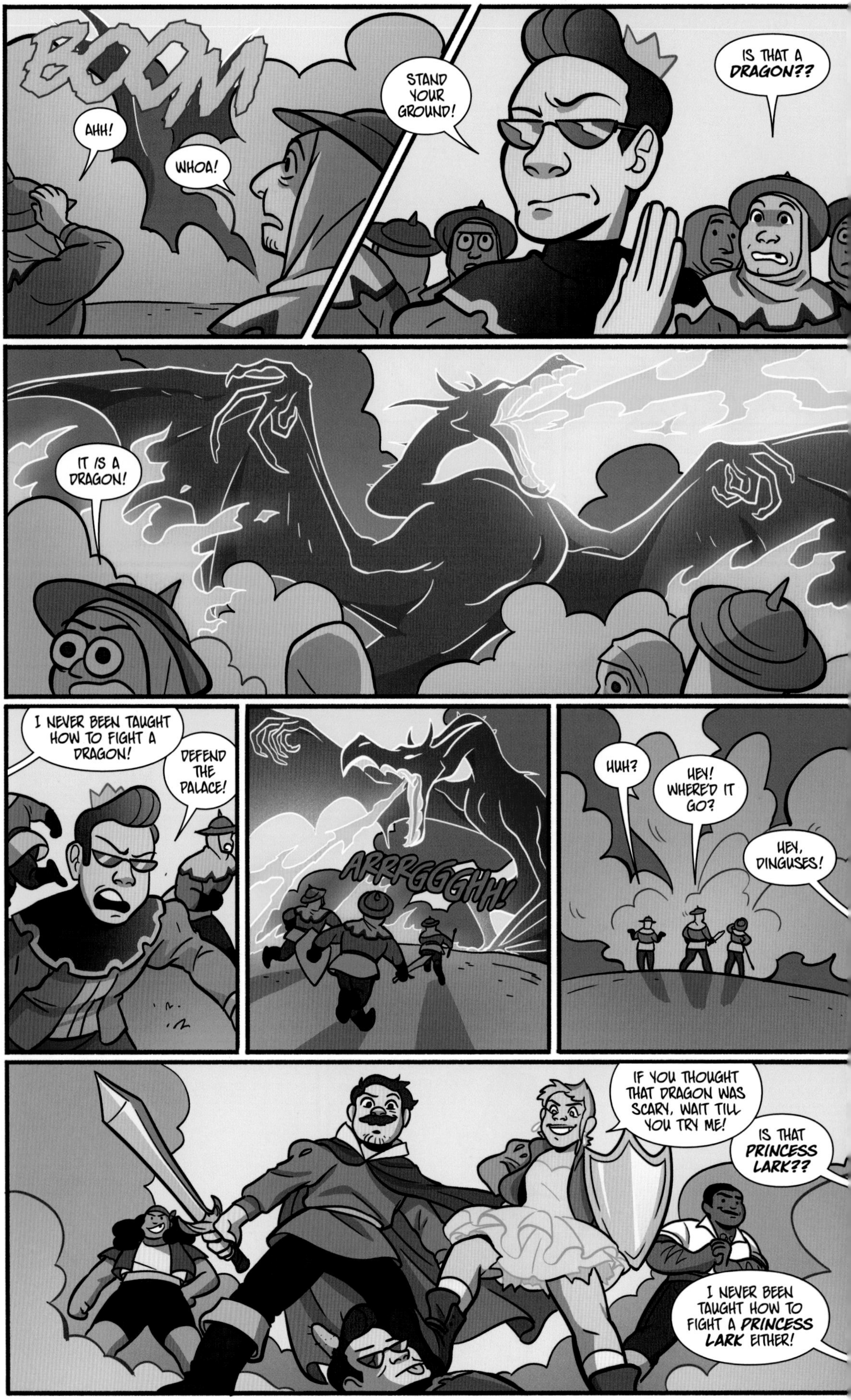
BOOM
AHH!
WHOA!
STAND YOUR GROUND!
IS THAT A DRAGON??
IT IS A DRAGON!
I NEVER BEEN TAUGHT HOW TO FIGHT A DRAGON!
DEFEND THE PALACE!
ARRRGGGHH!
HUH?
HEY! WHERE'D IT GO?
HEY, DINGUSES!
IF YOU THOUGHT THAT DRAGON WAS SCARY, WAIT TILL YOU TRY ME!
IS THAT PRINCESS LARK??
I NEVER BEEN TAUGHT HOW TO FIGHT A PRINCESS LARK EITHER!

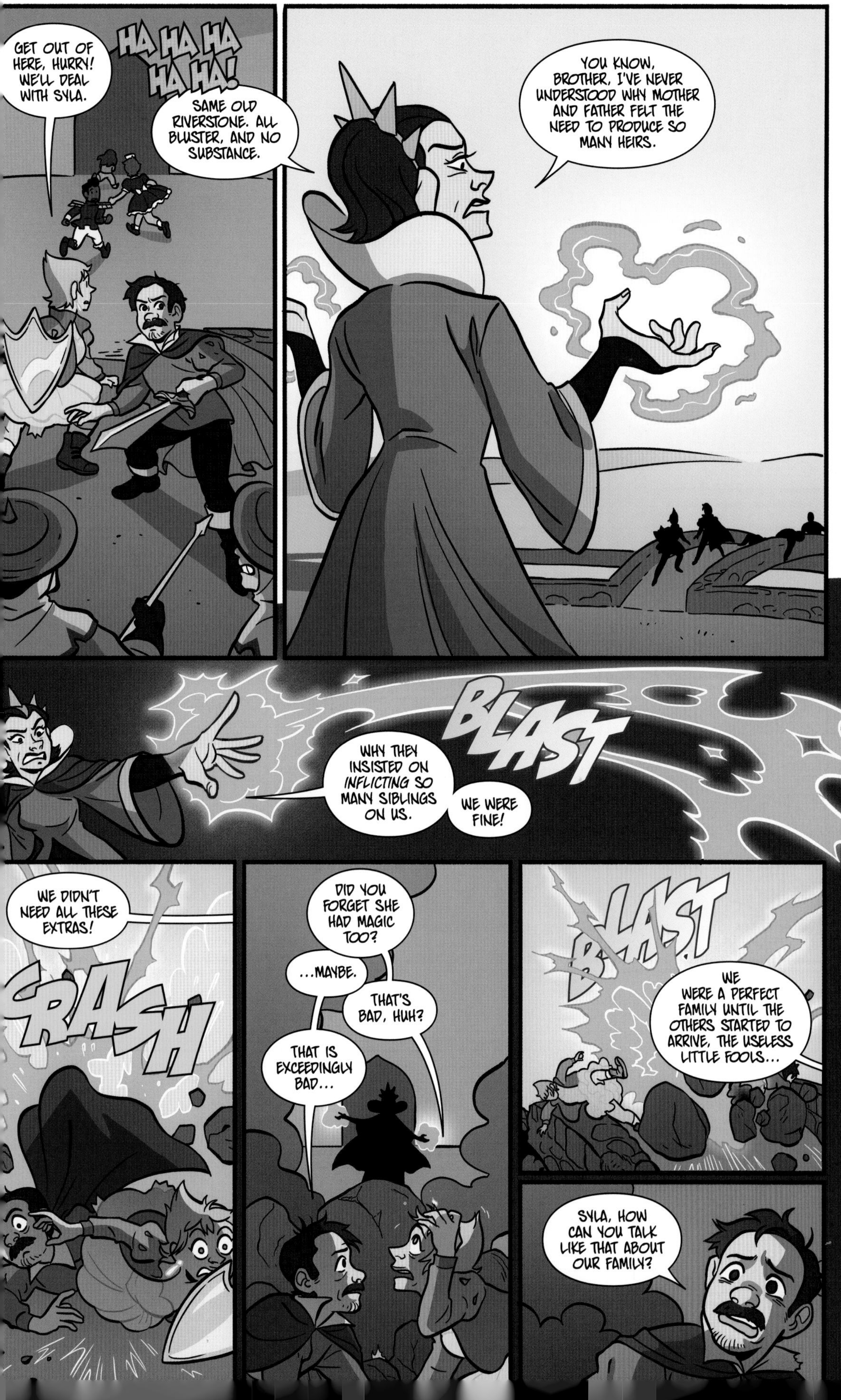
GET OUT OF HERE, HURRY! WE'LL DEAL WITH SYLA.
HA HA HA HA HA!
SAME OLD RIVERSTONE. ALL BLUSTER, AND NO SUBSTANCE.
YOU KNOW, BROTHER, I'VE NEVER UNDERSTOOD WHY MOTHER AND FATHER FELT THE NEED TO PRODUCE SO MANY HEIRS.
BLAST
WHY THEY INSISTED ON INFLICTING SO MANY SIBLINGS ON US.
WE WERE FINE!
WE DIDN'T NEED ALL THESE EXTRAS!
CRASH
DID YOU FORGET SHE HAD MAGIC TOO?
...MAYBE.
THAT'S BAD, HUH?
THAT IS EXCEEDINGLY BAD...
BLAST
WE WERE A PERFECT FAMILY UNTIL THE OTHERS STARTED TO ARRIVE, THE USELESS LITTLE FOOLS...
SYLA, HOW CAN YOU TALK LIKE THAT ABOUT OUR FAMILY?

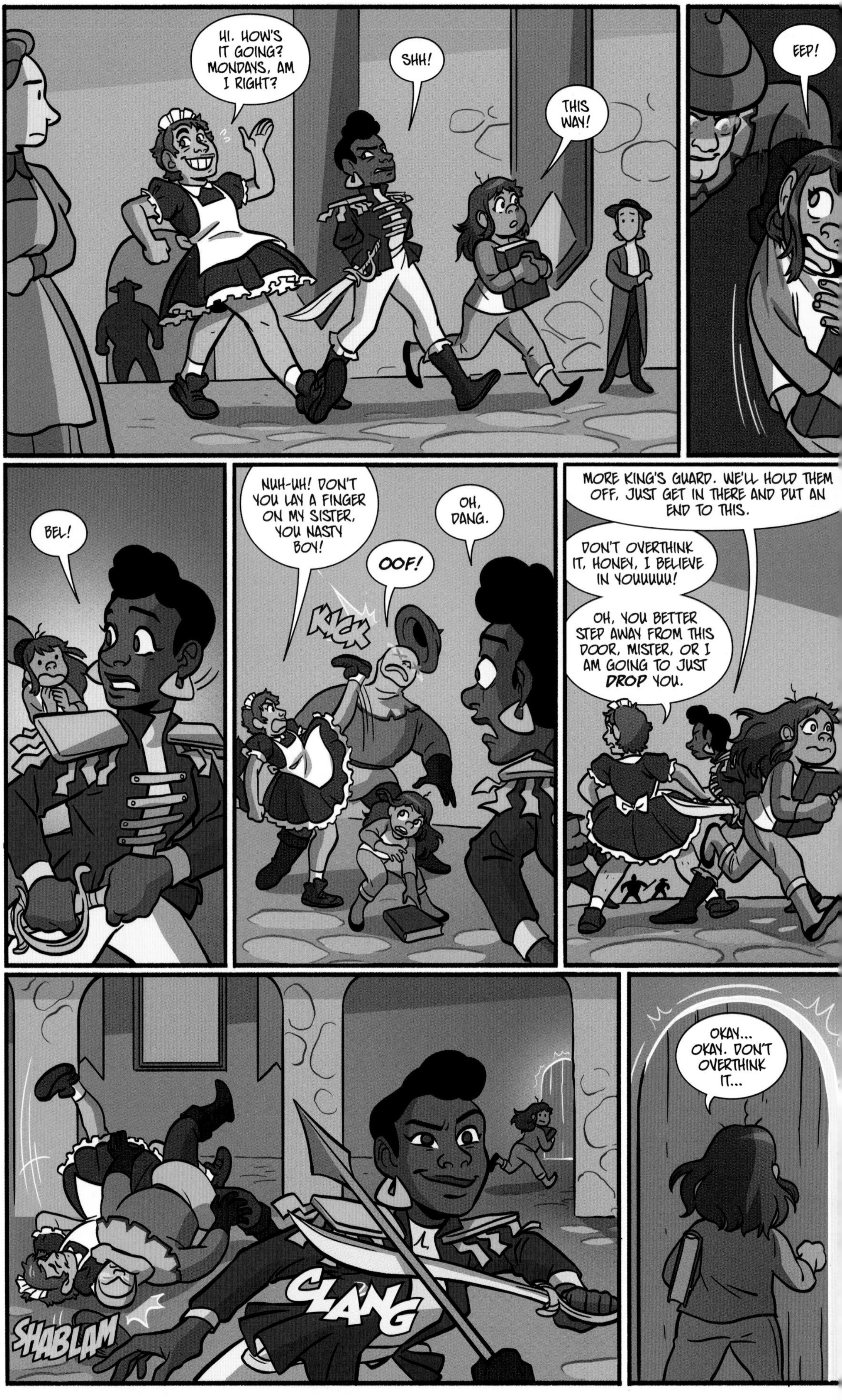
HI. HOW'S IT GOING? MONDAYS, AM I RIGHT?
SHH!
THIS WAY!
EEP!
BEL!
NUH-UH! DON'T YOU LAY A FINGER ON MY SISTER, YOU NASTY BOY!
OOF!
KICK
OH, DANG.
MORE KING'S GUARD. WE'LL HOLD THEM OFF, JUST GET IN THERE AND PUT AN END TO THIS.
DON'T OVERTHINK IT, HONEY, I BELIEVE IN YOUUUUU!
OH, YOU BETTER STEP AWAY FROM THIS DOOR, MISTER, OR I AM GOING TO JUST DROP YOU.
CLANG
SHABLAM
OKAY... OKAY. DON'T OVERTHINK IT...

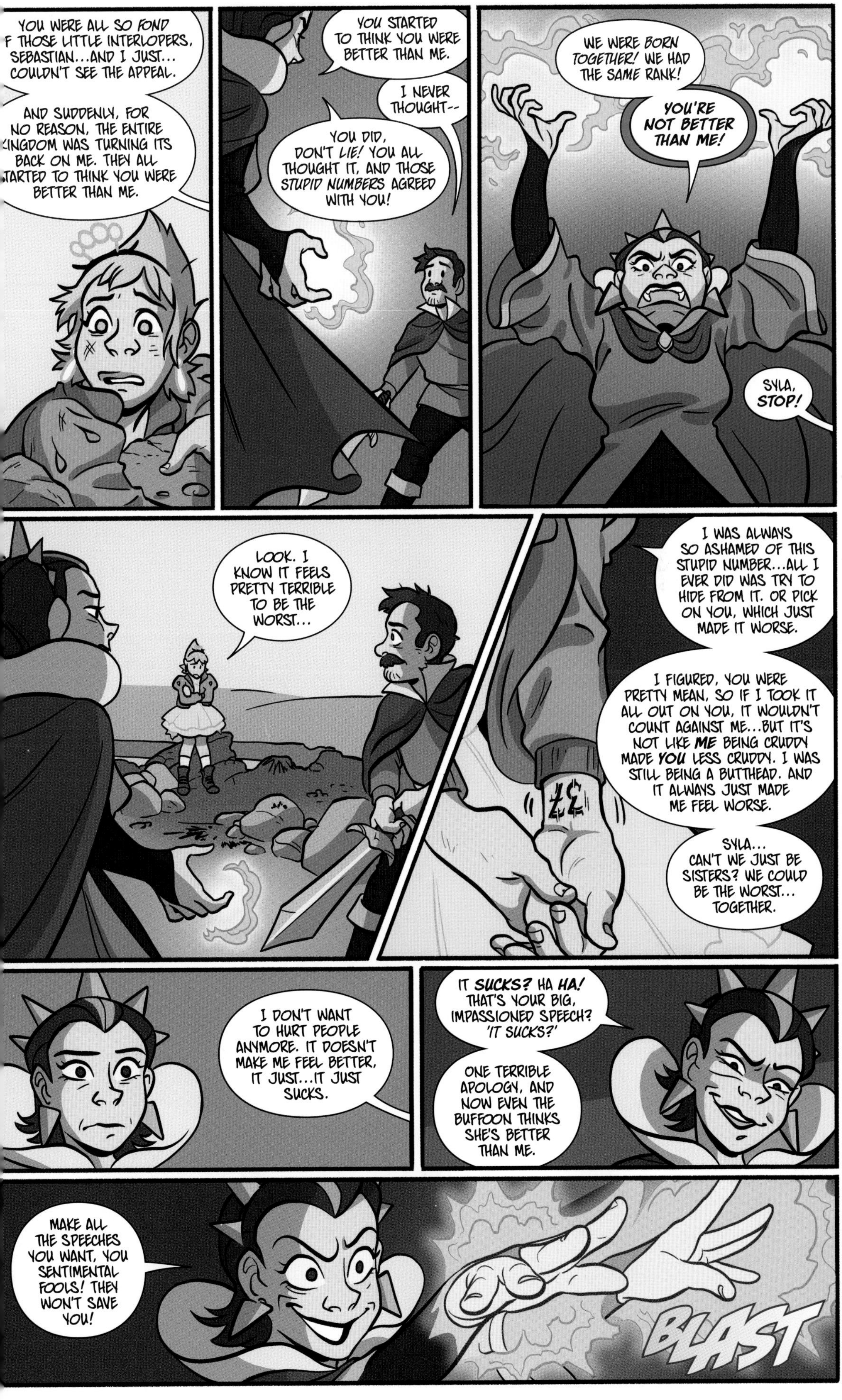
YOU WERE ALL SO FOND OF THOSE LITTLE INTERLOPERS, SEBASTIAN...AND I JUST... COULDN'T SEE THE APPEAL.
AND SUDDENLY, FOR NO REASON, THE ENTIRE KINGDOM WAS TURNING ITS BACK ON ME. THEY ALL STARTED TO THINK YOU WERE BETTER THAN ME.
YOU STARTED TO THINK YOU WERE BETTER THAN ME.
I NEVER THOUGHT--
YOU DID, DON'T *LIE!* YOU ALL THOUGHT IT, AND THOSE *STUPID NUMBERS* AGREED WITH YOU!
WE WERE BORN *TOGETHER!* WE HAD THE SAME RANK!
YOU'RE NOT BETTER THAN ME!
SYLA, **STOP!**
LOOK. I KNOW IT FEELS PRETTY TERRIBLE TO BE THE WORST...
I WAS ALWAYS SO ASHAMED OF THIS STUPID NUMBER...ALL I EVER DID WAS TRY TO HIDE FROM IT. OR PICK ON YOU, WHICH JUST MADE IT WORSE.
I FIGURED, YOU WERE PRETTY MEAN, SO IF I TOOK IT ALL OUT ON YOU, IT WOULDN'T COUNT AGAINST ME...BUT IT'S NOT LIKE **ME** BEING CRUDDY MADE ***YOU*** LESS CRUDDY. I WAS STILL BEING A BUTTHEAD. AND IT ALWAYS JUST MADE ME FEEL WORSE.
SYLA... CAN'T WE JUST BE SISTERS? WE COULD BE THE WORST... TOGETHER.
I DON'T WANT TO HURT PEOPLE ANYMORE. IT DOESN'T MAKE ME FEEL BETTER, IT JUST...IT JUST SUCKS.
IT ***SUCKS?*** HA ***HA!*** THAT'S YOUR BIG, IMPASSIONED SPEECH? *'IT SUCKS?'*
ONE TERRIBLE APOLOGY, AND NOW EVEN THE BUFFOON THINKS SHE'S BETTER THAN ME.
MAKE ALL THE SPEECHES YOU WANT, YOU SENTIMENTAL FOOLS! THEY WON'T SAVE YOU!
BLAST

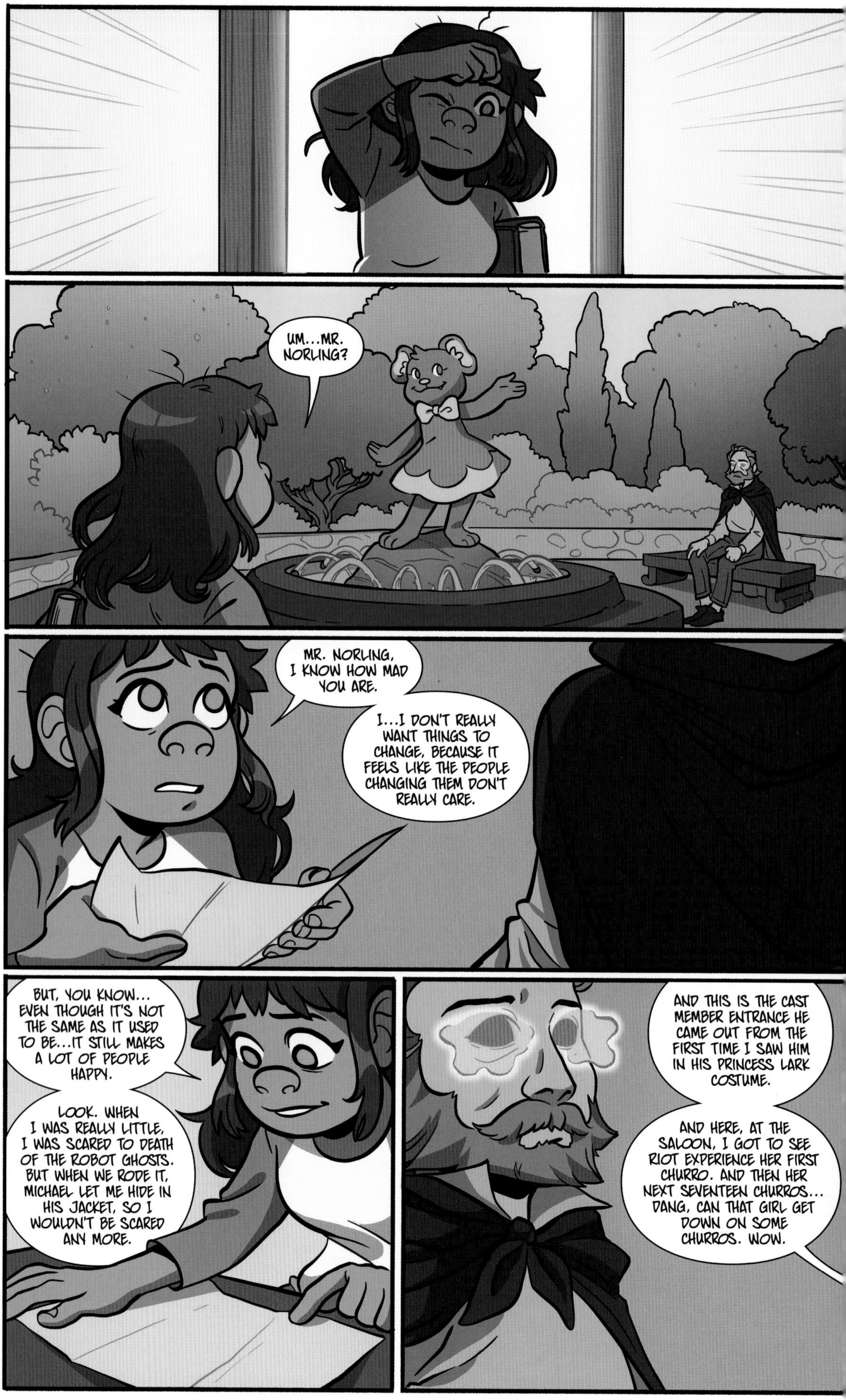
UM...MR. NORLING?
MR. NORLING, I KNOW HOW MAD YOU ARE.
I...I DON'T REALLY WANT THINGS TO CHANGE, BECAUSE IT FEELS LIKE THE PEOPLE CHANGING THEM DON'T REALLY CARE.
BUT, YOU KNOW... EVEN THOUGH IT'S NOT THE SAME AS IT USED TO BE...IT STILL MAKES A LOT OF PEOPLE HAPPY.
LOOK. WHEN I WAS REALLY LITTLE, I WAS SCARED TO DEATH OF THE ROBOT GHOSTS. BUT WHEN WE RODE IT, MICHAEL LET ME HIDE IN HIS JACKET, SO I WOULDN'T BE SCARED ANY MORE.
AND THIS IS THE CAST MEMBER ENTRANCE HE CAME OUT FROM THE FIRST TIME I SAW HIM IN HIS PRINCESS LARK COSTUME.
AND HERE, AT THE SALOON, I GOT TO SEE RIOT EXPERIENCE HER FIRST CHURRO. AND THEN HER NEXT SEVENTEEN CHURROS... DANG, CAN THAT GIRL GET DOWN ON SOME CHURROS. WOW.

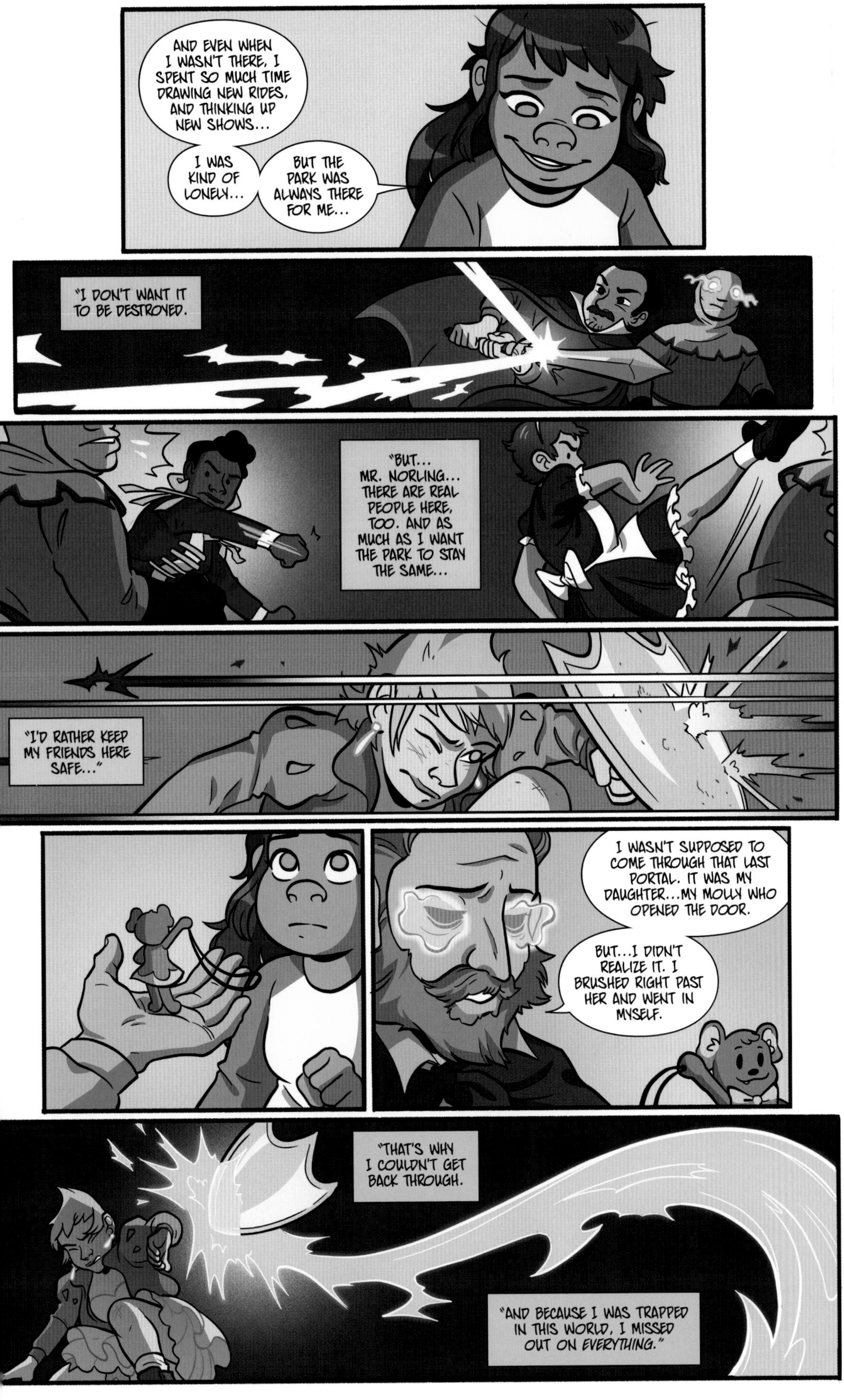
AND EVEN WHEN I WASN'T THERE, I SPENT SO MUCH TIME DRAWING NEW RIDES, AND THINKING UP NEW SHOWS...
I WAS KIND OF LONELY...
BUT THE PARK WAS ALWAYS THERE FOR ME...
"I DON'T WANT IT TO BE DESTROYED.
"BUT... MR. NORLING... THERE ARE REAL PEOPLE HERE, TOO. AND AS MUCH AS I WANT THE PARK TO STAY THE SAME...
"I'D RATHER KEEP MY FRIENDS HERE SAFE..."
I WASN'T SUPPOSED TO COME THROUGH THAT LAST PORTAL. IT WAS MY DAUGHTER...MY MOLLY WHO OPENED THE DOOR.
BUT...I DIDN'T REALIZE IT. I BRUSHED RIGHT PAST HER AND WENT IN MYSELF.
"THAT'S WHY I COULDN'T GET BACK THROUGH.
"AND BECAUSE I WAS TRAPPED IN THIS WORLD, I MISSED OUT ON EVERYTHING."

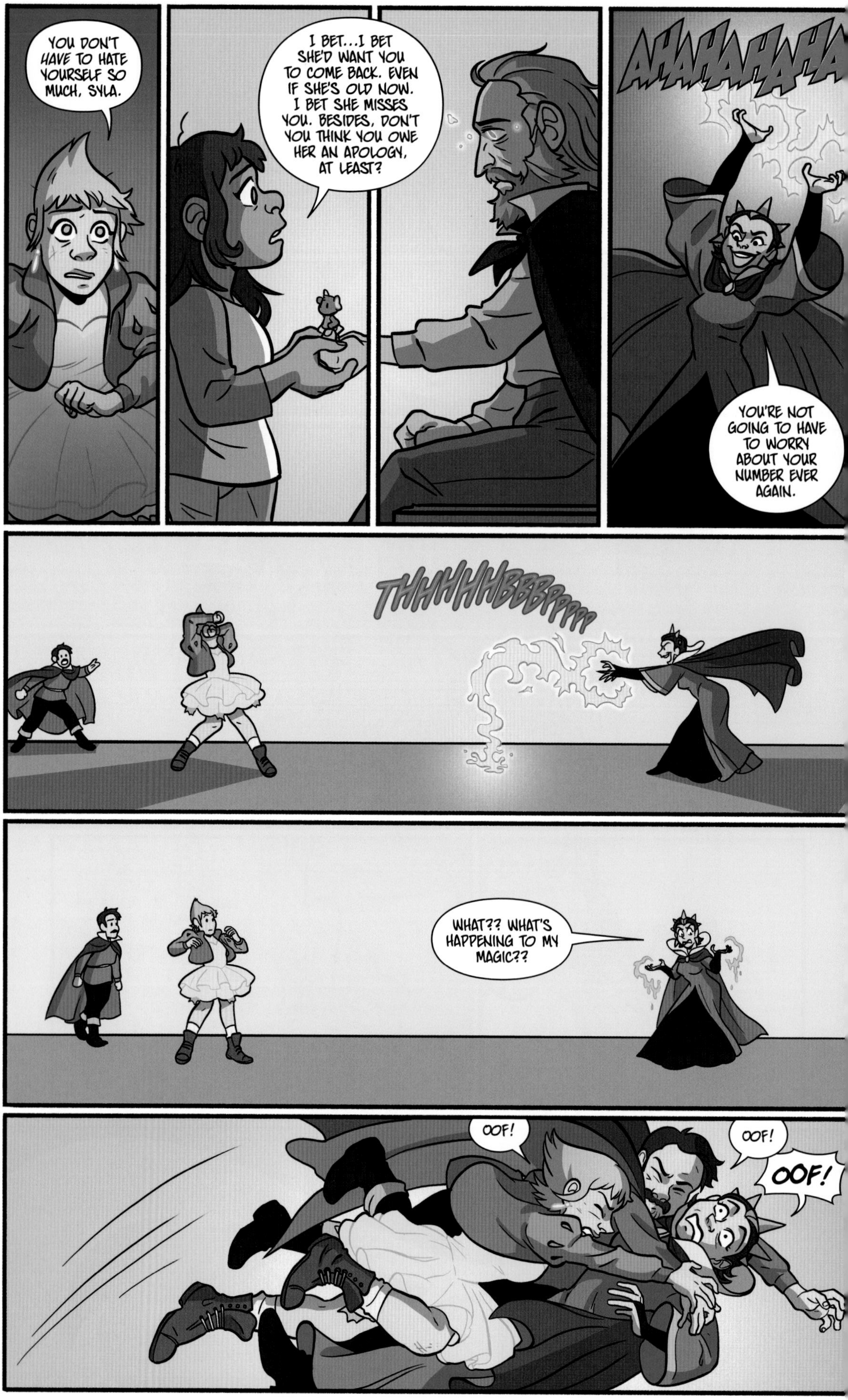
YOU DON'T HAVE TO HATE YOURSELF SO MUCH, SYLA.
I BET...I BET SHE'D WANT YOU TO COME BACK. EVEN IF SHE'S OLD NOW. I BET SHE MISSES YOU. BESIDES, DON'T YOU THINK YOU OWE HER AN APOLOGY, AT LEAST?
AHAHAHAHAHA
YOU'RE NOT GOING TO HAVE TO WORRY ABOUT YOUR NUMBER EVER AGAIN.
THHHHHBBBPPPPP
WHAT?? WHAT'S HAPPENING TO MY MAGIC??
OOF!
OOF!
OOF!

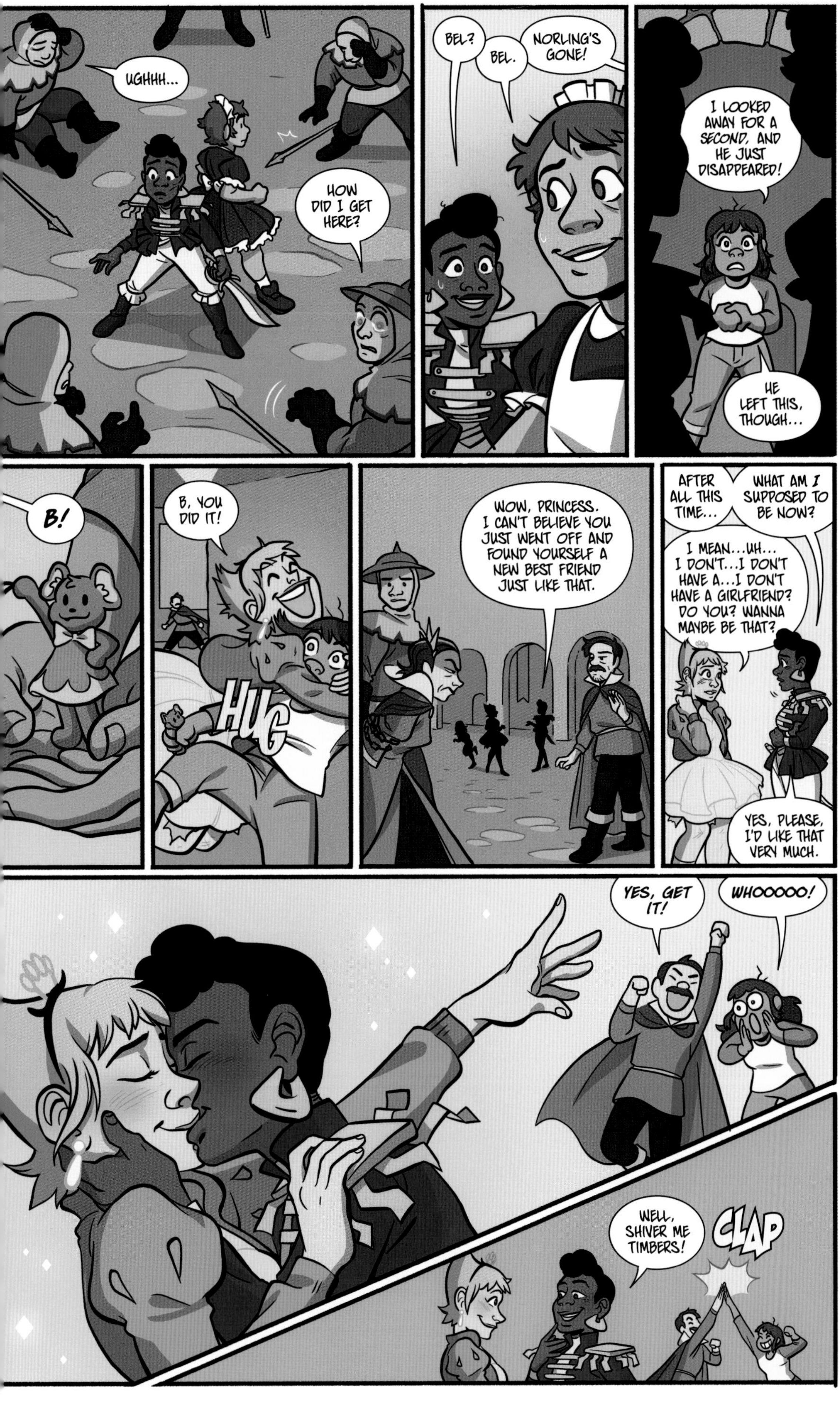
UGHHH...
HOW DID I GET HERE?
BEL?
BEL.
NORLING'S GONE!
I LOOKED AWAY FOR A SECOND, AND HE JUST DISAPPEARED!
HE LEFT THIS, THOUGH...
B!
B, YOU DID IT!
HUG
WOW, PRINCESS. I CAN'T BELIEVE YOU JUST WENT OFF AND FOUND YOURSELF A NEW BEST FRIEND JUST LIKE THAT.
AFTER ALL THIS TIME...
WHAT AM I SUPPOSED TO BE NOW?
I MEAN...UH... I DON'T...I DON'T HAVE A...I DON'T HAVE A GIRLFRIEND? DO YOU? WANNA MAYBE BE THAT?
YES, PLEASE, I'D LIKE THAT VERY MUCH.
YES, GET IT!
WHOOOOO!
WELL, SHIVER ME TIMBERS!
CLAP

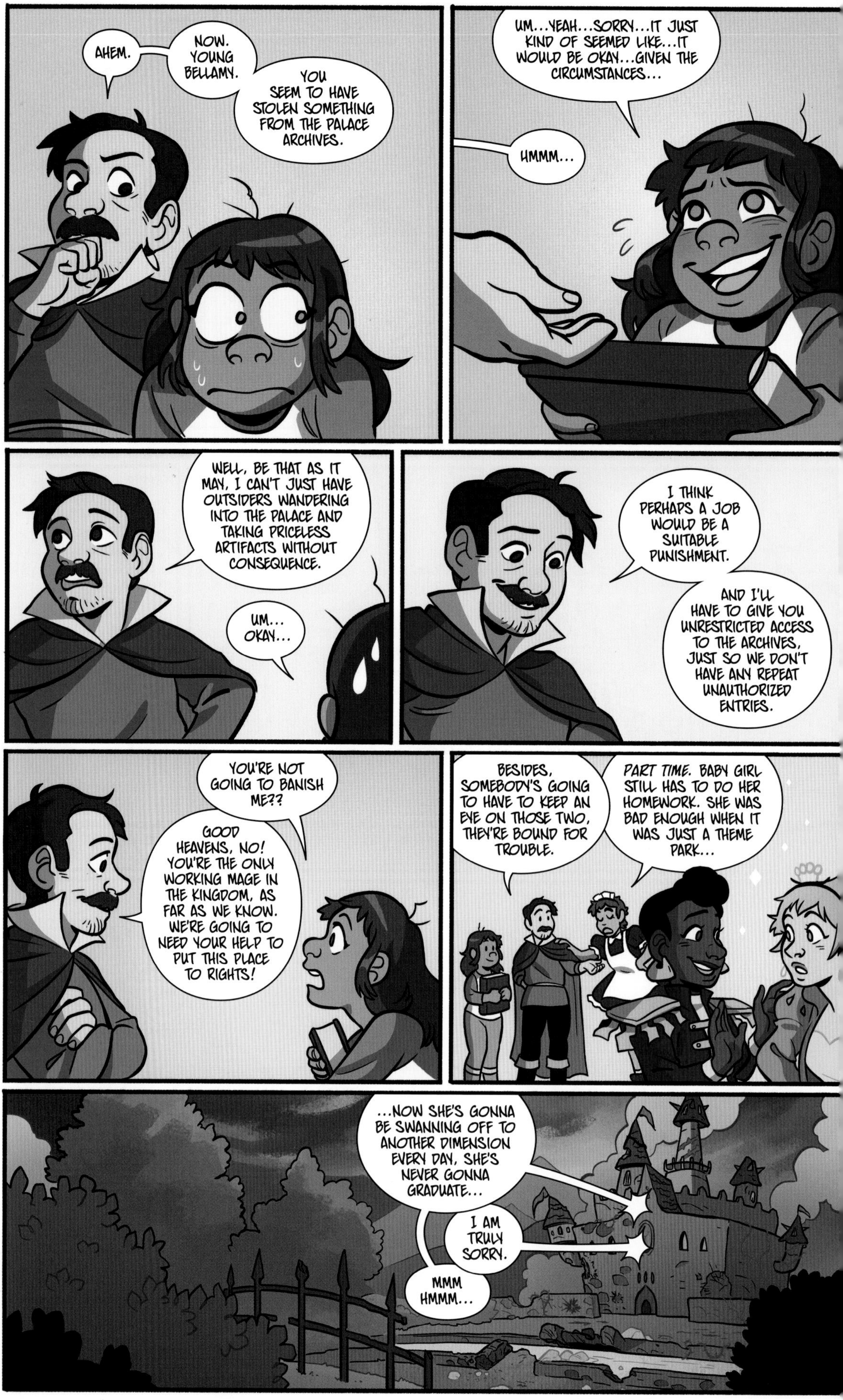
AHEM.
NOW. YOUNG BELLAMY.
YOU SEEM TO HAVE STOLEN SOMETHING FROM THE PALACE ARCHIVES.
UM...YEAH...SORRY...IT JUST KIND OF SEEMED LIKE...IT WOULD BE OKAY...GIVEN THE CIRCUMSTANCES...
HMMM...
WELL, BE THAT AS IT MAY, I CAN'T JUST HAVE OUTSIDERS WANDERING INTO THE PALACE AND TAKING PRICELESS ARTIFACTS WITHOUT CONSEQUENCE.
UM... OKAY...
I THINK PERHAPS A JOB WOULD BE A SUITABLE PUNISHMENT.
AND I'LL HAVE TO GIVE YOU UNRESTRICTED ACCESS TO THE ARCHIVES, JUST SO WE DON'T HAVE ANY REPEAT UNAUTHORIZED ENTRIES.
YOU'RE NOT GOING TO BANISH ME??
GOOD HEAVENS, NO! YOU'RE THE ONLY WORKING MAGE IN THE KINGDOM, AS FAR AS WE KNOW. WE'RE GOING TO NEED YOUR HELP TO PUT THIS PLACE TO RIGHTS!
BESIDES, SOMEBODY'S GOING TO HAVE TO KEEP AN EYE ON THOSE TWO, THEY'RE BOUND FOR TROUBLE.
PART TIME. BABY GIRL STILL HAS TO DO HER HOMEWORK. SHE WAS BAD ENOUGH WHEN IT WAS JUST A THEME PARK...
...NOW SHE'S GONNA BE SWANNING OFF TO ANOTHER DIMENSION EVERY DAY, SHE'S NEVER GONNA GRADUATE...
I AM TRULY SORRY.
MMM HMMM...

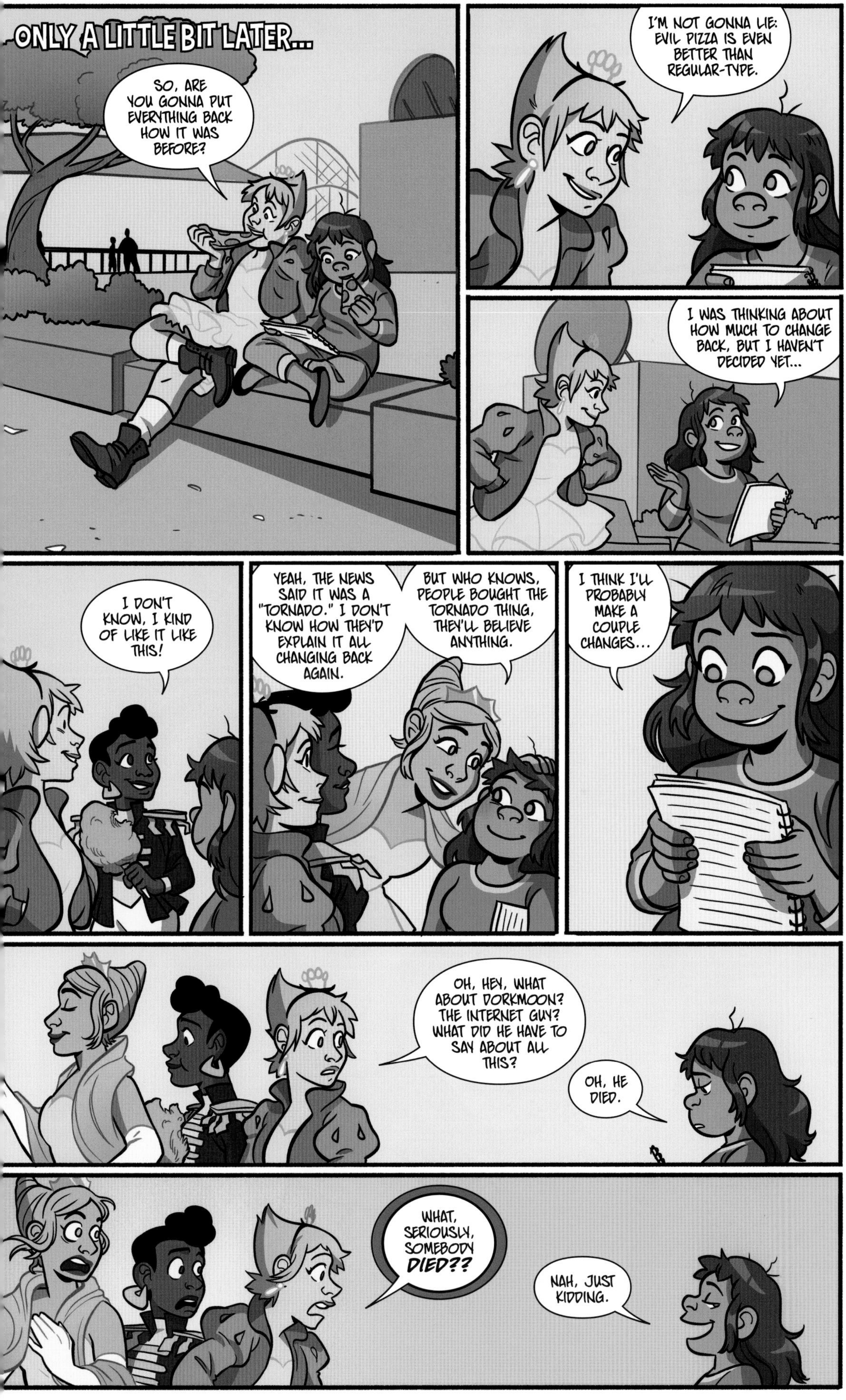
ONLY A LITTLE BIT LATER...
SO, ARE YOU GONNA PUT EVERYTHING BACK HOW IT WAS BEFORE?
I'M NOT GONNA LIE: EVIL PIZZA IS EVEN BETTER THAN REGULAR-TYPE.
I WAS THINKING ABOUT HOW MUCH TO CHANGE BACK, BUT I HAVEN'T DECIDED YET...
I DON'T KNOW, I KIND OF LIKE IT LIKE THIS!
YEAH, THE NEWS SAID IT WAS A "TORNADO." I DON'T KNOW HOW THEY'D EXPLAIN IT ALL CHANGING BACK AGAIN.
BUT WHO KNOWS, PEOPLE BOUGHT THE TORNADO THING, THEY'LL BELIEVE ANYTHING.
I THINK I'LL PROBABLY MAKE A COUPLE CHANGES...
OH, HEY, WHAT ABOUT DORKMOON? THE INTERNET GUY? WHAT DID HE HAVE TO SAY ABOUT ALL THIS?
OH, HE DIED.
WHAT, SERIOUSLY, SOMEBODY DIED??
NAH, JUST KIDDING.

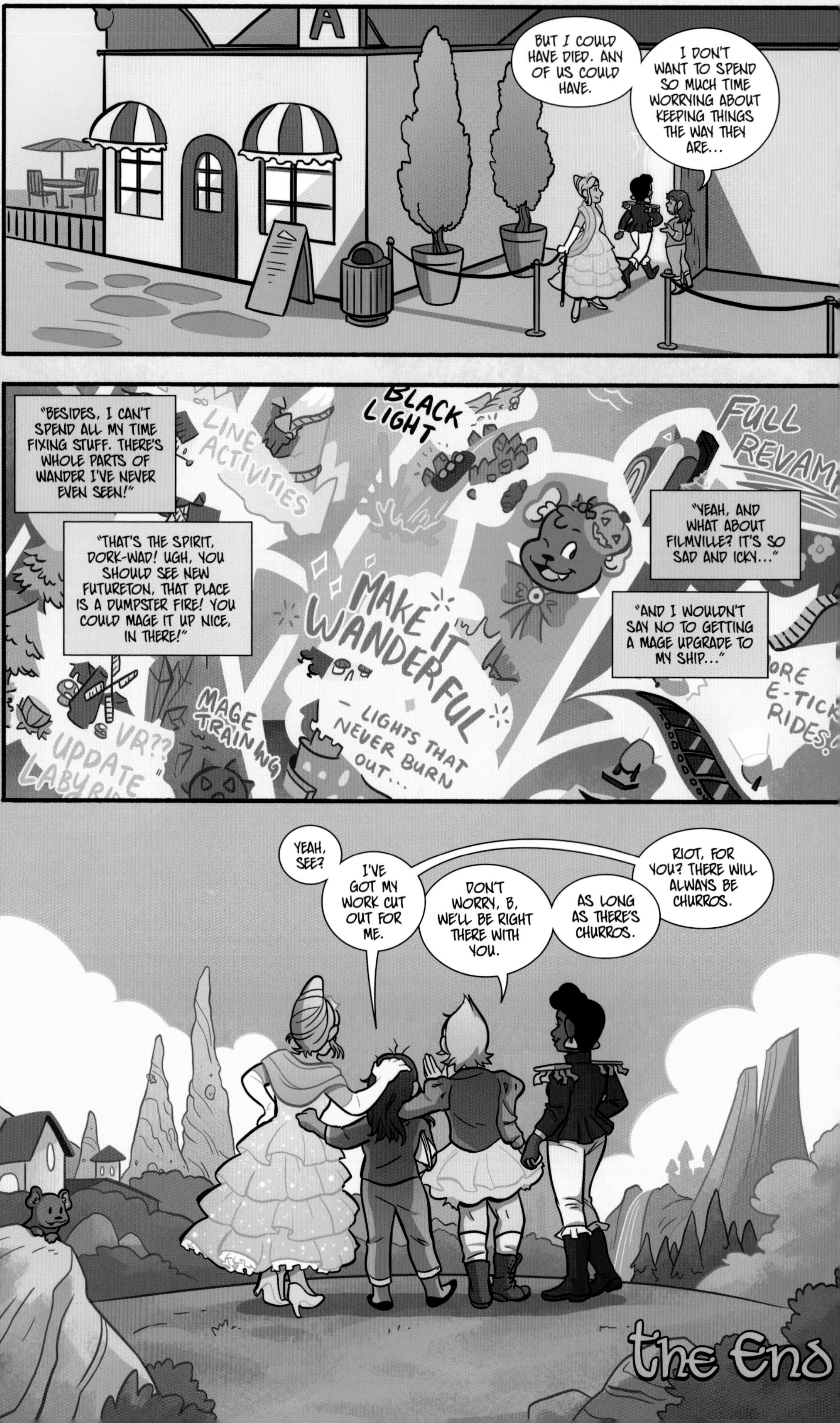
A
BUT I COULD HAVE DIED. ANY OF US COULD HAVE.
I DON'T WANT TO SPEND SO MUCH TIME WORRYING ABOUT KEEPING THINGS THE WAY THEY ARE...
"BESIDES, I CAN'T SPEND ALL MY TIME FIXING STUFF. THERE'S WHOLE PARTS OF WANDER I'VE NEVER EVEN SEEN!"
BLACK LIGHT
LINE ACTIVITIES
FULL REVAM
"YEAH, AND WHAT ABOUT FILMVILLE? IT'S SO SAD AND ICKY..."
"THAT'S THE SPIRIT, DORK-WAD! UGH, YOU SHOULD SEE NEW FUTURETON, THAT PLACE IS A DUMPSTER FIRE! YOU COULD MAGE IT UP NICE, IN THERE!"
MAKE IT WANDERFUL
"AND I WOULDN'T SAY NO TO GETTING A MAGE UPGRADE TO MY SHIP..."
- LIGHTS THAT NEVER BURN OUT...
MAGE TRAINING
VR??
UPDATE
YEAH, SEE?
I'VE GOT MY WORK CUT OUT FOR ME.
DON'T WORRY, B, WE'LL BE RIGHT THERE WITH YOU.
AS LONG AS THERE'S CHURROS.
RIOT, FOR YOU? THERE WILL ALWAYS BE CHURROS.
THE END

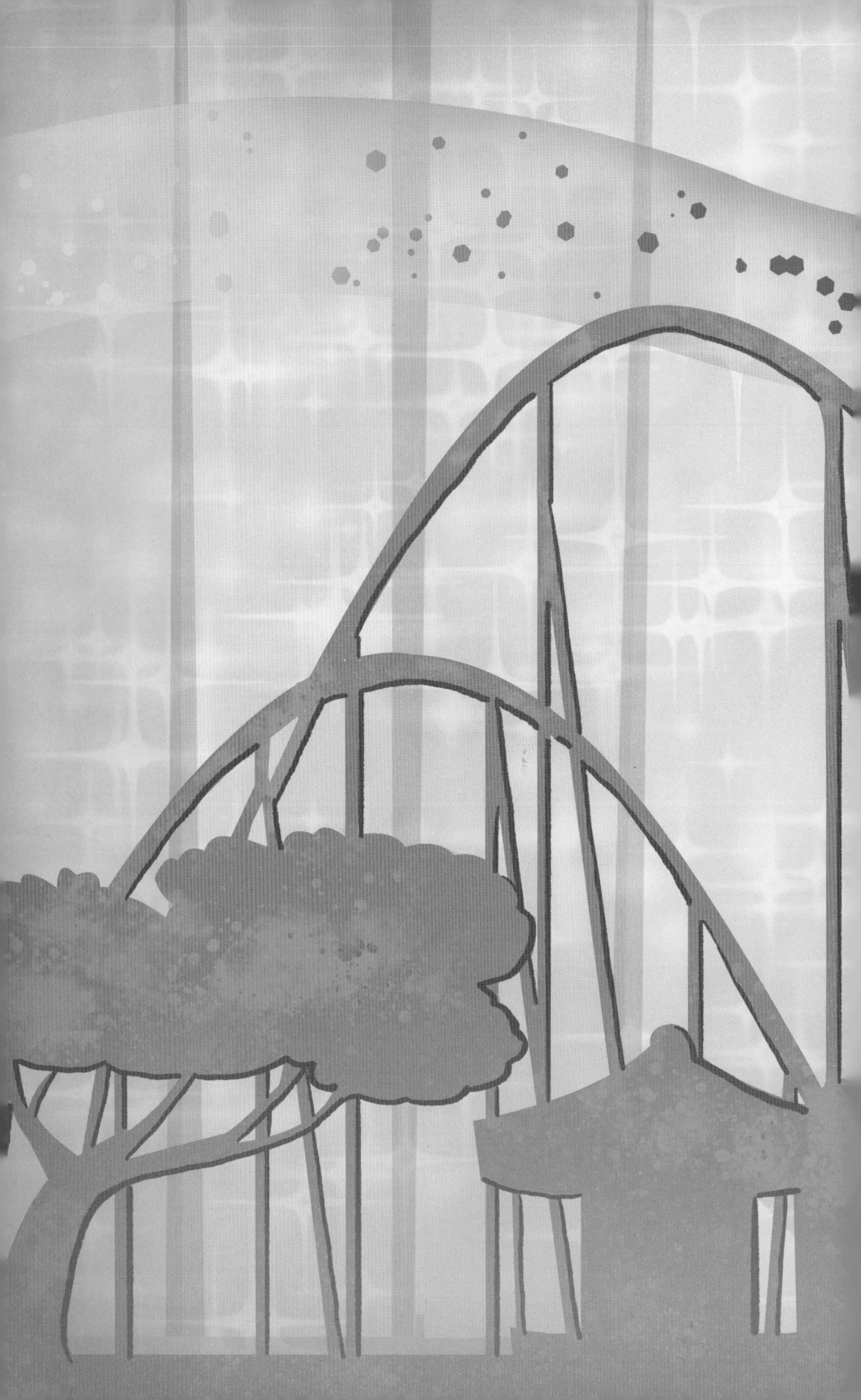

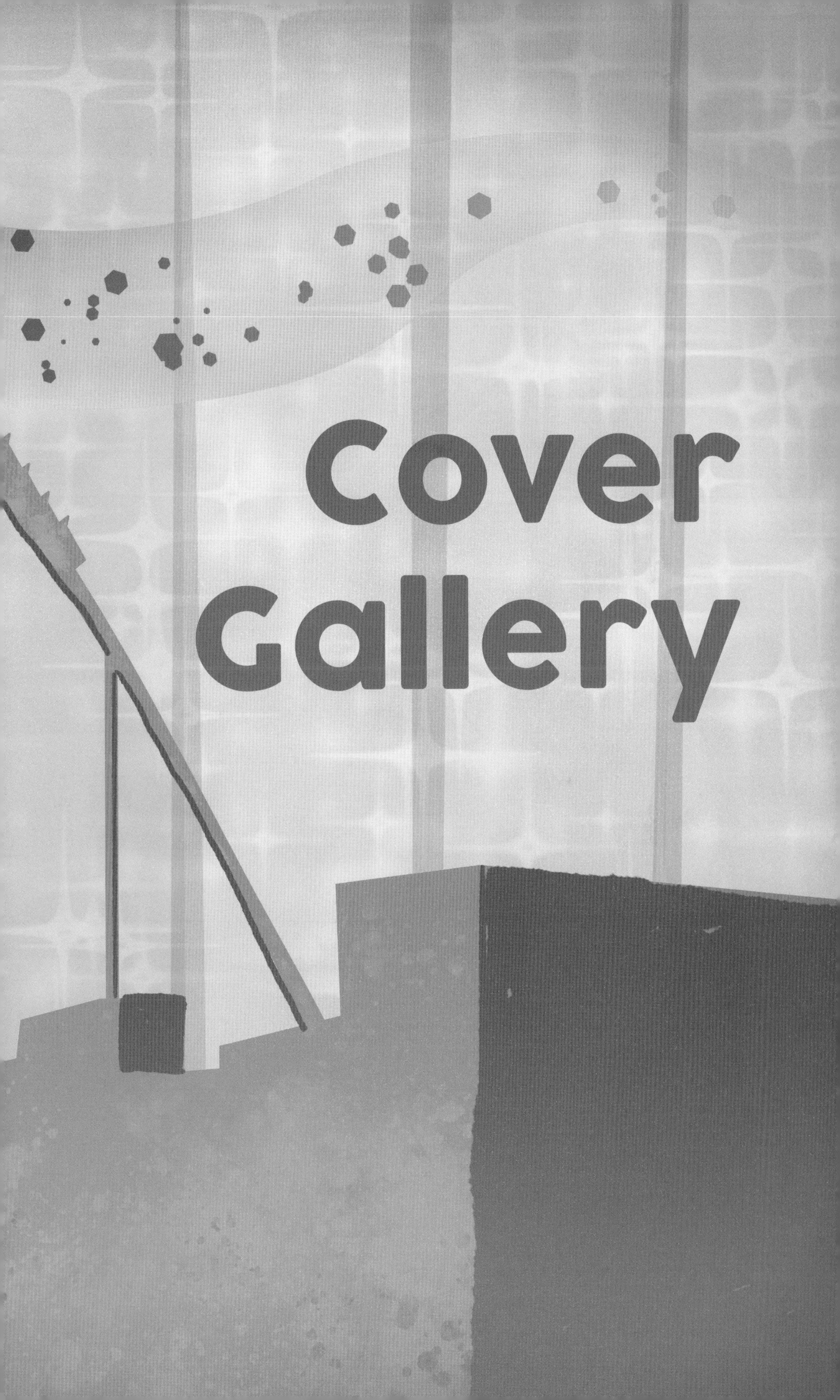
Cover
Gallery

Issue 1 Cover by
Maddi Gonzalez

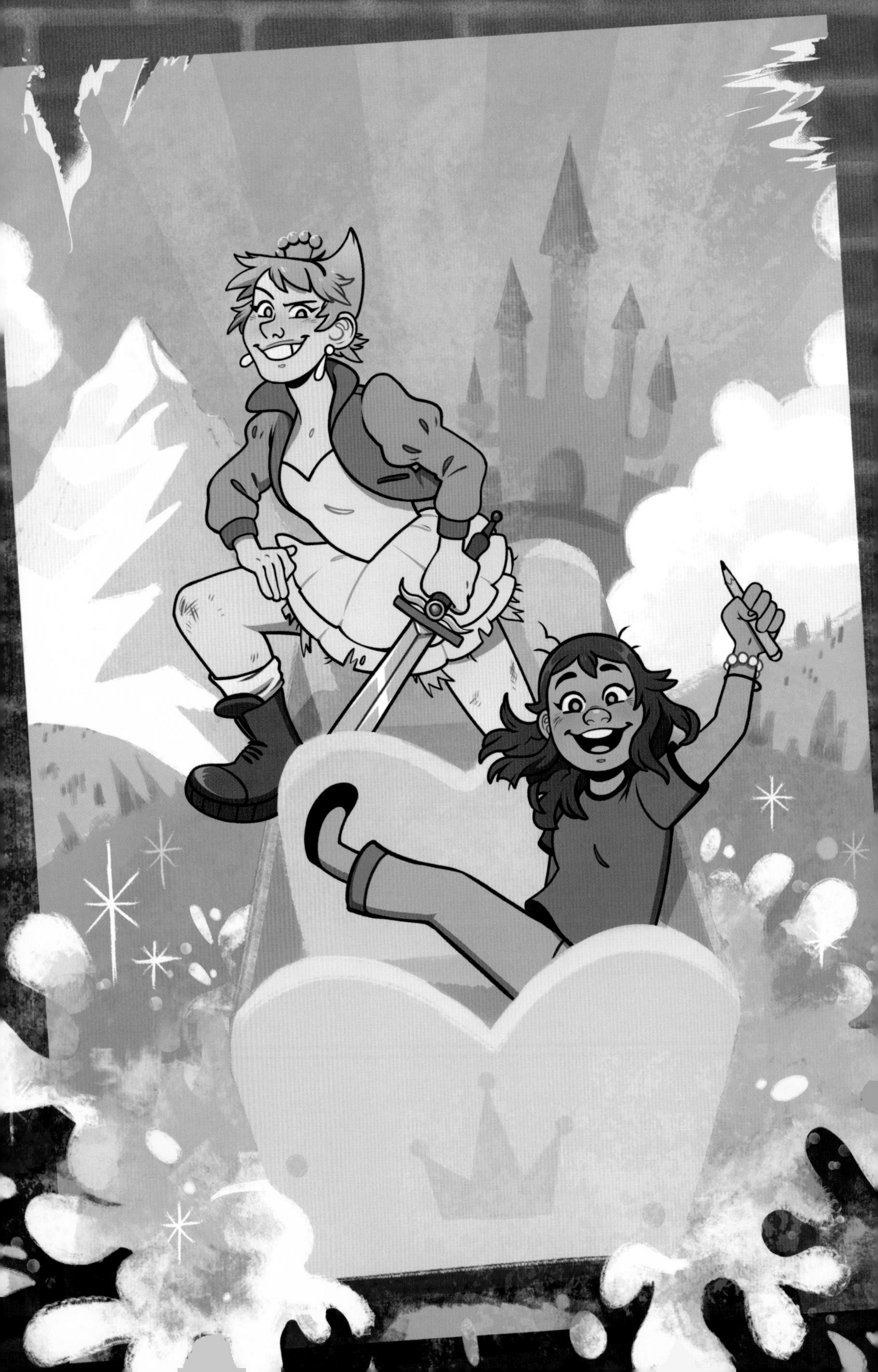

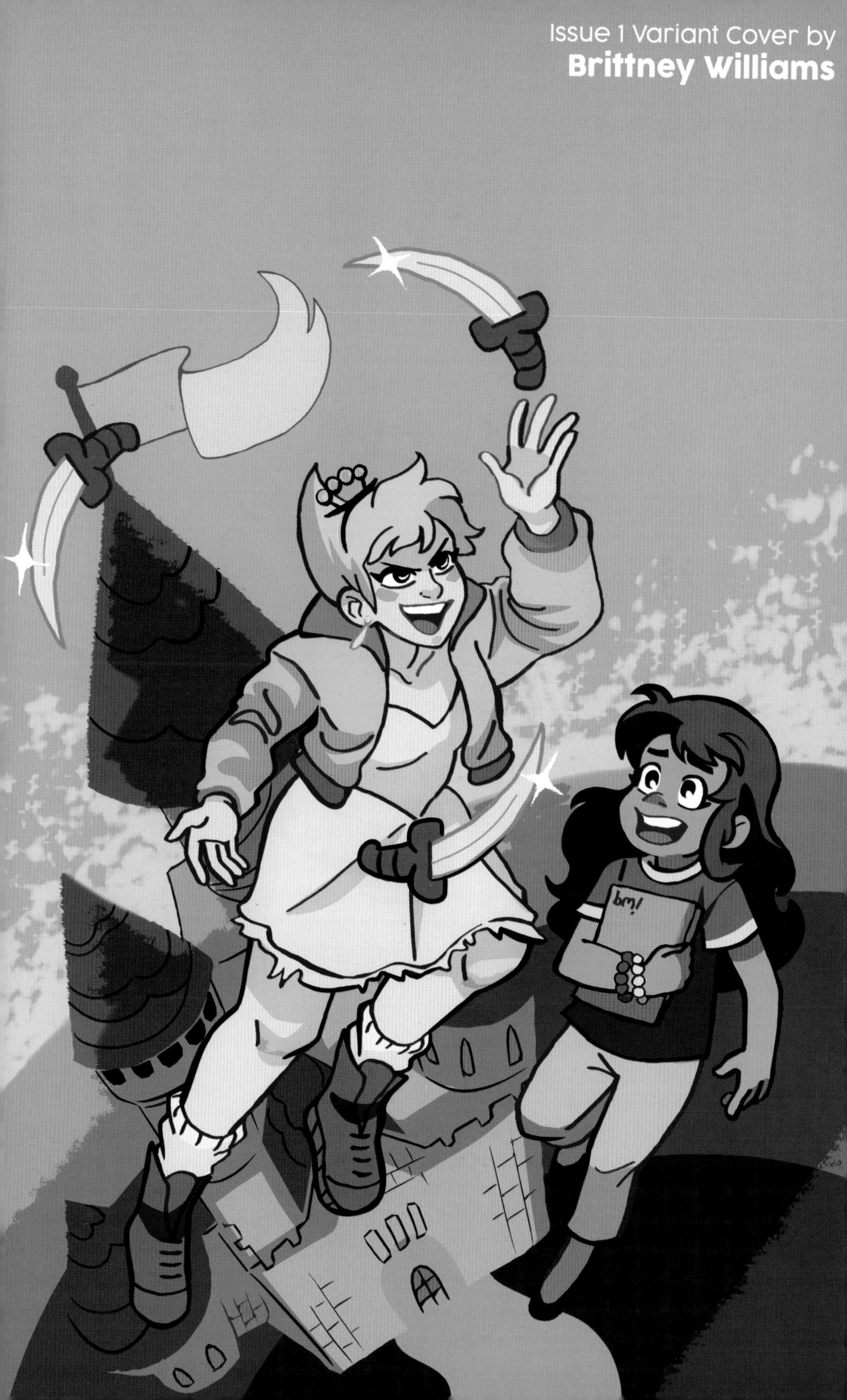

Issue 1 Variant Cover by
Brittney Williams

Issue 2 Cover by
Maddi Gonzalez

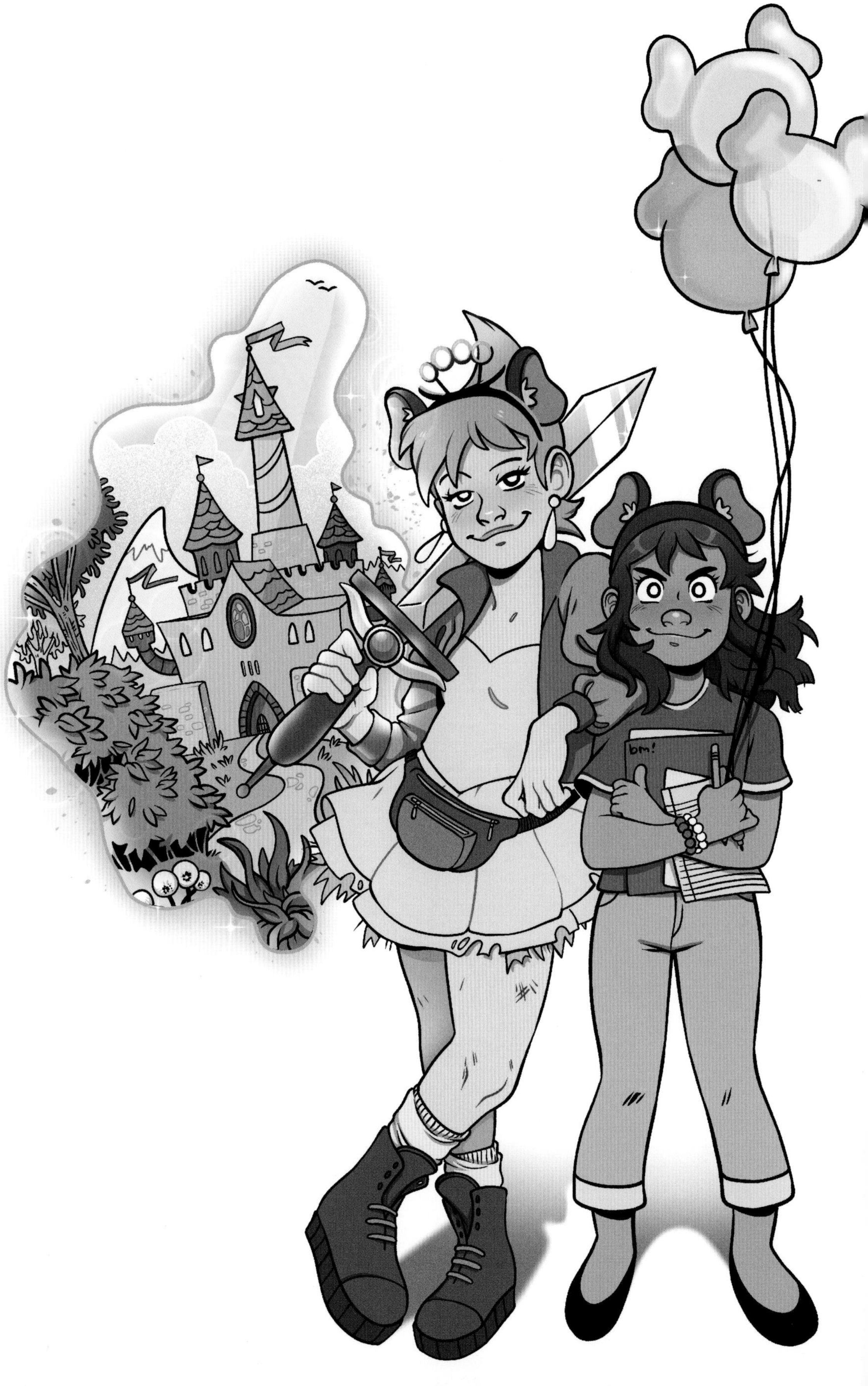
bm!

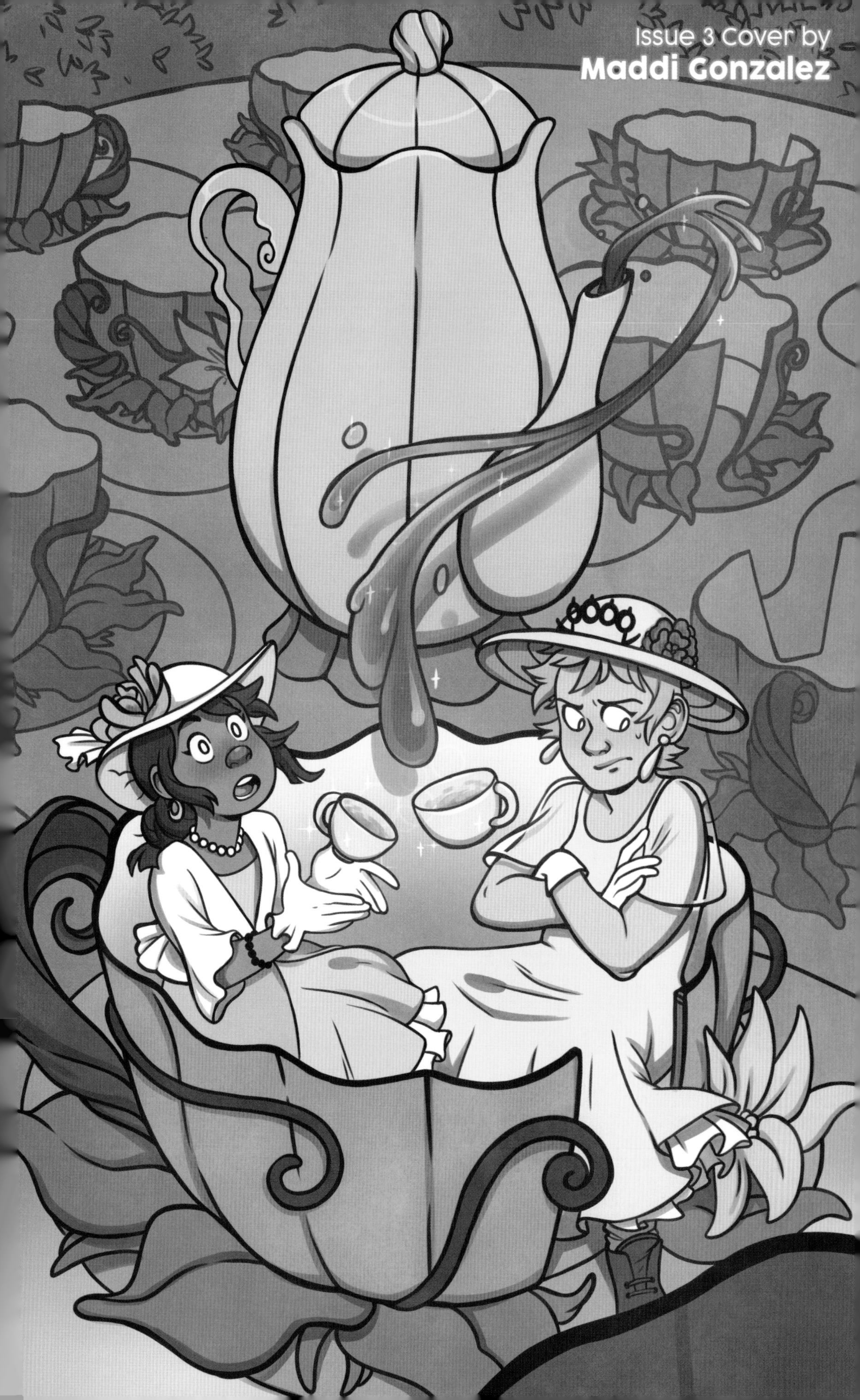

Issue 3 Cover by
Maddi Gonzalez

Issue 4 Cover by
Maddi Gonzalez

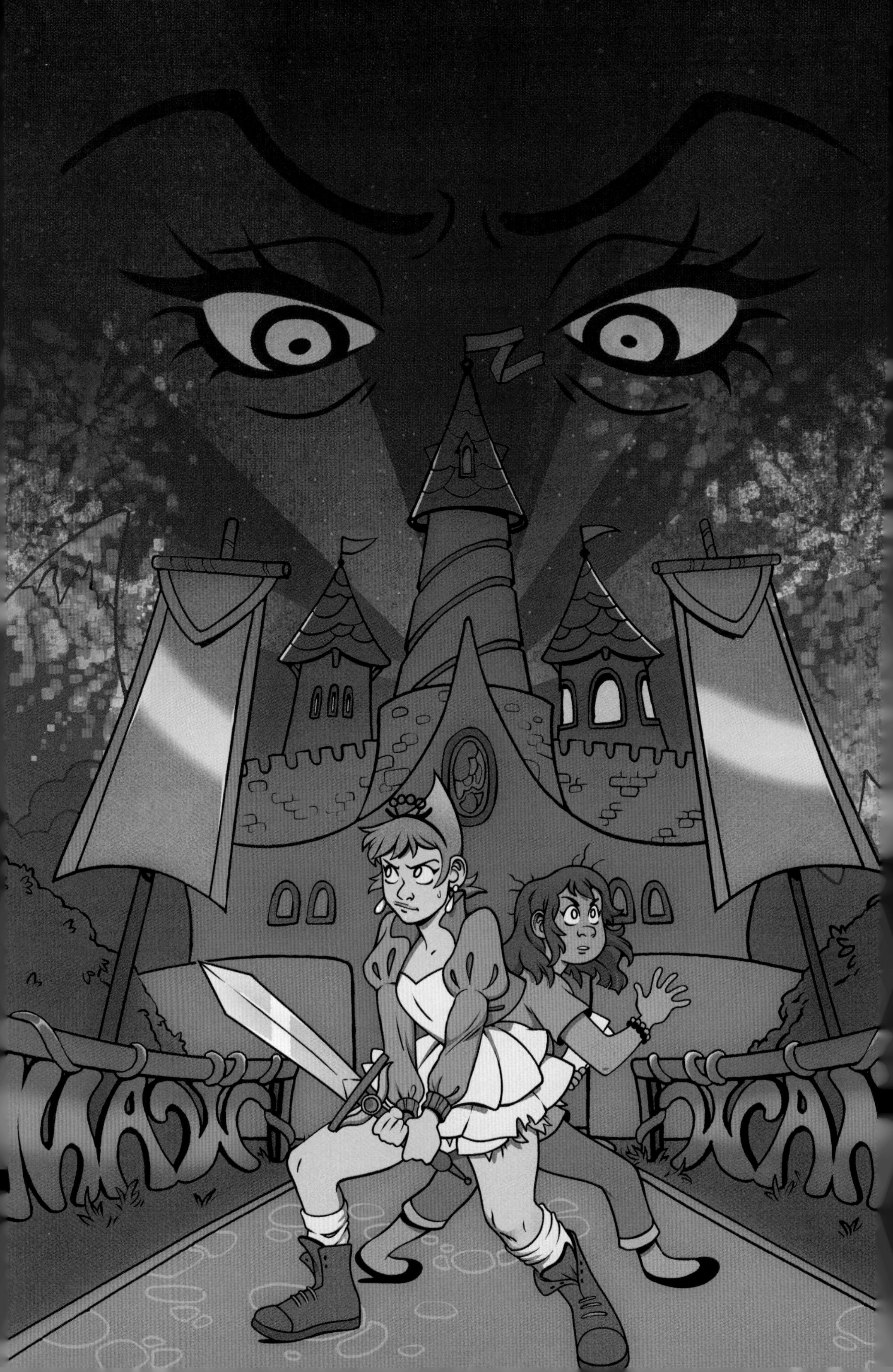

Hey! Thanks for picking up this book!

Now, put down this book and start clapping. A lot of people worked really hard for this book to exist. Like Maddi, who designed all these beautiful children, and drew three stunning books, despite life working really hard to try to stop her. Or Mollie, who stepped in for her, and knocked the final book out of the park. There were a lot of obstacles, and a lot of people involved in getting past them: Nimali, Ed, Shannon, Sophie, Michelle, Chelsea, Raven, Ilaria, Tasha, Cathy, Maarta, Cristina, Rebecca, Kieran, and Deron have all had roles in making this book exist, ranging from "supercolossal" to just "very big indeed." Are you clapping?

Okay, stop clapping, you look silly.

But seriously, thank you for making this book possible. I hope it made you smile. Yes, you: Teen at the school library. And you: Dad looking for something to read with his kids. And you: Adult who enjoys media for all ages. I hope you're out there, reading this, and knowing there's some weirdo out there, thinking about YOU, SPECIFICALLY.

And, not to make it awkward or anything, but: I love you!

Keep it Wanderful!
Jackie Ball

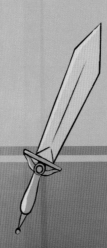

Sketches and Designs by **Maddi Gonzalez**

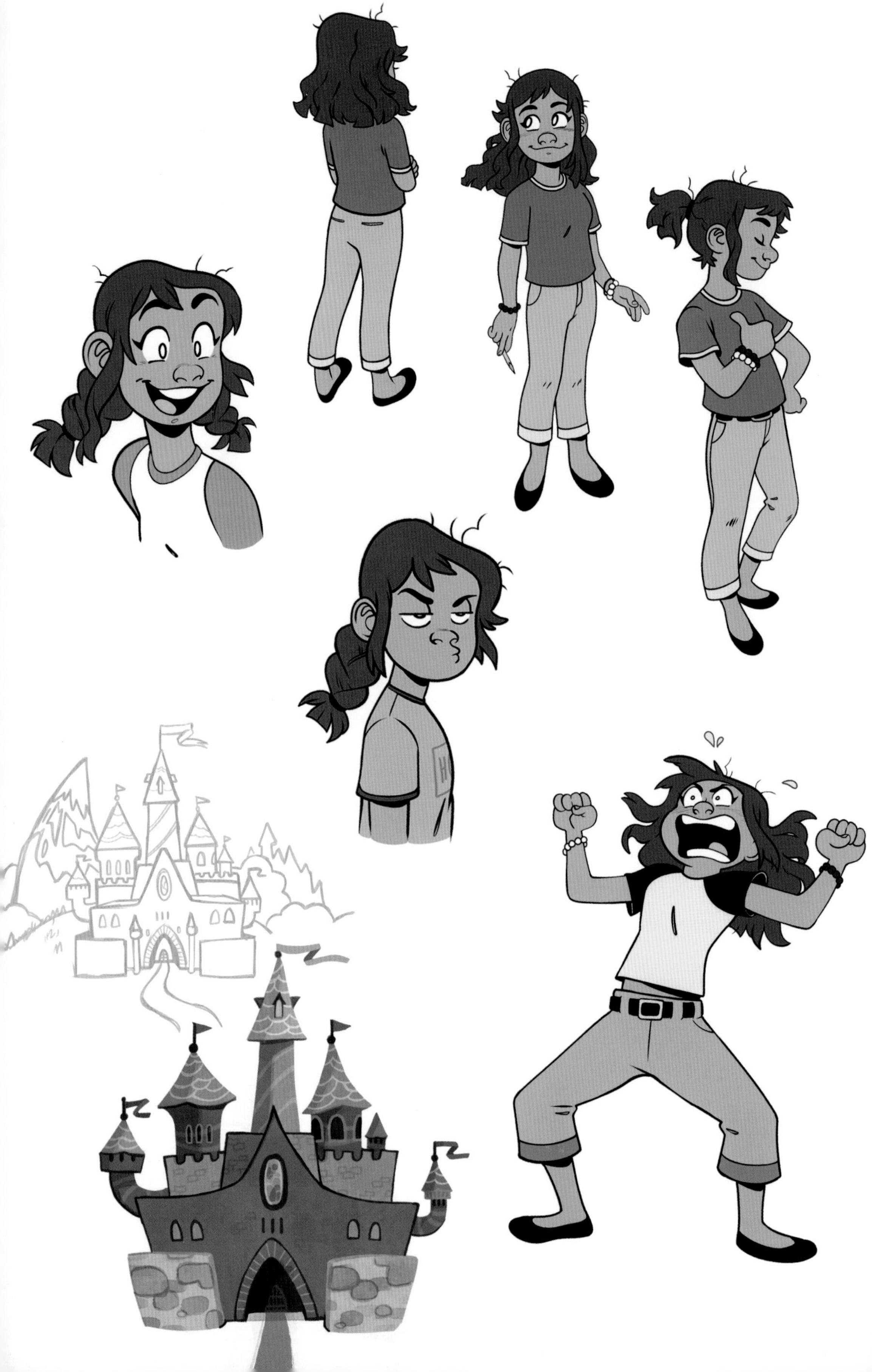

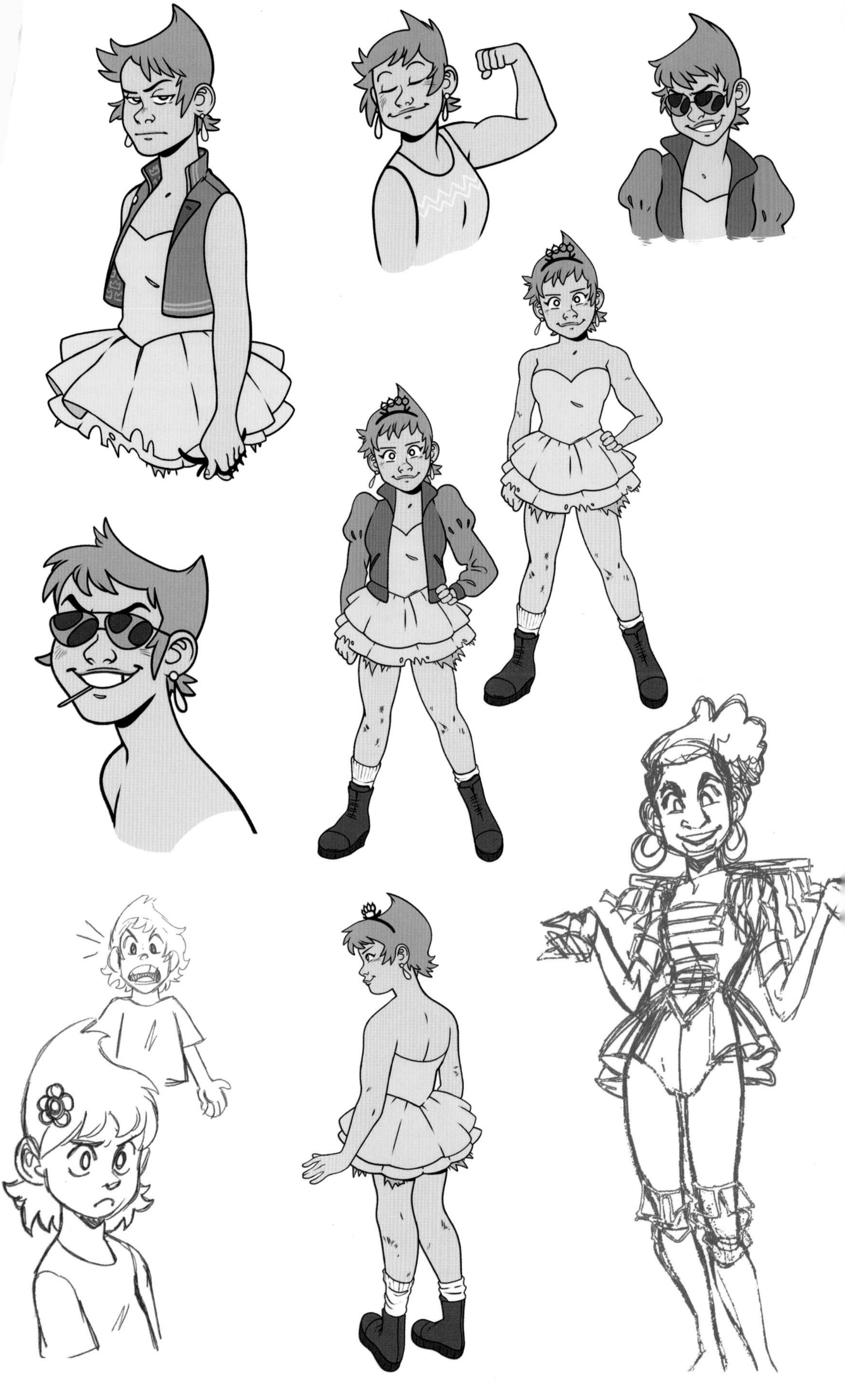

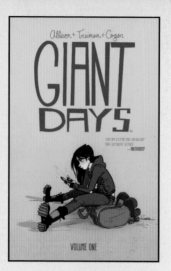

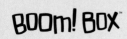